"Pitol is not just our best living storyteller, he is also the strongest renovator of our literature."

　　—ÁLVARO ENRIGUE, author of *Sudden Death*

"One of Mexico's most culturally complex and composite writers. He is certainly the strangest, most unfathomable and eccentric... [His] voice...reverberates beyond the margins of his books."

　　—VALERIA LUISELLI, author of *Faces in the Crowd*

"[*The Art of Flight*] is the most celebrated of Pitol's novels... It travels through readings—from Antonio Tabucchi to [William] Faulkner and Thomas Mann—through cities, films, notebooks, and recordings, melancholy memories, hypnosis, and dreams."

　　—*Letras Libres*

"The bountiful work of [Sergio Pitol] is one of the most original in the Spanish language."

　　—*El País*

"[*The Art of Flight*] combines cultural density with autobiographical vigor...a landscape that is classic, desolate, ironic, parodic, and very lively."

　　—CARLOS MONSIVÁIS

DEEP
VELLUM

THE ART
OF FLIGHT

THE ART
OF FLIGHT

—

Sergio Pitol

TRANSLATED FROM THE SPANISH BY
GEORGE HENSON

INTRODUCTION BY
ENRIQUE VILA-MATAS

DEEP VELLUM PUBLISHING

DALLAS, TEXAS

Deep Vellum Publishing
2919 Commerce St. #159, Dallas, Texas 75226
deepvellum.org · @deepvellum

ISBN: 978-1-941920-06-0 (paperback) · 978-1-941920-07-7 (ebook)
LIBRARY OF CONGRESS CONTROL NUMBER: 2015930299

—

Esta publicación fue realizada con el estímulo del PROGRAMA
DE APOYO A LA TRADUCCIÓN (PROTRAD) dependiente de
instituciones culturales mexicanas.

This publication was carried out with the support of the
PROGRAM TO SUPPORT THE TRANSLATION OF MEXICAN
WORKS INTO FOREIGN LANGUAGES (PROTRAD) with the
collective support of Mexico's cultural institutions.

—

Cover design & typesetting by Anna Zylicz · annazylicz.com

Text set in Bembo, a typeface modeled on typefaces cut by Francesco Griffo
for Aldo Manuzio's printing of *De Aetna* in 1495 in Venice.

Deep Vellum titles are published under the fiscal sponsorship of
The Writer's Garret, a nationally recognized nonprofit literary arts organization.

Distributed by Consortium Book Sales & Distribution.

Printed in the United States of America on acid-free paper.

Contents

—

INTRODUCTION BY ENRIQUE VILA-MATAS   III

I.   MEMORY

   EVERYTHING IS IN ALL THINGS   3

     YES, I TOO HAVE HAD MY VISION   3

     PAST AND PRESENT   7

     LUNCH AT THE BELLINGHAUSEN   12

     EVERYTHING IS ALL THINGS   18

   WITH MONSIVÁIS THE YOUNGER   27

     ONE DAY IN 1957   27

     THE RETURN HOME   37

     ANOTHER DAY, IN 1962   44

     NOW   53

   THE WOUND OF TIME   56

   DREAMS, NOTHING MORE   67

   TEST OF INITIATION   81

   DIARY FROM ESCUDILLERS   85

   A VINDICATION OF HYPNOSIS   103

   SIENA REVISITED   113

II.   WRITING

   THE NARRATOR   135

   THE DARK TWIN   154

   DROCTULF AND OTHERS   172

   THE MARQUISE WAS NEVER CONTENT

     TO STAY AT HOME   179

   ON RECONCILIATIONS   188

     AND THE WORD BECAME FLESH   188

WRESTLING WITH THE ANGEL   190

TRAVELING AND WRITING   200

AN ARS POETICA?   213

HERE COMES THE PARADE!   223

CHARMS   232

III. READINGS

THE GREAT THEATER OF THE WORLD   237

OUR CONTEMPORARY CHEKHOV   265

ŠVEJK   277

BOROLA AGAINST THE WORLD   292

TWO WEEKS WITH THOMAS MANN   298

THE GATES OF PARADISE   310

OUR ULYSSES   329

PEREIRA DECLARES   352

IV. ENDING

JOURNEY TO CHIAPAS   363

   I. THE BEGINNINGS   363

   II. WATER FROM THE SAME RIVER   376

   III. FROM THEN UNTIL NOW   385

V. TRANSLATOR'S NOTE   393

VI. BIBLIOGRAPHY OF TRANSLATED TEXTS   400

AUTHOR AND TRANSLATOR BIOGRAPHIES   402

PUBLISHER'S NOTE   404

INTRODUCTION

PITOL IN THE RAIN

By Enrique Vila-Matas

Life and literature are fused in Sergio Pitol. And I wonder now if there is anything more Cervantesesque than his passion for confusing life and literature. Somewhere in *The Art of Flight,* Sergio tells us that he is the sum of "the books I have read, the paintings I have seen, the music I have heard and forgotten, and the streets I have walked. One is his childhood, his family, some friends, a few loves, and more than a few annoyances."

I think about the streets I've had the chance to walk with him. There are streets, side streets, and backstreets traveled in Ashgabat, Veracruz, Caracas, Paris, Aix-en-Provence, Prague, Desvarié, and Kabul. And I'm reminded especially of a rainy day in Aix-en-Provence, where we went to pay tribute to Antonio Tabucchi. I remember the day because there was a pounding rain and Sergio was constantly losing his glasses; the latter was not at all unusual, his penchant for losing and then finding his glasses being legendary. That day he lost them several times, in various bookstores and cafés, as if that were a perfect antidote for not losing his umbrella. I recalled the day that Juan Villoro had found in Pitol's tendency to lose his glasses a clue to illuminating new aspects of his poetics: "Sergio writes in that hazy region of someone who loses his eyeglasses on purpose; he pretends that his originality is an attribute of his bad eyesight…"

For Villoro, Pitol does not seek to clarify but rather distort what he sees. In *The Art of Flight,* Pitol tells us that, on his first trip to Venice, back in 1961, he misplaced his glasses upon his arrival, he misplaced them while wondering if he would find death in Venice, death in the city of his ancestors. We also found death and mist, misplaced eyeglasses, and the compact fusion of life with literature on another rainy day, this time in Mérida, in the Venezuelan Andes. We had climbed to four thousand feet and, upon descending into the city, Sergio became alarmed because he thought his blood pressure was too high. We went into a pharmacy where a fourteen-year-old boy, who obviously didn't know what he was doing, took his blood pressure. "You have five thousand four hundred pesos of blood pressure," the boy said. Sergio grew faint and startled. "You should be dead," the boy added. "Ay!" Sergio screamed, and I can still hear today the echo of that scream unleashed in the middle of that Andean city. I explained to him that blood pressure was not measured in pesos and that, besides, the number didn't make sense, but Sergio remained peaked, and I ended up accompanying him to a nearby clinic where—true to his nature—he would forget his glasses. There, a nurse, who was dressed in an innocent yet almost obscene way (in an unbelievable miniskirt), after a brief examination, would only say that he was in no danger. "None," she told him. "Oh, Miss," Sergio added, "it's as if you had saved my life." Was that obscene nurse literature itself? Sergio always said that literature had saved his life. Shortly thereafter, he had to once again look for his glasses.

In these anecdotes of rainy days past lies the silhouette of his

Cervantesesque life, since, as he says, "Everything is all things." Reading him, one has the impression of being in the presence of the best writer in the Spanish language of our time. And to whomever asks about his style, I will say that it consists in fleeing anyone who is so dreadful as to be full of certainty. His style is to say everything, but to not solve the mystery. His style is to distort what he sees. His style consists in traveling and losing countries and losing one or two pairs of eyeglasses in them, losing all of them, losing eyeglasses and losing countries and rainy days, losing everything: having nothing and being Mexican and at the same time always being a foreigner.

Translated by George Henson

MEMORY

EVERYTHING IS IN ALL THINGS

YES, I TOO HAVE HAD MY VISION

It was enough just to leave the train station and catch a glimpse from
the vaporetto of the façades along the Grand Canal as they came into
view to experience the feeling of being one step away from my goal,
of having traveled years to cross the threshold, unable to decipher
what that goal was and what threshold had to be crossed. Would I die
in Venice? Would something arise that could in an instant change my
destiny? Would I, perchance, be reborn in Venice?

I was arriving from Trieste; I had not searched for Joyce's house or
for traces of Svevo, nor had I done or seen anything that was worthwhile. I had arrived in the city the evening before, and as I attempted
to find lodging in a hotel, an employee detected some anomaly or
other in my visa, an error in the expiration date, I believe, which
rendered my stay in the country illegal. I was allowed, reluctantly, to
spend the night in the hotel lobby. Early that morning I caught the
return train; when it stopped in Venice I decided to get off. It must
have been seven in the morning when I first set foot on Venetian soil.
I would spend the rest of the day there and continue on to Rome on
the night express. It is written that misfortunes never come singly:
after checking my bag at left-luggage I discovered I had lost my glasses;

3

I searched my pockets and ran to the platform, hoping to find them on the ground, but the sea of travelers and porters bustling about forced me to abandon my search. Most likely, I thought, I had left them at the hotel in Trieste or on the train car I had left in such a rush.

All of this must have taken place in mid-October of 1961. I suddenly found myself in the Piazzetta, eager to begin my tour. My near-sightedness in no way dulled the wonder. I arrived at the Piazza San Marco and drank my first coffee at the Caffè Florian, that place of legend profiled by every writer and artist who ever visited Venice. Next door to the Florian, I bought a guidebook. Seeing up-close—reading, for example—presented little problem. After the coffee, guidebook in hand, I began to walk. The details eluded me, the contours faded; immense multicolored spots, luxurious glows, and perfect patinas appeared all around me. I saw the sparkle of timeworn gold where most certainly there was flaking on a wall. Everything was submerged in mist, like in the mysterious *Views of Venice* painted by Turner. I walked among shadows. I could and could not see, I caught fragments of a shifting reality; the feeling of being trapped between light and dark grew increasingly more pronounced as a fine, trembling drizzle gradually created the chiaroscuro in which I was moving.

As the mist concealed my view of palaces, piazzas, and bridges, my happiness grew. I walked so long that even now I have the impression that the day encompassed a multitude of days. As I walked, ecstatic, I repeated over and over a phrase from Berenson: "Color is the greatest gift the Venetians have given us," words I remembered having read at the beginning of *The Venetian Painters of the Renaissance*. I return to the book today to verify the quote and discover that not only had I caused it to lose its nuance but I had also deformed and contracted it, as no doubt happened with everything I discovered in Venice during that first encounter. Berenson writes: "Their mastery over colour is the first thing that attracts most people to the painters of Venice. Their colouring not only gives direct pleasure to the eye, but acts like music upon the moods, stimulating thought and memory in much the same way as a work by a great composer." By shortening the quote I was attempting to approximate its meaning. Yes, color—that predominant gray I perceived, with backgrounds of ochre, sienna reds, bottle greens, and constant golds—not only became a source of pleasure for my weary eyes, it also stimulated my mind, my imagination, and my memory in an extraordinary way.

As I entered San Marco, the vastness of the space overwhelmed me. For a while I followed a group to whom a tour guide was explaining in laggard and pedantic French certain characteristics of Byzantine art. In that magnificent space I experienced the day's only moment of doubt. It was difficult for me to make up my mind whether its grandeur was an obvious sign of the splendor of Byzantium, or a first step toward the aesthetic of Cecile B. DeMille, that titan of Hollywood. During subsequent, more relaxing visits, I concluded, with Solomonic wisdom, that both poetics are interwoven in that glorious basilica in remarkable harmony. I then moved on to a room located in an adjacent palace, where I saw an exhibition of Bosch. It was trial by fire! I had to look at the paintings from a considerable distance, which for me meant stumbling into total darkness. Had my knowledge of modern art been less rudimentary, I would have been able to compare some of those paintings with Malevich's famous *Black Square* or with one of the enormous canvases in black by Rothko, of whose existence of course I was unaware.

I then set off for the Galleria. I toured its rooms overflowing with wonders: Giorgione, Bellini, Titian, Tintoretto, Veronese, and Carpaccio: the immense legacy of form and color that Venice has bequeathed to the world. I cannot remember if I followed a group, as I did in San Marco, or whether I relied on my guidebook, pausing before some of the paintings. Afterward, I become lost. All I know is that I walked aimlessly for several hours, wandered down countless streets, crossed the great Rialto Bridge several times, and other less majestic ones, even some in ruins that crossed the small canals in less affluent neighborhoods. I boarded the vaporetto on several occasions and continued moving; I drank another coffee at the Florian and ate gloriously in a trattoria I happened upon by accident. As I walked, I became lost from time to time in my tiny guidebook. I tried to find Palladio's buildings, those spaces that Hofmannsthal considered more worthy of being inhabited by gods than by men; I did not know then that outside of two or three churches the rest of his work is located on dry land, in Vicenza specifically. I thought I had found the Palazzo Mocenigo where Byron lived two years of scandalous orgies and prolific creation; the Palazzo Vendramin where Wagner lodged, and that other one where Henry James took an apartment in order to write The Aspern Papers. I began to imagine which one belonged to Juliana Bordereau, the centenarian protagonist who guards the much coveted papers, and the house where Robert Browning died, and the one where Alma Mahler attended to her daughter's deathbed, and the one where Schnitzler's daughter committed suicide just days after marrying. The very name of the city links the annals of love with moments of death. It is no wonder that one of the great titles of literature is *Death in Venice*. I saw towers, battlements, and balconies.

I saw pointed arches and columns, bronze horses and marble lions. I heard Italian and German and French spoken all around me, as well as the Venetian dialect, peppered with words from Old Castilian, which once upon a time my ancestors must have spoken in those narrow streets. I paused in front of the Teatro La Fenice, whose splendid interior I had just seen in a movie by Visconti. In the vestibule, a large poster by Picasso announced a recent performance by the Berliner Ensemble: *Mutter Courage*.

That night, as I boarded my train, I felt as though I knew Venice like the back of my hand. What a poor naïve devil! Fatigue was getting the best of me; all of the sudden I began to feel the incredible effort I had exerted that day: my eyes, my temples, the back of my neck, my joints all hurt. I struggled to open my suitcase to take out my pajamas. The first thing I pulled out was a jacket; I felt my glasses in one of the pockets. The miracle had been completed: I had crossed the threshold, the steel blue egg of Leda was beginning to hatch, and opposites were uniting at the bottom of tombs. Where was all this esoteric logorrhea coming from? I did not finish putting on my pajamas. I remembered a line from the end of *To the Lighthouse*: "Yes, I have had my vision," and I fell asleep. I repeated it again in the morning as I woke up, when the train was about to arrive in Rome.

PAST AND PRESENT

The year was 1965. I had been living in Warsaw for two years. One day the postman handed me a letter from Vence, a village in the South of France. It was signed by Witold Gombrowicz. Could it be a joke?

I could scarcely believe it was real. I showed it to some Polish friends, and they were stunned. A young Mexican who was living in Warsaw had just received a letter from Gombrowicz! It couldn't be! It was impossible! I nodded, ecstatic. "Like everything in Gombrowicz's life," I told myself.

He explained in the letter that someone had given him the Spanish translation of *The Gates of Paradise* by Jerzy Andrzejewski, which I had done, and that he found it satisfactory. So he invited me to collaborate with him on the translation of his *Argentine Diary*, which the publishing house Sudamericana was to publish in Buenos Aires. It was the beginning of a significant improvement in my living conditions. Suddenly, I began to receive offers from various places. The sources of my income were Joaquín Mortiz at Ediciones Era and the Universidad Veracruzana Press in Mexico; Seix Barral and Planeta in Barcelona; and Sudamericana in Buenos Aires. Until then, I had only managed to place a few translations here and there. From that moment on, in just three or four hours a day, I managed to earn a regular income that in Poland in those days was a tidy little sum. In addition to Polish literature, I was receiving offers to translate Italian and English authors. For the next six or seven years I worked primarily as a translator; the profession I had begun in Warsaw allowed me to live full-time in Barcelona and part-time in England.

As I recall that time, I do not think that "I was living another life," as people usually say, but rather that the person I'm talking about was not entirely me; instead, that person was a young Mexican who shared my name and some of my habits and idiosyncrasies.

One of the obvious bonds I share with that young man living in Warsaw is his inordinate love for reading. The freedom he enjoyed then is scarcely visible in his writings, but perhaps it was placed into a reservoir for later use, when, paradoxically, his spirit of freedom had withered. Recalling his irresponsibility, his cheek, his taste for adventure, produces in the writer of these lines a kind of vertigo.

I have trouble writing. My hand freezes when I recall the time when living was akin to being a noble savage and realize, without rancor, that society, its offices and its conventions, eventually achieved their mission. But not entirely! Perhaps my opposition to the ways of the world is more radical now, but it manifests itself in sullenness rather than joy—in convictions. It is no longer a mere emanation of nature.

During my stay in Warsaw I was master of my time, my body, and my pen. And while it is true that freedom in Poland was far from absolute, it is also true that the Poles took advantage as best they could, and with an intensity that bordered on frenzy, of the spaces opened up during de-Stalinization, especially artistic spaces. I owe to that period the pleasure of reading texts that would certainly have been different had I been living in my own country or in any of the cultural metropolises. Free from the burden of trends, from the *capillas*, Mexico's literary coteries, and from any pressing need for information, reading became an act of sheer hedonism. I read the Poles, of course, and everything in that world was discovery; I read what my friends sent me from Mexico: Mexican and Latin American literature. *Hopscotch* was a revelation. Other books that were treasures were Francisco Delicado's *The Portrait of Lozana*; a great deal of Tirso de Molina; Canetti's *Auto da Fé*; Musil's *The Confusions of Young Törless*; Tibor Déry's *Mr. G.A. in X*; Milan Fust's *The Story of My Wife*; and, in particular, the ample collection of the British Council library: Shakespeare and the other Elizabethans; the theater of the Restoration,

especially Sheridan and Congreve; Sterne's *Tristram Shandy*; Walter
de la Mare's *Memoirs of a Midget*; and, of course, everything, or almost
everything, by Conrad, the reading of whom was different in a Polish
milieu; and Henry James and Ford Madox Ford and Firbank and
many others. The difference between who I am now and who I was
then is defined by my passion for reading and my aversion for any
manifestation of power.

Around the same time as Gombrowicz's letter, I received another
from the publisher Don Rafael Giménez Siles, encouraging me to
write an autobiography. He had invited a dozen writers from my
generation and from the even younger one. He was interested, he said,
in knowing how we young writers perceived the world and, more
importantly, how we came to terms with our circumstances within it.

One aspect of the biographies would be their brevity, consistent
with the short journey made by their writers. I began to write the
account reluctantly and with very mixed feelings, but convinced of
the need to have a presence, however small, in my country. Unlike the
other authors included, I had written very little: two small books of
short stories. I was certain that my life, and not just my literary one,
had just started; nevertheless, I wrote the autobiographical essay out
of vanity, or frivolity, or inertia.

I finished the requested text in a few days. As I wrote it, I felt
trapped in an endless continuum. The recent episode was still very
close to me, within a stone's throw, and none of its lines had been
brought to a close yet. I could compare my past to one of those
extremely destructive hurricanes that strike a particular region with
ferocity and, then, for weeks, travel for thousands of miles, but without moving from the spot where they built their greatest strength, to

which they return time and time again to unleash their wrath. That was how I viewed my life: my childhood or what I tried to and could remember about it, my days at university, and a few trips, all of it was present in my memory as a single, rather confusing entity. The distance from Mexico, the perspective that it gave me, the strangeness of the new setting, helped to transform the past into a shapeless mixture of elements.

In late 1988 I returned to Mexico permanently. During my absence I published several books; some were translated into other languages. I received awards, all those things! I returned to the country with the idea of devoting my time and energy exclusively to writing. I felt an almost physical need to live with the language, to listen to Spanish all the time, to know it was around me, even if I did not hear it. The Mexico City I encountered seemed foreign and stubbornly complex. I persevered for four years without being able to assimilate it, nor assimilate myself to it. After I arrived, I began to receive publishing proposals; one was to rework that early autobiography, adding a second part that would bear witness to the previous twenty years. I had never reread it. When I did, I felt disgusted, with myself, and, above all, with my language. I did not recognize myself in the least in the image I sketched in Warsaw in 1965. I was struck immediately by a demure tone and false modesty that were irreconcilable with my relationship to literature, which has always been visceral, excessive, even wild. I sensed a plea for forgiveness emanating from the text for having been written and published. They were pages of immense hypocrisy. The writer's task seemed like a third-rate activity. In short, it would not have bothered me to declare—because at the time I believed it—that I enjoyed writing less than reading, or that it was an ill-defined and precarious experience compared to other things that life offered me. That would have been fine. What I found strange was the virtuous schoolboy mask I was hiding behind, in halftone, the hypocritical ramblings of the Pharisee.

Lately, I have been very aware that I have a past. Not only because I have reached an age when the greater part of the journey has been traveled, but also because I now know fragments of my childhood that until recently were off-limits to me. I can now distinguish the various stages of my life with sufficient clarity—the autonomy of the parts and their relation to the whole—which I was previously unable to do. I have begun to remember with respect and emotion not only my youth but that of others because of the innocence it represents—its blindness, intransigence, and destiny. That alone allows me to conceive of an infinite, unknown, and promising future.

LUNCH AT THE BELLINGHAUSEN

In 1978 or 1979 I spent a few months in Mexico City. At the time, I was a cultural attaché to our embassy in Moscow. I had saved my vacation days for two years so that my stay in Mexico would make more sense than on previous occasions, when I felt I was and was not in my country. Two months was a more respectable amount of time. During the first days of my stay I received a telephone call from Julieta Campos, then director of the Mexican PEN Club, inviting me to participate in a series of presentations of writers from various generations. In each session an older writer and a younger one, a literary newcomer, would read recent texts and then discuss them with the audience. She told me that she was thinking of pairing me with Villoro; we then talked about other things, some of which, with respect to the literary performance, were unclear to me.

After hanging up the phone it occurred to me that there was something about the proposition that did not make sense, that there was not sufficient distance between his generation and mine. It would have made more sense to be paired with Juan de la Cabada, Fernando Benítez, or Luis Cardoza y Aragón, my seniors. I was more than surprised when I learned a few days later that the Villoro with whom I would be introduced was Juan, Luis's son; I had been assigned the role of the elder. I was forty-five years old, but until fairly recently I was still being mentioned among Mexico's young writers. I suppose it was in part because of my absence, which made me difficult to identify, and the paucity of my work.

That was the first sign that things were no longer what they had been. That first public reading I did in Mexico gave me the opportunity to read a story that I had just written after several years of unbearable hibernation. It was also the beginning of a great friendship that binds me to Juan Villoro.

A mature author requires no introduction, or does he? The truth is the majority of my work appeared after that night when I passed the mantle to a very tall, hyperactive adolescent, who read with an impressive display of energy the story "El mariscal de campo" (The Field Marshal).

The act of reading, at that meeting of generations, a text that marked my return to writing made me feel, once the nightmare had ended and the celebratory teasing had begun, that I had reached maturity in a rather equivocal situation, that I had behaved like an adolescent writer and Juan like the master who was returning from all the experiences. I read with almost unbearable tension, without knowing if I would be able to make it to the end of a paragraph or even a sentence. I was afraid of having an embolism or a heart attack before getting to a stopping point, unlike the excruciating ease of the beardless youth who seemed to be conquering not just the audience but the entire world.

But in spite of the confusion, I was able to surmise that the equivocal relationship between age and writing would over the years become something eminently comical. The march toward old age, and, let's say it plainly, toward death, continues to provide unimaginable surprises, as if everything were an invention, a spectacle in which I am both actor and audience, and in which the scenes are characterized quite often by their parodic quality, like a laughable but also harsh theatrical illusion.

Let us look at an example:

I accompany Carlos Monsiváis to the Bellinghausen to meet Hugo Gutiérrez Vega, who had just arrived in Mexico to celebrate the New Year. Every time he returns to the country, whether from Madrid, Río, Washington, Athens, from whatever city his diplomatic career takes him, Carlos and I meet him at the same place to eat. Without fail, we begin to talk as if only a few weeks had passed since our last meal, which is one of the surest signs of friendship. On this occasion, he was coming from San Juan, Puerto Rico, where he is Consul General.

Hugo's magnanimity is known to everyone. I am indebted to him, among other expressions of affection, for having put me in contact with some friends of his from the University of Bristol, where I was lecturer for a year in the Spanish department. We are the same age; I think I am even a couple of years his senior, but this does not prevent me from remembering him as an older brother; in fact, he and Lucy were like a big brother and big sister—and extraordinarily so!—during my stay in England.

In short, we met and were glad to be chatting again at the Bellinghausen. After the obligatory comments—our ailments, our friends, the situation in the country—Hugo manages to turn the conversation to one of his favorite topics: Romania, or rather, Romanian literature. He is elated that the Latin Union of Romance Languages Prize, awarded a few days ago in Rome, was given to the Romanian Alexandru Vona, whom he knows well. He won it for a single novel, he tells us, which Vona finished writing in 1947 and was finally about to have published. The novel, *Bricked-up Windows*, has shaped his destiny. It continues to be his destiny! The few intimate friends whom the Romanian author had allowed to read the novel claimed that his narrative style revealed such a sublime and rigorous quest for form that, if one were to make comparisons, the only names that might come to mind would be the great writers of our century: Kafka, Joyce, Broch, or Musil. For decades, the novelist lived with the certainty that he would never see his work published. Nevertheless, he continued to care for it, refining it in secret. His first surprise must have been its publication in 1993 in its original language, Romanian; then came the translation to French, and now the prize awarded him unanimously by an exceptionally brilliant jury comprised of, among others, Vincenzo Consolo, Luigi Malerba, Antonio Muñoz Molina, Rubem Fonseca, and our dear friend Álvaro Mutis. And from Vona, Hugo bounces to other writers he knows—some personally, others by their work—because one of his greatest passions, perhaps the most eccentric, is, you may have already guessed by now, Romanian literature.

Hugo speaks with characteristic passion as he moves within his sphere; the names he cited elude me, with the exception of the most obvious: Cioran, Eminescu, Eliade, Gian Luca Caragiale; the same thing, I imagine, happens to Monsiváis. He recounts the exploit of a poet and Hispanist—was it Gialescu?—who, although gravely ill from osseous tuberculosis, devotes the rest of his life to translating Góngora's *Soledades* which he does so masterfully that today it is considered one of the most remarkable renderings of the Andalusian poet's work in any foreign language. From there, I begin to get lost, my mind wanders, and not because Hugo's discussion fails to interest me, rather because I discover that an old man, the doyen of all the world's old men, the quintessential Nestor, is waving ardently at me from at a faraway table. I watch him stand up suddenly and begin to walk, very slowly, dragging two feet that by all appearances are attempting to rebel against him; he moves his arms as if he were feeling his way or attempting to propel himself. He smiles as though our presence in the restaurant both surprised him and filled him with happiness.

He is wearing stylish clothes, greenish-gray flannel trousers and a slightly wrinkled checkered jacket, which adds a discreet elegance to his figure. His white mane is full and unruly. His face has a pinkish hue, like that of a baby, but scored in every direction with wrinkles of varying lengths and depths, which seems out of place with his infant-like coloring. He reminds me of the last photos of Auden: "My face looks like a wedding cake left out in the rain…" The only one among us who could not see him was Carlos, because this radiant specter of happiness was approaching from his rear. The names of classmates came to mind suddenly en masse; at that moment, I tried to imagine the face of a younger man, to return it to adolescence and assign it a name, but it was impossible.

Waiting on the tip of my tongue were all the platitudes that one says at moments such as this: "It's great to see you, old man, especially in such good shape! Obviously, life has treated you well, am I right? Now I know why our colleagues call you Dorian Gray. But they're wrong, you're in much better shape, much better of course," and other such nonsense, only to buy time and give the other person the opportunity to say something that will allow me to identify him.

He opened his arms just a step from our table, as I was about to stand and embrace him. Fortunately, I stopped; I would have made a spectacle of myself. The old timer walked past us without stopping, without even looking at us, his smile growing bigger, and his arms flailing even more. He stopped at the table right behind ours. I was saved from having to repeat such drivel and listen to him do the same. Someone at the table next to us said: "You're looking good, Flacus! Just look at him! I'm so jealous, Flacus!" And the salvo of hot air that the occasion demanded continued; the gamut of banalities that language has accumulated for such cases. I turned around to watch the show. It was a long table, with some ten people, everyone fawning over Flacus, who, with a content look he attempted to mitigate with words of modesty, responded: "Don't be so sure, not everything that glimmers is gold; I don't always feel as good as today; don't be so sure, you can't judge a book by its cover…!"

I breathed a sigh of relief. At that moment, I realized that we had all stopped talking. What was curious was that the three of us, Hugo and I from the beginning of the old man's march, and Monsiváis from the time he walked by the table, thought that he was a friend from our youth whom we were not able to place. Perhaps an actor from our generation, a young leading man with a brief but intense career, retired from the profession many years ago. But that possibility turned out to be, without our knowing why, unconvincing.

We devoured our dessert and downed our coffee, as if trying to escape that character who was so close to us. The suspicion that someone could at that very moment be saying the same thing about us made us a little uneasy to say the least. In short, one must grow accustomed to such discomfort upon reaching a certain age.

EVERYTHING IS ALL THINGS

After the first "vision," I returned to Venice at least a dozen times. I have wandered every corner of it, and read with interest and pleasure many of the texts that have been written about it, its history, its art, and its customs. There also exists a store of fiction set in Venice. In almost every one of these novels it is considered more than just a setting; rather, it becomes a character. Sometimes it is the protagonist itself.

Puritans, by training, by creed, or by temperament, tend to demonize it; in some, the rejection coincides with an irresistible attraction, and that duality is transformed into delirium. Ruskin passionately described each of its stones, and at the same time was horrified by the customs and traditions of its inhabitants. Evil dwells in the heart of Venice; it is a sea of abomination; its contaminating power is the work of the devil, they say. Should an innocent person manage to escape from there, he does so with a damaged soul. Some are even denied that privilege. They succumb; such is the case of Aschenbach from *Death in Venice*. Half of mankind allows itself to berate it, lecture it; they attempt to reform it, redeem it from its sins and vices; they demand it cease to exist in order to purge its sins; they rejoice in its decline; only its sinking—death by water—will succeed in purifying it.

Its defenders at times employ disconcerting arguments. Berenson becomes rhapsodic over its colors. He marvels at its extraordinary school of painting, the only one in Italy that lacks "primitives," because it was born with a handful of masterpieces. The celebrated aesthete asserts that Venice was the first modern European nation, but the reasons underlying this assertion seem rather paradoxical: "Since there was little room for personal glory in Venice, the perpetuators of glory, the Humanists, found at first scant encouragement there, and the Venetians were saved from that absorption in archeology and pure science which overwhelmed Florence at an early date. [...] As it was, the feeling for beauty was not hindered in its natural development." Venetian painting is created, and he insists on this point at various times, to be simply an object of pleasure.

What Berenson highlights—his admiration for beautiful and healthy bodies; his love for colorful and sumptuous decoration; the disposition toward pleasure, carnival; the permanent use of the mask and erotic extravagance—is what scandalizes Puritans. On the other hand, anyone who has the slightest propensity for sensuality will in *La Serenissima* feel as if he were in the Temple of Venus. It is no wonder Casanova is known world-over as the son of Venice.

Venice is boundless and unfathomable. There is always something to see on the next trip, because a church is under restoration, a painting is on loan, the museums are on strike, a thousand reasons. Each trip means corrections, amplifications, surprises, dedications, and demystifications. During my first trips Longhi did not even exist for me, yet today he is one of the painters I am most drawn to. I waited many long years to be able to see Carpaccio's amazing mural *St. George and the Dragon*. For many years, time and again, I walked the long route from La Fenice et des Artistes hotel, where I always stay, to the church of San Giorgio degli Schiavoni, and each time I encountered an unexpected obstacle: closed for restoration, admission denied due to some special ceremony, the walls draped in thick curtains without any explanation whatsoever. During my last trip, when I was finally able to see that and the other frescoes the San Giorgio holds, I felt as if I had at long last planted a pike in Flanders.

The first time, it bears repeating, I saw the city without seeing it. Instead I saw it in fragments, emerging and disappearing, with incorrect proportions and altered colors. The spectacle was at once unreal and marvelous. Over the years I have corrected that vision, each time more magnificent, each time more unreal. In some way my travels around the world, my entire life, have had that same character. With or without glasses, I've never achieved more than glimpses, approximations, mutterings in search of meaning in the narrow space that runs between light and darkness. I've dreamt that I was a voyager in that fantastic ship of fools painted by Memling, which I once contemplated with amazement in the Naval Museum of Gdansk. What are we, and what is the universe? What are we in the universe? These are questions that leave us speechless, and that we are accustomed to answering with a joke so as not to seem ridiculous.

We, I would venture to guess, are the books we have read, the paintings we have seen, the music we have heard and forgotten, the streets we have walked. We are our childhood, our family, some friends, a few loves, more than a few disappointments. A sum reduced by infinite subtractions. We are shaped by different times, hobbies, and creeds.

As I write these pages, I can divide my life into one long, enjoyable, gregarious phase, and another, the most recent, in which solitude seems to me a gift from the gods. For many years, going to parties, lunches, *tertulias*, cafés, bars, restaurants was a daily pleasure. The transition to the other extreme occurred so gradually I'm unable to explain the process's distinct movements. My years in Prague coincided with an intense inner energy. Writing became an obsession; I believe the unbearable social life that I was obliged to lead, for reasons of protocol, in some way nourished the novels I wrote there with anecdotes, episodes, gestures, phrases, and habits.

I live in Xalapa, a provincial capital surrounded by exceptional landscapes. In the morning I go out to the countryside, where I have a cabin, and I spend several hours writing and listening to music. From time to time I take a break to play with my dog in the garden. I return to the city for the midday meal, and in the afternoon I write again, listen to music, read, and sometimes I watch an old movie on videocassette. I talk to friends on the phone. After six p.m., except on rare occasions, nothing can make me leave the house. I am indebted to the architect Bernal Lascuráin, to his imagination, to his taste and his talent, for the pleasure of inhabiting these houses, each one built as a complement to the other. If I had to live under house arrest in them, I would be perfectly happy. I work until two or three in the morning. That rhythm of life which others might find maddening is the only one that appeals to me.

Those things of importance that happen to us in life are due to instinct, Julien Green says. "All sexualities are a part of the same family: instinct. But there is something in it that always escapes us, of which we are conscious. It is what makes our life exciting. Every human being carries a mystery of which he is unaware."What doesn't matter, I suppose, what is the same for everyone in the world, what makes an epoch trivial, is created naturally by society. We condition ourselves to it without realizing it; that is one of its great labors and the source of a thousand misfortunes. But then one believes he is behaving like a robot, acting mechanically, marching like a sleepwalker, like an army of tiny little men, and, in the end, it turns out that the force of instinct has worked in the opposite direction. As a child Rosita Gómez dreamt of being a stripper and ended up being an honest bank teller; she never learned to dance, not even waltzes. Marcelino Góngora dreamt of being in the mafia, the head of a criminal gang, the terror of the underworld, yet before the end of adolescence he was a sacristan in his village church. The book that someone intended to write, and for which he took countless notes for years, suddenly came to a standstill, ceased to be a project; something unexpected, beyond his control, began to take shape. That's how things work. Ask again what we are, where we are going, and a fist in the mouth will rid you of the few teeth you have left.

And from instinct, which is a mystery, I would like to shift to the subject of tolerance, which is an act of will. There is no human virtue more admirable. It implies recognition of others: another way of knowing oneself. An extraordinary virtue, says E.M. Forster, although hardly exciting. There are no hymns to tolerance, as there are, in abundance, to love. It lacks poems and sculptures that extol it. It is a virtue that requires a constant effort and vigilance. It has no popular prestige. If one says of a man that he is tolerant, most people instantly believe that his wife has cheated on him, and the rest make him out to be a fool. One would have to return to the eighteenth century, to

Voltaire, to Diderot, to the *encyclopédistes*, to find the true meaning of the word. In our century, Bakhtin is one of its paladins: his notion of dialogism allows for the possibility of responding to different and opposite meanings equally. "We only harm others when we're incapable of imagining them," writes Carlos Fuentes. "Political democracy and civilized coexistence between men demands tolerance and the acceptance of values and ideas different than our own," says Octavio Paz.

Norberto Bobbio offers a definition of the "civilized" man that embodies the concept of tolerance as daily action, a working moral exercise: The civilized man "lets others be themselves irrespective of whether these individuals may be arrogant, haughty, or domineering. They do not engage with others intending to compete, harass, and ultimately prevail. They refrain from exercising the spirit of contest, competition, or rivalry, and therefore also of winning. In life's struggle [civilized men] are perpetual losers. [...] This is because in this kind of world there are no contests for primacy, no struggles for power, and no competitions for wealth. In short, here the very conditions that enable the division of individuals into winners and losers do not exist."[1] There is something enormous in those words. When I observe the deterioration of Mexican life, I think that only an act of reflection, of critique, and of tolerance could provide an exit from the situation. But conceiving of tolerance as it is imagined in the Bobbio's text implies a titanic effort. I begin to think about the hubris, arrogance,

---

1 Translated by Teresa Chataway. Throughout the text, Pitol quotes from a variety of literary texts written in Spanish and in other languages. Because he does not cite the quotations, it is impossible to know the source of the translated quotations. For consistency, where possible, I have opted to use published English translations of all quotations. A full bibliography of these translations and their sources is included in the Appendix. Unless otherwise noted by a footnote, all translations of these quotations are mine. — *Trans.*

and corruption of some acquaintances, and I become angry, I begin to list their attitudes that most irritate me, I discover the magnitude of contempt they inspire in me, and eventually I must recognize how far I am from being a civilized man.

In the second entry of Lezama Lima's diaries, dated October 24, 1939, the Cuban writer writes of the relationship between Voltaire and Frederick II. In the beginning, the rapport between the monarch and the philosopher seemed perfect: "Both constantly lose all sense of measure in their praise." But a single criticism by Voltaire regarding the spelling mistakes that spoil Louis XIV's prose is enough to poison the relationship. A king is a king and therefore his greatness cannot be dishonored by a solecism or a spelling mistake; a philosopher, no matter how genius, is only a philosopher and should know his place. *Caesar est supra grammaticam*, that must never be forgotten. The age-old connection between writer and prince has been undermined by misunderstanding; it is a dangerous friendship. A novelist must learn to carry on a dialogue with others, but especially with himself, he must learn to scrutinize and listen to himself; this will help him know who he is. If he fails, instead of a novel, he will build a verbal artifact that attempts to simulate a narrative form, but whose breathing will be wrong. It will, perhaps, pick up something in the atmosphere. The author knows that he will please either Caesar or the masses, it makes no difference; he has written it for one of those two deities. A few years later, it will end up on the scrapheap. Literature is worse than *la belle dame sans merci*, that woman beloved and feared by the symbolists. When they play tricks on her, when she senses that she's being used for spurious reasons, her revenge can be ferocious.

To begin by invoking the annals of Venice and to end bogged down in a literature of lies is a vulgarity. This fact allows me to realize how far I am from the civilized man that Bobbio envisions. Rather than yield to that irritation, I would like to comment on the attitude of two writers who have been decisive as models for my life of retirement: Luis Cernuda and Julien Gracq. It is well known that temperament is destiny, and in temperament I feel that I belong to the same family as those writers. From the outside, and out of slapdashness, one might think that it is a question of authors determined to read life instead of live it. The truth is a little more complex and at the same time much simpler.

One might think that renouncing a large portion of the world's customs is a way to make arrogance, and occasionally pride, pass for humility. This is not the case. For me it's a matter of intense relaxation, a pure form of hedonism. Walking through my garden; seeing all my books collected at last, knowing that I have reached the desert island with more options than the ten titles demanded by polls; being far from everything—without refusing to observe the world—scrutinizing it, reading it, trying to decipher its signs, sensing its movements, is overall a pleasure. This does not exclude traveling, dreaming of walking once again the streets of Lisbon, Prague, Marienbad, Venice…

Venice has been a frequent setting in my literature. It is an imagined Venice like Hofmannsthal's, an ideal Venice, which produces in me the certainty of man's biological unity with everything that surrounds him and his mythical fusion with the past.

I once wrote:

"All times deep down are a single time. Venice comprises and is comprised of all cities, and the young tourist who, Baedeker in hand and eyes half-closed, stops to contemplate a whimsical façade on the Via degli Schiavoni, the collar of his raincoat raised to protect his weak bronchial tubes from the prevailing dampness, is the same young Levantine with almond eyes and curly hair who contemplates with amazement the riches of the market that runs along the recently erected Rialto Bridge, and also the slave with a coarse mop of dirty-green hair captured in a Kashubian village on the Baltic coast in order to dig the first palafittes of what would later become the most colorful, the most eccentric, the most spectacular of all cities. Each one of us is all men. I have been, the protagonist seems to proclaim, Othello and also Iago and also Desdemona's lost handkerchief! I am my grandfather and those who will be my grandchildren! I am the vast stone that lays the foundation for these wonders, and I am also its cupolas and estipites! I am a lad and a horse and a piece of bronze that represents a horse! Everything is all things! And only Venice, with its absolute individuality, could reveal that secret."

Xalapa, February 1996

WITH MONSIVÁIS THE YOUNGER

ONE DAY IN 1957

I'm waiting for Monsiváis in the Kilos on Avenida Juárez, opposite the El Caballito statue. We agreed to meet at two, have lunch, and go over the final pages of the text I was to publish in the *Cuadernos del Unicornio* (The Unicorn's Notebooks). I don't know how many times I've reread the proofs, but I'll feel more secure if he takes a look at them. Carlos was the first person to read the two stories that will make up the notebook; the first, "Victorio Ferri Tells a Tale," is dedicated to him. I see him almost daily, even if just in passing. We met three years ago—yes, in 1954—during the days preceding the "Glorious Victory." At that time we were participating in the University Committee for Solidarity with Guatemala; we collected protest signatures, distributed fliers, attended a rally together that began in the Plaza de Santo Domingo. We saw Frida Kahlo there, surrounded by Diego Rivera, Carlos Pellicer, Juan O'Gorman, and some other "greats." She was already living entirely against the grain; it was her last public appearance: she died shortly thereafter. From then on I began to see Carlos regularly: in the café at the Faculty of Philosophy and Letters; at a *cineclub*; in the editorial office of *Estaciones*; or in the home of mutual friends. More than anywhere else, I ran into him at bookstores.

Not long after we met, he came to my apartment, on Calle de Londres, when the Juárez neighborhood had not yet become the Zona Rosa, to read a story that he had just finished: "Fino acero de niebla" (Fine Steel of Mist), about which the only thing I remember is that it had nothing to do with the Mexican literature of our generation. The language was popular, but highly stylized; and the structure was very elusive. It demanded that the reader more or less find his own way. The fiction written by our contemporaries, even the most innovative, seemed closer to the canons of the nineteenth century next to his fine steel. Monsiváis brought together in his story two elements that would later define his personality: an interest in popular culture—in this case the language of the working-class neighborhoods—and a passion for form, two facets that do not usually coincide. When I expressed my enthusiasm after the reading, he immediately snapped shut, like an oyster trying to dodge lemon drops.

He had just finished reading when Luis Prieto arrived. He greeted Carlos warmly, and Carlos immediately shoved the pages into a folder, as if they were compromising documents. Luis told us that he had just come from Las Lomas, from a very entertaining gathering with a group of English philosophers, followers of Ouspensky; one of them, who was very rich, Mr. Tur-Four, or Sir Cecil Tur-Four, as the group's members referred to him, had proposed building a place for meditation—a temple, to be exact—The Eye of God, on the outskirts of Cuautla, where the community would be able to perform the necessary rites. Some thirty people had attended to express their gratitude. Luis said he didn't understand why they had invited him. It didn't surprise me; I had accompanied him on many of his adventures through the impenetrable labyrinth of eccentricity that lay hidden within the city at the time, a world that included locals and foreigners, teachers, notaries, archeologists, old Balkan countesses, Chinese restaurateurs, Italian mediums, famous actresses, anonymous students, choreographers, rural school teachers, and opulent collectors of African, Oceanic, and pre-Hispanic art that had traveled the world, exhibited in the most famous museums, but also others, much more modest, who collected cigarette boxes, beer bottles, and shoes. Luis was also a friend of two nuns who had been cloistered during the time of religious persecution; one of them, congenitally ill-natured, a Mexican, and daughter of an Englishman, Párvula Dry, who at the slightest provocation would recount to whomever was standing in front of her, even a perfect stranger, her thorny post-convent odyssey, her arduous journey toward the Truth. The other never spoke; instead she just agreed solemnly with whatever her spokeswoman said. Every time I saw them with Luis, Párvula Dry would repeat, in almost the exact same words, that if both she and the other, the former Mother Superior, had managed to find themselves, it was due not to psychoanalysis, to which they had both turned, nor to tantric Buddhism, which is a mere fallacy, nor to the teachings of Krishnamurti, from which they learned nothing, but to their discovery of Ouspensky's *Tertium Organum*. Luis was like a fish in water with these over-the-top characters. He eventually described the meeting in detail, the characters in attendance, the events that transpired; he told us that, in the middle of Mr. Tur-Four's report on the progress of the construction of The Eye of God, a very large man, monster-like in his obesity, fell suddenly into a trance and from his lips the Maestro, Ouspensky of course, violently insulted the patron and the two dissolute nuns who were manipulating him, whose mere presence, he said, sullied their Work.

He described the uproar that occurred in the room at these words and his astonishment when several of the participants, instead of attempting to silence the giant who continued his trance-induced tirade, began to savagely insult each other. Some fell into a trance and produced conflicting messages. A skeleton-like woman, who in her normal state sounded like a bird chirping when she spoke, emitted a thunderous voice with which she threatened the snake, the worm who claimed to be the Maestro's messenger, with expulsion from the sect, and added that the former nuns, slaves of papism in the past, had already been redeemed and that, like the magnanimous Sir Cecil Tur-Four, they were absolutely necessary to the revelation of the Truth. Some fell into convulsions only to hurl increasingly inappropriate insults at each other; Luis Prieto deepened his voice and in a cavernous tone announced: "The session has been suspended!" At that moment they all came out of their trance, stood up and, like good Englishmen, said their goodbyes with the greatest propriety imaginable, except for a single elderly woman who became flabbergasted and kept repeating in English, "Two-four, stop! Two-four, stop!" and who had to be carried out on a stretcher. Luis reproduced the session in so many different voices and so many details that it looked as if a demiurge were recreating that amazing theosophical pandemonium before our eyes. Until then, for as long as I had known Carlos, I had never seen him laugh so much, nor could I imagine that a person so introspective and ensconced in books would be so receptive to such madcap humor. It was the first time I heard his inimitable guffaw. Luis and I began to tell variations of the story, adding characters, exaggerating some scenes for effect, and, to my surprise, the neophyte not only laughed like Rabelais but also contributed very skillfully to the construction and deconstruction of that verbal puzzle, the great game, of which Luis's verbal synopsis had been only a starting point.

Those stories took place three years prior to the day I'm waiting for Carlos at the Kikos on Avenida Juárez. I wait for him as I read *'Tis Pity She's a Whore*, the intense, truculent, and painful tragedy by John Ford. Of all the works of Elizabethan theatre that I know, including those by Shakespeare, Ford's tragedy is one of those that most impress me. I began to read it when I arrived at the restaurant, and I'm almost finished when the incestuous brother explodes in anger upon discovering that he's been betrayed. It's a literary period that I frequent more and more. I would like to study it in depth, systematize my readings, take notes, and establish the chronology of the period. But the same thing always happens: at the moment of greatest fervor I become sidetracked by other subjects, other periods, and I end up not studying anything in depth. Carlos is always late, but on this occasion he goes too far; it's possible that he won't even show. I'm famished; I decide to order the daily special. I eat and continue reading Ford. By the time dessert arrives I reach the end, which leaves me terrified. At that moment Carlos arrives. He's coming from the Radio Universidad, where he took part, he says, in a taping on science fiction. He orders only a hamburger and a Coke. He places the proofs next to his plate and reads them in a few minutes as he eats. He makes one or two corrections. He then takes out a couple of pages from a book, marks through a few words, adds others, changes the last lines completely. He asks me to go with him to the *Excelsior*, which is next door, so he can deliver the piece that he just corrected; it will only take a moment. In no time we'll be at Juan José Arreola's house to deliver the proofs. Waiting for us there is José Emilio Pacheco,

THE ART OF FLIGHT

who today will submit his manuscript of *La sangre de medusa* (The Blood of Medusa), which will also be published in the *Cuadernos de Unicornio*. La Zaplana, Mexico's largest bookstore, is located on the ground floor of the building immediately adjacent to the Kikos; we're unable to resist the temptation to glance at the bookstore's tables and shelves. Each of us leaves with an immense package under his arm. We're proud of the rapid growth of our libraries (Monsiváis's will eventually exceed thirty thousand volumes). We return to the Kikos to ask them to sell us some cardboard boxes because it's impossible to move through the street or get on a bus with so many books in our hands. While they look for the boxes we drink coffee and examine our finds. During our four-year friendship, our reading lists have expanded and overlapped. We both purchased Conrad by coincidence that day. I pick up *Victory* and *Under Western Eyes*, and he picks up *Lord Jim, The Outcast of the Islands*, and *The Secret Agent*. We both read an abundance of Anglo-Saxon authors, I prefer English, and he North Americans; but the end result is a mutually beneficial influence. We leaf through our purchases. I talk about Henry James, and he about Melville and Hawthorne; I about Forster, Sterne, and Virginia Woolf, and he about Poe, Twain, and Thoreau. We both admire the intelligent wit of James Thurber, and we declare once more that the language of Borges constitutes the greatest miracle that has happened to our language in this century; he pauses briefly and adds that one of the highest moments in the Castilian language is owed to Casiodoro de Reina and his disciple Cipriano de Valera, and when I ask, confused by the names, "And who are they?" he replies, scandalized, that they are none other than the translators of the Bible. He tells me that he aspires one day to write prose that exhibits the benefit of the countless years he's devoted to reading biblical texts; I, who am ignorant of them, comment, cowering slightly, that the greatest influence I've encountered is that of William Faulkner, and there he checkmates me when he explains that the language of Faulkner, like that of Melville and Hawthorne, is profoundly influenced by the Bible, that they are a non-religious derivation of the Revealed Language. Suddenly, he points out that it's gotten late, that we have to rush to the *Excelsior* to deliver his piece. I ask him if it's "The Idiot Box," and he immediately changes the subject. "The Idiot Box" is a very acerbic column about television and its effects, which are very disconcerting to Carlos. Television! Who in the hell cares about television! Certainly no one I associate with. We arrive at the editor's office. The section chief, to whom he must turn in his piece, has gone upstairs to a meeting. He might be back in a half hour. We sit wherever we can. A journalist sitting next to us, talking on the phone, says that things in Mexico are getting worse because of the government's softness, that it's giving in more and more to union pressure, that if the authorities do not intervene and eradicate the leprosy, the country will unravel. We continue to talk about books, which implies that literature is the subject to which we constantly return, although frequently interrupted by bursts of commentary of all kinds—cinema, the city, problems that concern us at the moment, the university, our lives, friends, acquaintances, and enemies—until we arrive at that subject which most entertains and amuses us: our novel, to the writing of which we have devoted hundreds of hours of conversation, without ever having written a word. Our novel, we confess, is in some way determined by the parodic humor of the young Waugh. We also know that it is equally determined by the impudence and imagination of *La familia Burrón,* the comic strip by Gabriel Vargas, and by the daily fireworks of Luis Prieto. Before beginning our work, and to exercise our mind a bit, we make a succinct summary of what is being written in Mexico, the authors worth reading, those it's better to toss in the trash; those who pass are, of the contemporaries: Gorostiza, Pellicer, Novo, and Villaurrutia; *The Labyrinth of Solitude* and *Freedom under Parole* by Octavio Paz, which just came out; Juan José Arreola's prose and the two superb books by Rulfo. We feel a genuine veneration for *Pedro Páramo*. We've heard very good things about two novels, one recently published, another about to be, but already widely commented on: the first is *Balún Canán*, by Rosario Castellanos; the other, *Where the Air Is Clear*, by Carlos Fuentes. And we no longer have time to delve into our parodic novel because an employee approaches to tells Carlos that the section chief is about to leave; to our utter amazement he adds that he's been in his office for an hour. Carlos jumps up, hastily follows the employee and disappears behind a door. Ten minutes later he returns, calm. He's almost certain that his piece will appear in tomorrow's edition.

Night falls. A bus drops us at the corner of the Chapultepec movie house, just a short walk from where Arreola lives. When we arrive, he complains about our delay. José Emilio is about to leave. We convince him to stay awhile. Arreola is also about to leave. He has committed to attending the premier of Pirandello's *Henry IV* at Bellas Artes. He assures us that the next day he'll take the proofs to press. Our *Cuadernos* will appear very soon. He shows us a few sheets of stunning Dutch paper and gives us a lesson on watermarks. It's obvious that he's in a hurry to leave, but he agrees to sit for a moment to chat. He urges Carlos to submit material for a *Cuaderno*. José Emilio and I mention that he has a magnificent story. In unison we shout: "Fino acero de niebla!" Carlos bursts out laughing, covers his face with a cushion, and then promises vaguely that he's revising something he's about to finish. Arreola begins to talk about Pirandello, recalling the staging of his works when the great Italian companies toured Mexico; the best, according to him, was that of Mimi Agugli. He then turns to Louis Jouvet; he did not miss a single performance when his company was in Mexico, or in Paris, when he lived there. Theater is the genre that combines all literary perfections, he declares; he suddenly stands, marches around the room, and recites entire scenes while imitating all the characters from *Farce of the Chaste Susana* by Diego Sánchez de Badajoz; later, he retracts, in no way is theater the most import-ant genre, such a claim is an aberration; he then discusses poetry and thereafter takes out a volume of Proust and reads to us, in per-fect French, the chapter in which Albertine is surprised while asleep. Suddenly, a young man, visibly irritated, who has been listening to him, and who has remained silent throughout our stay, stands and barks that if he and Arreola do not leave at once they'll never make curtain time. We all go out into the street. Arreola and his companion get in a taxi, and the three of us—José Emilio, Carlos, and I—walk up the Paseo de la Reforma, turn right on Niza, and walk to a taquería next to the Insurgentes movie house, where we would often go at night to eat soup and sample the most delicious selection of tacos imaginable. While we eat, we return to the subject of literature, each of us reiterating our preferences. To the usual names, we add others: Alejo Carpentier and Juan Carlos Onetti, and, thanks to José Emilio, poets are also introduced: Quevedo, Garcilaso, López Velarde, Neruda, Vallejo, Huidobro, the Generation of '27. José Emilio eats quickly and says goodbye; he has to turn in a translation the next day. Some writers we barely know approach our table to sit and chat. They're obsessed with defining the topics our generation is obligated to address. They begin to enumerate their projects; they know what they must do for the next five years at least. We eat without paying too much attention to the ambitions of our newly arrived guests. Later, we discuss a fabulous book, James Boswell's *The Life of Samuel Johnson, LL.D.*, in which both biographer and biographee appear alternately as the remarkable characters they were, but they also prefigure traits belonging to Mr. Pickwick or, closer to home, to the comic strip character Don Reginito Burrón, which makes its reading even more enjoyable. We also discuss detective novels to avoid the formulaic and insipid conversation that dominates the table, and only out of politeness do we answer the questions that our acquaintances occasionally ask, without telling them that the only project that interests us is writing a satirical novel in which we would portray them as a bunch of grotesque and pompous idiots.

Perhaps we're aware that we'll never write a line of that novel, but perhaps we also sense that such a daily game can be one of the sources that will inspire our later work, that is if it is ever written. We cannot foretell the future, nor do we want to; the only thing that matters to us is the present and the immediate future; to think, for example, about what the coming days offer, how the complex situations that each of us confronts in his personal life will unravel, and with the same intensity, what books we will read in the days to come.

THE RETURN HOME

I return to Mexico in mid-1962. I'm excited to get back to my old habits and haunts. Nevertheless, I do everything possible to return to Italy. I do not have steady employment; I manage on a hodgepodge of jobs I do at home. After the absolute freedom I enjoyed in Rome, the idea of going back to an office is difficult for me to accept. During this time, I translate *The Monk*, the gothic novel by M.G. Lewis, which is published in installments in Salvador Elizondo's magazine *Snob*. I do readers' notes for Joaquín Díez-Canedo. Max Aub has given me small jobs at Radio Universidad: snippets to celebrate the anniversaries of famous writers; I also participate in a book review program, also at Radio, with Rosario Castellanos, José Emilio Pacheco, and Carlos Monsiváis. The Coordination of Cultural Diffusion, which oversees Radio Universidad, is enjoying a golden age under the direction of Jaime García Terrés. To start with, there is no censorship. Rosario Castellanos adds a very informal character to the program; everyone is able to express his or her opinion with no strings attached. We celebrate on the program the release of Carlos Fuentes's *The Death of Artemio Cruz*; we dust off the work of Martín Luis Guzmán, which of late the author himself has not even paid much attention to. We discuss the new postwar Spanish narrative, the existence of which has been difficult to accept in Mexico. The prevailing opinion is that since the fall of the Republic it is impossible for anything worthwhile to emerge; that a new literature can only be born with the disappearance of Franco. Discussing, much less praising, new authors like Sánchez Ferlosio, Goytisolo, Martín-Santos, Aldecoa, bothers a lot of people who believe that to do so legitimizes the Franco regime.

It's a nuisance but it's impossible to compromise with this kind of intolerance.

Since that day in 1957 I described before, many things have happened: there have been shockwaves that have provoked reactions against the government apparatus and its institutions; unexpected social movements have arisen; labor leaders have emerged who question the old codgers immobilizing the social organism. Corruption was condemned in many areas. There were protest marches and strikes nationwide; railway workers, teachers, telephone operators, and other union groups filled the streets and took control of them. There were impressive demonstrations. I remember one organized in support of teachers in which the participation of intellectuals was particularly important; there were not only young people but also those we considered our teachers. In a row ahead of Monsiváis and me were Octavio Paz and Carlos Fuentes, both functionaries of the Foreign Service. We marched in front of the Secretariat of Foreign Affairs just as the employees were leaving. Some diplomats applauded when they saw their colleagues in the march; others, horrified, could not believe their eyes.

The response was immediate: a disproportionate crackdown. From 1958 to 1960 riot police seemed to take control of the city, surprised, perhaps, by the obstinacy of students and workers who, in spite of the beatings, arrests, and torture, continued to express their dissatisfaction, handing out fliers, marching in the streets, singing subversive songs, ridiculing the government. The jails filled with political prisoners. Monsiváis, José Emilio, a dozen other writers, and I went on a hunger strike called by José Revueltas, in solidarity with the strike that Siqueiros and other political prisoners had undertaken in Lecumberri.

We were living day to day, with a recklessness that could only be attributed to naïveté. We took for granted that nothing would happen to us, and it was senseless to worry beforehand. We did not possess a desire to be martyrs—on the contrary. Personally, the experience helped me to rid myself of a feeling of over-protection that was beginning to hinder me. Somehow we understood that the country needed changes, that the political institutions were rusty, that it was unhealthy for a nation to be perpetually governed by a single party. But we did not expect the violent reaction from the groups in control. They were only able to respond to dialogue with beatings, arrests, and even murder.

Every time I reread *La segunda casaca* (The Second Turncoat), that remarkable national episode by Benito Pérez Galdós, I'm moved by a statement made by the protagonist Salvador Monsalud:

> I have always believed the same thing, and I very much fear,
> even after victory, that things in my country will continue to
> seem to me as bad as before. This is such a horrible mixture of
> ignorance, bad faith, corruption, and weakness that I suspect
> the evil is too deep for revolutionaries to repair. Among these,
> one sees everything: there are men of much merit, good heads,
> and hearts of gold; but there are also unruly ones who seek
> only noise and chaos; not to mention those filled with good
> faith yet lacking in intelligence and common sense. I have
> observed this group they are caught up in, unable to unite
> the greatness of ideas with the pettiness of their ambitions;
> I have felt a certain fear for principle; but after pondering it,
> I have concluded by affirming that the evils that revolution

may bring will never be as great as those as absolutism. And if they are—he continued contemptuously—they well deserve it. If all this is to continue to bear the name of nation, everything must be turned upside down, that common sense which has been offended be avenged, drawing and quartering such ridiculous idolatry, such foolishness, and barbarism erected in living institutions; there must be a complete renovation of the patria, no vestiges of the past should remain, and everything must be plowed under with noise, crushing the foolish who insist on carrying an outmoded artifice on their shoulders. And this must be done quickly, violently, because if it is not done this way it will never be done… Here the doors of tyranny must be torn down with ax blows in order to destroy them, because if we open them with their key, they will be left standing and will close again.

This is what Salvador Monsalud proclaimed, the unblemished hero, the character whom Galdós treated with the greatest sympathy, as if he wanted to share the same exploits with him. But, unlike Monsalud, we did not think it was necessary to change everything, to turn everything upside down, rather simply to ensure that the Constitution be followed, that our legislative practice be real, and not a mere pretext that gives rise to oratorical pirouettes and flourishes; that the rights of the citizens be respected, that the corrupt leaders and uncivil rulers disappear, those scourges capable of tarnishing any system, and through momentary disharmony reach social harmony. After the repression began we no longer thought the same; we wished, like Monsalud, for everything to be uprooted so that nothing would ever be the same, and one of the options that we envisioned was socialism, whether democratic socialism like Sweden or Finland, or real socialism like that of Eastern Europe, or even a socialism sui generis like that of China. It was the period of the "Hundred Flowers," not of the Cultural Revolution; I had just read a couple of very suggestive books: *The Long March*, by Simone de Beauvoir, and *Into China*, by the magnificent Claude Roy; both writers portrayed that world as a utopia in progress; an ideal vision built with real elements. In other words, the radical Monsalud, at first a purely literary character, ended up being our contemporary. We were tied to him by a common desire for justice, cleanliness, and decency. We also shared with him his doubts about what could happen after the change, if in fact there was one, and at the same time we were captivated by his adventurous life, not at all stifled by his political activity. We were anti-dogmatic by nature. E.M. Forster's book *Two Cheers for Democracy* became my spiritual guide; since then, I always have it by my side.

I can say with confidence that during those three years—1958, 1959, 1960—our lives did not take the same course as those of the positive characters in Soviet literature and film. I would dare to believe that the opposite was true, and the proximity of some closed-minded, rigid, and dogmatic revolutionaries was the best antidote. Our ability to live happily remained intact, even if the spaces had become more limited and enclosed; perhaps that very thing made them more intense. Friendship in those days became almost fraternity. Carlos and I continued to observe the tireless cycle of the human comedy: its glories, its agonies, its tricks, and its tragedies, but also its foolishness, its pettiness, its infinite capacity to embody the grotesque, the pretentious, and the seedy. We did everything possible so that the turmoil in the streets did not overwhelm our readings, and that in the event it did influence our conversations—it was impossible, not to mention undesirable, to avoid it—it did not excessively dominate or weaken them. We continued to go to the same *cineclubs*, cafés, theaters; we saw each other with the same or greater frequency, we discussed every imaginable subject, but literature especially.

Exhausted by some personal conflicts, anxious because of a fallow period that I had begun to associate with the political maelstrom, I decided to take a break and leave the country for a time; I thought about a trip to New York to recharge my batteries, or to Havana to witness firsthand that new revolutionary reality that certain well-known intellectuals such as Jean-Paul Sartre or Michel Leiris were celebrating, but I ended up traveling to Europe. I sold what I had—books and paintings—which allowed me to spend a few weeks in London, a few days in Paris and Geneva, and an extended period of time in Rome.

While I was away many things happened.

On my return to Mexico, I find a modified reality. The climate of official antagonism has increased, moving into other sectors. Financiers have not forgiven López Mateos for having defined his government as leftist, even if it was within the Constitution. The nationalization of industries, especially those of light and power, creates in these circles a feeling close to panic. China has been allowed to hold an exhibition in Mexico on the advances achieved by the Revolution. What exasperates them above all is this unprecedented foreign policy during the presidential sexennial. More than one hundred thousand people protest in front of the Palacio Nacional against free textbooks, which they consider an assault on the religious sensibilities of the nation.

Fliers are circulated revealing that the president's wife is a Protestant. Overnight, notices appear on the doors and windows of tens of thousands of houses that read: "In this house we are Roman Catholics, and do not accept either Protestant or Communist propaganda."

Moreover, a new and anti-dogmatic political thought has taken root. A group of intellectuals—made up of Víctor Flores Olea, Carlos Fuentes, Jaime García Terrés, Enrique González Pedrero, Francisco López Cámara, and Luis Villoro—founded a dissident publication: *El Espectador*, which carried a significant weight of opinion, especially among intellectuals.

At the same time, first imperceptibly then with an irresistible rhythm, a joyful spirit of carnival, of libertarian revelry, began to spread. Mexico is becoming a fiesta. My neighborhood, Juárez, is becoming the city's Zona Rosa, teeming with galleries, restaurants, and cafés where everyone meets. I've returned with the intention of staying only a brief time and of picking up some translations to do in Italy. My desire to leave, however, wanes with each passing day. Monsiváis and José Emilio have become important cultural figures in the city. Their talent and their immense capacity to work have opened many doors for them, both at the University and in cultural supplements and magazines, which at that time are the only venues available to writers. Carlos's program *Cine y Crítica,* which is broadcast by Radio Universidad, has become very popular, thanks in no small part to his cultural breadth and polemical character, but most of all to his humor, that never-ending rainstorm that falls on the desert of solemnity that characterizes our medium.

ANOTHER DAY, IN 1962

I go to Coyoacán to eat at the home of Vicente and Albo Rojo. José Carlos Becerra has arrived from Cuernavaca and says that he encountered military reserves on the highway. Twice they stopped his car and made him get out; they searched inside the car and the trunk. It wasn't anything personal, he says; from what he was able to ascertain, they were searching all cars and buses. The newspapers are reporting that in the last few days there have been uprisings in different areas of Morelos and that panic is spreading in Cuernavaca. They accuse an agrarian leader, Rubén Jaramillo, of having taken up arms. The poet Becerra says that the talk of panic is a lie; they're trying to create panic, perhaps as a pretext to arrest Jaramillo.

Monsiváis arrives during coffee. The get-together takes on a new life. Carlos remarks that the struggle between the solemn and the anti-solemn is beginning to cause tension in certain quarters. Lists are immediately made; everyone contributes names. In some cases, the opinion is unanimous; in others, there are doubts and reservations, nuances are noted. Examples are cited, of intellectuals as well as public figures, solemn in perpetuity, who, so as not to lose their clients, pretend to have loosened up. Luis Prieto comments that in the penultimate ordinary meeting of the association "Friends United for a Culture of Modesty," several members remarked that they were alarmed by the disappearance of their own presence in their homes as well as at their businesses; their grandchildren, and also their employees, servants, and gardeners were all talking in front of them as if they did not exist—which they attributed to having succumbed to an excess of solemnity. They meet the first Tuesday of each month,

Luis adds; the women in one of their homes, and the gentlemen in a room at the Bankers' Club. Every few months both sexes celebrate a plenary meeting at the country club. Luis had to go as a representative of the attorney De la Cadena, a friend of his grandfather since childhood, who could not attend that day because it was his ninetieth birthday, which he wanted to celebrate with family. He presented a letter that authorized him to vote for de-solemnization provided that it was carried out gradually and judiciously. During that session, they voted unanimously to ask their tailors to dress them in the latest style, not all at once, since that would be unbearable, but little by little, *pian piano.* The other decision, although it must be noted that it was not unanimous, was to be initiated into modern music because they know it to be the centerpiece of the anti-solemn view. For this session, the banker Don Arturo María Junco, certain of the outcome of the vote, had already contracted a movie projectionist with equipment necessary to show a film: "Modern music, *ma non troppo!*" he said. The projectionist chose films by Ginger Rogers and Fred Astaire. When the title appeared on screen: *The Gay Divorcee,* the uproar was overwhelming. A divorcee! And gay! A gay divorcee? Never! Could it be that they were members of an association called "Friends United for a Culture of Debauchery?!" Fortunately, the man from the theater had another film: *Pies de seda.*

"*Shall We Dance?*" Monsiváis said immediately in English.

"As the projection progressed," Luis continued, "something began to move inside the hearts of those watching. When it was over, they asked the projectionist to replay some musical numbers, and in one of them, Don Arturo María stood up and to everyone's surprise began to do a few discreet tap steps, then spun like a top, waving a lace tablecloth that he had removed from the table, tossing it into the air, and running rhythmically to catch it before it fell. He moved about with remarkable ease, as if during his entire life he had done nothing but dance. A musical number was replayed, and on that occasion four or five others began to tap with him, and although the difference between Don Arturo María and the new enthusiasts was astronomical, the audience's joy was absolute."

"But how can you be sure, Luis, that whatshisname had not danced before?" Someone added: "I assure you he's probably a smooth operator who's fooled his entire fraternity."

"He insisted he wasn't, and I have no reason to disbelieve him," Luis responds. "Even he seemed to be surprised by his exploits. He was ecstatic. This month I had to go back to the Bankers' Club because old man De la Cadena overdid it on his birthday and is being insufferable, and this time the meeting was entirely different. Most showed up in shoes appropriate for dancing with disheveled hair, which some had dyed, or so it seemed, and print ties that they would never have dared to wear before voting for modernization. And, you guessed it, to top it all off, they themselves demanded that *The Gay Divorcee* be shown. 'Modesty be damned!' they shouted. At the end, just as before, there was a replay of musical scenes and dancing. Don Arturo María was out of control and unrecognizable. At one point, he turned to his brother-in-law, Rafael de Aguirre, stuck out his hand and said to him: 'Hey, Fallo, now it's your turn to be Ginger for a while and I'll be Fred.' Don Rafael was horrified. 'What, you're going to be Fred?' he stuttered. 'That's right, and you're Ginger; you understood me perfectly.' I thought Don Rafael was going to collapse from an embolism, but his brother-in-law calmed him down: 'Remember, Fallo, in this kind of dance one barely touches the tips of the fingers; or didn't you notice? Did you watch the movie or did you fall asleep? In these numbers, each person twirls however he wants.' 'But what about my beard, Fatso? Won't it look bad if Ginger has a beard?' 'We'll all pretend that you don't have one, or that we don't see it, Fallo,' his cousin Don Graciano de Aguirre, the dean of the Association, said forcefully. That said, the poor devil began to remove the cilices that were torturing his legs; 'So I don't lose my agility,' he said, and also removed the scapulars because it seemed disrespectful to drag Our Lady of Pilar and above all the Virgin of Guadalupe into those dances. So they began to dance. Everyone else formed a semicircle and made choreographed movements with their arms and legs to enhance the couple's artistry. When it was over, they decided unanimously to hire a choreographer to teach them how to stage more complex numbers; upon hearing this, the projectionist took a card from his pocket and handed it to the dean. It read: 'Párvula Dry: Dance Teacher: Flamenco, Conga, Cuchichí, Mambo, and Other Rhythms.' 'We've entered a new era,' the dean said. 'Our Association has taken an historic step. On the one hand, it will improve our circulation, of which we're in dire need, but also, and most of all, we'll surprise our wives at October's plenary session. Can you imagine, gentlemen, the looks on their faces? They'll be so proud of us. Neither they nor anyone else will be able to brand us as solemn, do you realize? First thing tomorrow, I'll contact Doña Párvula Dry.'"

Luis's story is very famous, and it grows richer with each re-telling; characters we all know filter through it. The name Párvula Dry printed on the card becomes increasingly more important until she becomes the story's protagonist. Upon discovering the size of her pupils' fortunes,

Párvula Dry will take advantage of them, scam them, promise to take them on a triumphant world tour, when in reality the most she will do is book them in Barcelona's Bodega Bohemia, a Goyaesque dive where old variety singers are heckled and jeered by a ruthless public. Once there, she'll escort the group, now called "Friends United of the Voluptuous Terpsichore," in the front door then vanish out the back, only to reappear in Capri, where she'll buy a sumptuous residence that once belonged to Gloria Swanson; thus beginning a new chapter in her stormy existence. By the end, the story undergoes so many changes that it ends up making no sense, but we all amuse ourselves to death.

Carlos and I take a bus that drops us in Bucareli, not far from the Paseo de la Reforma, which works out beautifully because we're able to spend a moment in the Librería Francesa, where they have set aside for him two or three of the last issues of *Cahiers du Cinéma*; we stroll in the direction of the María Bárbara hotel, where the group Nuevo Cine is holding a meeting. Carlos's library, from what I've seen, has branched out; it continues to be fundamentally a literary library, but now has sections devoted to social sciences, anthropology, history of Mexico, cinema, photography. Mine no longer exists; having sold almost all of my books before leaving for Europe, and the few I bought in Italy—with the exception of a volume of Rivadeneyra's edition of *Tirso de Molina*, which I found by chance in a bookstore in Milan and brought with me to Mexico—are still in Rome, at Zamprano's house, in boxes and suitcases that await my return.

As we walk to the café we also stop at the Británica. Carlos buys a few English magazines and half a dozen books on pop music and photography that, he assures me, are indispensable. I find *The Gothic Revival* by Clark, a study of that genre known as the Gothic novel that emerged in England in the eighteenth century—replete with horror, eroticism, occultism, orientalism, sadism, and gruesomeness—in which Lewis's *The Monk* is set, which I'm translating at the moment. We finally arrive at the María Bárbara, to my surprise, before the meeting is scheduled to start, which gives us time to chat alone for a while, more or less seriously, something we rarely do.

I tell Carlos that I'm thinking more and more about staying in Mexico, and he encourages me to stay. He tells me that the struggle against solemnity that he has undertaken is more than just mere entertainment, or a simple act of amusement, although there is much of that. He's convinced that the years of the recent past, those in which the riot police were a permanent fixture in the streets, could only have happened by virtue of a fossilization of mindsets and, therefore, of institutions. Everything is frozen: legislation; the cult of heroes, transformed into concrete statues or fountains with meaningless quotations that refer to nothing real; the official rites of the revolution are as vacuous as everything else. The mindset of politicians has become a part of that same fossilized structure. We have to begin to laugh at everything, to the point of chaos if necessary, and create an environment in which the sanctimonious become worried, for a large part of their ills and ours come from their limitations. Laugh at them, ridicule them, make them feel powerless; this is the only way anything can change. A Sisyphus-like effort, no doubt, but one worth undertaking, and one that eases the monotony of life. If it is impossible to humanize the faces of reinforced concrete that politicians hope to acquire from their first measly little position, then at least it will be possible to expose some cracks. Young people are fed up will all the nonsense.

They won't even set foot in the Museum of Anthropology so they don't have to see the hieratic expressions of their leaders on the massive stone statue of Coatlicue, the Aztec goddess of creation. Everyone must learn to laugh at those ridiculous and sinister puppets that address the nation as if history were told through their mouth, not the living one, never that, rather the one they've embalmed. Anything new frightens them. When people finally see them for the rats they are, the parrots they are, and not as the magnificent lions and peacocks that they believe themselves to be, when they discover—of course it will take time!—that they are an object of ridicule, not of respect or fear, change will finally arrive; for that to happen they have to lose their base; they're prepared to respond to even the most violent insult, but not to humor.

This is what we're discussing when the friends Monsiváis is meeting arrive: José Luis González de León, Luis Vicens, José de la Colina, Paul Leduc, Tomás Pérez Turrent, Manuel Michel, Emilio García Riera, Juan Manuel Torres, among others. They're meeting to discuss cinema, and on this specific occasion to plan the publication of some *Cuadernos*. Juan Manuel Torres tells me that he's writing about the first divas—the Italians, la Menichelli, la Terribile-González, and la Borelli—and the erotic impulse they represent, which emerged around the birth of the cinema and is still present in it today. They then move to a long table at the back of the café to talk; I stay where I am and read the chapter about Lewis in the book I just purchased at the Británica. When they finish, we'll go to the *cineclub* to see Johnny Guitar, which is part of a season titled something like "The Tribulations of Eros."

Off we go. It's a rather idiosyncratic Western, in which the protagonists of the duel, an element that is essential to this genre, are two women.

The fight is not between a villain and a hero, that coarse but law-abiding cowboy who is usually John Wayne, Gary Cooper, or Randolph Scott. Instead the villain is an insufferable woman. The indispensable leading lady is Joan Crawford. The conflict is between the owner/ hostess of a saloon where the cowboys entertain themselves gaily and a raging puritan who devotes every waking moment to combating vice. For Joan Crawford there isn't a single moment of rest; the other woman harasses and pursues her, and lays the most treacherous traps for her until she is led to the gallows. At the last minute, with the noose around her neck, it looks as if a hero is about to save her, although I mostly imagine this and don't see it because of the commotion in the theater. We're sitting, as we have for several years, very close to the screen, in the third row on the right. From the beginning, we find the movie intensely amusing. The villainess's horrific tantrums and the palavering in which the heroine defends herself create a glorious dialogue. At times they sound like oracles; and others like grocers. Something about it is reminiscent of Ionesco's world and the humor of the early silent pictures. Our cackles echo throughout the theater, although we're surprised that ours are the only ones. The audience begins to shush us, insult us, and call for us to be thrown out of the theater. The commotion prevents me from enjoying the ending. When the lights turn on, a few spectators, almost all friends of ours, of course, curse at us. We're a couple of Pharisees, ignoramuses; our materialist distortion keeps us from detecting and appreciating a new treatment of Myth. Are we not able to see that the true face of hate is love? Has it escaped us that the relationship we saw on screen is governed by the concept of *l'amour-fou*? We've witnessed an extraordinary case of *l'amour-fou*, and two or three of our friends repeat in unison—

I'm not sure whether seriously or in jest—that *l'amour-fou* means mad love, yes: the mad, mad love proclaimed by the surrealists, with the great Breton in the lead. Did we even know who André Breton was?

We walk to the taquería next door to the Insurgentes movie house. We reflect with increasing pleasure on certain scenes from the movie and the frenzied intolerance of the priggish cinephiles. It's been a day blessed by laughter. I feel in optimum condition to go home and make some progress for a couple of hours on the gruesome and wanton story of Lewis's monk.

Suddenly a newsboy comes in with the latest edition of the paper. The headline takes up half the page. Rubén Jaramillo has been executed. We buy the paper. They talk about Jaramillo in the vilest of terms, as if he were a dangerous beast that has finally been hunted down. They've also killed his four children and his pregnant wife Epifanía. The tone is celebratory: another victory against the Bolshevist threat. Carlos gives me a brief summary of Jaramillo's life: he was a Methodist pastor who had fallen out with the Morelos government because of a series of abuses that took place in the countryside. He lived in a village near Cuernavaca, where the price of land has increased enormously. Land speculation had set its sights on them. Jaramillo became a natural leader of the region; he stopped the tenant farmers from being evicted. Holding the paper in my hands is degrading; it expels a foul odor. "Dead dogs don't bite!" it seems to shout. As we leave the restaurant, Carlos takes a taxi to return to Portales, and I walk few blocks home. My brief walk is enveloped in feelings of unreality, anger, and horror. Everything I've seen the last few days becomes a façade, which a harsh Mexico has taken it upon itself to smash to bits.

NOW

Not a single intellectual celebrated that crime, nor attempted to mitigate publicly the government's responsibility. The journalists at the service of the State made sure to do that. They seemed to become intoxicated with fame as they carried out the task; they knew the greater his infamy the higher their reward from the public treasury would be. Writers had yet to lend themselves to that task. That would come later; during the Salinas presidency it would become a succulently "lucrative" profession. Fernando Benítez devoted a supplement in *La Cultura en México*, which he edited at the time, to Jaramillo's murder. He visited the region of Morelos himself, with Carlos Fuentes and Víctor Flores Olea, where the events had occurred. The accounts they wrote were splendid and brave.

My desire to stay in Mexico disappeared that night. Soon after, I left the country. Carlos stayed and persisted in his projects, thanks to which he managed to accomplish a large part of the program he confided to me in 1962 at the María Bárbara. Since then, he's written brilliant books, needless to say; they are a testament to chaos, its rituals, its slime, its greatness, infamy, horrors, excesses, and forms of liberation. They are also an account of a Rocambolesque and ludic world, delirious and macabre. They are our esperpento. Culture and society are his two great domains. Intelligence, humor, and fury have been his greatest advisors. I'm convinced that the current catalyst to create, in spite of everything, a civil society, is due to his efforts.

In his own way, Carlos Monsiváis is a constantly expanding polygraph, a one-man writers' union, a legion of heteronyms that out of eccentricity sign the same name. If you have a question about a biblical text, all you have to do is call him—he'll answer it immediately; the same if you need a bit of information about a movie filmed in 1924, 1935, or whatever year you like; you want to know the name of the regent of the city of Mexico or of the governor of Sonora in 1954; or the circumstances under which Diego Rivera painted a mural in San Francisco in 1931, which José Clemente Orozco dubbed "Assitorium"; or the possible transformation of Tamayo's work during his brief Parisian period, or the fidelity of a line of poetry that may be dancing in your head by Quevedo, Góngora, Sor Juana, Darío, López Velarde, Gorostiza, Pellicer, Vallejo, Neruda, Machado, Paz, Villaurrutia, Novo, Sabines, of any great poet of our language, and the answer will appear immediately: not just the verse but the stanza in which it is located. He is Mr. Memory. He is also an incomparable historian of mentalities: an intensely receptive and sharp essayist—if you don't believe me, just read the pages he has written on Onetti, Novo, Beckford, Hammett; a remarkable movie critic; a student of Mexican painting who has produced excellent pages on Diego, Tamayo, Gerzso, María Izquierdo, and Toledo; and a lucid political essayist. He is the chronicler of all our misfortunes and our marvels, more of the former, considering that the Mexico in which we're living has been fertile in misfortunes and, in turn, the marvels appear exceptional as miracles often do; he is the documentarian of the extremely fertile gamut of our national imbecility. His weekly columns capture the statements of the great minds of our minuscule universe; in them speak financiers, bishops, senators, deputies, and governors, the President of the Republic, the "communicators," the cultured doyens. The result is devastating. Next to him, the discoveries of Bouvard and Pécuchet would look like the apothegms of Plato or Aristotle. To these attributes,

others can be added: bibliophile; collector of a thousand heterogeneous things; felinophile, Sinologist—Carlos Monsiváis is all this
and more. And, in addition, as readers may have already surmised: he
is my closest friend.

Xalapa, January 1996

THE WOUND OF TIME

"On the burning February morning Beatriz Viterbo died, after braving an agony that never for a single moment gave way to self-pity or fear, I noticed that the sidewalk billboards around Constitution Plaza were advertising some new brand or other of American cigarettes. The fact pained me, for I realised that the wide and ceaseless universe was already slipping away from her and that this slight change was the first of an endless series."[2] As the reader may have already noticed, this is the beginning of "The Aleph," that great miracle by which Jorge Luis Borges enriched our lives.

From a certain age, every change one discovers in the environment takes on an offensive character, an agonizing personal mutilation. As if with that change, someone were giving us a macabre wink, and the new advertising for American cigarettes, just like Beatriz Viterbo's death, were turning into an unexpected *memento mori*, an announcement of our future and inevitable death.

Thirty-five years ago, in Rome, I frequented a small bookstore in the Via del Babuino. It was run by a couple whose age was hard to discern, except that they were more young than old. I enjoyed

---

2 Translated by Norman Thomas Di Giovanni

chatting with them and hearing their recommendations. They were book people through and through. Their shelves reflected a confident and cultivated taste. Later on, each time I passed through Rome I would venture at least once to their store. It was impossible not to as it was on the way to the Piazza del Popolo. I watched them age without ever losing the conviction of their intuition and good literary judgment. The classics fit perfectly there with the new currents of thought and modern narrative forms. They had no patience for light literature, self-help books, or superficial theosophy. These genres fell outside their circle of interests; I imagine it would have disgusted them to welcome into their store readers who were addicted to those kinds of books.

So I saw them from time to time. On one occasion, I found only the woman behind the counter. Her husband, she told me, had died a few months before, from a blood clot, I think. Years later, on a different visit, I saw her sitting in a chair, with the look of someone who was completely detached from reality: she neither moved nor spoke; she didn't seem interested in anything; her stare was fixed and blank. A slightly younger woman attended to the customers; I think I heard her say she was a cousin. I told her about the relationship that had bound me to the store since I was a young man: my first Ariosto, my first novels by Pavese. She told me that her cousin had succumbed to a deep depression; no treatment had been able to bring her out of it. She was afraid of leaving her in the apartment alone, something might happen to her, she might need help. So every morning she dressed her and took her to the bookstore, and that brought her back to life. "Look how good she feels; she's spent her entire life here; being here cheers her up, of course it cheers her up." If the vegetative state

I witnessed could be considered a sign of revival, she must have felt awful at home, I thought.

In the spring of 1966, I spent a few days in Italy. When I passed the bookstore it was closed; what's more, it was nonexistent. The windows on either side of the door that night and day had displayed the latest titles had disappeared. The sign with the bookstore's name had disappeared. I felt the wound of time, its malignancy, with terrible intensity. That disappearance was a way of punishing the immense happiness of the young man who one day appeared there, rummaged through the bookshelves, and left with copies of *Orlando Furioso, Il campagno,* and *Tra donne sole* under his arm.

In every city where I lived I've experienced similar circumstances. Running into such changes diminishes not only the pleasure of traveling but also the concrete awareness of the past. Sometimes I have to go out of my way in order to avoid walking by a place where one of these incidents has happened... To not see, for example, in a city in central Italy that where there was once a theater there is now a discotheque whose flashing neon lights take the place of those that more discreetly announced Paolo Stampa and Rina Morelli in a play by Goldoni, or that in place of a middling café where I used to sit and write in Rome there now stands a tacky souvenir store for garden-variety tourists.

Still in Rome, for many years now I've stopped walking down that narrow street, which also leads to the Piazza del Popolo, whose eccentricity lies in one side being called Via della Penna and the other Via dell'Oca. It's the only street that I know like that. On one side of the street lived Alberto Moravia and Elsa Morante, and on the other there were two trattorias essential on my life's map: Mondino's and, a few steps away, Pietro's. Mondino had fought in the International Brigades during the Spanish Civil War; afterward, for the rest of his life, he was a diehard anti-fascist. He ran his trattoria with his wife and son. Together they cooked and served. Customers ate at long tables around the stove. The clientele was made up of students, young intellectuals, theater students, poor artists, and foreign scholars. They were divided between communists and existentialists. They all had a single common hero: Sartre, who at the time was very close to the Italian Communist Party. His *Criticism of Dialectical Reason* was the most oft-quoted book among the patrons. Philosophy and, above all, Marxism were constant topics of discussion. At times there were discussions that threatened to erupt into war. Someone would then tell a joke, and laughs would win the day. It smelled like sweat, smoke, onion, and olive oil. When I had no money, I ate for free because it gave Mondino great pleasure to talk about Machado in Spanish and for me to listen to him recite Machado's poetry, which he knew by heart. At night I would eat at the neighboring trattoria, Pietro's, a Calabrese who detested bohemian culture, the young crowd, extremist ideas, and, therefore, Mondino, I suppose. There I would meet María and Araceli Zambrano, other literati, important journalists and filmmakers, but seldom famous people, because the establishment was rather modest. The central figure was María, who had in fact transformed the trattoria into a salon. Prominent Hispanists and intellectuals, as well as visitors from Spain and Latin America who were passing through Rome, would sit around her. Whenever a group of young Spaniards came in, María would light up. She'd talk to them about her Republican youth, about her teacher Ortega y Gasset, about the writers of her generation, the Civil War, defeat, and then exile. She became a tragic

THE ART OF FLIGHT

figure: Hecuba, Cassandra, and, of course, Antigone. Swathed in the smoke of her cigarette, looking up, the words would pour out, as if a higher spirit inhabited her body, had possessed her, and was using her mouth to speak. She did not raise her voice. She spoke as if in a trance, inhaled her cigarette, and paused to exhale the smoke. Just then, before beginning the next sentence, the atmosphere became charged with an almost unbearable intensity; the young Spaniards looked as if a sacred current were running through them, and me along with them, as well as the entire restaurant, whether the dinner guests understood Spanish or not. She did not like to end on a note of pathos. Once attained, she would transition effortlessly to recounting anecdotes about Cernuda, Lezama Lima, or Prados, with whom she maintained intimate correspondence. I imagine that when the young people returned to Spain, what they remembered most of Rome was the moment they had seen and heard María Zambrano. At times, I could not withstand so much intensity, and I would leave there with a fever and spend several days ill in the boarding house where I lived. María and Araceli have died, as have Mondino and Pietro. Their trattorias today have other names and another look. Above all, the atmosphere of elation and generosity, of frenzy, and of anguish and hope that characterized Rome *prima del miracolo economico* has disappeared. Revisiting the past means, among other heartaches, contemplating a world that is, and at the same time has ceased to be, the same.

Take Mexico, for example. Think about the changes that have occurred in the last half-century—the devastation of the capital, the degradation of the atmosphere, the moral pollution—and you will have a vision that borders on catastrophe. A dystopia staged by an expressionist director. When I entered university, the city was inhabited by four and a half million people; today that number seems to top more than twenty, and I say "seems" because no one can provide an exact figure. Any common memory, every possible collective imagination, tends to be smashed to bits in these circumstances; the social link that replaces their functions is crass TV, the creator of timid mythologies.

I would like to move beyond, to the extent possible, apocalyptic visions; and pause instead on areas of imprecise determination, on small details: writing, reading, dreams, anything that eschews the grandiose, the plaintive, an apostolic zeal, and didactic pontificating.

I spent several years outside the country. Traveling to Europe meant going to Veracruz, boarding a ship, and crossing the ocean. If someone wanted to take a more luxurious trip, faster and with fewer stops, he had to go to New York, and sail from there on one of the spectacular floating cities of the time: the *Queen Elizabeth*, the *Île de France*, the *Leonardo da Vinci*, for example. When in 1988 I decided to return to Mexico for good, passenger ships had ceased to exist several years before and were reduced to serving as cruise ships in the summer.

It is hardly surprising that during that long period of absence my memory would occasionally relive unusual episodes that were both fond and forgotten. A letter from Mexico could momentarily recover images I thought lost: a dusty, yellowed, and sometimes implausible *hic et nunc* managed to emerge from among the deceased, radiant and adorned with every possible prestige. Even an encounter with someone who had traveled through Mexico could cause my immediate surroundings to disappear and transport me back to the infernos or paradises of the past. Every instant recovered from oblivion turned suddenly into a concentration of the universe.

Time and space knew extraordinary permutations. As if by alchemy the Café Viena on the Paseo de la Reforma would appear in my memory: its atmosphere, its furniture, and the indisputable aroma of Central European pastries. It was only much later, when I had the opportunity to frequent similar establishments on my march through Europe's imperial cities—Vienna, Budapest, Prague, Zagreb, Salzburg, Marienbad, Karlsbad—that I realized that Café Viena was a tiny outpost of Habsburg culture. My memory returns me to a long table in the back of the café, beneath an immense rectangular mirror. Don Manuel Pedroso holds court, surrounded by a flock of lads who were probably between eighteen and twenty years old. A genuine interest in what they are hearing and an intense zest for life lessens their slight tendency toward snobbishness. They listen captivated as their mentor talks about Góngora, Balzac, Hobbes, and Dostoyevsky; about his time as a teacher in Seville and Madrid; about episodes and figures from the Spanish Republic; about theories of love in Stendhal and Proust; about studying philosophy and law in Germany; the emergence and height of expressionism, the Bauhaus, Rilke, and the Duino Elegies, of which he's committed long fragments to memory; about the Italy of Burckhardt, Goethe, Berenson; about the charms of Slavic, French, Andalusian, and Mexican women. He invites his friends to converse with us; one day he brings Américo Castro, who's passing through Mexico, and talks to us about Cervantes and Tirso de Molina, and declares that he disagrees entirely with the thesis he had espoused on Tirso in his youthful prologue to the comedies published in Espasa's *Clásicos Castellanos*, that his ideas about Spain's Golden Age had changed radically, and not just the Golden Age but also the whole of Spain's cultural formation. He was the most important visitor our *tertulia* ever had and, much to the annoyance of Pedroso, we listened to him rather with sarcasm and inattention because of the ridicule to which Borges had subjected him in *Other Inquisitions.* At Professor Pedroso's *tertulia,* the logos and its rigors coexist in total harmony with the trivial; Alicia Osorio, Lupina Mendoza, Ivonne Loyola, Carlos Fuentes, Víctor Flores Olea, Luis Prieto, and yours truly listen to the maestro intently, we celebrate his wit, we agree, question, dare to raise objections, which the maestro himself encourages. Finally, we say our goodbyes, aware that life is full of wonder, among other reasons, because we know that we will meet again next Saturday in the same café where, unbeknownst to us, our destiny is taking shape.

Memory works with the same oblique and rebellious logic as dreams. It rummages in dark holes and extracts visions that, unlike those of dreams, are almost always pleasant. Memory can, at the discretion of whoever possesses it, be colored by nostalgia, and nostalgia produces monsters only by exception. Nostalgia lives off the trappings of a past that confronts a present devoid of attraction. Its ideal device is the oxymoron: it summons contradictory incidents, intermingles them, causes them to merge, and brings order in a disorderly way to chaos. Mine relives the enthusiasm I felt as I left Bellas Artes after hearing Arrau, Rubenstein, Callas, and the Teatro Tívoli—no less venerated—where the audience's pleasure became frenzied before the gyrations of the famous "exotic" dancers of the time—Su Mu-Key, Tongolele, Kalantán; or the Lírico after applauding the legendary Josephine Baker; or the endless walks through the city's many different neighborhoods where I talked nonstop with Luis Prieto, Lucy Bonilla, Gustavo Londroño, Carlos Monsiváis, Luz del Amo, Ricardo Regazzoni about books, movies, politics, or private matters; we argued, fought, and always reconciled as we made fun of the false (and even genuine) glories of this world…Everything was real, everything was true and, unfortunately, unrepeatable.

Not too long ago, I went through some of my books while preparing them for re-publication, a task that has never been pleasing; I was surprised to discover that a place from my childhood appeared on several occasions, a place it would never have crossed my mind to think about, a setting that entered my writing surreptitiously, which served as an unconscious frame to a mysterious event: a crime that was never completely solved. It surprised me because in real life I had only been there on two or three occasions while I was still very small. Upon recalling those excursions, upon dislodging them from the place where my memory was hiding them, they burst into my conscience as one of the most startling episodes of my childhood. The place is the Ojo de Agua where the river Atoyac is born; a few days ago I discovered that it was one of the sacred places of the Totonacas.

I was living at the Potrero sugar mill. Some families used to organize occasional excursions to the region's picturesque sites, among them the natural spring at Ojo de Agua. The round-trip—bathing in the river, the picnic—took an entire day. We rode in a Jeep until we arrived at the village of Paraje Nuevo, and, from there, we walked on foot along the paths that the peasants cleared for us with their machetes in the middle of the jungle. One of the high points of the trip was crossing the river on a rope bridge.

It was like crossing a bottomless abyss; it's possible my childlike eyes magnified it disproportionately, as tends to happen. The bridge lacked the usual board planks common to hanging bridges. Instead there were just three or four ropes braided together. My feet slid slowly along the bottom rope as my hands held the upper one. There were probably twenty or twenty-five of us, including the children. There were some young American couples; the American women were wearing pants and seemed to possess the same sporting ability as their husbands. The Mexican women would not have dared wear pants even if they were threatened with being thrown from the cliff. I remember that they were carried across, tied to the men's arms, some shouted, terrified, while others laughed hysterically. We children rode astride the adults' shoulders, or tied to their backs. The operation took a good amount of time, because in addition to our crossing, large straw baskets containing food, drinks, plates, silverware, and other paraphernalia had to be transported across. We then crossed another patch of jungle until we arrived at a spot, the other climatic moment, from where we were able to contemplate paradise: the spring, located beneath a curtain of rocks that my memory reproduces like a great Wagnerian scene. As we neared the place we began to perceive certain mysterious movements in the water and in the brush along the bank. They slowly began to take shape and definition; they were otters, the marvelous water dogs that had inhabited the region from the beginning of creation. If they had stayed there, nothing would have happened to them; there was a tacit agreement not to disturb them. The peasants in the region watched over their pups and occasionally, when the time was right, sacrificed a few males to sell their pelts.

Not long ago I decided to return to that sanctuary, to the magic garden from my childhood. It's possible to travel to Paraje Nuevo today by car and continue in the same vehicle along dirt roads all the way to the river's edge. There are scarcely any vestiges of the original jungle left. It has been replaced by sugar cane. There are no longer any difficult passes. The atmosphere of mystery has disappeared. At a certain moment, I decided not to continue; I turned around and retraced my steps. I didn't dare go as far as the spring. Everything had deteriorated in an unbearable way. The animal life had disappeared, just as the vines from my childhood and the giant ferns, the huge climbing plants with enormous leaves, which back then surrounded the pool and climbed up the mountain, had disappeared. The natural world that existed until a few decades ago and took centuries to be created is now just a memory, just like the Babuino bookstore, the Mondino and Pietro trattorias, the Café Viena, the Tívoli, the Lírico, and so many other things.

Xalapa, May 1994

DREAMS, NOTHING MORE

Happy dreams tend to be scarce and difficult to remember. We awake from them with a smile on our lips; for an instant, we relish the slightest fragment our memory retains, and our smile quite possibly grows into a full laugh. Yet as soon as we get out of bed that happy dream disappears forever. At no time during the day does it occur to us to repeat or build on the happiness that we experienced.

On the contrary, the others, the distressing dreams—the terrifying ones, the monstrous nightmares—are capable of not leaving us alone, even for several days. They demand that we undertake an anxious search that is seldom crowned by complete success. We cling to any loose thread in an attempt to piece together the plot, and, little by little, dark, tangled fragments begin to appear, vague parodies of scenes, scraps we take advantage of to reconstruct the oppressive nighttime experience. We're fully aware that we're fabricating a narrative act that corresponds only in part to the ominous atmosphere that upset us at night. Specialists say that the function of these disturbing dreams consists of externally discharging unnecessary energy, of a poisonous kind, created, for some strange reason, by our own organism. Dreaming implies a defense or an omen. Dying means the end of one period and the announcement of a better one. A rebirth! We have undergone an internal cleansing without having willingly participated. Later, as we search consciously through the dream's residue, we weave it into a story to which we attribute pertinent faces and gestures to give shape to the ghosts that multiply beneath the surface. As we recognize them, but now completely awake, we destroy them, annihilate their evil powers, and we push them out of our psychic space. If this were not so, what sense then would the effort invested in recovering and reuniting the lost fragments make? Only a collective masochism, more widespread than desirable, could sustain that possibility. And I don't think things are heading in that direction.

I must have been twenty or twenty-one years old (I'm guessing because that was when I began to live by myself in an apartment on Calle de Londres) when an unknown figure, who seemed to encapsulate the infinite spectrum of human evil, began to appear in my dreams. His face displayed nothing but evil. At first glance, he might have looked like an ordinary man, but glancing at him a second time produced fear—being close to him, speaking to him, even more. I awoke terrified. Hours later, when I went down to the street, I recognized the sinister individual about whom I had dreamt. I was dumbfounded. I had read something in Jung about the premonitions contained in certain dreams. The Swiss author related the experience of some patients of his who had dreamt about a catastrophe and had later been the victim of a similar accident. A parapsychological premonition. I thought that the dream was trying to forewarn me of a demonic force that was surrounding my home. I had not dreamt of an imaginary being but rather a real one, whom I had seen with my own eyes a few yards from the building where I lived. That afternoon,

I visited a psychologist friend of mine, and I told her about the incident. She believed that I had possibly seen someone who had, perhaps because of a single detail, transformed into the frightening person of my dream. That is, by some mechanism of identification, I had erased the original features of the man I dreamt about and had attributed to him those of the individual who passed by me on the street. Since then I am aware that a large part of what we believe we remember are in fact inventions after the fact, and that this condition makes them indispensable for analytical work.

One never dreams so much as when undergoing psychoanalysis. He wakes up at any hour of the night and writes down on the first piece of paper within reach what he just experienced in the shadows. It would seem that dreaming only makes sense upon relating the experience to the psychoanalyst and scoring points in his analysis. One of the patient's greatest pleasures is subjecting himself to the exercise of interpreting what he has dreamt, sketching a first exegesis and listening to the analyst solicit another interpretation because the first one seems too obvious, or too flat, or too vague; then explaining one after another until the moment arrives when the patient is no longer talking about his nightly visions but rather certain real problems he has approached by way of the dream without realizing it. And that, I imagine, can only happen when one is under the almost silent tutelage of a specialist; I doubt anyone is willing to subject himself to the same effort when he's alone. Most commonly, the dreamer re-examines his visions alone for a few minutes and tries to make sense of them by mere formula; in reality, he doesn't attempt to interpret the dream, he doesn't try to find its meaning, he resigns himself to submitting to the process of putting it in order so he can recount it to the first person he traps. And then, upon recounting it to a third person, upon giving it some kind of coherence, an exercise of fictionalization, of distancing, of "defamiliarization," is unintentionally produced, which in and of itself can be therapeutic.

It seems to me that people abuse the word *oneiric* when describing phenomena that escape the usual notion of reality. It's said that *The Garden of Earthly Delights* and the *Haywain Triptych* are marked by an oneiric register. In those paintings, as in all paintings by Bosch, there are people with more legs and arms than necessary, men and women with roots on their feet and thorny branches on their head, make-believe animals, rats ridden by riders as monstrous as they are, bodies made up of nothing but a disproportionate head that is sprouting a pair of feet, outlandish machines, gnomes hatching from bleeding eggs, men birthing flocks of crows from their anuses. Anyway, we're all accustomed to describing those excesses as oneiric, just as we classify as oneiric "The Nose," that brilliant short story by Gogol in which one morning a man wakes up without a nose and spends the ensuing days looking for it, then making it return to where it belongs. The nose continuously disguises itself in an effort to evade its owner, until one day it becomes a powerful field marshal, without anyone on the streets of Petersburg exhibiting the slightest surprise at its metamorphoses.

Could someone possibly dream such fantastic and extravagant worlds as those? I can't even imagine it. My personal experience is so limited that it cannot conceive of anyone in his right mind being able to arrive at such enviable excesses. Perhaps alkaloids or other chemical stimulants could provoke such images. In any case, I would venture to say that the starting point of the works of Bosch, as well as those of Gogol, lies in wakefulness, not in dreaming: they are the fruits of imagination and fantasy. Oneiric mechanisms are different. I have never in my dreams seen myself with a body and face different than my own. My organs are always where they should be, and during the course of the dream I never turn into a jaguar, or a vampire, or an axolotl. I don't float in the air; on the contrary, I fly in a plane like God intended. I take in everything around me, but I'm more than a mere camera. I'm a camera, and I'm myself, lost, pursued, trapped, and judged.

Borges recounts a dream that leaves me very disturbed because it refutes the rule I maintain. The writer dreamt that he had met a friend who seemed to be hiding his right hand; at a certain moment Borges realizes that it has turned into a bird's claw.

If anything characterizes my nightmares it is their infinite ability to cause anxiety. They are not as rich in motifs as Bosch's paintings. They only differ from reality in time and space, as well as their combinatorial capacity, which in dreams exhibit a dizzying freedom. One can be in one place that turns into another and then another and so on infinitely, and talk to an interlocutor who during the conversation demonstrates the ability to mutate. A is X, and then Y, and then R, only to become A again. Nothing can ever be taken for granted or trusted.

When I returned to Mexico at the end of 1988, for several years I always dreamt that I was in European settings, even in some that in reality I do not know, like Oxford or Copenhagen. It was impossible for me to recognize those cities but I knew I was in them, in the same way that I knew that a house was in a certain region of Italy, or Spain, or Portugal without any local element appearing to verify the attribution.

I have noticed that in the last few years there is less action in my dreams; what gives them the character of nightmare is knowing that I am dreaming and am not able to awaken. I repeatedly try to wake up but it's pointless, I can't get out of the hole even though there isn't anything unusually terrifying inside; what is frightening is not being able to avoid it. Monotony deforms reality and creates an uncertainty that is nothing but the door to terror. It is in that moment of torment when a voice I recognize awakens me and announces that the orange juice and coffee are ready. All the suffering, the fear and anguish disappear as if by magic in the face of the quotidian with which the day begins. Is that not enough to drive anyone crazy?

From 1968 on I've kept a dream diary. It's remarkably narrative in nature. It contains a main story and an underground world that nourishes it. The agonizing nature arises from the desire to escape from what I have dreamt and the impossibility to do it. Let's take a look:

24 APRIL 1994

I'm about to open the door of my house when a young man walks up to me and asks if I'll let him walk Sacho this evening. The proposition suits me because I have to write an article that I should have already finished. He comes by the house at five, the time of the evening walk. He tells me that he'll take the dog to Los Berros Park. Sacho leaves with him willingly, which surprises me considerably. But he doesn't return at the agreed time. The next morning, very worried, I go out to ask the neighbors if they know anything about Sacho, if they've seen him with a young man with such and such description, and no one knows anything about the dog or his companion. At noon, Sacho shows up at the house in terrible shape, thirsty and irritable. He's alone, wearing a leather collar that isn't his; something about the collar attracts my attention, but I don't know exactly what. It has an engraving that suggests something dangerous. About that time, the murder of a local politician is made public. Rumors spread throughout the city. That night, on the evening news, I find out that a suspicious person had been walking a dog where the crime was committed. A newswoman describes the dog, which sounds exactly like Sacho. I am absolutely convinced that the criminal, or one of his accomplices, is the one who took Sacho. I can't figure out what led me to allow a stranger to take him. My anxiety grows as the day passes. They might suspect that Sacho is involved in a conspiracy and that even I might be in league with these criminals. What's more, Sacho is behaving very rudely; I've rarely seen him so unpleasant, as if he were resentful and blamed me for unpleasantness that took place the evening and night before. But, where could he have spent the night? Could he lead me there? And what would be accomplished by trying? I'm at a total loss. I tell myself that the whole thing is a dream; I struggle to leave the dream before the police come to question me, but I can't. It's precisely Sacho's barking that awakens me from the never-ending dream. He's very irritated. I'm barely able to put on his collar and make him go outside for his morning walk.

17 AUGUST 1995

I've rented an apartment in a small city on the coast, perhaps in Spain, in a region unfamiliar to me. The building is humdrum, squat, devoid of ornamentation. From time to time I run into a sullen-looking married couple on the street; both of them dressed without any sense of style, as if they were hiding behind tasteless clothes, but who, in spite of everything, carry themselves with a certain degree of dignity. Both are wearing mouse-gray raincoats that accentuate their anonymity. One day we happen to meet in the lobby as we collect our mail;

later we begin to say hello, to make conversation about the weather, we even begin to take walks together. We talk about books, history, architecture, but without ever going beyond the usual banalities. We never talk about ourselves, our professions, our past, not even why we chose to live in such a lackluster building. To say "we" speak is an exaggeration; the husband is the one who does all the talking, he's a pale man, on the cusp of old age, always smiling but with a sly, dirty smile that produces a feeling of rejection, at least in me. I never pay too much attention to what he says; nonetheless, I don't mind going out with them; on the contrary, I prefer going out with them to being alone. On one occasion, when the husband went upstairs to retrieve something from the apartment, something, I don't know what, drove me to say to his wife:

"Your husband knows so much about so many things! I never get tired of listening to him!" It was an obviously foolish comment because his wife looked at me stunned.

"I would never have imagined," she replied, "that you were so limited. He seems like a complete idiot to me."

From then on, she almost never went out with us, and the few times she did she never failed to show disgust when her husband spoke. Walking alone with him grew tiresome. I had nothing in common with anything he said, although he assumed that I shared his opinions. I began to avoid him, but he contrived ways to run into me. On several occasions I refused to go with him; he would pretend not to hear me and continue rambling beside me. The situation became insufferable. One day, I ran into his wife at the pharmacy and complained about the harassment that her husband was subjecting me to. She looked at me with contempt and told me that I deserved it, that for weeks I did nothing but egg the moron on. After that, I made the guy feel like he was insufferable, that I preferred to stay home, or take my walks alone. At first, he didn't lose his composure, sometimes he would act like a martyr and comment somewhat wryly on my arrogance; later, he began to suggest in a veiled way that I should watch out, that he might harm me, that I shouldn't underestimate his capabilities, that if he wanted to he could have me kicked out of the building; what's more, out of the city, maybe even the country; his dark smile, his evil stare grew in those moments. Little by little, the dream begins to transform into a nightmare; the action grinds to a stop, his threats, whispered in an unctuous tone, become constant. I know it's just a dream, but I can't do anything to stop it. I seem to be condemned for the rest of my life to be unable to get away from him, to try to avoid his presence unsuccessfully, to listen to his threats, as if everything had become an endless cycle, without escape, and that was the circle of hell where I belonged.

21 APRIL 1992

I've moved to Rome, where I just bought a house. It must be on the outskirts of the city; it looks very poor: the furniture is sparse, old, rickety, and dust-covered. Suddenly, I see an electric cable sparking. The sparks erupt into small flames and begin to scorch a beam. I live alone, with no one to help me in cases like this. I leave to go look for an electrician, but the situation doesn't seem to concern me very much, as if the short circuit were as unimportant as an armoire door that doesn't close correctly. I go out onto the street with a ladder in one hand and a suitcase in the other. I notice that Sacho has followed me; I let him come with me because it's time for his walk. I hide the ladder and the suitcase in a clump of flowers, in a small, rather plain traffic circle. I discover an entrance to the Pincian Hill, and I enter with Sancho through a gate that is unfamiliar to me. We walk by an aviary; massive cages house thousands of beautifully colored exotic birds. We begin to climb the hill; as I walk by a little store, I start to crave some bread and cheese. They won't allow Sacho to come in, so I leave him on the sidewalk with instructions not to move while I'm gone. I leave him by a back door by mistake; I take advantage of the opportunity to walk around and enjoy the scenery. At a given moment, I discover that I'm lost. I walk around aimlessly, uneasy; I can't stop thinking about Sacho. I walk into a café and tell everyone inside about my circumstance, that I lost my dog, that I can't find him. I ask them to reorient me so I can return to the entrance of the part of the Pincian where the aviary is. A young man offers to take me, saying he knows the way perfectly because he's a bread distributor for all of the businesses along the way. Before leaving, he selects, with a fatal lack of urgency, two huge loaves of bread, and then, as we walk, he explains to me how important bread is to the Romans, in particular that kind of heavy, dark bread; he says that by eating it they take communion, they reaffirm their identity. I listen to him in desperation. I mention that we've gone the wrong way, that I'm feeling farther and farther away from the place where Sacho lies abandoned. He replies smugly that he knows these surroundings better than anyone, that we're taking a direct route. We walk silently for a long time. As we turn the corner, Saint Peter's cupola appears in front of us. The Vatican! I'm absolutely convinced that I've followed a mad man or someone totally irresponsible, which is the same thing. I insult him, and he leaves eating his bread. I can't understand how we could have passed the river without noticing. We've walked through half of Rome; I'm farther than ever from my poor dog, and it's starting to get dark. I'm certain that he's also desperately looking for me. In the worst-case scenario, someone will appreciate his coat, realize what a good dog he is, and take care of him. Sacho won't have to wander the streets. I, on the other hand, won't be able to survive his getting lost. I'll feel guilty for having abandoned him. I remember that I left a suitcase and a ladder somewhere, unusual objects to carry along when going to look for an electrician; I also remember that my house had caught fire. So many hours have passed that nothing will be left but ashes. I went out to the street without identification, or perhaps they're in the lost suitcase. I have no friends in the city to go to. I'll go to the consulate tomorrow to request assistance going home. I'll return to Mexico penniless; but I don't care about that, the real tragedy is returning without Sacho.

At that moment, I wake up in despair, feeling that the rest of my life will be bleak, that I'll never recover, that it's all been my fault. I have a hard time convincing myself that I've been resurrected, that is, that I've returned to reality, that I'm in my room, that the agony that I just lived was a mere dream; at that moment, I discover that Sacho is asleep just three feet from my bed. I look at the clock, it's very late, an hour after his walk time. Because it's Sunday we're alone in the house. I immediately put on his leash, and we take our usual walk through the center of Coyoacán. He turns his head every so often as if to make sure I'm there, as if he had dreamt that I had gotten lost in an immense park in a strange city.

2 JULY 1993

I've been living in a house in the country for some time, in some uncertain region of Italy. It's a large house, tastefully furnished, extremely comfortable; a place where writing is a delight. From my desk I can see a beautiful cherry orchard, and at the end of the orchard, a cabin, where a Mexican professor of Italian literature lives as a guest. He spends his vacation there while finishing a translation of a classical drama. When he arrived, I offered him a room in the main house, but he opted for the solitude and independence of the cabin. At midday, he comes to eat with me and some other people, because there are always guests in the house; they come to eat lunch or dinner, have drinks, engage in conversation, spend the weekend, several days, an entire season. I like the house, the scenery, and the way of life. Not far from the house, on the bank of a river, a child's corpse appeared one day. Someone had strangled him and thrown him in the water. A young literature student who arrived in the region recently discovered the body, already in a state of decomposition, and notified the police. All evidence points to his innocence. On the day of the murder, as determined by the pathologist, he was out of the country. He has proof and witnesses. Nonetheless, a cloud of suspicion begins to grow around him. No one in the village believes in his innocence, which becomes evident at every turn.

One night I'm hosting a very formal dinner, like when I was a diplomat, with some twenty guests around the table. At opposite ends of the table are myself and an elderly doyenne of emphatic gestures and expressions, possibly an actress. Suddenly, the student bursts into the dining room. He's terrified; he says that he's being followed, that they want to kill him. In a magnanimous gesture the elderly woman orders him to sit beside her. He'll be safe there. Seconds later, a peasant, also very frantic from the chase, enters the room and stands before a window, covering it with his imposing body. His motionlessness intensifies the fierce look on his face. Two men appear in the kitchen door and stand in front of the two other windows. Suddenly, the room is filled with men and women shouting, among them the gardener and cook; they're carrying knives, clubs, and ropes in their hands. They form a sinister circle around us. The young man, overcome with fear, stands, attempts to flee, but they manage to restrain him and take him outside. I explain the situation to my guests, about the murdered child, the discovery of his body. I insist that the evidence supports beyond doubt the lad's innocence. I'm still speaking when we hear a horrible scream coming from the orchard. We're frozen with fear, silent. The execution has taken place. The cook, the gardener, and a man I don't know appear and withdraw to the kitchen without saying a word. Their hands and clothes are covered in blood. I interrogate my guests with my eyes; I'm convinced that one of them is the murderer, but I don't know which one. Our silence lasts a few minutes, until broken by the elderly woman:

"Petrilli never liked me. My Amneris was much better than her Aida. It's not unusual. From the beginning of rehearsals, the relationship between the sopranos, mezzos, and contraltos turns into a fierce battle."

They begin to serve the consommé. My dinner guests talk about opera, singers, conductors, and performances that are memorable for their splendor or for their disaster, about *Turandot*, *Der Rosenkavalier*, *Tosca*, and *Così Fan Tutte*. I too take part, after all I'm pretending to be a good host, but little by little the lynching of the student, the faces contorted by hatred, the blood-soaked hands, begin to hang over the guests like an unbearable weight. The conversation that began with so much exuberance becomes subdued. The guests stare and scrutinize each other, ask trick questions. The suspicion that the boy's murderer can be found at the table takes over. I'm terrified that someone might suspect me. I could offer irrefutable proof of my innocence. But what would it matter? The student also had proof, which did nothing to help him escape execution. My anxiety intensifies. I can't wake up.

Xalapa, March 1995

TEST OF INITIATION

Imagine an eighteen-year-old youth who suddenly decides to become a writer and consumes the better part of his nights scribbling literary articles. His tastes, you must understand, are unintentionally ecumenical. He writes about Eugene O'Neill and his theater, about a novel by Rabindranath Tagore, *Home and the World*, which he had just read, about a trip to Mexico told by Paul Morand. His interests are as varied as his ignorance is vast. Needless to say, the judgments he makes are not conspicuous for their originality, and his prose is only slightly less than flat. Undoubtedly, none of his pages exceed the level of a school assignment. Someone, perhaps a friend from law school, surprised by his talent, suggests that he send his articles to the cultural supplement (rather shoddy, in fact) of an important daily where a friend of his father works, and he embraces the suggestion with enthusiasm. Once the articles are submitted, his friend naturally assumes the role of advocate and spokesman, making an exaggerated defense of his writings, of his love for reading, and of other personal qualities that are unrelated. If they accept his writings, the author thinks, he will have taken the first step on a path toward the stars.

Several months went by without a single article appearing in the supplement. Having recovered from such a chilly reception, the budding literato gives up his night job. He's still too green for literature: a sound conclusion. But one Sunday he goes out to buy newspapers in the provincial city where his family lives, and where he usually spends all his holidays. On the way home he decides to stop at a café and leaf through one of the newspapers he's carrying under his arm. From the front page of the cultural supplement, the title of one of his articles leaps out at him, the one in which he commented on O'Neill's theater. The sense of excitement that some authors claim to experience when they see their first published text and their name printed below the title eludes him. The exact opposite happens. He's momentarily paralyzed; then, slowly, a feeling of shame that ends in nausea pours over him. The mere thought of returning home with the newspaper seems impossible. He suddenly realizes that he's become an unclean animal, and at that moment he has the evidence that proves it. He's afraid to go home. He feels incapable of enduring a single comment; the most discreet praise, any sign of surprise or celebration of his talent, unknown to his family, would drive him hopelessly mad, at least that's what he believes as he stares blankly at the newspaper. Finally, he decides to tear out the page, fold it up, and hide it in his jacket pocket. He leaves the rest of the supplement on the table. When he reaches the dreaded place, he deposits the papers in the living room, and slips off to his room where he stays locked up the rest of the afternoon. He rereads the article without grasping its meaning. "Without understanding a lick," was all he could think of to say. But this time, unlike in the past, the expression fails to reassure him. Only in a handful of old translations of foreign novels has he run across these words. To read that Nastasya Filipovna, desperate and exhausted, implores her prince to speak with greater clarity, otherwise to leave her in peace lest she not understand "a lick" of the lofty and passionate sermons with which he overwhelms her, or for Emma Bovary to repeat in one of her final heart-rending meditations, that she has not understood "a lick" about life, not only destroyed the desired pathos but also rendered laughable the situations written to move the reader. He is only able to discern the titles scattered throughout the article because they're written in a different font and in bold: *The Great God Brown, Mourning Becomes Electra, Desire under the Elms, The Emperor Jones, The Hairy Ape, Anna Christie,* and a few others. Those dramas that have so impressed him seem as hollow and ridiculous as his own prose. He wants nothing more than to disappear from the world, to invent a chilling story to persuade his brother that he desperately needs to borrow money so he can travel to Veracruz, where he will board the first boat weighing anchor and become lost in the world without leaving the slightest trace. Or just plain die. He doesn't even dare pour his heart out to his grandmother, his usual confidant.

The afternoon dragged on, like a nightmare. But, to his surprise, no one discovered the crime. No one came by the house or called to congratulate him. The apathy toward literature from those around him left him perplexed and disappointed. The remaining articles he submitted appeared the following Sundays. He had returned to Mexico City; his friends' comments left him undaunted. He did not care whether anyone read them or not, whether anyone liked them or not, even if it wasn't entirely true. In any case, he did not succumb to the vice of writing again for some time.

Over the years he has come to believe that he would have preferred to be discovered that Sunday when his guilt was made public.

Not only that, but also to be mocked and condemned; everything would have been easier, cleaner. His relationship with the world could have been cleared of many cobwebs. Now, more than forty years after that incident, he's content with merely acknowledging the event. He tries to examine the circumstances, to elaborate a few hypotheses. Why was that rite of initiation bathed in horror? Did it have something to do with a late detachment of his umbilical cord, a bloody separation of his body from those around him? He arrives at the conclusion that the exercise is becoming a pointless guessing game, that to continue it would send him into a labyrinth of astonishment. He would become lost in marshes without ever touching solid ground.

Perhaps he owes to that experience his inability to write at home, as if it were an activity to be avoided at all costs. Writing in the same space where he lives was for much of his life equivalent to committing an obscene act in a holy place. But that's anecdotal. What is certain is that his fall into uncleanness that characterized, at the end of his adolescence, his confrontation with the word, his printed word, has conditioned his most personal, most secret, most unwitting manner of writing, and has transformed the exercise into a joyful game of concealment, an approach to the art of flight.

Xalapa, December 1994

DIARY FROM ESCUDILLERS[3]

(At the end of 1968, I left the Mexican embassy in Belgrade, where I was carrying out my first diplomatic mission. I refused to continue to collaborate with the Mexican government after Tlatelolco. I returned to Mexico and found the atmosphere to be unbreathable. A female friend promised to help me find a job in London as a translator at The Economist, *which was about to begin publishing in Spanish. It was almost certain that I would begin working in October. I would be able to spend the summer in Poland as a guest of Zofia Szleyen. My attendance at a conference on Conrad, I thought, would allow me to obtain a visa. I stopped in Barcelona to deliver the translation of* Cosmos, *by Gombrowicz, to Seix Barral, which I had almost finished, thinking it would only be a matter of a couple more weeks' work. I arrived in Barcelona on June 20, 1969, at midnight, at the Francia station. I did not know the city. I asked the taxi driver to recommend a pleasant and moderately priced hotel. He took me to a place out of this world, which ended up being a hostel on Calle de Escudillers. I was planning to wait there for some money that was being sent from Mexico to continue*

---

3 Known as Escudellers in Catalan, Franco mandated the change of all Catalan street names during his dictatorship, hence Pitol would have known the street as Escudillers in 1968. Today, the street is once again known by its original Catalan name, Carrer dels Escudellers. —*Trans.*

*my trip, as well as the invitation to the conference in Warsaw, or the personal
invitation from my friend Zofia, without either of which I would not be
able to obtain a Polish visa. Instead of the three weeks I intended to spend
in Barcelona, I stayed three years. The memory of those times, of wonderful
friends, of constant surprises still moves me today. My time there, in spite of
the initial snags and a few spectacular surprises that at the moment seemed
like the impending Last Judgment, only to end up disappearing into the air,
constituted a daily exercise of freedom.)*

BARCELONA, 22 JUNE 1969

One A.M. It's raining. My tiny room traps all the noise from the
neighborhood. A very acute depression this afternoon...tremors. I'll
never drink again. It must be the hangover from a monstrous cognac
drunk, or some horrid liquor they passed off as cognac. After I settled into the room I went out and toured all the city's bars near the
hostel. Limitless excitement about the city's nightlife. I walked without stopping along La Rambla and Escudillers, driven by curiosity
or rather by the necessity to become acquainted with what will be
my neighborhood for the next few days. I still haven't been able to
tackle *Cosmos*. I wrote two letters. One to Neus, another to Díez-
Canedo, giving them my address for the checks I'm expecting. The
trip to Spain was very exciting. As the train approached the border,
I heard songs of the Fifth Regiment, which some teenagers were
singing in the compartment next to mine. To interrupt the climax
I made small talk with a plump, toothless French girl seated across
from me. Collioure, Perpignan, Argelès, names I heard spoken so many
times by Don Manuel Pedroso, by Max Aub, Garzón del Camino,
Ara and María Zambrano: a crescendo of excitement. By the time

I arrived at the border, I would forever hate the French girl, who was missing two front teeth, because of the contempt she expressed for the Spaniards and their songs. "To us they're primitive, they think they're going to save the world with their songs, no matter what they do, they'll always be primitive," smiling as she said it, her lips creased like the Mona Lisa, hiding her oral cavity.

Yes, my neighborhood is bustling, which is fine, although it seems like they go overboard just a bit. Something tells me this isn't my city. I find it excessively noisy, deafening, and insane in its hyperactivity. The *guardia civil* stopped two hippies this afternoon beside my hotel and beat them mercilessly. A group of them walk along La Rambla frequently; a mix of intelligent and delicate faces with others that are excessively barbarian: young people of both sexes decked out in Afghani, Indian, or Nepalese blouses and jackets, alongside others who barely cover their flesh in rags; Germans, English, French, Scandinavians; they barely speak to Spaniards. They hang out in the Dingo, a bar located beside the Plaza Real, which is also beside my hostel. My room, because of its modesty, takes me back to Vittoria, Rome, 1961. Apparently, I'm neither maturing nor making progress.

23 JUNE

No, I do not get this city. Yesterday afternoon I went to the movies. I did the same today. Double feature: one of the movies was the really ancient *Ahí está el detalle*, with Cantinflas. A way of escaping reality, it seems, of blotting out the racket where I live. I'm starting to feel a bit like a coward. I walk a lot, but I never leave La Rambla or Escudillers. My biggest entertainment: watching the expressions and habits of the exotic hippies, who also never leave the Plaza Real and its surroundings, and who usually hole up in the Dingo. Racket, scandal at all hours, enough to drive anyone crazy! I should have changed hotels the day after I arrived; instead I sent everyone this address, and now I have to grin and bear it until my correspondence gets here. You can get by here on a few pesetas a day.

7 JULY

Terrible insomnia. I fall asleep around seven or eight in the morning, which causes me to stay in bed until evening, and I wake up furious that I've wasted the day, which makes it impossible to have any kind of normal work schedule. I visited Pepe and María del Pilar Donoso. We talked at length about friends from Mexico, about Pepe's illnesses, the novel he's writing. The plot, which he explained in broad terms, is fascinating. I ask them about their life in Barcelona, and they respond vaguely, as if they wanted to avoid the subject. New friendships: a young married couple, both writers; he works at Seix Barral; she's finishing university. The extreme seriousness they've established between themselves surprises me. Last night I finished my revisions of *Cosmos*, by Gombrowicz. I'm in a panic, at wit's end. My money situation is getting dire. The trip to Warsaw appears uncertain. Not many letters from Mexico. Today I'm going back to Jean Franco's book. The hippies are an enigma to me, an amazing phenomenon. The only thing I knew about them came from the press. I saw them in London a few months ago, but there the city absorbed them, despite openly shooting heroin in the metro and public toilets. In Barcelona they stand out from the rest of the city, its customs, Spain, even in this neighborhood that is the height of obscenity, but an obscenity of another kind, that has taken centuries to create. This mix of multiple nationalities, unlike anything else I've ever seen, is a novelty I still haven't been able to digest. I exchanged a few words in the Dingo with a hippie with hellishly dirty, iodine-colored hair. They walk around in groups; in general they're boring and sullen. This one seems more independent, more upbeat, and bordering on a sense of humor. I'm starting to get used to Barcelona; but to be completely comfortable I'd need a more obvious element of foreignness, like other European cities I've lived in. A greater distance from the language and customs could help me adjust to the paralysis I'm experiencing.

WEDNESDAY, 9 JULY

I woke up today at three in the afternoon, yesterday at four thirty, which is definitely not normal. I work until two in the morning and then I'm completely tense for five or six hours, unable to sleep, not even able to read. In this way, time seems to dissolve in my hands. A waste that reminds me of the worst times of my life, the most squalid I've ever lived, and even worse. I haven't seen any of Barcelona, I don't know it. Actually, what has made me this way, paralyzed, frozen, is my lack of resources, perhaps even the expectation of an impending departure. I feel sick. I'll inquire about a doctor that's not too expensive. On Monday I'll receive a partial payment for translation of *Cosmos*. I have to finish the Jean Franco translation in twenty days. Is it crazy to stay in Barcelona, in this hovel, in this disgusting neighborhood, drowning in debt?

11 JULY

Today, at noon, I witnessed a murder, just two meters from me, on the corner of Los Caracoles. Both the murderer and the victim were probably a little over twenty. I mean, I think he killed him. He plunged a knife into his stomach. Afterward, the hotel owner's nieces, the girls who do the cleaning, asked me: "Did a lot of people gather around? Did they catch the thug? He didn't get away, did he?" I didn't know what to tell them, I still don't know for sure what happened. The only thing I remember is that the guy who was stabbed fell against the wall, then, looking more surprised than anyone, tried to throw his body forward, but wasn't able to. Instead, he doubled over like an accordion that was closing. Did I really witness them pull the bloody knife from his body, or am I making it up? My memory is blurry. I kept walking. I went inside a secondhand bookshop, where the smell of mold made me queasy. I'm sure I bought *Jacob's Room*, by Virginia Woolf, in an edition by Janes that I wasn't familiar with. But the truth is when I got back to my room I didn't have it.

SUNDAY, 20 JULY

I saw a live broadcast of the first men on the moon. They looked like giant pandas. It was as if I were not seeing them. There was no element of surprise because I had already read about it in my childhood, but in a more attractive form, in Verne and in Wells. I had also seen it happen with more glamour in the movies. Today makes a month since I arrived, and I still don't know Barcelona. Brutalizing work. Activities this month: translations of Gombrowicz and Jean Franco. Permanent lack of money. Friendship with the De Azúas. Little news from Mexico. Too many movies and weekly visits to the Donosos' home. Urgent needs: a few days at the beach, clothes, books, money, friends, a doctor.

22 JULY

I talk to Ralph, the hippie with the iodine-colored hair. He reminds me of someone, but I can't think of whom. In spite of the fact that his features are very manly, there's something beneath them that reminds me of a woman I know, but I'm not able to put my finger on it. There's an excessive concentration in his expressions; he wrinkles his face even when he laughs, which hints at a fit of hysteria. Our conversation is extremely chaotic: "What do you study?" "Oh, that was four years ago. Since then I've lived *on the road*: Nepal, India, Turkey"; he remains silent, lost in a daydream. He suddenly adds: "I did a lot of business in Tétouan. There's no one here who can help me." "Is that a good business, hash?" "Quiet, man, I don't do it here. It's six years in prison. I may go to London soon." "It's an expensive city," I tell him. "Nothing's expensive for me. I don't have any money, it's all the same. If I'm hungry, I beg for pesetas. I'll show you a place where you can get soup for six pesetas. But you have to take a bowl or a cup." A long silence, I drink three cognacs, one after another. "I live in the cheapest neighborhood in the city," he adds. "Twenty-five pesetas a day, that's nothing." I'm still waiting for money from Mexico. I owe the hostel two weeks' rent. Whose expression is that? Where have I seen those gestures? Perhaps at the movies, Jean Harlow, in *China Seas*, but imprinted on a man's face. No one could imagine the chill that ran through me when he mentioned the six-peseta soup, honestly, taking your own bowl. As he said it to me, he seemed sure I'd be taking advantage of it soon. The invitation from Warsaw hasn't come. Tonight we'll go see a film by Richard Lester with John Lennon and Michael Crawford.

THURSDAY, 24TH

Wonderful movie! An excellent film by Lester, very Brechtian, a plea against war in the vein of Chaplin's *Monsieur Verdoux*. Talking to Ralph always turns out to be predictable and at the same time overwhelming. At times his face is monstrous. "Have you been to Madrid?" I ask him. "What's it like?" He answers: "Really bad. The people are mean. They won't give you money. They tell you, go get a job! They threw me in jail for a month, you know? Here in Barcelona the people are nice, kind of silly." He says he pays his room and board by selling blood at a clinic. I thought the pricks on his arms were from heroin. I'm not convinced that they're not. Sometimes a wild look comes over his face. I've become destitute. The money from Mexico hasn't arrived. I owe the hostel again. I'll start the prologue to Conrad's *Nostromo* tomorrow. And my novel? I'll start it tomorrow too.

SATURDAY, 26 JULY

I didn't sleep last night trying to organize my schedule. I was still awake at four in the morning. If I got into bed, I wouldn't be able to fall asleep until well into the morning, and then I'd stay in bed most of the day. I decided not to sleep at all. I started work on my novel; what I read seemed utterly stupid. Does it make any sense to continue it? Perhaps the death of the old woman with elephantiasis is ruining the whole thing. What if I changed the ending? The scenes in Venice will hold up better, although they still require a lot of work. Later I began to read Mann, the *Mountain,* for the third time in six months. The first book by Mann I read was *Doctor Faustus*, about fifteen years ago. A task that at times seemed impossible. Nonetheless I continued. When I finished, I felt drunk. I had cleared the highest hurdle and crossed the finish line without suffering a single scratch. Then I set out to read the rest of his works, with the exception of his

Joseph tetralogy. None impressed me as much as *Faustus*. I tried several times since adolescence to read *The Magic Mountain*. It was a book that we had at home and was widely recommended. I was never able to make it beyond page fifty. But during a long trip I took on a Yugoslavian freighter a few months ago, I was finally able to read it from start to finish. When I got to the last word I closed the book, and the next day I started to reread it, this time closely, which was the happiest reading I can remember. I've less than fifty pesetas in my pocket, and the money still hasn't arrived. I have to pay rent again. No one writes me from Mexico. I haven't heard from Zofia; I'm afraid she's going through hard times in Warsaw, where a wave of officially sanctioned anti-Semitism has erupted. Maybe that's why the invitation hasn't arrived. Not being able to spend the rest of the summer there, which would cost me nothing, would spoil my plans and put me in a financially difficult situation. What a life! Horrible! Things being as they are, within a year I'll have finished my first novel. I'm constantly changing the title.

SUNDAY, 27 JULY

The novel is turning out to be very hard for me. A lot more than I expected. I write chapters then undo them. It's turning out to be a structural novel, if you can call this kind of novel that. I've gained something by not killing the protagonist. I redid the first two chapters, and now I'm revising the third, where Paz Naranjo and Gabino Rodríguez appear furtively, as does Carlos Ibarra; this way, all three stories will begin to intersect. There's a line from *Hamlet* that would make a good title. I do not have it handy. Something like *The Music of a Flute*. So just like that I'm back to being poor?

And miserably so! In a way I would never have guessed in my wildest imagination!

SUNDAY, 2 AUGUST

I worked on the chapter dealing with the meeting between Carlos Ibarra and Ángel Rodríguez, and Paz Naranjo's reaction. A truly difficult chapter. I half-heartedly outlined a few pages. I'm no longer anxious about my poverty, but it doesn't allow me to work like I should. I would need an apartment, and I only have ten pesetas in my pocket. I've not received confirmation of my trip, nor payment for the Jean Franco translation. In the event I do not go to Warsaw, I'd still have to stay two months in Barcelona to reorganize my finances. That's good. When I saw this moment approaching, I was unable to sleep. The mere thought of the day when I'd be peseta-less kept me awake all night. I asked Ralph if poverty scared him. "No," he answered instantly. "When you don't have money, you learn to do without things." And that's what's happening to me now. Last week the thought of running out of toothpaste left me petrified; when it finally ran out I brushed my teeth with soap. The only thing I know for sure is you won't see me standing in a soup line. There are things that I can't do: wash my own clothes, for example. I prefer to sell something, the few books I have left, and keep paying for laundry service, or walk around dirty, plain and simple.

17 AUGUST

Last week went from bad to worse. I'm still waiting for payment for the translation of Franco's book. On the other hand, Era sent me a check, but for some reason I never fully understood, the bank refused to cash it. I had to return it and ask for it to be reissued. What's more, the telegram from Poland still hasn't arrived. All this time I've had to work in unbearable conditions. I just finished translating *Behind the Door*, a novel by Giorgio Bassani. The book interested me very little, and I imagine the results are very poor, but I get paid tomorrow and will be able to catch up on the back rent. The horrible light, the noisy neighborhood, the sleepless nights, the chaotic schedule, and the agonizing wait for the mailman, have all become routine these last two months. It's not surprising I suffered a breakdown all of a sudden. One day, I was unable to work. Everything hurt. I went to bed with a very high fever and the feeling that I had a rock in the pit of my stomach. The next day I received a telegram from Díez-Canedo. He had wired me five hundred dollars. My fever went away immediately. I went to the bank. Apparently the transfer process is very complicated: first the money arrives to Madrid, then goes to a currency exchange office, which transfers a payment request to Barcelona. In all, it means waiting a few days. I left the bank, bought the laxative recommended to me by the hostel owner's nieces; I took it and have spent three days with horrible stomach pains. If I'm not able to collect the money, and if the invitation from Zofia doesn't arrive, I'll never be able to leave this hellhole. What a bloody nuisance! Sometimes I feel like postponing the trip to Poland and renting a furnished apartment. On Craywinckel, at the foot of Tibidabo, for example, in the building where the De Azúas and Myriam Acevedo live. That wouldn't be bad at all. First, I'd have to spend a week at the beach. I desperately need a change of atmosphere, a bit of rest, and the sea air. What a wonderful, incredibly generous person, Félix! Thanks to his help at Seix Barral I've managed to survive.

23 AUGUST

In Los Caracoles. I'm writing these lines beneath an autographed photo of Mistinguett. I'd like to have more friends, become better organized. How many times have I written, thought, and said the same thing? The trip to Poland still seems possible. But it's not that important anymore. I just want to write. Suddenly everything that lay hidden and managed to survive being crushed beneath the awareness of poverty has come to life again. A desire for everything! An appetite for everything! All I need is to learn how to sleep decently again. I continue to work on the Conrad introduction. Translating in such a compulsive way has become mind-numbing. Will I be able to incorporate Ralph and his four years "on the road" into my novel? Make him perhaps a character in a chapter that's a reflection on radical exile? I survived! Yes, I'm alive. Yes, yes, yes, yes.

SATURDAY, 30 AUGUST

Dreadful days. Reading Mandiargues's *La Marge* strengthened my resentment for the vast and sickening bordello that is my neighborhood. Last night I witnessed an especially grotesque spectacle in a dive where I drink coffee. A black lad, who looked like a doll, was having a drink at the bar and looking out onto the street. He was dressed impeccably, his face touched up with makeup, possibly under the effect of some drug, his pupils dilated beyond description. He must have been rich; he was dressed like a king. It seemed as if his only possibility in life was suffering. He exuded it. The display of such suffering was able to thrive in numerous literary sources; there was a great deal of the hysterical exhibitionism from Tennessee Williams, but more of the languid affectation of M. Delly. A little black princess of the moor. He was surrounded by an escort of battle-hardened Arab bodyguards; one raised the cup to his mouth, another wiped his lips with a napkin, he seemed to not even notice them, his eyes were fixed on the door, as if he were waiting for someone, a lover or a drug supplier. The five or six bodyguards surrounding him stared menacingly at the clientele, like thugs. Now, as I write this, it occurs to me that he might have been kidnapped, and they were waiting for the ransom that would set him free. How gruesome! His servants displayed too much servile respect for that to be true. In any event, it's rare to find such a flamboyant character and entourage in an out-of-the-way place like this. Perhaps I'm writing this just so I do not have to deal with what happened in the Dingo…A week ago when I was there a guy walked up and sat at my table: his face wasn't completely unfamiliar; maybe because it was a look that had been practiced carefully so everyone would recognize it. He said hello matter-of-factly, and commented that we had not seen each other since our rendezvous in Lausanne, a city I've never even set foot in. He was drunk, or at least pretended to be. I asked where he was from. "Ecuador," he replied. "You look like you're Catalan." "Well, I'm not." I was beginning to dislike his presence at the table, his tone. I asked for my bill. Then he said: "Okay, let's go somewhere else." "I'm not going anywhere; I'm out of money." "Come have another drink." "Thanks, but I can't with this headache." His tone changed abruptly. He whistled between his teeth menacingly: "Go and tell them at your company right now that I need money. I want twenty thousand dollars and an Argentine passport." At that moment several sinister-looking guys came into the bar; one of them seemed to be motioning to the man who was talking to me, who got up and walked, randomly and after making a complicated detour, to the table where the others had just sat down. A minute later, a huge brawl broke out, but in a made-up, theatrical sort of way, which my "acquaintance from Lausanne" took part in. So I took advantage of the opportunity to slip out of the place, frightened to death. It seemed obvious to me that I had been mistaken for someone else. And in police novels those kinds of mistakes usually end you up in the morgue. Tomorrow will be my last day in this neighborhood. I'm moving in the opposite direction. It's wonderful being able to escape! Every cell in my body rebels against the existence of this disgusting labyrinth: against the limping, midget, haggard-looking, hunchbacked whores who fill its streets when night falls. Against the charade that rules the sex trade. It will be marvelous to escape tomorrow to my apartment in Craywinckel! It feels like pus that's impossible to wash off has splattered all over me. I wouldn't care in the least if someone decided to dynamite all of this. "I shall latch onto my God who destroys me!" This statement might not even be five percent true, but today I'm in complete agreement with that five percent. I'm an absolute prude.

11 SEPTEMBER

A month full of surprises and goings-on. I receive late payments from everywhere. I'm living in my new apartment, very much like a ship's bow. Félix and Virginia came by to pick me up for dinner at the home of Beatriz and Óscar Tusquets. They're about to start a new publishing house. I was delighted to meet them and have the opportunity to talk to them. They invited me to collaborate in their new endeavor. After a long conversation, we discussed and discarded various projects;

in the end we agreed to create a new collection: The Heterodox, for writers and texts alike. They gave me their address, and as a first step in the collaboration they commissioned a translation of a selection of letters by Malcolm Lowry. That's good news. First, I have to translate *The Good Soldier* by Ford Madox Ford, which Planeta commissioned a few days ago. It will appear in the collection *Great Authors of Our Century*. I can hardly believe that I'm living in this beautiful apartment, in such a pleasant neighborhood, sleeping on clean sheets, meeting such stimulating people, receiving so many offers of work. I close my eyes, see the dirty hippies, the ignoble streets, my squalid room, and the only thing that occurs to me is to quote a sentence from Galdós that María Zambrano used to repeat frequently: "The clouds moved and everything became a caricature." I need to stick by my decisions, not to return to Mexico right now, forget England for the moment, and stay longer in Barcelona, and devote myself fully to publishing and to literature.

14 SEPTEMBER

Carmen Balcells held a boisterous reception in a luxury hotel for Max Aub, who, from what I'm told, has returned to Spain for the first time since his exile. The *gauche divine* showed up in force. I felt happy. Max introduced me to Carlos Barral, Castellet, Gil de Biedma, to everyone. Later a discussion with Azúa at Los Caracoles ended very bitterly. Federico Campbell arrived today from Rome, and we had a long, delightful conversation about mutual friends in Mexico and Italy. I authored five articles for Seix Barral. I became a member of the Council of Reading a few days ago. My novel, unfortunately, has been interrupted. A piece of news left me dumbfounded. My brother Ángel called from Mexico to tell me that Francisco Zendejas had published news of my death in *Excélsior*, to the obvious consternation of my family. Suddenly I'm frightened by the possibility that it might be an omen, so to cheer myself up I tell myself, and to a certain extent it works, that the person who died was a shadow that I barely recognize today, and who was a prisoner the entire summer in the Escudillers. After Ángel's call I was so nervous that I went up to Myriam Acevedo's apartment to have a cup of coffee. I mentioned, among other incidents from my past life, the encounter with the man in the bar who said he had met me in Switzerland. Something he said to me had a profound effect on her, something like, "Tell your company that I need an Argentine passport and for them to deliver twenty thousand dollars to me." She insisted on knowing what company he was referring to. I told her twenty thousand times that I didn't know, that that was what had frightened me, because it all had been a case of mistaken identity. Then out of the blue she asked me: "Do you know a spy? Are you sure that one of your friends isn't a spy?" "I suppose so," I told her. "Possibly in Warsaw or in Belgrade, or right here, people come up to me to try and find out what I think about the regime. But you can't know if they are spies," I said. "Yes, but one can find out. Examine your friends," she added. And so on for a long while; I went down to my apartment with a greater sense of unease than when I left. Surely she and her husband must feel hounded by informants who want to know what they are doing in Spain, if they plan to return to their country, etcetera, and that must have her very neurotic. "Don't talk about anything to anyone; you don't know what kind of world you're moving in," was the last thing she said to me.

FRIDAY, 19 SEPTEMBER

I took a blood test just in case. "Everything's perfect," the doctor said, smiling. Amazing!

SATURDAY, 27 SEPTEMBER

I was finally able to finish the prologue to *Nostromo*. I situated it primarily in the political realm, which I believe to be the novel's central theme. It's a work of great unevenness. Conrad talks too much about Nostromo's remarkable qualities, about his invincible influence on individuals and the masses; however, once he introduces him, he inflicts on him a monotonous tone, a pedantry that serves only as a prop. He appears pretentious and insipid, limited, capable of nothing but clichés. The love scenes, as is almost always the case in Conrad, seem to take place between cardboard figures. The "passionate" dialogues between Nostromo and Viola, in spite of the air of panpipes and tambourines that the author imprints on them, and perhaps because of that very thing, are less than flat. I dined last night with Beatriz and a group of her friends, writers, translators, theater people, all young, at Can Masana, and when she introduced me she commented to someone that I had lived in Peking. Lived in China? For most of them it's next to impossible to obtain a passport to cross the French border. I mentioned in passing my disappointment; the climate I endured there for six years, the steps toward the Cultural Revolution, the fanaticism, the absolute intolerance. I said how after eight days traveling by train, upon arriving to Moscow, I felt as if I were in the middle of Babylon. To some of them it seemed like an exaggeration. When I told them that I had just lived for three months in Escudillers they were almost more surprised than by my stay in Peking;

the atmosphere immediately became more relaxed. Fortunately, they must have thought they were not talking to an ideologue but with a mad man. Once again, I felt like a survivor. *Boudou Saved from Drowning*, I could have shouted; but I didn't, so as not to seem pedantic.

The truth is I wouldn't trade Barcelona for any city in the world.

A VINDICATION OF HYPNOSIS

Suddenly, during a pause in his monologue, Federico Pérez cautioned me not to become too lost in circumlocution. I should lay everything on the line, he said. I replied that I had already done that the very day I made the appointment by phone. I was trusting that his treatment by hypnosis, about which I had heard great things, would help me give up smoking. If I had gone into too many details at the beginning of my explanation, it was to clarify what my relationship with tobacco was and had been. I do not remember his exact words, but he did allude to the evasiveness and circumlocutions in my speech. He added that he thought it was a manifestation of insecurity, a defense mechanism behind which I was hiding. I do not know if the doctor's intervention, his interruption and description of the structure of the story, which unbeknownst to me had become unnecessarily and painfully labyrinthine, was part of the treatment, an attempt to stimulate a particular reaction, the beginning of subjugation. I defended myself with literary arguments. I took refuge in the fact that my writing was fundamentally built on those devices. That is its visible expression. I feel incapable of describing any action, no matter how simple, in a direct way. I said that other writers were able to do that, which did not mean I was less competent than they. In my case, plain and naked exposition, without flourishes, without detours, without echoes or shadows, fatally diminishes the efficiency of the story, converts it into a mere anecdote; a vulgarity, when all is said and done. From the very beginning, what I had always done was scatter a series of points onto the blank page as if they had fallen there by chance, with no visible relationship between them; until one suddenly began to spread out, expand, sprout tentacles in search of others, and then the others would follow its example: the points would become lines running across the page to find their sisters, either to subordinate or serve them, until that initial group of solitary points morphed into an increasingly complex and intricate character, with gaps, creases, ironies, blurrings, and glaring darkness. That was my writing or, at least, the ideal of my writing. I could have added, but I restrained myself, that my exposition could be the reflection of a specific way of conceiving literature, or rather, that the apparent loss of direction in language had created in me a second nature from which I could not escape. To the extent that I did not know how to talk about anything, not even the weather, without detours, and that, in itself, had nothing to do with personal insecurity, as it is usually understood, but rather with a lack of confidence, abstract, of course, in the possibility of communication and persuasion in the ontological loneliness of being. The narrator who, as a rule, appears in my novels rehearses several starting points in the pursuit of a truth, a revelation, and in the effort will lose his way a thousand times, stumble constantly, and will maintain the pace with great difficulty between suffering hallucinations and sleepwalking, only in the end to declare himself defeated. He will come to know that absolutes do not exist, that there is no truth that is not conjectural, relative, and, therefore, vulnerable. But searching for it, no matter how ephemeral, partial, and inconstant it may be, will always be his objective. The narrator might be Sisyphus and Icarus at the same time. His only certainty is that along the way he might have touched a few strands in a marvelous and deplorable tapestry, obscured sometimes by ominous stains or by a sudden and immediate iridescence that, upon seeing it, gives meaning to his efforts.

Of course, apart from demonstrating to Federico, whom I expected to miraculously free me from nicotine, an oral expression polluted by some stylistic processes, I refrained from adding everything else. It seemed like an abuse to ask a doctor to return my lost health to me and to blurt out to him on an empty stomach a speech on the radical solitude of man and the impossibility of attaining by rational means the truth or of arriving at it by approximations and estimates. The pretentious enunciation of those clichés was considerably watered down. Federico allowed me speak a bit more about the history of my tobacco use and its tribulations. Then he explained in a cursory way what his method consisted of and, just like that, I was hypnotized. At that moment, the most profound experience I've known in my adult life began. I've tried to decipher it on various occasions and after a few lines, I give up. The only thing I can do, and I won't try to do any more, is transcribe the process.

We were discussing how Federico Pérez began to hypnotize me. He gave me the instructions necessary to cross the threshold of my inner self; at a given moment he discovered that I was in a trance and could therefore begin the treatment. I should add that I submit to any curative experience with the credulity of a child. I become the tamest lamb that anyone ever imagined. All personal resistance disappears.

Allopathic or homeopathic doctors, magnetists, shamans, acupuncturists, *curanderos*, it doesn't matter: I surrender my faith immediately and entirely to them. Any hint of skepticism disappears. The afternoon of 14 October 1991, the same thing happened, except magnified. I knew through Juan Villoro, his brother-in-law, that Federico worked miracles, and that he had broken the creative paralysis produced by writer's block, as if the void that existed between the page written several years ago and the most recent one had never existed. I was convinced that if he had achieved that, freeing me from nicotine would be child's play for him. A woman in Prague with magnetic powers had passed her hands over my chest a few times and the desire to smoke had disappeared instantly, as if my fingers had never touched a cigarette. A few years later, on a plane, someone offered me one, I lit it almost without realizing it, and the torture began anew. Suddenly, while I listened to Federico's words, I began to feel in my chest and on my arms the same heat that invaded me when the magnetist in Prague passed her hands a few centimeters from my body.

I went to Córdoba yesterday. I spent a good while going through family photo albums with my uncle Agustín Deméneghi and my cousin Luis. In them, I found two photographs that I brought home. One is of my mother and my sister Irma, taken shortly before their deaths; I'm almost sure that it's the last photo of my mother. She's leaning on a white automobile; the landscape is rustic, and she has in her arms a beautiful little girl of three or four years of age. My mother's face is sullen, severe; she had made decisions that would change her life, and ours, my uncle told me. Her demeanor is different than in other photographs I know of her. Her seriousness contrasts with the radiant happiness of the girl who's holding out her arms to the person taking the picture. The other photo is of my sister Irma, sitting on a tricycle, taken a few days later. The transformation is startling. She looks like another girl, whose only similarity to the other is her extremely blonde, straw-like hair; but no trace of the happiness that previously lit up her face remains. In the few days that separated one from the other something monstrous had happened: the death of my mother. That would explain the tragic withdrawal. My tiny sister, a year younger than I, was not able to survive that tragedy. A few weeks later, she would also die. Looking at those portraits fills me once again with an inextinguishable anger and pain.

Federico Pérez asks me to remember a few moments in my life I consider to have been important. And suddenly, without having to make the slightest effort, a curious mix of images begins to parade before me, as if an invisible projector were reflecting them before my eyes. They are significantly enlarged photos, where even the minutest details appear with surprising clarity. There is no chronological order, or any other sort, to their appearance; at least I'm not able to find the threads that unite them. Especially because they pass before me with dizzying speed. I appear with family members, with friends, in the middle of the crowd. The chronology seems to have gone berserk. One image may be from a few days ago, the next from fifty years ago, only to jump forward twenty years, then repeat scenes of three days in a row. I move back and forth in time without any perceptible meaning. I see myself as a child, adolescent, old man, elementary pupil, student in law school, diplomat, teacher, hard worker, shirker, happy, worried, furious, sick, riding a chestnut horse, in the cabin of a German ship, on the deck of the *Leonardo da Vinci*, in the theater, on the street, extremely drunk, in the middle of the snow, under the

India's sun, hospitalized in a cast from head to toe, reading a book whose title I can't make out because my fingers are obscuring it, in Venice, in Potrero, in Istanbul, Cadaqués, Córdoba, Palermo, Moscow, Marienbad, Bogotá, and Belize, in places that I can't even identify. I seem to see thousands of people around me, a mass of people whom I don't know or don't remember, people walking down the street where I walk, who eat in the same restaurant where I'm eating, on a train, mere passersby, and, of course, friends and family. In spite of the fact that I'm in a trance, it still amazes me that none of those images alludes to an important moment in my life, as Federico Pérez had asked me to do. On the contrary, it's nothing more than a bewildering collection of banalities. They lack sound: there's no noise or words. Their power is purely visual. They're photographs, it must not be forgotten. Unlike dreams, or the memories we evoke or that assail us unexpectedly, the details in these portraits that hypnosis offers me are very precise. I identify jackets, sweaters, coats that I wore on such and such occasion, whether bought at Harrods or in the wool market at Santa Ana Chiautempan in the state of Tlaxcala. The details of the clothes acquire almost hyper-realistic effects. I'm fascinated. Then, all of a sudden, just as the terrifying visions of the Apocalypse must have appeared unexpectedly to Saint John, an image looms before my eyes and stops; it doesn't allow another to replace it; in fact, it's the last image of the session. The only difference is that it has movement. My brother Ángel and I are sitting on the floor, watching doves come and go from the sunny terrace where we are. I must have been about five years old, which would make my brother eight. We're wearing short pants. I recognize the house and the landscape around it. We're on the outskirts of Atoyac, a town in Veracruz, at the home of

Pepe Conzzati, a young friend of the family. I recognize the place because in the years that followed I went there many times with my uncle and grandmother. But on the day that corresponds to the image, and in the days that followed, we never saw the owner of the house. Perhaps he left very early and returned at night after we were already asleep. We only see an old woman, the *sirvienta*, who comes out to the terrace where we spend the better part of the day to get us and takes us inside at mealtime. She probably also puts us to bed. We stay at the house for several days, which frees us from all funeral services. Just as in the other images, there's no sound in this one either. My brother and I are sitting, as I said, on the terrace, facing each other, with our legs outstretched on the ground. Ángel looks like a corpse. His face is terrible: his eyes are opened wide. He gets up and goes to sit by me, and I begin to cry. I can't hear my words or my crying; I can only see it. At that moment, I am no longer the hypnotized patient looking to give up smoking. I feel possessed by the little boy I was and who is before my eyes. Apparently I no longer need the image; I become the crying boy. I know that I've gone with my mother and my brother and our little sister Irma to spend a few days with my uncle. His house is in a place called Potrero. My grandmother has also arrived from Huatusco. For a few days, everything is happiness. More than anyone else they celebrate Irma, the youngest; they lift her over their heads, kiss her, and she laughs, laughs, laughs…One day there was a lunch in the house's garden. Several people came: the Mosses, the Scullys, the Cárdenases, and I suppose the Celmas too, who were my uncle's best friends. Some of the guests decided to go that afternoon, after lunch, to Atoyac, to swim in the river, in a place called Idiot's Pond. My uncle, my grandmother, Ángel, and I left later in the car to meet them at the pond. As soon as my uncle stopped the car, two peasants race to tell him something that he repeated to my grandmother. They started running down a path that snaked the length of the river. Surprised by their behavior, my brother and I followed as best we could. I fell several times, my brother helped me up. We arrived after everyone else to a wide clearing, under immense trees, with leaves so intensely green they were almost black; mango trees, I think. The family friends and several ranchers from the region were moving helplessly from one side to the other, some dressed, others half-dressed, some still in bathing suits. My grandmother was crying; some women were hugging her, restraining her so she wouldn't run to my mother's body; they were all crying; some peasant women, standing next to the group, were wailing. My uncle was trying to remove the water from my mother's body. Ángel and I were snatched from the ground by surprise. A very tall man began to run with us in his arms. We're now in his house. We haven't seen him again. A very old woman feeds us and puts us to bed at night. My father is already dead and now my mother is too. I don't know if this is our house. The old woman tells us that we won't see her again until we die. We spend our days on the terrace watching the doves. I want to die. I don't know what I say, but Ángel gets mad, he shakes me by the arm and then he starts to cry like me. I feel my face bathed in tears, I shake uncontrollably; they are real convulsions. In the distance, I hear Federico Pérez's helpful voice. I begin to come out of a deep hole. The convulsions begin to abate. My face is soaked from crying; I feel tears running down my cheeks, toward my mouth, my neck. Federico's voice and his proximity slowly soothe me. As soon as I can speak, I repeat incoherently everything I experienced in the trance. I tell Federico about the experience, from the first innocuous images to the pain from which I am still unable to free myself. I'm entirely out of hypnosis, or so I think, but the echo of the terror continues to stun me.

Federico gives me new instructions: walk slowly until you arrive to the hotel, breathe deeply, and be careful when crossing the street.

"If when you arrive to your hotel," he says, as we say goodbye, "you feel bad, call me. If tonight, no matter what time, you feel bad, don't hesitate to call me at home. You can count on our help at any moment."

I went out into the street. Still stunned, I began to walk slowly. The walk from Federico's house to my hotel normally takes a half hour at a relaxed pace. I was sure that the walk would exceed my energy. I thought about walking three or four blocks and then taking a taxi. All I wanted to do was lie down, take a sedative, and forget about the hypnosis, its revelations, and its results. I kept walking, and with each step I felt, almost physically, that a wound my body had harbored secretly for more than fifty years was beginning to heal. As I progressed, I could feel the improvement. The only thing I was conscious of was that I was leaving an illness behind me. I began to realize that I had lived all those years just to prevent that monstrous pain from repeating itself, to block the circumstances that might provoke it. My life's meaning had consisted of protecting myself, fleeing, wrapping myself in armor. Suddenly I noticed on the sidewalk ahead a bougainvillea that was climbing a tree and flowering in its branches. It looked like a marvelous spectacle unlike anything I had seen before. My fatigue disappeared as if by magic. When I arrived at the hotel, everything had bloomed. I went directly to the restaurant, I ate like a barbarian, everything tasted exquisite; I arrived to my room, lay down on the bed, and began to read an interview with Cioran. I jotted down in my notebook: "We're a terrible mixture, and in each individual coexist three, four, five different individuals, so it's normal that they don't agree with each other"; it wasn't relevant, but it soothed me; and with that news I fell asleep.

The next morning I awoke with an unfamiliar feeling, as if my dialogue with myself were different. Many things had become coherent and explainable: everything in my life had been nothing more than a perpetual flight. There had been fantastic experiences, yes, extraordinary, which I could never regret, but they had also been a nucleus of agony that demanded that I close them off and look for new ones.

My debt of gratitude to Doctor Federico Pérez del Castillo, who allowed me to understand this, is infinite.

Xalapa, August 1994

SIENA REVISITED

For Laura Molina Montmany

I must confess that I am deaf in my left ear, which produces in me mood changes that, at their worst, could be confused with idiocy and also dementia. If at a social gathering, especially a dinner, the guest to my left is by nature very talkative, I'm already lost. I say the wrong thing, instinctively, by chance; imprecisions and nonsense abound, until the failed interlocutor slowly moves away, tired of repeating his questions and of hearing answers that have little or nothing to do with the questions. This is the source of incredible inhibition for me, and once inhibited, tense and fearful, I'm no longer responsible for my behavior.

In the spring of 1993 I took a brief trip to Europe to celebrate my sixtieth birthday. I chose three cities that were foundational in my life: London, Rome, and Barcelona. Warsaw was missing. I wanted to be in Rome at the same time as Augusto Monterroso and Bárbara Jacobs at the presentation of the Juan Rulfo Prize for Latin American and Caribbean Literature, which was being presented to Monterroso. I wrote to Lia Ongno, who at that time was finishing a translation of one of my novels, to let her know that I would be in Rome the day of the award, certain that she, as translator of the honoree, would be present, and that way we could meet and find time to resolve some questions regarding the text about which she had written me. Lia, on her end, informed Antonio Melis, head of the Faculty of Letters at the University of Siena, an old friend of mine, about my upcoming trip to Italy, who, in turn, sent me a fax, inviting me to give a lecture in his department, where, I should add, the chair of Portuguese Studies is held by Antonio Tabucchi, the person who introduced Pessoa to Italy, his translator and commentator, and, most importantly, an exceptional novelist.

I visited Siena briefly at the beginning of 1962, having spent the December holidays with my mother's family. Christmas in Bologna and New Year's Eve in Bonizzo castle. At the end of the last century, my great-grandfather Domenico Buganza crossed the ocean with his three daughters, Preseide, Agnese, and Catarina, the youngest, who was my grandmother, to educate them in Italy. Only two returned: my grandmother and her sister Agnese. The other, the oldest, married in Italy, and has since then lived in that castle, from which she has scarcely moved during her very long life.

Two or three days before my arrival, they gave my *tía* Preseide calming infusions to soothe her nerves, in preparation for her great-nephew's surprise visit from Veracruz. When I introduced myself, she stood up and threw herself into my arms with the force of a hurricane, only to make me repeat again and again the important events from the family history that had happened on the other side of the Atlantic during her sixty-year absence. Except during the war years, correspondence between her and my grandmother had never been interrupted. Still she wanted to hear firsthand everything she had read over the years. She asked me about ranches, towns, people whom

I'd never heard mentioned; I answered as best I could, which is to say clumsily. Suddenly she looked at me with contempt; she must have thought that she had before her an impostor who was pretending to be, who knows to what ends, the grandson of Catarina Buganza-Buganza, her youngest sister. At times she'd grow tired and would send me to the garden or to see the collection of Etruscan pieces that belonged to her granddaughter's husband, on display in another part of the castle, or she'd ask her son-in-law, Noradino, a mathematician and *tía* Argia's husband, to take me to see the surroundings, the river banks where my aunts and grandmother had strolled so many times at the beginning of the century. The truth is that apart from the snow there was little or nothing to see except a thick, milky white mist that obscured everything. I can remember, while almost half-asleep, taking a pair of car trips, one to Ostiglia, a small city, plunged into darkness and the closest to the castle, that according to my uncle had been, during some period, I do not remember which, the outer limit of the Roman empire; the other, to a small architectural jewel—or did it just seem that it was because I was able to see churches and palaces that were not covered in fog?—Mirandola, whose most illustrious son was none other than Pico della Mirandola. I spent those days enveloped by a very intense emotion. I sensed in those settings the presence of my grandmother; my grandmother the child, my grandmother the adolescent, my grandmother on the eve of returning to Mexico. I wrote her a letter from Ostiglia relating my reunion with the family, the conversations with *tía* Preseide, of which she, my grandmother, was the primary topic of conversation; I comforted her, reassured her that I was on my best behavior, drinking moderately, minding what I said. I told her about the condition of the property; a section was heavily damaged, but for years they had stored the materials needed to begin the work behind the garden in large sheds: tons of old Saracen bricks, acquired primarily in Calabria and Sicily from ancient buildings now in ruins, all to be used for the restoration.

The night of January 1, after dinner, very late, I said goodbye to the family; to my elderly great-aunts and uncles forever, as they would die shortly afterward. Early the next morning, my *tío* Noradino took me to Ostiglia, in whose tiny railway station we said goodbye. I boarded a beautiful toy train, a relic from the early days of the railway, I imagine: two small cars with seats lined with a thick threadbare velvet but still very elegant. I don't believe that small narrow gauge train could have ever, not even in its prime, reached a heady speed, and by early 1962, many decades of work, wars, and bad times had rendered it nearly inoperable, and, with the mountains of snow that were covering the tracks that day, reduced it to an almost total inertia at times. The trip to Bologna took longer than expected. At the station in Ostiglia, when we said goodbye, my *tío* Noradino gave me a beautiful black leather wallet, full of enormous, meticulously folded bills. "To start off the year," he said. I thanked him profusely for the unexpected gift that helped me not only to start the year but also for much longer. When I arrived in Bologna, the train on which I had reserved a seat had already departed, and I had to wait for another one that night. As they unloaded an automobile from a freight car, I tried very hard to bribe a railroad employee on that same platform to secure me a berth or, at least, a seat in first class; I was afraid to travel in a crowded second-class car with that much money in my pockets. People were returning to Rome and to the cities in the south in droves after the holidays; the platforms were packed. The young owner of the automobile that had been removed from the train asked me where I was going. I told him Rome, and he offered to take me to Siena, which meant taking me a good distance. He was on his way back from London, where he had attended an international theater festival. He had spent the New Year in Paris, taken the train to Bologna, where he had agreed to pick up the car that belonged to a family member. We talked about theater. He had finished his law degree, if I remember correctly, but he had not yet taken the bar. He possessed that good education characteristic of young people from well-to-do liberal families in which knowledge and pleasure are understood to be naturally integrated. He told me that the theater festival for the most part had been political, and that it was quite good. And that led us to talk for a while about politics. He was a socialist, a fervent admirer of Pietro Nenni, and was convinced that an intermediate force between the Christian Democrats and the Communist Party was necessary for Italy's good political health. If the votes for the socialists and communists were combined, he said, the victory against the right would be convincing. In some areas—health, education, and international politics—the two parties voted frequently on the same side; but if that happened in every case, if they managed to merge into a single political organism, the socialists would run the risk of being absorbed, as had happened in Poland and Czechoslovakia, by the other party. As we approached Piacenza, my host informed me that we would be passing through the city center, which meant I would be able to see the Carthusian monastery by daylight and contemplate the works of Luca and Andrea della Robbia, which I had never seen. I remember the pleasure that the architectural structure of the *certosa* gave me, in which the color of the majolica was a cry of joy. I was completely ignorant insofar as applied arts, which I considered a trivial form of decoration. I owe no small part of my education to the many trips I took hitchhiking across Italy that year.

Between Pistoia and Siena, our conversation revolved primarily around two subjects: English literature and Italian art, in particular the primitive and the Renaissance painters. Before entering law school at a very young age, he had spent a year in London to learn the language and to experience living away from his family. During that time, and for several years before, my readings were preferably English. I made a comment about the Italian influence in English literature; not just beginning with the Romantics, who were fleeing the philistinism of their country in droves, but long before, since the Renaissance. Their debt to Bandello, for example, was noteworthy, and a considerable part of his work was set in Italian cities, and I cited in passing, since we were on our way to Siena, a commentary by Robert Greene about the city's raucous university life, where he heard about practices that took place as a matter of routine and that would have been unimaginable in his country. My travel companion politely corrected the name, believing that I was citing Graham Greene, and I explained to him that no, I was referring to Robert Greene, a contemporary of Shakespeare to whom some scholars attributed the authorship or, at least, his collaboration in the writing of *Titus Andronicus*, who in his youth traveled throughout Italy and probably stopped for a time in Siena, which he cites as a compendium of all the excesses of the pagan world. The young law student became a bit confused. He changed the conversation to more pedestrian topics and suggested that upon our arrival in Siena I stay at the station; since the snow had begun to fall again and we were progressing at a cautious speed, we would arrive late at night; so I should check my bag and rest for a while in the waiting room. There wouldn't be any problem because it was a station with little activity; then, at daybreak, I could go out and walk through the city since the colors of the murals and palaces were illuminated at that hour in such a way that only then would I be able to experience the hue that the entire world knows as sienna red in all its splendor. He suggested I visit the cathedral before leaving the city and the art museum to see the masterpieces of Sienese painting, those by Simone Martini, Ambrogio, and Pietro Lorenzetti, and especially those of Duccio di Buoninsegna, the founder of the Sienese school, and its most important proponent. He recommended that I write down the name so I wouldn't forget it. I replied without pretension that I knew who he was, I had seen one of his pieces in the National Gallery in London, and that I knew the majority of his works in reproduction. And then I blurted out, also casually, some ideas by Berenson, whose books, which I had become acquainted with and studied in Mexico, I always carried with me during my trips to Italy. I talked about the sumptuousness of his greens and metallic golds, of the technique he had inherited from Bizancio that he managed to make them look more like bronze bas-reliefs than paintings. Duccio was extraordinary, I insisted, no one doubted it, but he lacked Giotto's genius, whose work summarized those tactile values, which for Berenson were everything. And then there was another silence similar to the one that followed my comment about Robert Greene and his memories of Siena.

During the first months of my stay in Italy, I often experienced the feeling that people expected me, and all young Latin Americans, to possess a wealth of hardened, tropical views, different ways of thinking, myths, rebellions, and new strategies that would perhaps help redeem the Old World: the *aggiornata* representation of the *beau savage* with Borgesian memories and flashes of Che Guevara. It flattered and at the same time disappointed them to feel their culture being recognized. Those adventures through the Renaissance, the Enlightenment, and the avant-garde, after all, belonged to them. The claim seemed absurd to me, and sometimes I responded with provocations, but the European experience made me conscious, in spite of the sincerity of my intentions, that I ran the risk of learning everything solely from books, by rote, a self-indulgence that lacked the foundation that the necessary environment provides. It's not that I was interested in submitting to any methodology, nor that I had academic ambitions; nothing interested me less than weakening the hedonistic nature of my readings, their purely casual organization. Nor was I going to ignore my almost innate disposition to seize everything the world had to offer. That was not the point; I intuitively understood that I needed to affirm the source of my own language and culture. I could recite a list of palaces and churches built by Palladio or Brunelleschi, and on the other hand, I possessed overwhelming gaps in the Mexican baroque, the truncated horizon of the Olmec and Maya, to cite just a few examples. I knew that I needed to capture that past in order to move freely in the world. It was the marrow needed to sustain the complex being I aspired to be. Without an affirmation of his language, the traveler loses the capacity to aspire to translate the universe; he will become a mere interpreter on the level of a tour guide.

Once in Siena, my traveling companion telephoned a few friends at whose home we had dinner, and then he accompanied me very late to the station, where our paths parted. I spent a few hours in the waiting room. I wasn't able to sleep. That wait was like a reality check that rendered phantasmagoric my memory of the family rituals of Bonizzo, the complicated medieval maneuvers to heat the beds for the purpose of keeping them warm at night, the beauty of the spaces, the marvelous dinners prepared under the direction of my *tía* Argia, the good manners, the fire in the hearths, the Etruscan pieces. In contrast, I was enveloped in the smoke of dreadful cigarettes, coarse accents, and endless guffaws. It was like stepping onto foreign soil. There were few who slept. Men and women of different ages killed time recounting episodes of their lives, family intimacies, jobs and job searches; the youngest talked about unrealistic projects, recounted with a joy and innocence that managed to transform the most scabrous passages—and believe me there were!—into dialogues of pastoral purity.

I left there at dawn to go see the walls, awash in sienna red. I ate breakfast and walked to the museum, ready to experience ecstasy before the Byzantine splendor of the great Duccio. But it was still a holiday and no museums were open. I could have stayed in Siena a couple of days, but I could not resist the temptation of going to Rome, of introducing myself to Canova, to tell Araceli and María Zambrano and their friends about my family experience in Bonizzo, and to find out how they had spent the holidays, and to make plans for the following days. I thought I would return very soon. So I decided to walk only a bit through the city's center, to enjoy its splendor and a while later take the bus that would leave me in Rome.

Thirty years had to pass, however, for me to again see the walls of that exceptional city.

I returned to deliver a talk on my most recent novels at the Faculty of Arts at the University of Siena during the course of an afternoon devoted to Hispano-American culture. The event would begin at five or six in the afternoon; I would speak, then there would be a music program organized by the students, perhaps a discussion, and it would conclude with a dinner at a home not far from Siena.

I had arrived in Florence, where I called Melis to coordinate our trip to Siena, the day before the event. She would come by, she said, to pick me up at my hotel the next day at seven in the morning. Later, I called Antonio Tabucchi's number in Florence. I was told that he was at his home in Vecchiano, a town near Pisa, and they gave me his telephone number. I tracked him down shortly thereafter; I told him that I was in Florence and that the next day I was leaving with Professor Melis for Siena, where that evening I was to meet with the students. He replied that he already knew, but regrettably was not going to be able to attend. He had to get some papers in order and then take care of some tax-related matters, which had him very anxious. He had no idea when he might be able to leave his appointment, but he suggested I go to Vecchiano from Siena and stay a few days at his home. He assured me that I would like the region and that there were sites of interest in Pisa. I explained to him that I would be delighted to accept his invitation, but my schedule was very tight. I would be leaving Siena the morning following the event; I was to be present when the award was presented to Augusto Monterroso in Rome and then return to Barcelona, where I had already committed to meet Jorge and Lali Herralde. In short, we would have to see each other another time.

I had admired Tabucchi since Anagrama had published *The Woman of Porto Pim* and *Indian Nocturne*. I awaited the arrival of each of his books after their release in Italy, and I arranged for their immediate delivery.

I had written about them. I would have liked immensely to talk to him about one of his novels, *The Edge of the Horizon*, which reminded me of Conrad at his best, as elusive and multivalent as *The Secret Sharer. The Edge of the Horizon* possesses that absolutely intimate quality nourished by the everyday fantastic found in the best of Tabucchi's stories. The reader is witness, and in a certain way accomplice, to a secret battle that takes place nonstop between allusion and elusion. The more precise the details, the more mysterious the story becomes.

I spent the rest of the day at the Uffizi. The long stroll itself through the visual splendor of the Renaissance made the trip worthwhile. Everything there is magnificent. I lingered in the hall of the Sienese three hundred, as if I were anticipating what I would see the next day. Two of the works on exhibit, the *Madonna in Maestà*, by Duccio di Buoninsegna, and Simone Martini's *The Annunciation with St. Margaret and St. Ansanus* left me so amazed that when I thought of Siena the referent was not my conference but rather the previous visit I made to the Museum of Art. After the Uffizi Gallery, I walked through the city for a few hours; when I arrived at the hotel, I fell into bed like a ton of bricks.

I left Florence for Siena at 7:00 A.M., accompanied by Antonio Melis. The first news that met me was so awful that I rejected it out of hand, as if I had not yet awakened and were trapped in a nightmare. It was the 27th of May, 1993. Antonio turned on his car radio, where we heard the confirmation. A huge explosion had occurred the night before at the Uffizi, which resulted in seven deaths, several injuries, and the destruction of part of the building. We made the drive from Florence to Siena in a state of shock. Melis tried to clarify for me somewhat Italy's labyrinthine political and social reality: the collapse of the Christian Democracy, whose monopoly on power had lasted more than a half century, corruption, the judicial proceedings against politicians, the ties to the mafia, drug trafficking; in short, everything that had rocked Italy for a couple of years. The catastrophe that had taken place that day could be one of the consequences of that fall into disgrace. It was perhaps an effort to destabilize Italy, to strike at its most sensitive sites, to deter the police investigations into the nexuses between political and criminal power, or, if not, to live with its consequences. I arrived in Siena very distraught. The idea of having been in those precincts for several hours, shortly before the explosion, at perhaps the same time as the criminals as they studied the last details, added to my unease. If it were a nightmare, I would feel as if I were being watched, investigated, surrounded, I would end up feeling guilty, yes, I would doubt myself, rack my brain trying to prove my innocence without being convinced myself. Someone would swear that I had been seen in the car disguised as a taxi or an ambulance that introduced the dynamite into the museum. We all know how nightmares are. When we arrived in Siena we learned that only a few paintings had been affected, and none destroyed. The deaths and injuries were the result of the dynamite having been placed in a section where part of the museum's custodial staff lived.

Antonio Melis drove me to the university and introduced me to Lia Ogno, who then took me to the hotel where I would be staying, which was not very far. I had most of the day free. I walked with Lia through the city's medieval center, through wonderful alleys, through plazas whose preservation seemed miraculous. We said goodbye in the main Piazza del Campo. I picked up my pace and looked for the museum. I needed to embrace it. The gate to the entrance was draped by an enormous black fabric. All museums and art centers in Italy were closing their doors for two days in mourning and protest for the attack against culture carried out in Florence.

Once again, I had been forbidden the opportunity to experience the masterpieces of Sienese painting. Two of the attractions that had made my trip to Siena appealing had vanished. I would not see Duccio de Buoninsegna's *The Kiss of Judas*, nor would I meet in person Antonio Tabucchi. Talking to him, learning his points of view, hearing his interpretation of some of his texts had become so essential to me, as compulsive as it had been for the American editor, a matter of pride and dishonor, of life and death, to have in his hands the letters that the celebrated Jeffrey Aspern had written to Juliana Bordereau in the novel by Henry James.

But in the end I did see Tabucchi. I shudder as I relive the episode. Recalling my behavior still causes me stress. Since this book in a certain way is a collection of reparations and regrets, an attempt to allay anxieties and cauterize wounds, I'll take the liberty of sketching in a few lines the circumstances of the encounter.

That afternoon I held my talk with the students and teachers. I spoke before a warm audience about my career as a writer, my ties to Italy, my recognizable influences, some philias and many phobias, viable and impossible projects. During the course of my talk, I saw Tabucchi enter through the door in the back. I recognized him immediately; I had seen pictures of him in his Anagrama editions and in the press; so I could not have been mistaken; he entered with wife María José, a very beautiful woman, with a splendidly intense expression. At the end of the talk, we introduced ourselves. Previously our relationship had been mediated by correspondence and numerous phone calls. The invisible presence of Jorge Herralde, our friend and mutual editor in Barcelona, served as a point of reference. The musical performance was about to begin. Speaking before the audience had left me extremely thirsty and rather fatigued. I asked if there was anywhere I could get a coffee; I needed at least two cups immediately. He said we could go somewhere, that there was a pleasant café near the university. I do not know if it was the excitement of the day, or the fear of not being able to hear him due to the deafness I mentioned earlier and responding foolishly to questions, but the fact is as soon as we sat down, after commenting briefly on the morning's terrible news, I began to talk about his latest book, a short, smart, and delightful text about the imaginary dreams of characters to which he was devoted. It was the book of a curious, sharp, and refined intellectual, and, at the same time, one not locked away in an ivory tower—an author in solidarity with life. The twenty characters who were dreaming represented very diverse signs that the author, by bringing them together, was reconciling: Apuleyo, Rabelais, Goya, Leopardi, Stevenson, Rimbaud, Chekov, Pessoa, Mayakovsky, García Lorca, and Freund, among others. The book's title was *Dreams of Dreams*; it had been released very recently in a beautiful edition by Sellerio. I began almost immediately to talk nonstop, without allowing him to contribute; I began to list authors whose dreams would be worth imagining; Henry James, for example, must have some very complex ones, locked in a labyrinthine and elliptical syntax that trying to follow would have driven even the most competent psychoanalyst insane. It would have been an arduous task not only to decipher one of his dreams but also to understand his language, not become lost in the many folds of the single, never-ending and surely dark sentence in which he described them.

And Borges's dreams! Lezama Lima's, Góngora's, and I don't know how many others! I spoke nonstop until we realized that time had flown by and we needed to return to the university so we could at least be present at the end of the musical performance. We returned. The concert ended, and the preparations began that would lead us to the house in the country where we were invited to have dinner. The Tabucchis invited me to ride with them in their car. Naturally, I sat in the front seat, which meant that my good ear faced the window and the deaf one toward Tabucchi and, partially, María José, who was sitting in the backseat.

They asked me the usual questions that well-mannered people ask: how my trip had been, where I was coming from, how did I feel in Italy, those necessary preliminary questions that tend to relax the interlocutor, create a climate of trust and, at the same time, the necessary conditions for what will become the body of the conversation. I answered that I had flown from Mexico to London, from there to Rome, and then traveled to Florence by train, where I met Antonio Melis with whom I drove to Siena.

I should have stopped there. Or perhaps I could have described my shock that morning upon learning about the destruction of a place where I had been a few hours before the catastrophe, a place that should be considered invulnerable for having endured five centuries of wars, invasions, floods, and sackings, from which it had always emerged intact. That would have been the correct thing to do, would it not? But the events did not transpire that way. After relating my itinerary, as I have already said, I began to talk about my experience in the taxi that drove me from my London hotel to the airport. I said that the driver struck up a conversation, perhaps out of politeness, to keep me entertained during the long ride, which made me rather uncomfortable in the first place because of the effort required to hear and make myself heard in those vehicles of such excessive dimensions, and because as a rule English cabbies speak with accents very difficult to understand, each one more exotic than Cockney, in which one loses words and entire sentences. The driver was a man of more or less my age, portly, and with a face similar to the one in those classical illustrations by which we've come to know Mr. Pickwick. He began to talk about his experiences as a tourist. He recalled with disconcerting precision, like an English incarnation of Borges's Funes, the names of all the hotels in which he had stayed, the restaurants where he had eaten, the dishes he had ingested, as well as their condiments, the brands of cigarettes, soaps, and toilet paper, and the price in local currency of each of these products, which he immediately translated into pounds sterling. He had been to Mexico on one occasion and recalled everything I had never noticed. He did not show the slightest artistic or historical curiosity for the countries he had visited, nor excitement for the landscape; no human interest in the inhabitants of those places nor curiosity about their problems. Everywhere he went he amused himself by finding the English products that were on the market and finding out their price, comparing it to the price in London and in the process determining the profits made by the merchants. To be honest, I was fed up; I answered in monosyllabic words; I wanted to read the morning paper, but cutting him off in mid-sentence would be very awkward. So I reconciled myself passively to not encouraging the conversation. He told me that he walked as much as he could, both while traveling and in London. He thought that society had begun to break down because people had become unaccustomed to walking. I do not know if in response to one of his questions or *motu proprio* I told him that I took a walk twice a day; that I walked my dog an hour in the morning and another hour at night. He asked me the name and breed of my dog. His name is Sacho, and he's a wonderful bearded collie. You should have heard the fuss! He told me the story of his dog, also a bearded collie, with which he had lived for fifteen years. When she died, several years earlier, he suffered an extreme depression. He stopped working; a time arrived when he did not leave the house, he thought the end was near. A few Sundays he mustered the strength to go to Mass, it turns out he was Catholic. On one occasion, shortly before the end of mass, he heard a voice that said to him: "She's fine where she is and is taking care of you from there." His depression disappeared; he was able to return to a normal life and to work. His emotion seemed authentic, even after so many years. I adored him. I could have traveled to the ends of the earth to hear the everyday details of his relationship with his dog. Just then we were arriving at the house in the country. "It has an air of Chekov," was Tabucchi's comment.

We dined outdoors, on a terrace; I ended up sitting in the middle of a small group of professors and beside María José and Antonio Tabucchi. I do not know how I came up with the topic, what provoked it, whether the Devil made me do it, but suddenly I heard myself telling the story about the escape and death of Carranza—yes, the departure of Don Venustiano from Mexico City and his tragic final hours!—the arrival of the president and his entourage to Buenavista station, the commotion, the chaos that reigned, the hundreds of coaches, one containing the national treasury; another the official archives, the first desertions, and then, during the trip, the different attacks of which the presidential train was a target, the lack of water and coal for the engines, the telegram from the governor of Veracruz refusing to recognize him as head of State, the impossibility of going on and of turning back, his flight on horseback to the village of Tlaxcalantongo, the final bullet that cut short his life.

Where was all of this going? To talk for two hours in great detail about the flight and death of a Mexican president from the revolutionary period whom no one knew, on the terrace of a country house near Siena! Suddenly, I realized that the only person in the group speaking was me; by then we were having coffee, and the guests were beginning to say goodbye.

I would have liked for Tabucchi to clarify moments from *The Edge of the Horizon*, to talk about one of the stories that I liked most, "Saturday Afternoon," to know more about his interest in Portugal, in Pessoa, to talk, if he wanted, about what he was writing. I emerged from what seemed like a trance and was horrified, more embarrassed than I had ever felt. I apologized as best as I could and added that I was usually rather quiet, which is true, that the parrot I had become was a side to my personality that I did not even know. And María José, with a smile for which I shall forever be thankful, told me that she thought my story about the old president was both tragic and beautiful. Tabucchi presented a small book to me before I left; the text of a lecture he had given not long before in Tenerife. When I got back to the hotel, I read it in one sitting, and once again I was impressed by the quality of his intelligence. I felt even more embarrassed.

In short, it was one of those nights when one would rather be shot.

Xalapa, April 1996

WRITING

THE NARRATOR

Thinking about the foreboding moments of a work of fiction inevitably takes me back to that famous interview in which William Faulkner confessed that the inspiration for one of his novels came from seeing the "drawers" of a little girl who was attempting to climb a tree. Day after day, he would see those panties and that tree at the most unexpected times. He would pour himself a whiskey, and the intimate garment would appear among the ice cubes; he would try to read a newspaper, and the little girl's thighs would appear floating on the printed page; he would see a puckered and wizened neighbor woman walk down the street, and could not help but superimpose the small buttocks of the girl who was climbing the tree on the behind of that dismal advertisement against lust. That initial image would begin at some moment to branch out. It occurs to me that one day the writer must have imagined a little boy beneath that tree who struggled between shame, humiliation, and the animal need to stare at the naked legs and intimate garment of the little girl who was his sister. There, in a nutshell, is the essence of one of the most extraordinary novels of our century, which recounts Quentin Compson's erotic attraction for his sister Caddy and its tragic development.

Its title: *The Sound and the Fury.*

At times, this first incitement surfaces, for a moment or for several days, then troubles the eventual author, only to later withdraw inexplicably into one of the blackest holes of memory, waiting for the opportune moment to reappear with accumulated strength. No one can predict how long the inspiration will take to mature. It can be a matter of days or decades. At twenty, Thomas Mann sketched the outline of a novel that he would write fifty years later, *Doctor Faustus*, a book that would be enough to guarantee immortality for any author.

The paths to creation are imprecise. They are full of wrinkles, mirages, delays. They require the patience of a saint, a good deal of abandonment, and, at the same time, an iron will in order to not succumb to the traps the unconscious lays to block the writer. It is well known that the struggle between Eros and Thanatos always lies at the root of creation. But the end of the battle is always unforeseeable.

I spent my childhood at a sugar mill in Potrero, Veracruz, a place, without a doubt, as unhealthy as the farms in New Guinea, the Upper Volta, or the Amazon must have been during the same period. Between brief intervals of physical activity there were long periods during which I was bedridden with fevers caused by malignant tertian malaria. Reading became my only pleasure. I gladly and by necessity became a full-time reader. From the usual childhood readings— all of Verne, *Treasure Island*, *The Call of the Wild*, *The Adventures of Tom Sawyer*—I dove into the novels of Dickens, and then, without delay, into *Creole Ulysses* by Vasconcelos, *War and Peace*, the Mexican poets of the *Contemporáneos* group, Freud, Proust, D.H. Lawrence, and foreign languages. I read everything that fell into my hands. I reached adolescence carrying an almost unbearable weight of readings.

If one adds to this the fact that I lived at my grandmother's house, and that the only people who frequented the house were her sister-in-law, her childhood friends, and, occasionally, her near one-hundred-year -old nanny, who did everything possible so the conversation would avoid any contemporary topic and remain frozen in a kind of vanquished utopia, a subverted Eden, the world before the Revolution, when one could travel to take waters, not just in Tehuacán but also in Italy—to reclaim a health that ultimately served no purpose, since the time that was worth living had been left behind, lost and destroyed—my subsequent destiny can be understood. If one adds to the accumulation of poorly digested readings the incessant flow of oral literature intended to keep the house removed from the present, and thus from reality, it is not at all surprising that at some point I would pass from the category of reader to that of aspiring writer.

I arrived in the capital at sixteen to take classes at the university. Although I enrolled in law school, I spent most of my time in the Faculty of Philosophy and Letters. If it is true that the latter was, overall, much more attractive than law—going from classes on the history of historiography to those on medieval Italian literature, and from the history of modern art to the literature of the Golden Age, was infinitely more pleasing than attending classes in law school, where I was forced to listen to incomprehensible disquisitions on business law or civil procedure—, it is also true that I owe the direction of my destiny toward and for literature to law school, and in particular to one teacher, Don Manuel Martínez de Pedroso, professor of Theory of the State. The students who were most committed to the study of law, the most organized, those with the best grades in all their subjects, disoriented by the absence of a previously established syllabus and the

THE ART OF FLIGHT

maestro's refusal to designate a textbook, defected two or three weeks after the beginning of the term. Don Manuel Pedroso was one of the most cultured persons I have ever known, and perhaps, for that reason, there was nothing bookish about him. His sense of order was demonstrated in the most oblique way one could imagine. Once only a handful of faithful remained in his class, the maestro from Seville would begin his paideia in earnest. He imparted it in the most heterodox way conceivable at that time—and possibly any other—for the teaching of law. Pedroso would talk to us about the ethical dilemma embedded in Dostoyevsky's "The Grand Inquisitor"; about the antagonism between obedience to power and free will in Sophocles; about the notions of political theory expressed by the Henrys and the Richards in the historical dramas of Shakespeare; about Balzac and his dynamic conception of history; about the points of contact between the Renaissance utopists and their antagonists—which for Pedroso were only superficial—the theorists of political thought, the first visionaries of the Modern State: Juan Bodino and Thomas Hobbes. Sometimes in class he would lecture at length about the poetry of Góngora, whom he preferred to any other Spanish-language poet, or about his youth in Germany, where he carried out the first Spanish translation of Das Kapital and Frank Wedekind's *Spring Awakening*, one of the first expressionist plays to circulate in the Hispanic world; about his activities during Spain's civil war during which, from the beginning, his title of *marqués* did not prevent him from placing himself at the service of the Republic; about his experiences in the terrifying Moscow of the Great Purge, where he was the last ambassador of the Spanish Republic. He frequently thrashed us with caustic sarcasm, but he also celebrated our victories. Pedroso urged us to read, to study languages, but also to live. He enjoyed the stories we'd share with him, inventing some details and exaggerating others, about our nightly rounds through a circuit of dives from which we miraculously escaped unscathed. One of the triumphs of the Mexican baroque manifested itself at the time in the complexity of the capital's nightlife, governed and lived with unbounded imagination. It seems that the sense of danger one experienced upon entering one of those dives was the product of impeccable staging and *mise-en-scène*, spaces that were in no way innocent but also enormously entertaining and not at all dangerous. With Pedroso, the temptations of the world lived in harmony with the rigors of knowledge. Humor was one of his key traits. Even the most dramatic episodes of the civil war could, just before reaching the height of pathos, be transformed into an endless parade of scenes of indescribable comedy. When the term ended, one knew the theory of the State with greater clarity than those students who deserted to drink from more canonical waters. Carlos Fuentes and Víctor Flores Olea have written excellent pages about him.

Reading Jules Verne had fueled in me a certain desperation to travel and become lost in the world; perhaps compensation for my childhood seclusion. In early 1953 I traveled abroad for the first time. It was a trip to South America. I planned to disembark in Venezuela, travel through Colombia and Ecuador to reach Peru, where I would embark again for Mexico. Letters of introduction from Alfonso Reyes provided immediate access to various Venezuelan intellectuals and foreigners residing in Venezuela. While there, I met the essayist Maríano Picón Salas, the most respected Venezuelan on the continent, Alejo Carpentier, Juan David García Bacca, and many others. In my early days in Caracas, Carpentier's novel *The Kingdom of This World*, which had been published in Mexico, appeared in bookstores, whose reading, of course, left me dazzled. Carpentier became one of three Hispano-American authors who, during my university years, constituted my personal Olympus; the others were Borges and Onetti, to whom I have added half a dozen other names. What attracted me most to the Cuban writer was his rhythm, the austere melody of his phrasing, an intense verbal musicality with classical resonances and modulations that came from other languages and other literatures. To the quality of his language Carpentier added the allures of the Caribbean, its intricate geography, its fascinating history, the crossroads of myths and languages, political reflection; all of which was integrated into perfect plots. *Explosion in a Cathedral* is one of the most extraordinary novels in the Spanish language, a tale about the influence of the Enlightenment on the islands and the continent, and a bitter and profound reflection on political ideals—revolution, its triumph, its transformation into *raison d'État*—ideals held in public proclamations but denied and fought in practice. I never encountered the same tension in anything Carpentier wrote later.

Venezuela was suffering at the time under the cruel and obtuse military dictatorship of Pérez Jiménez. I remained in Caracas for several months instead of undertaking the ambitious itinerary I had previously outlined. I celebrated my twentieth birthday there. I wrote an occasional article for *El Papel Literario*, the cultural supplement edited by Picón Salas, as well as a few poems I hoped to publish as soon as I returned to Mexico. Love poems, of course. My guardian angel protected and saved my literary future: I misplaced the poems. When I reread them thirty years later, I was petrified; to say they were atrocious would be to praise them. Had I published them, it is very likely that my relationship to literature would have been dealt a mortal blow. In any case, I lived for the first time the incomparable experience involved in creation. During those months, I witnessed a political and social unrest that was all but nonexistent in the circle in which I moved in Mexico.

When I returned home, I enrolled in a course in dramatic theory and technique with the intention of learning to write theater. I was certain that my vocation was pointing me in that direction. The playwright Luisa Josefina Hernández assigned us some Greek tragedies and gave us the task of adapting their themes to our century, to create Mexican Electras, Orestes, Iphigenias, and Oedipuses. I sketched my dramatic outlines in accordance with her instructions, and when I began to develop them I was surprised that, instead of a tragedy, a short story was taking shape. They were twilight recreations of life on ranches and haciendas of my native Veracruz, in which I summarized the family mythology that I had assimilated for as long as I could remember. An inexplicable alchemic impulse, which I felt incapable of resisting, caused the dialogues and stage directions to disappear and, in their place, a narrative web began to take shape, which included the history of those foreign families, whose arrogance I surely exaggerated, scattered around Huatusco and its surroundings, where my great-grandparents had settled a century before.

At twenty-five I published my first book of stories: *Tiempo cercado* (Corralled Time) and thus began to expel the toxins I had accumulated since childhood. Living in Veracruz meant being periodically engulfed in the fiesta. At the time, however, I was unable to discern what I would later learn in Bakhtin, namely that the feast makes up the primary and indestructible ingredient of human civilization;

it may weaken, it may degenerate even, but there will never be a force that can eclipse it completely. "The feast," says the Russian philosopher, "has no utilitarian connotation (as has daily rest and relaxation after working hours). On the contrary, the feast means liberation from all that is utilitarian, practical. It is a temporary transfer to the utopian world."[4] Although I was immersed in the feast, I did not allow it access to those tales of Veracruz that suffered conspicuously from its absence; in those stories, evil appears as a factotum; it constitutes a closed universe, univocal, reluctant to recognize, much less celebrate, "the world's inexhaustible mutation." Those family histories that depict the deterioration of immense houses that are possessed over time by humidity, weeds, and the devil held for me a single virtue: they allowed me to cut an umbilical cord that refused to be severed. When I wrote my first books, *Tiempo cercado* and *Infierno de todos* (Everyone's Hell), which brought together those tales whose somber tone and rigid literary devices did not reconcile with the exuberant nature from which they emerged, I learned how to tell stories, to recreate some of the characters that my grandmother resurrected as she spoke about her lost Huatusco. But, above all, I rid myself of a world that belonged only vicariously to me, and I felt obligated to recount exploits and disasters closer to my experience. My guardian angel during that time was William Faulkner, whose Yoknapatawpha County I attempted to recreate among the coffee plantations, palm trees, and dark tropical rivers.

During the time I wrote those stories, I traveled to New York. It must have been 1956. Only in recent years have I realized the vast education those two very different trips provided me. I have

---

4 Translated by Hélène Iswolsky

since gone to many museums, but none of those visits succeeded in repeating the wonder produced by those in New York, above all the Museum of Modern Art. For weeks I was appalled by the scale of my ignorance but took delight in the extraordinary surprises that my efforts to diminish that ignorance afforded me. What a difference between *Guernica* in its natural state and its miniature reproductions in magazines or cultural supplements! I discovered many of the trends in contemporary art, and I was won over or unsettled (which, in the end, is the same thing) by some of them. During that period the Expressionists did not yet enjoy the prestige they enjoy today. It was difficult to find them outside of a few German museums. On a wall of the Museum of Modern Art hung *The Departure*, the first of the new triptychs painted by Max Beckmann. Unlike traditional polyptychs that narrate a story—the tragic life of a martyr, the road to conversion of an excessively degenerate pagan that ends up becoming Pope, the exploits of a warrior who subjects vast territories to catechization, the vicissitudes of an emperor desperate to hold his empire together despite the push of an enemy infidel—where each panel represents a segment of the story so that the whole can provide us with the complete vision, Beckmann's triptychs are flooded with strange figures engaged in unfathomable acts. A rich tapestry emerges before our eyes where certain signs are repeated over and over like pillars of a personal mythology. No sum is possible, and, therefore, the progressive sequence of a story is never achieved. In the triptych I am referring to, the side panels are a catalogue of sordid and brutal acts. In the left panel, a sinister-looking villain is torturing three people—two men and a woman. One has been mutilated: his hands cut off, the stumps still bloody. In the right panel, a young woman holding an oil lamp is walking with the corpse of a half-nude man trussed vertically to her body: the corpse is positioned head-down, the feet reach the woman's neck, and the head the floor; behind her a bellboy is walking blindfolded, carrying a big fish in his hands. Beside him, a modestly dressed character is playing a drum energetically. The radiant central canvas stands in contrast to the sordidness going on in the side panels: a man wearing a crown and a woman holding a baby in her arms are standing beside a mysterious male figure with his face covered. The blue sky and sea shine as if it were varnish, in contrast to the absence of sunlight and the violence cloistered on the sides. I imagine the triptych's title, *The Departure*, refers to that scene. The couple and their son, the king and queen of creation, are abandoning the cruel, turbid, and incomprehensible world that surrounds them. The brightness of the colors in the center, accentuated by the space in which the royal protagonists are situated, immediately attracts the observer's eye.

The many acts encapsulated in one of Beckmann's works can, at first sight, produce a mistaken effect. It could be taken for the illustrations of a literary work. However, the sensuality of the color and the extraordinary power of the line undo that mistake. It is not painted literature but pure painting: it is natural that people use these elements to try to create a personal story. When explaining to a friend the panel on the right where a corpse, naked from the waist down and trussed to the body of a beautiful woman, beside whom a man, who doesn't even see them, is playing a drum, Beckmann states: "The body tied to you is a part of yourself, the corpse of your memories, of your wrongs and failures, the murder everyone commits at some time in his life—you can never free yourself of your past, you have to carry that corpse while Life plays the drum." If someone who had not read Beckmann's explanation stood in front of the triptych and translated that fragment similarly, I would slit my throat. Each spectator must decipher the elements as best he can, drawing on life lessons or personal experiences; this, which seems inevitable, does not mean enriching or impoverishing the aesthetic pleasure. Of course certain general elements catch the eye: an anxious tension between the power of Life and the presence of Death, and other indirect tensions resulting from a series of confrontations between closure and openness, health and illness, dignity and humiliation. I cannot think of any other feature at the moment, but deep down I would want to discover some sort of coherence in that tumultuous collection of figures and enigmatic situations; I would turn it into stories, into plots that would have nothing in common with the painter's version.

I lingered before that triptych for a long time, filled with amazement and contradictory feelings that alternated between fascination and rejection. Over the years, I have been able to see a large part of Beckmann's work in German museums and in international exhibitions of Expressionist art, and I've consulted some excellent monographs. But the image that lingers in my memory is that of my first encounter, my astonishment before the accumulation of so many unlikely elements in the same space. On certain occasions, after looking at Beckmann's paintings, I've felt the temptation to incorporate into my stories situations and characters whose mere proximity could be considered scandalous; to establish, in a fit of bravura, the threads necessary to set into motion all kinds of incompatible incidents until they could be shaped into a plot. Dreaming about writing a novel replete with contradictions, most only superficial; to create from time to time zones of shadows, deep fissures, abysmal caverns, so that the reader can travel on his own the story's vast spaces.

It pleases me to imagine an author who isn't intimidated by the thought of being demolished by critics. Surely he would be attacked for the novel's extravagant execution, characterized as a worshipper of the avant-garde, although the very idea of the avant-garde for him is an anachronism. He would withstand a storm of insults and foolish attacks from anonymous frauds. What would truly terrify him would be that his novel might arouse the interest of some foolish and generous critic who claimed to have deciphered the enigmas buried throughout the text and interpreted them as an shameful acceptance of the world that he detests, someone who said that his novel should be read "as a harsh and painful requiem, a heartrending lament, the melancholy farewell to the set of values that in the past had given meaning to his life." Something like that would destroy and sadden him, would cause him to toy with the idea of suicide. He would repent of his sins; condemn his vanity, his taste for paradox. He would blame himself for not having clarified, just to achieve certain effects, the mysteries in which his plot delights, for having not known how to renounce the vain pleasure of ambiguities. Over time, he would be able to recover; he would forget his past tribulations, his longing for atonement, such that when he starts writing his next novel he will have already forgotten the moments of contrition as well as his efforts to make amends.

And he will return to his old habits; he will leave unexplained gaps between A and B, between G and H , he will dig tunnels everywhere, will put into action an ongoing program of misinformation, he'll emphasize the trivial and ignore those moments that normally require an intense emotional charge. While writing, he dreams with delight that his tale will confuse law-abiding citizens, reasonable people, bureaucrats, politicians, sycophants and bodyguards, social climbers, nationalists and cosmopolitans by decree, pedants and imbeciles, society matrons, flamethrowers, fops, whitewashed tombs, and simpletons. He aspires for the ubiquitous mob to lose its way in the first chapters, to become exasperated, and to fail to grasp the narrator's intention. He will write a novel for strong spirits, whom he will allow to invent a personal plot sustained by a few points of support laboriously and joyously formulated. Each reader would find at last the novel he has at some time dreamt of reading. The opulent, the incomparable, the delectable Polydora will be every woman of the world: the proto-semantic Polydora, as her refined admirers, as if spellbound, are wont to call her, but also the dandies—what are you going to do!—, the distinguished Mrs. Polydora, as she is known to officials, wealthy merchants and professionals, unlike the masses, who call a spade a spade and refer to her simply as "the best ass in the world." For some she will be a saint, for others the mother of all whores, and to a third group both things and many more. The bewildered reader will discover that not even Father Burgos, her long-suffering confessor, knows how to react to the abrupt spiritual oscillations of this untamed lady whose conduct he curses one day only to bless her exalted piety with his tears the next. And what about Generoso de Chalma, the famous bullfighter, her lover, her victim? That abominable figure might be a hero and a buffoon, a mystic, a labyrinth, the powerful head of a drug cartel, the innocent victim of a cruel vendetta, and a despicable snitch in the pay of the police, depending on how the reader's whims or emotional needs sketch him. The only thing that the potential addicts of this novel could agree on would be to confirm that the times we live in, the same as the narrative, are abominable, cruel, foolish, and ignoble, awkward to the imagination, to generosity, to greatness, and that none of the characters, neither the best nor the worst, deserve the punishment of living in them. I have never written that novel; unfortunately, I am not that hero. But by just remembering Beckmann's first triptych, I would have liked to be.

If my visits to New York's Museum of Modern Art dazzled me by showing me the courage of the contemporary artists in their relentless pursuit, the emotion I experienced in the vast spaces of the Metropolitan in contemplation of the Titians, Rembrandts, Vermeers, Goyas, and other splendors it contains was no less. I learned that nothing remarkable in the arts can happen if a connection is not established with past achievements; irrefutable proof of this is Picasso's portrait of Gertrude Stein, housed in this very museum. By failing to maintain a living dialogue with the classics, the artist, the writer, runs the risk of spending his life reinventing the wheel. I know nothing more reductive than the cult of style. The task of the writer consists of enriching tradition, even if he venerates it one day and comes to blows with it the next. Either way, he will be aware of its existence. This is why problems of form, techniques, and possibilities of genres, and their capacity for transformation have both attracted and interested me.

Instead of fading after my first outings, the urge to travel became more obsessive. I began 1961 with a strong sense of annoyance. I was sick of my circumstances and also the world. The press was reporting the unrest that was beginning to alter some young writers in different parts of the world, one of those fevers that appears every few years. They were leaving home, security, work, and undertaking to travel the globe. They were leaving New York and California to settle in Mexico and then taking the leap to Tangier or Marrakesh. Or they settled in Paris, Rome, Capri, Rhodes, Santorini, and sometimes even in a small shantytown in the Philippines or Ceylon. I felt corned in Mexico; I got the bug, sold almost all my books and some paintings, and I hit the road. In the middle of June I boarded a ship in Veracruz and crossed the ocean. I spent a few weeks in London, a few days in Paris, and finally settled in Rome. Like Cervantes, I thought I had reached the undisputed center of the Universe. There I met María Zambrano, who among other things introduced me to Galdós, on whom she was writing memorable pages at the time. I made several trips around Italy, but always returned quickly to Rome, as if any minute spent away would be wasted. For the first time, I felt healthy and immensely free. I was twenty-eight years old and extremely eager to conquer the world. The result of that stay was my return to writing. One night, in a middling café, I began to outline a story that, for better or worse, I am still writing. That trip that was supposed to last a few months lasted twenty-eight years, my age when I arrived in Europe.

My time abroad can be divided into two periods: one that was anarchic, insane, amazing, and always extraordinarily enriching that lasted twelve years; and another, as a member of the diplomatic corps, which spanned the remaining years. During the first, I supported myself however I could and managed to survive with minimal assistance, classes, and editorial activities. I lived in Rome, Peking, Warsaw, Barcelona, and London, each of which left a different mark on my life. In Barcelona I translated for Seix Barral, and at Tusquets edited a collection called Heterodoxos. I remember fondly the work sessions with Beatriz de Moura and other friends in which we spoke with intense enthusiasm about our projects. During a period where the political atmosphere was decidedly orthodox! Of every three or four titles, the censors allowed us to publish maybe one. We lived and worked ignoring the dictatorship. When a Heterodox saw the light of day we celebrated with devotion. During that time, Anagrama was born, and at its first book launch I met Jorge Herralde. We became fast friends. I have translated several books for him, written prologues for others, and later published all my novels with his press. Thanks to the Herralde Prize my work began to be noticed in Mexico. I met Lali Gubern at Leteradura, her wonderful bookstore, and even now the existence of that open space in a period of extreme intolerance seems miraculous. Immediately after being paid for a translation at Seix Barral, I went to Leteradura and headed without hesitation to the table displaying the attractive books from De Donato, the collection that included the Russian formalists and avant-gardists; some of the books I most value: Victor Shklovsky's *Theory of Prose*; the *Complete Theater* of Mikhail Bulgakov; the three volumes on Tolstoy by Boris Eichenbaum—all came from that splendid table. I visited Luis and María Antonia Goytisolo, Cristina Fernández Cubas, Carlos Trías, Félix de Azúa. On two occasions, I exchanged a few words with Enrique Vila-Matas, although our friendship was born and grew far from Barcelona: in Warsaw, in Paris, in Venezuela's Mérida, in Morelia, Xalapa, and Veracruz. My second period abroad spans my diplomatic life in Paris, Budapest, Moscow, and Prague. The bond that links both experiences, and which, more precisely, unites every moment in my life, has been literature.

In his diaries, Leo Tolstoy noted that he could only write about what he had known and lived personally. His admirable work draws on the experiences he accumulated during his life; it is a kind of parallel biography. Shortly before his death, the aforementioned Max Beckmann wrote: "I can only say that in art everything is a matter of discrimination, address, and sensibility, regardless of whether it is modern or not. Truth should emanate from work. Truth through nature and a self-discipline of iron." Like Tolstoy, I can only write about what I have lived. My narratives have been a logbook that records my movements. A spectrum of my preoccupations, happy and unfortunate times, readings, perplexities, and jobs. And, like Beckmann, I am convinced that the lived must submit itself to a process of discrimination. The selection of materials must coincide with the appearance of a form. From that moment on, the form will determine the work's fate, without giving a damn whether it is modern or not.

For years, I used the settings I visited as a backdrop against which my characters compare who they are (or rather, what they imagine themselves to be) to other values. Usually they are Mexicans living abroad, filmmakers attending a film festival, politicians on vacation in Rome or Venice, Mexican students passing through Vienna, Warsaw, or Samarkand. The cheap exoticism that surrounds them barely matters; what is important is the moral dilemma they contemplate, the value judgment they must make once free of their traditional support, their habits, the alibis that for years they have used in an attempt to numb their conscience.

During my last six years abroad I was an ambassador in Prague, which implied permanent dealings with representatives of power—foreign and domestic officials at the top, in the middle, at the bottom—and with some ambassadors, all with imperial pretensions. They as well as I expressed ourselves in an official and stratified language that feigned grandeur: a conceited language, completely devoid of humor.

Shortly after my arrival in Prague, I was invited to an exhibition in celebration of the centenary of Egon Erwin Kisch, who lived in political exile in Mexico during the Second World War. There I saw photos of Kisch with Diego Rivera, Frida Kahlo, Dolores del Río, José Clemente Orozco, and Carlos Chávez, with Polish princes, Mexican politicians, German communist leaders, Spanish refugees, and two Hollywood movie stars, Buster Keaton and Paulette Godard, all gathered at a single celebration. I was struck (and no other verb seems more exact) with the idea to write a novel set in Mexico in 1942, the year in which Mexico declared war on the Axis powers. The novel should at all times be a comedy of errors, an amusing story of mistakes that would inevitably lead down crime alley. Evoking that time, consulting the edition of photographs by the Casasola brothers, remembering the sayings and expressions that were in common use during my childhood, was like a holiday for me. In two weeks, I had the general outline of the novel completed. *El desfile del amor* (Love's Parade) seemed to construct itself. I was surprised to see it come together, dictate its own laws and obey them, create its plots and subplots, its hidden relationships. I seemed to hear the protagonists' voices, detect their specific timbres. I was merely a secretary taking dictation. *El desfile del amor* introduced me into an area where until then I had only dabbled superficially: parody. I felt transported to the fields of Gombrowicz, those of Bustos-Domecq. As the official language I heard and spoke every day became increasingly more rarefied, to compensate, that of my novel became more animated, sarcastic, and waggish. Every scene was a caricature of real life, that is to say a caricature of a caricature. I took refuge in its laxness. The complete transformation of my narrative world began in earnest.

When I finished the novel, I began to jot down a few notes about a possible story that could take place in the town of Tepoztlán, where I would also use vague memories of Rome and Istanbul, a scatological story, with dislocated language, an homage to the absurd, the Spanish *género chico*, that owes much to barracks humor. It was *Domar a la divina Garza* (Taming the Divine Heron). It was followed by another, *La vida conyugal* (Married Life), where in the very proper and measured language employed at the family dinner table when there are respected guests, I describe forty years of joyous marital breakdown. Shortly after finishing it, I discovered that *El desfile del amor, Domar a la divina garza,* and *La vida conyugal* formed a natural triptych, without any preconceived idea. The function of the communicating vessels established between the three novels suddenly seemed clear: it tended to reinforce the grotesque vision that sustained them. Everything that aspired to solemnity, canonization, and self-satisfaction careened suddenly into mockery, vulgarity, and derision. A world of masks and disguises prevailed. Every situation, together as well as separate, exemplifies the three fundamental stages that Bakhtin finds in the carnivalesque farce: crowning, uncrowning, and the final scourging. Perhaps the origin of this trilogy goes back almost forty years ago, when I saw the first triptych by Beckmann. As always happens in writing, that long meander, from a few images lost in my memory to setting them down on paper, continues to be a mystery to me.

Mexico City, November 1991

THE DARK TWIN

For Enrique Vila-Matas

Justo Navarro writes in his prologue to Paul Auster's *The Red Notebook*: "You write life, and life seems like a life already lived. And the closer you get to things in order to write them better, to translate them better into your own language, to understand them better, the closer you get to things, the more you seem to distance yourself from things, the more things get away from you. Then you grab onto what's closest to you: you talk about yourself as you approach yourself. Being a writer is to become a stranger, a foreigner: you have to start to translate yourself. Writing is a case of impersonation, forging an identity: writing is passing yourself off as someone else."

I recently reread *Tonio Kröger*, Thomas Mann's coming-of-age novel, which I had long since forgotten; I considered it a defense of the writer's loneliness, of the necessary segregation from the world to accomplish the task destined for him by a higher will: "One must have died if one is to be wholly a creator."[5] *Tonio Kröger* is a bildungsroman, the story of a literary and sentimental education. But the divorce between life and creation that Kröger proposes forms only the initial phase of the novel; the result of that education favors the

---

5 Translated by David Luke

opposite solution: the artist's reconciliation with life.

The Romantics abolished all dichotomies: life, destiny, light, shadow, sleep, wakefulness, body, and writing meant for them only fragments of a hazy, imprecise, but in the end, indivisible universe. The exaltation of the body and the passion of the spirit were their greatest desires. The romantic poet conceived of himself as his own laboratory and battlefield. In this story from 1903, Mann incorporated one of the ideals of the period: the idea of ethics as aesthetics, distancing the spirit entirely from all earthly vulgarity. Symbolism is a late offshoot of Romanticism, at least one of its trends. Tonio Kröger is a writer of bourgeois extraction; it fills him with pride to live only for the spirit, which implies a rejection of the world. He fulfills his destiny with the guilty conscience of a bourgeois who is ashamed of the mediocrity of his environment. Hence his asceticism is carried out with almost inhuman rigor. At the end of the novel, following some experiences that connect him to life, Kröger reveals to his confidante, a Russian painter, the conclusion to which he arrives: "You artists call me a bourgeois, and the bourgeois feel they ought to arrest me… I don't know which of the two hurts me more bitterly. The bourgeois are fools; but you worshippers of beauty, you who say I am phleg-matic and have no longing in my soul, you should remember that there is a kind of artist so profoundly, so primordially fated to be an artist that no longing seems sweeter and more precious to him than his longing for the bliss of the commonplace. I admire those proud, cold spirits who venture out along the paths of grandiose, demonic beauty and despise 'humanity'—but I do not envy them. For if there is anything that can turn a *littérateur* into a true writer, then it is this bourgeois love of mine for the human and the living and the ordinary. It is the source of all warmth, of all kindheartedness and of all humor."[6] End of quote. Tonio Kröger, German writer.

If I confused my recollection of the novel with the image of the writer's total reclusion, his isolation, it is due in no small part to one of his phrases, "One must have died if one is to be wholly a creator," which has been quoted a thousand times as an example of the writer's decision to not commit to anything but himself.

Even if such an attitude is eventually rejected by Tonio Kröger, it is still not surprising to find its echo in Mann's own reflections on old age. His autobiographical pages show his astonishment in the face of his popularity; the warmth with which he is treated by family, friends, and even strangers does not appear to reconcile with the reclusion that was necessary for him to complete his work. The reaction of the elderly Mann is much more convincing than Kröger's final confession, where his love of humanity disguises a declamatory and programmatic tone that fails to touch the depth of the complex relationship between writing and life. "You move away from yourself when you approach yourself…," Navarro says. "Writing is impersonating someone else."

I cannot imagine a novelist who does not use elements of his personal experience, a vision, a memory from childhood or the immediate past, a tone of voice captured in a meeting, a furtive gesture glimpsed by chance, only to incorporate them later into one or more characters. The narrator-writer delves deeper and deeper into his life as his novel progresses. It is not a mere autobiographical exercise; writing a novel solely about one's own life, in most cases, is a vulgarity, a lack of imagination. It is something else: a relentless observation of one's own reflections in order to be able to realize multiple prostheses inside the story.

6 Translated by David Luke

No matter what, the novelist will continue to write his novel. Never mind that other non-literary works may demand his time. He will focus on his story and will make progress on it in his spare time, on weekends, or holidays, but, even if he himself doesn't realize, he will at all times be implicated secretly in his novel, inserted into one of its folds, lost in its words, pushed by "the urgency of fiction itself, which always carries a certain weight,"[7] to quote Antonio Tabucchi.

I imagine a diplomat who was also a novelist. I would place him in Prague, a wonderful city, as is well known. He has just spent an extended holiday in Madeira and attends a dinner at the Portuguese Embassy. The table is a vision of elegance. To his right sits an elderly doyenne, the wife of the ambassador of a Scandinavian country; on the left, the wife of an official from the Embassy of Albania. The tone of the ambassador's wife is imperious and decisive; she speaks to be heard by those sitting around her. The writer, who has just arrived from Madeira, remarks that he has gotten the better of winter by two months. But he has just begun to talk when she commandeers the conversation to say that the best years of her youth were spent precisely in Funchal. She began her speech not with the city's gardens, nor in the beauty of the mountains, the seascape, the mild climate, nor with the virtues and defects of its inhabitants, but with its hospitality. She declared that tourism in Madeira had always been very exclusive and as an example of refinement commented that at the Reid they served tea with cucumber and butter sandwiches on dark bread, as was *de rigueur* in the last century; she spoke at length of her stay on the island where she lived during the war; she said that her father had always been a prudent man, so when the conflict seemed inevitable

---

7 Translated by Tim Parks

he decided to move with his family to Portugal, first to Lisbon and later to Madeira, where they settled permanently.

"That is how he was," she continued, "so excessively prudent that we spent five years away from home without our country ever having declared war. It was as if Madeira remained outside the world; correspondence and newspapers arrived with such delay that when news finally arrived, it was already so outdated that one could scarcely be bothered. We settled in Funchal, which goes without saying; where else on the island would we have done so?"

The guests around her ate and nodded; they were only permitted an occasional comment of amazement or agreement, at most a fleeting question that would encourage her to continue her monologue. She spoke of an outing she once took accompanied by her mother to greet countrymen who were going through difficult times. On that afternoon, she wore an absolutely delightful dress of silk chiffon by Edward Molyneux, a combination of lilac flowers on an ocher background, a pleated skirt, which required yards and yards of fabric for its construction. She met that afternoon the man who would become her future husband, making a vague gesture toward the other end of the table where the ambassador, immersed in gloomy silence, was seated. For a moment, the writer was perplexed; something in the man's face had changed over the holidays.

"We crossed Funchal until we arrived at a mansion on the outskirts that had seen better times, on whose terrace lay in deck chairs two youths covered in bandages and in casts from head to toe, taking air; both were convalescing from an accident. They lived there with their parents, a sister, and an English nurse who attended them. They belonged to an old family from my country, yes, the best kind of people, with large sums of money deposited in banks in different countries, although to see them no one would have thought as much; it was a house with little furniture, frighteningly ugly; the garden had become overgrown and where it was not overrun by weeds there were huge holes, like volcano craters."

The dinner guests' attention began to wane. Upon noticing signs of retreat, the old woman raised her voice even more and cast disapproving glances at the deserters, but she was defeated; conversations in small groups or pairs had already spread. Determined, she addressed the writer exclusively, hinting that he should consider it a privilege to hear such intimacies and memories of a place she considered off-limits to strangers.

"I approached the lounge chairs where the young men were lying" she continued, "and one of them, Arthur, quickly raised his partially plastered arm with his free hand, grabbed my big porcelain brick-colored buckle and pulled me to him, moaning and gasping; the pain from the effort must have been tremendous. 'A sudden outburst of amorous passion,' my mother, who was very wise, commented later. It may have been, but I think the poor, ailing creature was glad to see an impeccably dressed young woman, wrapped in beautifully colored fabrics, since he was always looking at his mother and sister—the nurse does not count—who were dressed like prisoners, which, I can assure you, was almost a crime in Funchal, whose elegance rivaled that of Estoril itself. Ah, such wonderful salons, and terraces, and garden parties! My greatest amusement at soirées was guessing the designers. Who had dressed the Princess Ratibor? Schiaparelli! And General Sikorski's niece? Grès! She was transformed into a Greek sculpture. And the very rich Mrs. Sasseson? None other than Lelong! Yes, Sir,

Lucien Lelong himself! My mother and I devoted our time at those parties to detecting which was an authentic Balmain, Patou, or Lanvin, and which were copies made by the Island's prodigious seamstresses. Those were moments of splendor. One needed the Gotha within reach to avoid taking risks; one could be ruined at every step with the central European and Balkan titles. Of Arthur's many wounds the only truly serious one was his knee, which had been shattered in a dynamite explosion. That is why the poor fellow still walks with a limp and not because of sciatica as he would have people believe, much less the bouts of gout as the Finnish doctor has been spreading. Yes, Arthur fell in love with my buckle; he loved the color, and asked me to wear it with all of my dresses. It may seem rather immodest on my part, but the belt buckle made him walk again; he began to stand; of course, he fell almost every time, howling in pain; we yelled to him amid applause that nothing could be learned without suffering. Now look at him, he's like a colt! Were it not for me, he might well be prostrate in his deck chair."

At that moment someone interrupted the storyteller, and the novelist took the opportunity to meet the woman who was eating silently to his left. She smiled at him widely and repeated the same words she had said at the beginning of the dinner, which is to say she pointed to her plate and said in broken English, "Is good." It pleased him enormously that a mere two words could make up a conversation because he was deaf in his left ear, and conversations on that side were almost always torture for him; misunderstandings often occurred, his responses seldom coincided with people's questions; in short, it was a nightmare.

The admirer of Madeira once again demanded his attention, and he, to extricate the monologue from the exhausting world of fashion, asked if the two young men had been injured in military action. The woman looked at him sternly and haughtily, and finally answered that the Finnish doctor, not the current but the previous one, had spread a malicious rumor that Arthur and his brothers had exploded the dynamite in order to avoid their military obligation, which was both slanderous and preposterous; none of them feared recruitment for the simple reason that their country was neutral. They had transported the dynamite in a small boat in order to eliminate an islet that was obstructing the view from the house. The oldest brother died, the other was paralyzed for life, and Arthur, the youngest, barely survived. He dreamt of devoting himself to organizing and directing safaris in Central Africa. When he recovered, contrary to what everyone might expect, he devoted himself to studying, and later joined the Foreign Service.

They were now having dessert; the woman from Albania touched his arm slightly, pointed to her plate and said, "Is good," and then, expounding for the first time that night, added, "Is very many pigs," or something that sounded close, and began to laugh delightfully. The wife of the Nordic ambassador appeared insulted. Not wanting to lose her preeminence, she made a comment about desserts in Madeira, especially those at the Reid and the Savoy, but the writer, infected by the gratuitousness of the Albanian woman's humor, suddenly interrupted the ambassador's wife with a comment about Conrad, his travels and his layovers, and said that he would have liked to know what he said when talking to ladies in Southeast Asia.

"Who?"

"Joseph Conrad. I imagine he must have occasionally received invitations; that he must not have spent all his life talking to merchants and sailors, and that he also spoke to wives, daughters, the sisters of British officials, of shipping agents. What do you think he talked to them about?"

The woman must have thought his deafness had caused him to become lost, and that it was necessary to assist him:

"The Portuguese women dressed with impeccable taste, some in Balenciaga, but their conversation did not always match the *hauteur* of their attire; they always seemed uninteresting to me, not to mention they were also incredibly stingy. They demanded prompt and impeccable work, but for payment they were a calamity. Well, all of them, not just the Portuguese, were dreadfully tightfisted," she exclaimed with sudden bitterness. "The war was a pretext to exercise their greed. They wanted to be queens, and they almost were: princesses, countesses, wives of bankers, in exile, yes, but with their fortunes safe, all of them, without exception, were unable to appreciate the work that conferred their elegance. They were willing to waste an entire morning in order to begrudge a dressmaker the few *escudos* needed to survive. Yes, Mr. Ambassador, I shall not take it back: they were all dreadfully tightfisted."

The hosts stood; the twenty-two guests followed suit, and they all moved slowly toward the salon to take coffee and liqueurs and smoke at their leisure. The writer approached, not without a certain morbid curiosity, the husband of the woman to whom he had listened throughout dinner, an elderly man who looked as if he were made of knots arranged haphazardly on bones, a face composed of arbitrarily positioned pits and protrusions, a porcelain prosthetic eye capable of disturbing even the most phlegmatic interlocutor, and a leg that lacked movement. He spoke as intensely as his wife in the presence of two functionaries from the Portuguese embassy who listened to him dispassionately about the preparations for the upcoming wild boar hunt in the Tatras, which only six or seven very skilled hunters would attend. The writer realized for the first time that he was looking at him with his prosthetic eye, which he always had covered with a black patch. The writer was surprised that the old codger, one-eyed and quasi-paralytic, was awaiting the event with such strange enthusiasm. As soon as he was able, the writer interrupted to say that he had just spent the holiday in Madeira and that he had taken advantage of the time to relax and read. He did not dare add "to write" because the porcelain gaze from the fake eye and the glimmer of confusion that emerged from the real one transformed instantly into a dark horror that bordered almost on dementia. The embassy staff took advantage of the moment to slip away and attend to another solitary guest.

The old man recovered his wits; he asked mockingly, as if he had not heard the writer's words, if he had decided to participate in the boar hunt, if he had oiled his old rifle and counted his cartridges, but, just like his wife, he did not wait for the answer and between groans added that they would leave from Bratislava the following Friday at four thirty in the morning, and that the hunt would last two days. The writer attempted to add that he only went on pheasant hunts, more than anything else because of the accompanying accoutrements: campfires in the snow, hunting music, horns, dinner at the castle. The old man frightened him again as he stared at him with the brutal coldness of his prosthetic eye and the maniacal fury of the other, and just when he expected to be labeled decadent, or "artistic," he was surprised to hear the old man say, his voice stifled, almost unintelligible, that he too had once been to that inferno, that he recalled with horror that abominable island, although the verb *recalled* was perhaps not appropriate, because he never recalled that desolate place, unless someone was foolhardy enough to mention it to him, which, as it were, rarely happened. He was very young then, naive, uncorrupted, you might say, he did not know how to defend himself, much less possess the physical capabilities to do so, when a pack of hungry she-wolves, of she-wolves that were hyenas and vultures, attacked him, beat him with belts and straps, threw him to the ground, bit him, and took advantage of him and his purity. That dark confidence ended with a groan, and then, without saying goodbye, he turned, leapt toward a group of guests most certainly to remind them that the wild boar hunt was to take place next week in Slovakia. He then turned suddenly with military precision, retraced his steps, and faced him once again, as if the conversation had never ended.

"Don't think," he said with an expression marked by sullenness, "that I did not notice my wife's unusual garrulousness at the table tonight. She did not allow anyone to speak, is that not right? One can never understand women; they spend the whole day immersed in the dreariest silence, and then, when least expected, they turn into magpies. What had her so excited?"

The writer commented that it had been a very instructive conversation; that in an environment as rigid as diplomacy, where women were accustomed to talking about trivialities, it was refreshing to meet a woman who could discuss such interesting topics.

"Topics? What topics?" he asked, as if carrying out a police interrogation. "Answer immediately! To what topics are you referring?"

"Your wife reveled in imagining what Conrad said to European

women, the English in particular, in the Malaysian ports. She specu-
lated on how Conrad might describe the dress of those long-suffering
colonial women."

"What are you saying, what, about whom was she talking?" It was
evident that the response had flummoxed him.

"About the great Joseph Conrad, your wife's favorite novelist."

The old man made a violent gesture with his hand, which could
be interpreted as "go to hell!" and he withdrew, hopping like a giant
cricket.

Once home, the writer recalled the woman's monologue about her
elegant youth in Madeira and her husband's subsequent comments.
It seemed as if he had heard two versions of the same highly dramatic
situation without having understood much about it, not even what
about it was dramatic. And that was precisely the kind of exciting
element necessary to create, to begin to invent, a plot. The enigmas
were many: a dynamite explosion that takes place on a boat, the absurd
explanation of wanting to blow up a reef to improve the view of
a house where no one was interested in aesthetics, the couple's relationship, the buckle, the belts, the woman's coldness during this part
of the story and, at the same time, the almost crazed excitement with
which she described the chiffons and silks and brocades. A few days
later, he remarked to some colleagues how strange the encounter with
the couple made him feel. He learned that the Finnish doctor had said
once that the ambassador's wife had been a dressmaker in her youth,
a woman who could reproduce a dress from a mere photograph. He
tries to invent a story; the porcelain eye torments him; he begins to
imagine scenes and even begins to give them dialogue; the ambition of
the dressmaker, spurred by a greedy mother, to trap the suffering boy,

heir to a large fortune. He imagines the girl and her mother as third-class guests at some get-togethers, admiring the dresses from the great ateliers of Paris, as well as those they had cut and sewn with their own hands. Whenever they discovered one of theirs they would exchange looks of complicity and joy.

A writer often listens without hearing a word spoken; other voices trap him. The voice of a real person disappears or becomes mere background music. Sometimes a few words send him to one imaginary character or another. Other times—and that's what's so surprising!—the writer doesn't even know that the voices he tries to incorporate into a character, or a plot, are not intended for that story, that lurking under the plot exists another one, waiting for him.

The day arrives when he sits down to work. He has failed to resolve the enigma of the dynamite; he looks for the relationship of the explosive with the craters in the garden of the house in Funchal. Surprisingly, out of the blue, a new character has emerged, a young theosophist who joins the dressmaker and her mother in their daily outings to visit the patient. Sometimes, only the two young women make the visit. Others, the theosophist goes to the injured young man behind her friend's back. The discovery of the young theosophist girl is tantamount to discovering a gold mine. He sees her, hears her, and knows what she's thinking. Her body is very small, her head larger than it should be, but she is far from a monster; at least not physically. There is something about her, however, something frightening: her rigidness, the harshness of her look, her sullen appearance. A fluid contempt for the world seems to exude from each of her pores. The author sees two young women of markedly dissimilar appearance walking down the road that leads to the mansion where the injured man lies: one is blonde and tall, a bit ungainly, well dressed; the other, the theosophist, is wearing a blouse and skirt of an almost military cut. At that moment, she recommends ferociously to the dressmaker something new and wicked to do to the patient. Anyone who saw them would think they were an ostrich and wild boar crossing, without noticing—so lost were they in thought—a flower garden's beauty.

When the novelist finally begins his story, Funchal and its surroundings, all of Madeira and its characters, disappear completely. Only his new discovery, the theosophist, survives. There she is: sitting in a restaurant in the lobby of the Hotel Zevallos; yes, facing the main square in Córdoba, Veracruz, where she moves much more naturally than on the flowering avenues of Funchal, which is not to say that she has become pleasant or polished or relaxed, nothing of the sort. The world is revealed to the writer at that moment. He has begun to translate himself. "Writing is a case of impersonation, forging an identity: writing is passing yourself off as someone else." At that moment, he is now that someone else. By transplanting the location, the young woman maintains her physical characteristics and is still a theosophist. She has returned to her hometown after living with her mother and sister in Los Angeles, California for twenty years, where the three had feverously read Annie Besant, Krishnamurti, and, above all, Madame Blavatsky. Upon her mother's death, she travels to Córdoba, which she left when she was six or seven, to claim an inheritance. She stays at the home of family friends, perhaps distant relatives. Everyone knows her as "Chiquitita," a nickname from her childhood and one that fills her with a heavy rage that she dares not show. Her resources are negligible, which is why she doesn't leave the family who has welcomed her; every day she notes in a diary her petty expenses. She has forbidden herself any kind of luxury. A lawyer friend of her mother advises her to contact one of the opposing parties, her *tío* Antonio, for example, who is the most amenable. The same lawyer is responsible for arranging the interview. Chiquitita follows his instructions and meets her uncle for lunch one day in the lobby of the Zevallos. He addresses her nonchalantly, as if everything between them were perfect. "What a gorgeous niece I have!" he says as he greets her, adding: "You look much better in person, *caramba*, I mean, what a beauty!" But the young woman at no time lowers her guard; she frowns sullenly throughout the meal. She's the same prickly person she ever was. Watching him drink glass after glass of beer during the meal repulses her. She reprimands him somewhat severely, commenting on the incompatibility of drunkenness and legal affairs. Her uncle laughs, amused, and calls her cutie pie, kitten, and pipsqueak. At the end, over dessert, her relative agrees to talk about the matter they met to discuss. He insists that he doesn't see the need to go to court, the case should be settled amicably, as should all things among family; that she must, however, understand that the property in dispute does not belong to her, that before leaving Córdoba her mother was compensated appropriately, that while she was alive she received a monthly payment. Just then, he's about to add that in spite of everything the family has considered giving them a sum, the amount of which would be determined when they signed a waiver renouncing their claim, but doesn't manage to say it because Chiquitita beats him to the punch. She berates him with a string of disconcerting adjectives and a tone so sarcastic and petulant that the brute becomes enraged and responds with a remark so vulgar that it frightens her. He can be heard shouting, so every local will know, that if anyone in

Córdoba remembers her mother, it's because of her whoring-around, that he personally would see to it that she and her sister don't see a penny, that he would prove that they were both daughters of someone other than his brother, her mother's husband in name only, and that therefore they had no right to any part of the inheritance. He then adds sarcastically that the best thing she can do is find a husband, or an equivalent, to scratch her belly and support her. Suddenly, the beast of a man gets up and leaves the restaurant. Stunned, Chiquitita remains at the table, not so much because of the violent way she's been treated, or because of the references to her mother's loose behavior, nor because she discovers that recovering the portion of the assets that belongs to her is going to be more—much more!—difficult than she imagined, not even because of the scandal involved, but because of the mere inability to pay the tab. Overcome by rage, and on the verge of tears, she asks the waiter if he'll accept the watch that hangs around her neck for a half hour, the time needed to go where she's staying and pick up the money to cover the bill.

The novelist thinks about his heroine's ensuing movements; he begins to mentally style the language; he imagines he will finish the story in a few days and return to the abandoned plot in Madeira, its characters, the dressmaker (now rid of her theosophist friend), the dynamite explosion, the exercises the injured young man does to regain movement, his falls, the cruel discipline to which he is subjected, unaware that Chiquitita's triumphs and tribulations during her stay in Córdoba would not end anytime soon, that the story he had just started would turn into a novel he would have to live with for several years and where perhaps there might appear a young farmer from Tierra Blanca, Veracruz, who was left paralyzed and blind in one eye mishandling dynamite, and an astute seamstress determined to have him and his property. Over time, the novelist will come to forget that the story came from a dinner at the Portuguese embassy in Prague. And were the social event ever able to penetrate his memory, he would only vaguely remember an ambassador's wife, probably French, for having unleashed an endless monologue about Parisian haute couture and its most celebrated names. In short, he would consider this incident as one of many moments of diplomatic routine during which he overheard exasperatingly detailed descriptions of locations and situations only to forget them a moment later, and he would never connect it with the appearance of Chiquitita, her misfortunes in Córdoba, and her intrepid fight to defeat—by human intervention, unimaginable tricks, and astral assistance—her enemy relatives until recovering the portion of the inheritance that belonged to her as well as a portion that did not. A novelist is shocked at the sudden appearance of an uninvited character; he often confuses sources, the migration of the characters, the transmutation of karma, to quote Chiquitita and also Thomas Mann, who understood those surprises very well.

The last novel by José Donoso, *Dónde van a morir los elefantes* (Where Elephants Go to Die), carries an epigraph from William Faulkner that illuminates a novelist's relationship with his work in progress: "A novel is a writer's secret life, the dark twin of a man."

A novelist is someone who hears voices through the voices. He crawls into bed, and suddenly those voices force him to get up, to look for a sheet of paper and write three or four lines, or just a couple of adjectives or the name of a plant. These features, and a few others, cause his life to bear a striking resemblance to that of the deranged, which doesn't bother him in the least; on the contrary, he thanks his muses for having transmitted these voices to him without which he would feel lost. With them he goes about drawing the map of his life. He knows that when he is no longer able do it, death will come for him, not the final death but living death, silence, hibernation, paralysis, which is infinitely worse.

Xalapa, July 1994

DROCTULFT AND OTHERS

I

Borges points out that it was on page 278 of the book *Poetry*, by Benedetto Croce, that he found an abbreviated text of the Latin historian Paul the Deacon that deals with the fate and death of Droctulft, the reading of which moved him profoundly. On the surface, it is a simple story; at its core, it is exemplary: Droctulft, a barbarian and fierce Lombard, marches with the men of his tribe toward the south. A common, one might say utilitarian, desire drives them: to sack the rich cities of the south; and another desire, more animal, more pleasing, and perhaps more intense: to destroy them. Upon contemplating Ravenna, the warrior switches sides and dies in defense of the city he had planned to attack. Borges's text is brief and bears the title, "History of the Warrior and the Captive." In the paragraphs dedicated to the warrior, the reader perceives a sense of amazement and an emotion that the author rarely lavished on his writing. It would seem that he had immediate circumstances in mind, perhaps related to that fatal discord that marks our history, one of whose poles is civilization and the other barbarism.

"Let us imagine" Borges says, "*sub specie aeternitatis*, Droctulft, not the individual Droctulft, who no doubt was unique and unfathomable (all individuals are), but the generic type formed from him and many others by tradition, which is the effect of oblivion and of memory. Through an obscure geography of forests and marshes, the wars brought him to Italy from the banks of the Danube and the Elbe, and perhaps he did not know he was going south and perhaps he did not know he was fighting against the name of Rome. Perhaps he professed the Arianist faith, which holds that the Son's glory is a reflection of the Holy Father's, but it is more congruous to imagine him a worshiper of the Earth, of Hertha, whose covered idol went from hut to hut in a cow-drawn cart, or of the gods of war and thunder, which were crude wooden figures wrapped in homespun clothing and hung with coins and bracelets. He came from the inextricable forests of the boar and the bison; he was light-skinned, spirited, innocent, cruel, loyal to his captain and his tribe, but not to the universe. The wars bring him to Ravenna and there he sees something he has never seen before, or has not seen fully. He sees the day and the cypresses and the marble. He sees a whole whose multiplicity is not that of disorder; he sees a city, an organism composed of statues, temples, gardens, rooms, amphitheaters, vases, columns, regular and open spaces. None of these fabrications (I know) strikes him as beautiful; he is touched by them as we now would be by a complex mechanism whose purpose we could not fathom but in whose design an immortal intelligence might be divined. Perhaps it is enough for him to see a single arch, with an incomprehensible inscription in eternal Roman letters. Suddenly he is blinded and renewed by this revelation, the City. He knows that in it he will be a dog, or a child, and that he will not even begin to understand it, but he also knows that it is worth more than his gods and his sworn faith and all the marshes of Germany.

Droctulft abandons his own and fights for Ravenna." The barbarian dies in its defense; the city entombs him with honors. Borges concludes: "He was not a traitor (traitors seldom inspire pious epitaphs); he was a man enlightened, a convert."[8]

This text seems to me to be the greatest tribute that one can pay to civilization. The best of Rome evokes the triumph of order over chaos, the proliferation of avenues and gardens, of valleys planted methodically with vineyards and olive groves, highways, aqueducts and amphitheaters, but also the creation of coexistence for the sake of law where man may be wolf to man, as Plautus said, and then Hobbes, and then half the world. Justinian is still present in our contemporary legislation.

There is one aspect of the Roman legacy that especially touches me: its permeability to other cultures. For years Rome sent its best sons to the School of Athens, and incorporated their deities, rechristening the large cast of the Greek Olympus; indeed, the cult of worship to those gods coincided with others: Isis and Osiris, Mantra, and also with the beliefs of Christians and Jews; and even in periods of persecution that religious coexistence was never successfully eradicated. That character of synchrony in diversity is what really interests me about the Latin world. Narrowing boundaries and enclosing oneself inside them has always been synonymous with impoverishment.

II

Literature has never felt at home among dogmatic strictures; it rebels against even the very canons it creates once it considers them

---

8 Translated by James E. Irby

unnecessary. It also becomes nonconformist when one tries to situate it within a single region. The desire to abolish cultural boundaries takes place at the very moment someone fixes the actual borders, those necessary to the tribe, to the *raison d'État*. The Renaissance circulated ideas, themes, styles, tones, and methods. One of its highest attributes is universality. Marsilius of Padua and his disciples translated Plato; Shakespeare rewrote texts by Bandello; Cervantes was seduced by Italian innovations and also, according to what is known today, by Arab narrative forms to which he was introduced during his captivity in Algiers; Juan Ruiz Alarcón wrote a masterpiece, *The Suspicious Truth*, which Corneille rewrote with the title of *Le menteur* and much later Goldoni with the title *Il bugiardo*; there were variants of *La Celestina* in many languages; Garcilaso and Boscán introduced Italian meter in Spain, not without receiving the occasional scoff from the guardians of the Spanish language. Later, during the romantic fever, what poet did not want to be Manfredo and Lara and the Corsair and Don Juan? Good and mediocre, superb and dreadful, reduced to bleak student lodgings, or installed in the library of a magnificent palace, in Puebla or in Morelia, in Lisbon or Coimbra, in Paris, in Petrópolis, Vilnius, Milan, Seville, and Naples, both in metropolises and lost villages; Byron's verses dazzled, enlightened, and enchanted an ardent pleiad of youths enamored of poetry and also of their own youth, of love, and of death. At the end of last century, the Hispano-American *modernistas* began to imitate by way of apprenticeship the French Symbolists, only to discover later their own registers, and thus were able to change poetry in the Spanish language. The influence of Darío, Borges, Neruda, Lezama Lima, Vallejo, Rulfo, and Onetti, to mention only a few, has produced among us a vast legion of imitators, probably mostly bad; what really matters is that this work establishes a level of quality that is impossible to ignore. It would be an aberration, after reading Rubén Darío, to claim that the Spaniard Núñez de Arce is a great poet. One can—and should—write in a way that is different and even antagonistic to these writers. The mere existence of a great creator erases many of his contemporaries and multitudes of predecessors whose mediocrity only becomes obvious after the appearance of a greater figure.

The totalitarian mentality accepts diversity with difficulty; it is by its nature monological; it allows only one voice, which is emitted by the master and slavishly repeated by his subjects. Until recently, this mindset exalted national values as a supreme cult. The cult of the Nation produced a paralysis of ideas and, when prolonged, an impoverishment of language. The cards, somehow or other, were in plain sight, and the game was clear. But the outlook has changed recently. That same mindset suddenly seemed to grow weary of exalting the "national" and its most visible symbols. It claims to have modernized; it discovers the pleasure of being cosmopolitan. Deep down, it is the same, even if the rhetorical adornments look different. It now encourages contempt for the classical tradition and humanist training. It tolerates only superficial reading. If this trend succeeds, we will have entered the world of robots.

I defend the freedom to find encouragement in the most diverse cultures. But I am convinced that these approaches are only productive where there is a national culture forged slowly by a language and certain specific customs. Where there is little or nothing, subjugation is inevitable, and the only thing that is created is a desert of vulgarity. Those who have never hidden their disdain for the risk that inheres in a living culture, their distrust of imagination and games, may feel satisfied. Vulgarity becomes the norm. I am convinced that not even the lack of readers can banish poetry. Without that conviction, it would be unbearable to continue living.

III

On several occasions I have associated my fate with that of Droctulft. If in certain periods Russian and Polish writers, in others, the English, the Central Europeans, the Latin Americans, Italians, or the Spanish Golden Age, have played a hegemonic role in my education, it has never occurred to me that this might transform me into a writer foreign to my own language. Something of them was possibly incorporated into my literature after passing through different filters to some area of my conscience, not the deepest, not in those secret folds of being where the first experiences of the world or the embers of first loves reside, where the true source of imagination is found. Writing is enriched by reading. Who doubts that! But the act only becomes fruitful if it is able to brush the shadow of a personal experience, a specific stereotype, perhaps a genetic memory. The writer is doomed from the start, even the one who has changed languages, to respond to the signs imprinted on him by culture. "We are all the past," I return to Borges, "we are our blood, we are the people we have seen die, we are the books that have made us better, we are gratefully the others." And that confidence in what we are prevents us from distorting those situations; it would seem ridiculous to us if someone sat down at his worktable with the awareness of being a Colombian, Brazilian, or Mexican writer. That is already assumed and deep down doesn't even matter, because the very instant he begins to write the only thing he must know, what really counts, is that language is his homeland. And keeping that in mind, the rest are trifles.

Xalapa, November 1995

THE MARQUISE WAS NEVER
CONTENT TO STAY AT HOME

For Margo Glantz

A feeling of disaster is haunting the world. The novel records it and, in doing so, is resplendent. The more rotten it smells in Denmark—and today Denmark seems to be a large part of the universe—the more indispensable the novel becomes. Ultima Thule: a reflection of an indomitable impulse to survive, of the preservation of form over chaos, sacrifice over apathy, spirit over unformed matter—the novel is that and more. Fueled by extreme tensions, witness to violent upheavals, nourished at times by caviar and quail and other times by carrion, it reappears on the international stage today with enviable health. It blooms with a fullness that roses would envy. Behold it: protean, generous, bold, ubiquitous, skeptical, cheeky, and unmanageable. Each crisis of society causes it to regenerate. When necessary, it sheds its skin. It grows with adversity. It is experiencing today one of its greatest moments and, as a result, there are probably those among us who are beginning to predict its next extinction. Perhaps they have already chosen its coffin and burial place. This prophecy is part of the customs of our century. Each time the novel is reinvigorated, someone announces its death knell. The truth is no one can defeat it.

Ortega y Gasset announced its death, as did Breton. Paul Valéry alluded to it in passing with a phrase that became instantly famous. André Breton reproduces a comment by Valéry that refers to his refusal to write one because he is incapable of anything as banal as "The Marquise went out at five o'clock." Is it possible that the author of *The Graveyard by the Sea* might have, out of politeness, uttered this sentence just to please Breton—who scorned this literary genre—that is, by chance, just to move the conversation along and thus avoid a lull? Or, perhaps at that moment, Valéry was thinking of some of the novelists fashionable at the time, Paul Morand or André Maurois, for example, in whose pages one might always see a marquise leave her home at five o'clock to take tea at the Ritz, perhaps a few minutes late? God only knows!

The truth is, "The Marquise went out at five o'clock" is an ideal incipit for stimulating the affectation of a certain type of reader who rejoices at hearing about marquises, princesses and baronesses, as well as the Cinderellas who, after enduring every imaginable hardship and humiliation, end up marrying marquis, princes, or barons. The absence of her ladyship's name in itself instills a degree of confidence; it takes for granted that the novel is about the marquise, or one of the marquises, from the neighborhood. Perhaps reading about the Marquise de La Rochefoucauld or the Marquise de Varennes would have intimidated the reader a bit, but a simple marquise inspires confidence; there is something comforting in her concise, almost homespun simplicity, an aroma of hot chocolate and freshly baked cinnamon buns.

It is also possible that Valéry, distracted by other interests or busied by other subjects and other times, did not recognize that the novel was no longer what it once was, and that far from Morand, Maurois, and Montherlant, who had their own appeal, new writers in France and, above all, in other latitudes were determined to transform narrative language and were beginning their novels in a very different way:

> Stately, plump Buck Mulligan came from the stairhead,
> bearing a bowl of lather on which a mirror and a razor lay
> crossed. A yellow dressing gown, ungirdled, was sustained
> gently behind him by the mild morning air. He held the
> bowl aloft and intoned: Introibo ad altare Dei.

There is an explicit coarseness present in this paragraph. Its reading does not produce a delightful chill heralding the appearance of a marquise on the street. Instead of a lady dressed by Molyneux or Schiaparelli, frantic to arrive promptly for an engagement, which could well change her life, with the handsome son of an Italian banker, or to go to her jeweler's shop to have him adjust the setting to one of her famous emerald stud earrings, or to the office of a seedy pawnbroker to hock them then and there, we find ourselves in the presence of a fat man, a few pedestrian barber utensils, and an untied yellow gown that establish a pronounced oxymoron, that is still very funny, with the liturgical Latin: "*Introibo ad altare Dei.*"

Let's consider the beginning of another novel:

> He—for there could be no doubt of his sex, though the
> fashion of the time did something to disguise it—was in
> the act of slicing at the head of a Moor which swung from
> the rafters. It was the colour of an old football, and more or
> less the shape of one, save for the sunken cheeks and a strand
> or two of coarse, dry hair, like the hair on a cocoanut.

The reference to the gender of the protagonist, his aggressiveness toward the head of a Moor hanging from the rafters, the similarity with an old soccer ball immediately produces in us a slight bewilderment. What world have we entered? The brutality of striking a head, whether of a Moor or anyone else, immediately dissolves, and is made unreal by the levity of the narrative tone. There is instead a kind of peculiar humor that is enhanced by comparing the head to a soccer ball and his dry hair to a coconut. We cannot be sure whether the exquisite lady wished to leave her home at five to witness such an uncommon spectacle. She was not prudish, no, nothing of the sort, rather she lacked humor and was therefore extremely disquieted by certain eccentricities; she did not know how to behave, and that was the worst thing that could happen to her. Instead of going out that evening she was left to play with a pair of moss-green kid gloves, waiting for a telephone call that never came. In the end, she was so prostrate with anger that she could have chewed the gloves to shreds.

The first quote is from 1922. They are the first lines of James Joyce's *Ulysses;* the second, from 1928, belongs to the beginning of Virginia Woolf's *Orlando.* A few years later, in the heart of Europe, Vienna to be precise, a young military engineer began a novel that would fill four large volumes that would remain unfinished on the author's death. A novel that still radiates throughout universal narrative:

> A barometric low hung over the Atlantic. It moved eastward toward a high-pressure area over Russia without as yet showing any inclination to bypass this high in a northerly direction. The isotherms and isotheres were functioning as they should. The air temperature was appropriate relative to the annual mean

temperature and to the aperiodic monthly fluctuations of the
temperature. The rising and the setting of the sun, the moon,
the phases of the moon, of Venus, of the rings of Saturn, and
many other significant phenomena were all in accordance with
the forecasts in the astronomical yearbooks. The water vapour
in the air was at its maximal state of tension, while the humidity was minimal. In a word that characterizes the facts fairly
accurately, even if it is a bit old-fashioned: It was a fine day
in August 1913.

You have probably recognized it by now; this is the first paragraph
of Robert Musil's *The Man Without Qualities*, published in 1930.
A stunning twist, a one-hundred-and-eighty degree turn, has occurred
in writing. It would seem to be a section of a scientific essay, or rather
a weather report written by a highly skilled employee. However, it is
a novel. In these ten lines, full of isotheres and isotherms, of monthly
aperiodic fluctuations and phases of the moon, of Venus and of the
rings of Saturn, in addition to other phenomena that are incomprehensible to us mere readers, a mystery is communicated, in just eight
words of quiet language, that, in the end, clarifies for us that it was
a beautiful day in August 1913. This wordy pomp and, moreover, its
subsequent clarification, grates on the nerves of our acquaintance, the
marquise. For as long as she can remember, she has detested those
Teutonic witticisms that, in her view, demonstrate a monumental
lack of tact and taste. That beautiful day, she did not go out at five or
any other time; she spent her time leafing through some magazines
and writing several drafts that she angrily crumpled up, until she was
finally able to write a dry, so very, very dry letter, in which she ended

a long-standing romantic relationship. She then began to laugh like a mad woman, took sedatives with champagne, and soon had to be put to bed.

And on the other side of the Atlantic, a North American, a Southerner to be exact, began one of the most beautiful novels ever written as follows:

> From a little after two o'clock until almost sundown of the long still hot weary dead September afternoon they sat in what Miss Coldfield still called the office because her father had called it that—a dim hot airless room with the blinds all closed and fastened for forty-three summers because when she was a girl someone had believed that light and moving air carried heat and that dark was always cooler, and which (as the sun shone fuller and fuller on that side of the house) became latticed with yellow slashes full of dust motes which Quentin thought of as being flecks of the dead old dried paint itself blown inward from the scaling blinds as wind might have blown them. There was a wistaria vine blooming for the second time that summer on a wooden trellis before one window, into which sparrows came now and then in random gusts, making a dry vivid dusty sound before going away: and opposite Quentin, Miss Coldfield in the eternal black which she had worn for forty-three years now, whether for sister, father, or husband none knew, sitting so bolt upright in the straight hard chair that was so tall for her that her legs hung straight and rigid as if she had iron shinbones and ankles, clear of the floor with that air of impotent and static rage like

children's feet, and talking in that grim haggard amazed
Voice until at last listening would renege and hearing-sense
self-confound and the long-dead object of her impotent yet
indomitable frustration would appear, as though by outraged
recapitulation evoked, quiet inattentive and harmless, out of
the biding and dreamy and victorious dust.

These are the first lines of *Absalom, Absalom!*, the brilliant novel that
William Faulkner published in 1936. If our friend—I imagine that by
now we can allow ourselves such familiarity—had gone out that day
at five to take part in the conversation that Quentin Compson held
with Miss Coldfield, she would surely have been on tenterhooks. She
had dealings in recent years with many highly esteemed Americans:
the Gereths, the Prest-Coovers, Mrs. Welton, and Howard Blendy,
a young diplomat of whom she was a trifle enamored. Aristocracy of
another kind, so to speak; rich, sophisticated, lighthearted, quite the
opposite of that sleepwalking couple from the South that reminded
her of a pair of ill-tempered crows who mumbled in some nonsensi-
cal language. Her education—although she's not entirely sure about
this—is firmly rooted in Descartes, which, combined with other
limitations that the reader has probably noticed, cause her to rebel
against that ecstatic verbal delirium. To hear that children's feet have
an air of impotent rage and that the summer dust was "biding and
dreamy and victorious," affects her in such a way that she could have
slapped anyone who dared repeat those words to her.

Several years passed, almost forty since *Ulysses* appeared, until, in
1960, Julio Cortázar took Paul Valéry's remark and crushed it with
joyous abandon. The first sentence of *The Winners* reads:

"The marquise went out at five," Carlos Lopez thought. "Where in the hell did I read that?"

Our poor, dear, old, powdered marquise! The years have taken their toll on her. She had imposed on herself a long and strict internal exile, and had completed it with exemplary rigor. The Argentine writer's attack had wrested her out of her lethargy.

She lay awake all night, plagued by two opposing impulses. On the one hand, she felt the temptation to repair to a convent where she would take a vow of perpetual silence. An innate pride compelled her to punish the world by turning away and making her contempt known. The sacred music, the smell of wax and incense, the proximity of angels, the locks of hair on the floor around her, the coarse habit of cloister, the tears, all of it, everything, drew her closer to God. It was possible, she thought, hopeful, that some writer understood the nobility of her gesture and would one day be tempted to write: "The marquise went out at five o'clock. A simple black tailleur by Patou accentuated her elegance as she left the house alone. A car took her to the gate of the convent that would house her earthly body for the rest of her days." An instant later, she recalled the allegations against Ives-Etienne, her niece's fiancé, who was also a distant nephew of hers, a brash and insolent boy, though not devoid of a certain charm, who, to the astonishment of his entire family, sympathized with the so-called popular causes. Suddenly, the old woman saw herself marching through the streets, erect like a steel stiletto, her left fist raised. She heard her voice suddenly become powerful, her cries of hatred for militarism, and her commitment to the fight in Algeria. Her brave decision to betray her class to march arm in arm with the downtrodden and the oppressed moved her to tears. Her courageous attitude would certainly inspire some author, who would one day write: "The marquise went out at five o'clock only to fall all at once into a sea of flags." And then he would describe with elegance the moment she leaned her arm on the arm of a metal worker to continue the march. They were wrapped in the music of *L'Internationale*, and they felt protected, secure in their cause, convinced that victory was near.

For a moment some other ideas swirled around her feverish mind. She dreamt, for example, that she was the heroine of libertine novels; she smiled ambiguously as she thought of certain terribly lascivious images, but those visions did not last, and the woman returned stubbornly to the previous dichotomy. At times she trembled, sobbed, admired the courage that was needed to cloister herself in the strictest order of silent nuns and, immediately, was even more dazzled by her own erect figure, rallying from a platform of the *Mutualité* to a throng of workers and students, or by the feat of having chained herself to the bow of a ship that would deliver arms to Southeast Asia. But such is life. Clinging to the possibility that she would once again grace the pages of some yet-to-be-published extraordinary novel, her heart grew weak, faltered, until a sudden blow shattered it completely.

The next day, the marquise went out at five o'clock. She did it inside a modest coffin. So far, to my knowledge, no one has recorded her departure.

Xalapa, July 1994

ON RECONCILIATIONS

AND THE WORD BECAME FLESH

"In the beginning was the Word," says the Gospel of John. I do not know if that was the first, but surely it is the highest praise language has ever received. "In the beginning of all literature we find form," declared the young Shklovsky during the second decade of the twentieth century, the brilliant theoretician from the Russian Formalist School, which revolutionized linguistic and literary studies. And around the same years, Stephen, James Joyce's adolescent artist, will discover that "in the virgin womb of the imagination the word was made flesh." That is to say, he sets the moment when the creation of form begins through language, the emergence of literature.

Perhaps the greatest enlightenment of my youth was the language of Borges; reading it allowed me to turn my back both on the telluric as well as the bad prose of the period. I read him for the first time in *México en la cultura*, the remarkable literary supplement edited by Fernando Benítez. The Borges story appeared as an illustration to an essay on fantasy literature by the Peruvian José Durand. It was "The House of Asterion"; I read it with amazement, gratitude, and boundless wonder. Upon arriving at the final sentence, I had the feeling that an electric current was running through my nervous system.

The words: "'Would you believe it, Ariadne?' said Theseus, 'the mino-
taur scarcely defended himself,'" said in passing, as if by accident,
revealed the hidden mystery of the story: the identity of the strange
protagonist and his resigned sacrifice. I was speechless. I never imagined that language could reach such levels of strength, subtlety, and
strangeness. I left immediately to look for books by Borges; I found
almost all of them, covered in dust, on the shelves of a bookstore;
during those years, one could count the Mexican readers of Borges
on two hands.

Literary genres and their transmigrations emerged from the union
between form and language. The novel, by its mere existence, is representative of freedom; everything in it is possible provided the following
elements are present: lively language and the intuition of a form. The
novel is the polyphonic genre par excellence; it recognizes only the
limits demanded by these two components: word and form, to which
we may add another: time, a specifically fictional time. And one more:
a proximity to society, its records: the never-ending round: the human
comedy: vanity fair, all that.

Xalapa, May 1995

WRESTLING WITH THE ANGEL

For Marek Keller

The undersigned, a writer who vaguely sensed his vocation for literature in a sugar mill in Veracruz, also encountered—and violently so!—the dark upheaval that afflicted Tonio Kröger in Wiesbaden: the struggle between the temptation of the world and the solitude essential to the creative process. That is, a hunger for the world and at the same time its rejection. For Kröger, steeped in a tradition where, for centuries, energy and discipline have been revealed to be a mere extension of nature, arriving at the correct solution seems no longer to possess merit. The world of Veracruz, as is well known, has virtues and charms that the Germans do not know, but that makes it prone, as few are, to all sorts of temptations. To resist a desire, whatever it may be, signifies a loss, being no one, living in error. The effort to reconcile life experience with the practice of writing made me feel oppressed for many years, disorganized, diminished. Now, when the world has become smaller to me, to the point of almost vanishing, that apparent struggle has become for me disconcertingly trivial. Either way, it has left a mark on my life. It has been a source of agony, but also, secretly, the most extraordinary creative stimulus.

I try to reproduce an afternoon in Warsaw, where the fragile balance between life experience and discipline threatens to cause crisis at any moment. From the top floor of the Hotel Bristol, I watch the lively crowd that roams the Krakowskie Przedmieście, perhaps the city's most beautiful avenue. People stop to admire the lilacs in the park beneath my room, to take some sun, eat pastries and ice cream, talk. The park's layout is rectangular; the front, which is narrower and borders the Krakowskie Przedmieście, is civilized, a tamed garden where benches abound so that passersby can rest and mothers can watch their children run on the sandy trails. The back of the park is deep: a tangle of wild bushes, a bit of English forest, they say, where games less innocent than children's are played. My desk is situated at an angle in front of the window. The sun illuminates my workplace from the left, as the manuals recommend.

As a rule, I would rise late, study Polish for a couple of hours, walk around town until mealtime, and, then, from four on I would sit down to work and would not leave the hotel until nine or ten at night, occupying the time preparing an anthology of contemporary Polish short stories, reading, selecting, translating, and constantly revising my translations. I would also devote time to working on a collection of stories I intended to send to Mexico. At night, I would socialize or read. While working, I would get up occasionally to make coffee, which, as a rule, I would drink on the large stone window ledge.

On the afternoon in question, the spectacle in the street and garden was both attractive and troubling. A sunny day in mid-May. The lilacs have appeared, a floral vision that is the first certain announcement of spring. The movement of the passersby is very festive. It must be Friday, when the activity is greater than any other day of the week. The heavy furs, the leather and simple wool coats have disappeared to make way for lighter clothing or trench coats. Most of the men are no longer wearing hats; the women wear hats made of straw or light fabric, adorned with small bouquets of artificial flowers. Among the young people of both sexes, one frequently sees sunglasses that protect their almost transparent blue or green eyes from the timid spring sun. On the balconies of nearby buildings, geraniums are in bloom.

During one of the breaks I devote to coffee, I see three young men enter the garden at about the same time but from different points; one is wearing a military uniform, one is obviously a university student, and the third seems, I don't know why, to be a boy who has just arrived from the provinces to carry out a commission in Warsaw or, perhaps, determined to remain in the capital indefinitely and set in motion, like Lucien de Rubempré, the still unclear threads of his ambition and transform his will into supreme law. To be someone! What does it mean for him to reach such heights? He is very young and possesses an imagination as passionate as it is limited. To become the husband of the daughter of a Rockefeller or an Onassis, should they one day decide to holiday in Poland? Or, at the very least, marry a less famous heiress, the daughter of a Polish millionaire living in Hamburg or Chicago, the owner of a beautiful cottage on the Baltic coast? This is his plan. Indeed, he considers any other attempt to shape his future to be pointless. I can also see three beautiful girls sitting on three different benches in the garden. One, a charming blonde would justify her presence there by the fact that she works in the bookshop across the street; she's waiting for the cashier—with whom she commutes daily on the trolleybus back to her neighborhood—to leave work; another, even more blonde, would tell whomever bothered to ask that she studies French literature and is waiting for some friends who will be there at any moment with the necessary books so they can do a translation exercise together that afternoon; the third, not as young but more attractive, with a full, perfectly shaped figure and short black hair that reveals a perfect neck, who's wearing nicer clothes and shoes made with better materials, would say curtly that she was unable to resist the temptation to enjoy a few minutes of sun while she waits to go to a movie; she would say it in a contained, intense, and somewhat dismissive tone, which suggests a sensuality that the two blondes lack and which always causes the listener to want to divert his gaze toward the more gifted parts of her body; she would then add in a stern, almost pedagogical voice, that she's attending an international film festival at the Skarpa cinema, without mentioning that her husband would be waiting for her there just before the function begins.

The ambitious young provincial sits at the opposite end of the same bench where, facing the sun, the beautiful woman with raven hair is seated. She opens in front of him a copy of *The Banner of Youth* or *Life of Warsaw*; she flips through it with disinterest only to let it fall on her lap and lights a cigarette that she smokes with obvious suggestiveness. Then, with an angelic face and oblivious air, he apologizes to his bench mate and shows her a page from the newspaper as if asking her a question. She turns toward him with a stern look of surprise on her face; she examines the paper and proffers a dry response. Little by little, the seriousness disappears from both their faces. He makes a comment and his smile grows wider; she raises a delicate, reproving finger and shakes it at the young man as if indicating that such things can be said in his village but never in a city like Warsaw, much less to a woman he doesn't know, but he eventually wins her over with his laugh, and they finally engage in a playful conversation.

The young man gets up, takes a few steps around the bench and sits down again, but this time he sits next to his neighbor so he can speak quietly. He probably says something to her about being lonely in the strange city, his fears, and his uncertainties.

After finishing my coffee, I return to my desk and begin to organize my papers. I am translating a story by Iwaszkiewicz entitled "Tatarak." My dictionary tells me that the word means "aromatic calamus" or "sweet rush," and that it is an aquatic plant that grows in lakes and ponds of the Baltic region. It is a magnificent story; the ending is tragic and filled with an intense and contained despair; it is about a romantic relationship or, more specifically, the development of a physical passion between a mature woman and a boy whose only attraction is his youth and the naturalness of his manner. Death is lurking throughout the story, but we only notice it at the end, when the boy appears trapped by the roots of the sweet rush. Quotidian lives, worthy, wasted, onto which their owners try to imprint an essential decency. The erotic element is very powerful, but its strength lies in the bowels of its language; the characters may not be aware of it, but their movements, their destiny, seem to be governed by it. All of a sudden, the twilight atmosphere causes me to think, obliquely, of the movie *Senso* by Visconti. Both the story and the film share a blurred sexuality. They are stories *en travesti,* or, at least, so it seems. The differences are vast: instead of the hysteria, the operatic madness of the film, there is in the story only opaqueness, a quasi-muteness, one of the greatest qualities in all of Jarosław Iwaszkiewicz's work. I work with great pleasure, resolving doubts, trying to maintain the same breath that the prose has in Polish. I get up to make sure I have an ironed white shirt and that my black shoes are shined, because that night

I'm going to the theater with Zofia Szleyen to see her translation of *The Youthful Deeds of the Cid* by Guillén de Castro. I'll pick her up an hour before the function for a light dinner. Going to the theater has been, since childhood, a substitute for a visit to paradise. This past year in Warsaw has been magnificent; in addition to the excellent Polish productions, I've seen the Royal Shakespeare Company, and also the Piccolo Teatro di Milano, the Stabile di Genoa, the Maly Theatre of Moscow, the Piraikón of Athens. No less! It is perhaps the only distraction about which I have no regrets; the stage fascinates me, gives me ideas, and renews my energy. The angel of order has taken it upon himself to organize a perfect day for me. Going to the theater is an immense source of pleasure, yes, but it's also an intellectual activity: I feel no remorse.

I get up again; I go to the bookcase just to make sure I have *The Youthful Deeds of the Cid*. Before returning to my work, I pause again at the window. I sit for a moment to take in the view. Night is about to fall, but there's a clarity in the air that outlines the figures perfectly. The characters have changed. The benches in the garden have new occupants, younger, more casual and playful, with binders and folders under their arms or piled on benches; without a doubt, they're students. The garden paths seem busier. Suddenly, there in the back, where the thick hedgerow usually conceals the lovers, I'm able to make out one of the couples that was beginning to form during my previous break. They say goodbye with an unconvincing formality. Who could it be but the fellow from the provinces and the sensual woman who had to meet her husband at the door of the cinema Skarpa? He walks toward the Krakowskie Przedmieście, she toward a side alley, the one that passes directly beneath my window.

She walks with an air of superiority; just steps from the sidewalk, but still within the garden, she stops, opens her purse, takes out a hand mirror, looks at herself, then, satisfied, returns it to her purse; not a single hair has been left out of place. She looks at her watch; she thinks perhaps about her husband, about the scene that awaits her, but this only accentuates her smile, reinvigorates her step, and renders her triumphant; she has become a lioness. By contrast, the young man seems to take pleasure in his disheveled appearance. He's walking in shirtsleeves; he flips an old summer jacket around with one hand as if it were a mill blade. His seraphic appearance is gone; his tousled hair and the loss of sexual appetite in his step announce his conquest with satyric pride—and how!—mission accomplished. He whistles as he walks. A few steps later he casually touches the crotch of his trouser to make sure the buttons are correctly fastened. A warm breeze, with all the aromas of spring, penetrates the window; the murmur of life begins to arrive to my studio with greater intensity. I sit down in front of my papers, but it's hard for me to concentrate.

Minutes later, I close the dictionary and put away the drafts my translation of "Tatarak." I consider myself fanatical about literary work and life. The combination of these qualities is a source of terrible conflicts. I take another folder out of the armoire, unfold other papers on the table, the material I'm about to send to the poet and translator Díez-Canedo: *Los climas* (The Climates), a book of short stories. With each revision, I discover new atrocities, and I make generous corrections. A never-ending process! The story that interests me most is about a hallucination suffered by a young Mexican who visits his friend, Juan Manuel Torres, in Lodz and returns by train to Warsaw, consumed with fever, one particularly cold winter night.

He sits across from an elderly woman who reminds him of a family member, his aunt, whom he knows only from photographs, one of his grandmother's sisters, who according to family tradition died at sea returning from her honeymoon. The account fuses two stories—the most visible: the journey by train of the feverish boy, his incoherent travel impressions, the encounter with his friend and his discovery of Poland; the other: a hallucination caused by delirium, where the elderly woman on the train is the supposedly dead sister of his grandmother. Reality and delirium treated with the same language. It was the first story I wrote in Poland; I have rewritten it a thousand times, but I find that the language still possesses a repulsive mawkishness and that the "gothic" story, in order not to fail, should be written in an almost transparent language, where unreality is inserted into the real without the seams being visible. I begin to cross out and super-impose words, add lines, omit adjectives, and an insidious anxiety gets the better of me, a sudden sense of claustrophobia. I tell myself that the Spartan rules I've imposed on myself are more appropriate in a notary office, in a government agency, anywhere except where a writer works. Does being locked up in a room, leafing through dictionaries, omitting or adding a word here and there not already imply a betrayal to literature? I have spoken ad nauseam of the importance of literature in my life. I have added that if I am still in Warsaw it is because I find the ideal atmosphere for writing here. But write about what, if the material that could nourish a story is down there, in the park, on the street, in the corner coffee shop? The places where life is, those things that don't happen in this garret where I force myself as punishment, as penance, to lock myself up in front of a typewriter and dictionaries. Would I perhaps have to keep rummaging forever into my childhood and write about my life as a child in Potrero and an adolescent in Córdoba for the rest of my life? I am sick of it. My freedom begins in the stories that I am now correcting.

It is well known that there is no tide without a counter-tide, action without reaction. And the undertows tend to be brutal. Perhaps in a bar, on a walk, in a party, I will suddenly regret not being in my garret, where I could take notes on the Shakespeare of Jan Kott, whose recent reading left me in awe, and study in an orderly fashion the Romantic poets, crucial to Polish literature, and then leap to Witkiewicz, Gombrowicz, and Bruno Schultz, and, in addition, read Borges, Cortázar, Neruda and Vallejo, Cervantes, Bernal Díaz del Castillo, Paz, and Fuentes, and write letters that I owe, and, above all, write stories, make up stories, write, write, write instead of drink like a Pole and go about life from binge to binge, instead of ruining my health, altering my nervous system, wasting my faculties, time, and energy only later to fully become the loser that at this moment I feel predestined to be.

I indulge in these sad meditations as I put my papers in their respective folders; I hasten to shave, get dressed and put on a tie. "The angel of order is still with me," I feel reassured knowing that soon I will dine with Zofia; I'll listen to her speak at length about her truest loves: Cervantes, Lope, Valle-Inclán, Lorca, and, above all, Tirso, whose *Don Gil of the Green Breeches* is by far her favorite work. And I find myself in that perfect dream when the phone rings. It's Marek Keller. He has a performance tonight, he says; he'll leave an invitation for me in the box office; afterward, there will be a party at Maja Berezowska's house—"that old libertine," as good people exclaim whenever anyone mentions her name. I am certain it will be an extremely entertaining gathering; just thinking of the radiant mob that awaits me that night is enough to feel overcome with joy. I know from experience that after the party someone will improvise another more modest one with fewer guests, and that perhaps the night will end in a raucous tour of those spots in Warsaw with the worst reputation. Almost without realizing it, I call Zofia to beg off and invent something so absurd that it ends up being convincing. I race to the theater where Marek's *Mazowsze* is playing; afterward, I'll allow myself to fall into the much anticipated well of chaos from which I will likely not emerge until breakfast time tomorrow.

Xalapa, May 1995

TRAVELING AND WRITING

For Julio Ortega

I amused myself recently rereading some fragments in an autobiographical notebook written some thirty years ago. I was hoping to
find in its pages the atmosphere that enveloped the first years of my
stay in Europe. A well-known editor of the time, Don Rafael Giménez
Siles, invited a dozen young writers to tell their life stories. He seemed
to be convinced that such an act would encourage a generation even
greener than ours to find its path to literature. I doubt that those
allegedly exemplary lives have fulfilled that purpose. The project was in
many ways ridiculous; those of us who were chosen were engaged, to
varying degrees, in an intense sentimental and literary education that
in no way corresponded with a desire to trawl the enigmas of the past
and use them to interpret the signs that governed our fate, let alone
serve as examples and mentors for the very young writers whom in
due time would take our place. I wrote those notes in Warsaw in early
1966. I had left Mexico five years earlier, visited several countries, and
prolonged my stay mainly in two cities, Rome and Warsaw.

As I reread the text, I was left suddenly with this question: "Why
do I get chills every time I think about returning to my country,
which, of course, will have to happen, like it or not, someday?"

Then I mentioned the circumstances that had prompted me to undertake this journey and to extend it indefinitely. It began with a sense of professional frustration: I was working at a publishing house where all my projects were systematically thwarted. It infuriated me to see that the practice of literature and the inevitable squabbles that resulted from it often concealed a noticeable intellectual disdain and hinted at aspirations that had little or nothing to do with literature. Some young intellectuals were beginning to seek a more intimate relationship with power than with the muses. My feelings toward political opposition groups, particularly the left, with whose ideals I identified most, were decidedly contradictory; I wanted them to grow stronger, but at the same time their methods seemed confusing to me, limited and far removed from any element of reality. More than anything, the empty rhetoric of official discourse sickened me, as well as the conformity of large swaths of the population to the restrictions of our democratic life and the backwardness of the country. I said all that to myself then, and it was true. But now I am able to see that in large part the state of frustration was related to having published a few years earlier a first book of stories that went unnoticed, and that after that I had stopped writing.

In mid-June 1961, I left Veracruz on the German ship *Marburg*. One morning, in the middle of the ocean, the bulletin we were given at breakfast announced that the ship, just as all units of the German merchant navy, would have to forego the originally scheduled stops (Le Havre, Antwerp, Rotterdam) and proceed without delay to a German port, where it should await further instructions. The officers, waiters, and German passengers showed signs of nervousness that we had not previously seen in them. We were treated with a condescending arrogance. They were custodians of secrets that concerned us, but were apparently forbidden to reveal. They had suddenly become our masters! That morning, among the passengers, there began to circulate a wide range of rumors, all catastrophic. That a new world war was about to break out was the first. Soon it had morphed into the aforementioned catastrophe had already begun. In the blink of an eye, the passengers' imaginations had plunged into delirium. As the day went on, the recent destruction of Rotterdam was accepted as fact; thereafter, it was confirmed that there had been a coup d'état in Rome and that the Vatican was under siege; that the Pope had been physically assaulted as he attempted to leave his apartments; that in Zurich, Frankfurt, and Milan banks had suspended operations; that Rotterdam was not the city destroyed by bombs but Marseille; that it had not been Marseille but Dresden; that it had not been Dresden but Rotterdam; not Rotterdam, on the contrary, someone had heard from a very trustworthy source, a German woman, that the cities destroyed were Marseille, Bristol, and Salerno. In the bar, groups of passengers gathered around the radio for hours, trying to tune in to European stations, none of which confirmed the rumors that were spreading on board. There was talk, yes, of a very serious conflict emerging between the two German States, the division of Berlin, which, in the opinion of the more discerning passengers, was an attempt to prevent widespread panic. After dinner, the Captain brought us together to inform us of the itinerary change and the reasons that had necessitated it. We would disembark in Bremerhaven, the port closest to Bremen. The line would cover our passage by rail to our initial ports of destination, if by then the trains were still working as scheduled. The Cold War, he said, savoring the news with delight, was no longer cold, and we were standing on the threshold of a serious conflict with unpredictable consequences. In a single night they had built a wall dividing Berlin, making prisoners of all the inhabitants of the eastern sector. He fired off sentences with a dryness that scarcely matched the profusion of gestures and grimaces that accompanied them. All of a sudden, he had become one of the most baleful characters of the expressionist cinema. At every turn he interrupted his rant to receive from a subordinate's hands cards that, we supposed, contained the latest news sent by telegraph. After reading the messages, his words became drier, his gestures more outrageous; he was a ventriloquist's dummy whose movements escaped the master's control. I was traveling with passage to Antwerp, where I would board a ferry that would take me to England. If the circumstances were as bad as they seemed, the Captain added, and if it were not possible to leave from Bremen, he recommended that we immediately contact the consular representatives of our respective countries. Deep down, I was as excited as the German officers, my blood raced with the same muddy drunkenness as theirs. I was ecstatic to find myself in one of those moments that could become a turning point of history. It did not occur to me in the least that my freedom, much less my life, might be in danger if war broke out. On the contrary, in radical opposition to my pacifist ideas, I considered the opportunity to be the beginning of a chain of exciting new events capable of wresting me from the stupor I was experiencing. Like the Germans from Marburg, I felt an exhilarating charge of electricity run through me, except, unlike them, I was convinced that the outbreak of war would once again mean the defeat of Germany and the beginning of a new world. At moments the session took on an intensity of Wagnerian proportions. Conversely, during the next four or five days, the last of the trip, the conversations turned melancholy. I ate with Belgian and Dutch passengers; the exuberance of the first day had waned; wild rumors were no longer circulating; nobody ventured hypotheses. They behaved more with the resignation of hostages than that of free men. Of our arrival to the German port, I remember, above all, the harried confusion of the landing and the difficulties hours later loading the luggage onto a crowded train that was departing for Holland. I did not receive passage to Antwerp but to a small Dutch port from where a ship would leave for Dover. Before leaving Bremen, I was able to visit a magnificent exhibition of recent works by Picasso with a young Swiss couple I had met on board. With the greatest irresponsibility, we abandoned our trunks and suitcases in the lobby of a completely deserted gallery and toured for a while its sepulcher-like halls. "It would be easy for us to steal a picture," the husband told me, and for a moment the idea worked us into to a frenzy. Everything was possible during what we believed to be a time of war. Fortunately, it was not.

The motive for that trip had been a reading of Bernard Berenson on some peculiarities of the Byzantine legacy in Sicily, illustrated with splendid photographs of the monumental apse at Cefalù. However, just before leaving, I decided to remove Italy from my trip in response to a bitter argument with some elderly aunts, for whom that country, that of our ancestors, was a beacon whose light reached all the way to their home in Colonia del Valle, allowing them to forget at times the thick darkness in which they claimed to be stagnating, in the land of Indians where our ancestors had mistakenly settled. Chance governed, above all else, my stay abroad. I lived, as I have already said, many years in Europe and, yet, I was never able to see the Byzantine apse at Cefalù or the Flemish paintings that I would presumably find in Antwerp. One morning in Paris, in early August 1961, almost without realizing it, I found myself in line at the Italian consulate to apply for a visa to travel to the country I had sworn never to set foot in, and from which, after arriving, it was a year before I was able to extricate myself.

The prelude to my arrival in Europe was marked by that grave international disturbance that involved the building of the Berlin Wall. Many extremely important events took place over the next thirty years; among others, ultimately, the collapse of that wall. But I never witnessed any of them. Either they had just occurred when I arrived somewhere, or they were about to happen as I was about to leave. Only once did I find myself in the middle of a popular uprising. It was in Istanbul. I was traveling with an Englishwoman and a Polish friend as absent-minded as me. Suddenly, we saw an agitated and raucous crowd that spilled out into the streets and squares of the city's center. There was a constant sound of gunfire; occasionally, groups of police, guns drawn, would stop our taxi, force us to get out, and subject us to a rather thorough body search. The driver acted as if it were a cheerful routine. There was no reason to take the incidents seriously, he told us with a reassuring smile. In the restaurants, the waiters quickly lowered the metal shutters, and we remained locked in for a while, hearing knocks at the door and screams from outside. The headwaiter approached the table with a beaming smile. Nothing was going on, boys playing games, mischief, excessive happiness, everything was in order; it would only be a matter of minutes until we could leave. The same thing happened in the Grand Bazaar, in the museums. There was merrymaking everywhere, singing students, boys roused by the mere joy of being young. Public order was perfect. Under the circumstances, we visited everywhere that the Baedeker guidebook recommended. Any excess was possible, we thought, in that unlikely city, although the noisy eccentricity of local customs and celebrations had begun to wear on us. Days later, far from Turkey, while reading *Le Monde*, I discovered that my trip to Istanbul had coincided with an attempted coup. The tourist services had worked to perfection, just as in *Death in Venice*, where everyone, from the manager of the grand hotel to the most humble gondoliers, did everything possible to exaggerate the festive mood so that the tourists would not suspect the city was being ravaged by the plague. In those days of peril, ignorance of civil drama stripped all meaning from the facts. Nothing that I read later about *"les émeutes de Stamboul"* existed as a real experience for me. However, perhaps because of that ambiguous and oblique quality, I introduced Istanbul into one of my novels as a scene that was not intended to be convincing in any way, and the trip on the *Marburg*, as well as the landing in Bremen, more precisely, have only served me as anecdotes, unable to crystallize into a narrative.

In Europe, I held various jobs, and at times I managed to survive without one. I moved frequently from one side of the famous wall whose appearance marked my arrival to the other. The thread that ties these years together, I've always known, is literature. All my personal experiences, in the end, have converged. For many years, my experiences traveling, reading, and writing merged into a single experience. The trains, the boats, and the airplanes have allowed me to discover worlds that were either wonderful or sinister, but all of them were surprising. Travel was the experience of the visible world; reading, on the other hand, allowed me to undertake an inner journey whose itinerary was not confined to space but rather let me move freely throughout time. Reading meant accompanying Mr. Bloom to the taverns of Dublin at the beginning of this century, Fabrice del Dongo through post-Napoleonic Italy, Hector and Achilles through the streets of Troy and the military camps that for many years surrounded it. And writing meant the possibility of embarking toward an elusive goal and fusing—thanks to that dark, inscrutable, and much-talked about alchemy one comes closer to the process of creation—the outside world and that subterranean one that inhabits us.

I was in Germany recently. Passing through Wiesbaden, I set out to find the house where Turgenev lived and wrote most of his work. Suddenly, I came across a raucous protest of neo-Nazi youths who were celebrating the second anniversary of German reunification with a bloodcurdling uproar. The disgust I felt as a result of a protest fraught with violence caused me to abandon my search for the palace where the Russian writer had lived. The next day, at more or less the same time, I was in Milan walking to the church of Santa María delle Grazie to once again see *The Last Supper*. As I approached the dazzling stonework of that noble building, one of Bramante's best, I was barely able to contain my excitement. I felt like applauding in front of everyone to celebrate that remarkable triumph of form. In a full state of grace, the march I had witnessed the day before in Wiesbaden crossed my mind. It is impossible to imagine a more crushing disparity! It was revealed to me once more with an almost physical intensity that in the face of a permanent irradiation of works of art, in the face of its finality and fullness, everything else is incidental, tangential, and superficial. Works of art express, and do so once and for all, the best energy humans are capable of producing.

Any political episode pales or becomes diluted before the splendor of a work of Palladio, Giorgione, Orozco, or Matisse, in the same way that before a literary work one discovers everything common and irrelevant contained in the language of practical politics, of business, of worldly ceremonies, that language that Galdós defined as "the daily diet and training-school of ordinary minds."[9]

Shortly after having settled in Italy, Bernard Berenson said that man is the perfection of the universe; the spirit, the perfection of man; and art, the combination and summary of all human perfections.

I think about Mikhail Bakhtin, about the many years that the Russian thinker was confined to a tiny village lost in the immensity of the Siberian tundra where he was serving a sentence of banishment. Knowing how to read and write allowed him to survive; in a region of illiterates, he was in charge of drawing up the administrative documents of the local kolkhoz. The living conditions might have been very different from those of Berenson, who wrote in a beautiful castle in Tuscany with the aid of a private library of forty-five thousand volumes, surrounded by paintings and *objets d'art* and a circle of friends that included several of the most eminent figures of our century. The conclusions of both humanists, however, are similar: ultimately, the spiritual life is the only one that counts. Only the fruits of thought and artistic creation truly justify man's presence in the world. With an energy characteristic of the Titans, Bakhtin was able to establish a delivery network so that some friends and disciples could send him the materials needed for his research. These were highly specialized books, in six or seven languages, difficult to obtain in Stalin's Russia. With them, he was about to finish while in Siberian exile

---

9 Translated by Robert Russell

a refreshingly learned book: *Rabelais and His World*, an erudite and passionate defense of the body and the human spirit against all forms of repression and intolerance. In it, the Russian humanist outlines an idea that several decades later thinkers as diverse as the Spaniard María Zambrano and the Pole Leszek Kolakowski would take up: against the discourse of power, the philosopher and the poet would impose the supreme efficacy of the jester's devices. The steely rigidness of the Prince—his immense power—would be ineffective to the halting step, the astonished gaze, and the vacuous smile of the clown. Nothing irritates the powerful like the ridiculing of their gestures and words, to be transformed not into an object of worship but one of mockery, among other reasons because their language usually exists on the edge of parody. By making a handful of minor alterations and intensifying a few gestures, Chaplin was able to transform a speech by Hitler into a perfect example of the grotesque. Over time, the circumstances surrounding Bakhtin's life will be remembered as one of many heinous periods that history insists on repeating with mediocre imagination. His books, on the other hand, will remain as an immense triumph of intelligence.

What exploit by Napoleon could be compared in splendor or permanence with *War and Peace*, the *National Episodes*, *The Charterhouse of Parma*, or *The Disasters of War*—works that paradoxically grew out of the existence of these exploits?

For the writer, language is everything.

Form, structure, and every element of a story—plot, characters, tone, gestuality, revelation, or prophecy—are all products of language. It will always be language that announces what paths to follow. Robert Graves said that the primary obligation of the writer is to work without granting himself a truce in, from, with, and about the word.

The exceptional moments in literature occur when the author, no matter what course he follows when starting a work, manages to immerse himself into the deep currents of language in order to, in this way, lose his own identity. E. M. Forster suggests that at the core of every great creation beats a longing for anonymity. In the imaginary world of Tlön, dreams Borges, "there is no concept of plagiarism: it has been established that all books are the work of a single author who is timeless and anonymous." "Every poet," Octavio Paz concludes, "is only a pulse in the river of language." A literary work is revealed as genius when the author succeeds in finding the dark current that carries vestiges of everything spoken since the time language was born, that is to say at the moment the writer feels he is transcribing a dictation, when the word makes its appearance even before being convened. If that moment is produced, life is saved! Thus the best pages of literature possess something at once luminous and unfathomable. All of us, as readers, have witnessed at some time this wonder. Speechless, astonished, excited, we have been conscious of the miracle that emerges from a page, one in which language and instinct have merged and the will of reason is overtaken by an energy that is greater, a page whose beauty is absolutely impossible to explain in its entirety. I am thinking of a very short story by Chekhov: "The Student."

Like Berenson, I have concerned myself with the construction of "the house of life," that is, the effort to understand the relationship between the individual and society, and the wish that this relationship be governed by the concepts of virtue and justice. Four years ago, shortly after returning definitively to Mexico, the wall that was a prelude to my first landing in Europe collapsed. A hopeful air spread across the world. It seemed that at last an age of freedom, fullness, tolerance, and prosperity had begun for everyone. At the same time, a dangerously narrow view was integrating the idea of democracy into a purely commercial mechanism: free trade. The results are obvious. The press repeats the unwelcome words everywhere: crisis, unemployment, recession, disillusionment, instability.

I returned to a Mexico very different from the one I left in 1961. It's clear that there exist today signs of a civil society that was unthinkable when I left. It is an encouraging phenomenon that coexists with images of profound devastation: an uninhabitable city, a degraded landscape, an almost nonexistent sky. In Coyoacán, in the Plaza de la Conchita, upon opening the door of my house, I have seen doves fall like rotten fruit, poisoned by acids that contaminate the air. And in the main square, also in Coyoacán, I have witnessed scenes similar to others I witnessed some fifty years ago that lay hidden in the depths of my memory. There were the squalid Indian women dressed in rags who arrived at the coffee plantations during harvest time, the same ones who arrived at the end of the workday, kneeling beside their husband or children whose hair they carded with furtive and stern expressions. Seeing them in Coyoacán, dedicated to the same labor, I once again seemed to hear the snap of lice crushed with thumbnails. The indigenous women of my childhood spoke Popolaca or Mixe; those of Coyoacán—possibly Otomí. Instead of cutting coffee, they sell poorly executed weavings while their offspring beg for alms around them.

Do those ghostly presences that appear around my home not prove the futility of a language that conceives of itself as velvet-like and triumphant, even when it does not cease to be a regrettable stammer?

Traveling and writing! Activities that are both marked by chance; the traveler and the writer will only be certain of the departure. Neither of them will know for sure what will happen on the way, let alone what fate awaits them upon their return to their personal Ithaca.

Xalapa, March 1993

AN ARS POETICA?

For Ednodio Quintero

I was invited to attend a biennale of writers in Mérida, Venezuela, where each of the participants was to explain his own concept of an *ars poetica*. I lived in terror for weeks. What did I have to say on the subject? The best I could do, I told myself, would be to draft an Ars Combinatoria. Or, more modestly, to enumerate certain issues and circumstances that in some way define my writing.

Regrettably, my theoretical grounding, throughout my life, has been limited. Only later in life, during a stay in Moscow, did I begin to take an interest in the work of the Russian formalists and their disciples. I met Viktor Shklovsky, who invited me to his studio where I listened to him talk for an entire morning. I was speechless! I was at a loss to explain how I had been able, until then, to do without that universe filled with brilliant provocations. I decided to study, as soon as I finished with the Russians, the fundamentals of linguistics, the various theories on form, to address the Prague School, then structuralism, semiotics, the new currents, Genette, Greimas, Yuri Lotman, and the Tartu-Moscow School. The truth is, I never got beyond the study of Russian formalism. I did read, with indescribable pleasure, the three volumes that Boris Eichenbaum dedicated to the work of Leo Tolstoy,

Tynyanov's book on the young Pushkin, Shklovsky's *Theory of Prose*, since his literary theory was also based on concrete works: those of Boccaccio, Cervantes, Sterne, Dickens, and Bely. My interest grew more intense when I got to Bakhtin and read his studies of Rabelais and Dostoevsky. When I attempted to delve into more specialized texts, the so-called "scientists," I felt lost. I was confused at every turn; I did not know the vocabulary. It was not without regret that little by little I began to abandon them. From time to time I suffer from abulia, and I dream about a future that will afford me the opportunity to become a scholar. Lacking any knowledge in classical rhetoric, how could I dare lecture on an *ars poetica*?

In Mexico, during my adolescence, I was a devoted and frequent reader of the work of Alfonso Reyes, which includes several titles on literary theory: *El deslinde* (The Demarcation), *La experiencia literaria* (The Literary Experience), and *Al yunque* (To the Anvil). I read them, I imagine, for the pure love of their language, for the unexpected music I found in them, for the ease with which he suddenly illuminated the most necessarily obscure topics. In a poem to the memory of the Mexican writer, Borges declares:

In his labors he was helped by mankind's
hope, which was the light of his life
to create a line that is not to be forgotten
and to renew Castilian prose.[10]

His modesty was such that even today few are aware of his extraordinary achievement: transforming—and in the process reinvigorating—

---

10 Translated by Harold Morland

our language. As I reread his essays, I continue to be amazed by a prose that is unlike any other. Cardoza y Aragón maintains that anyone who has not read Reyes's work cannot claim to have read his.

I owe to our great polygraph, and to several years of tenacious reading, my passion for language; I admire his secret and serene originality, his infinite combinatory ability, his humor, his talent for inserting everyday expressions, seemingly at odds with literary language, into a masterful exposition on Góngora, Virgil, or Mallarmé. Even though I may have been deaf to the theoretical reason present in Reyes, I am indebted to him for introducing me to the various fields to which I might otherwise have been slow to arrive: the Hellenistic world, medieval Spanish literature, the Golden Age, Brazil's *sertão* novels and avant-garde poetry, Sterne, Borges, Francisco Delicado, the detective novel, and so much more! His tastes were ecumenical. Reyes carried himself with a slight air of confidence and extreme courtesy, moving with an insatiable curiosity through many different literary spheres, some unenlightened. He complemented the hedonistic practice of writing with other responsibilities. The teacher—because he was that too—conceived of sharing with his flock everything that delighted him as a kind of ministry. He was a patient and hopeful shepherd who endeavored to, and in some cases succeeded in, cultivating generations of Mexicans; my generation's debt to him is immeasurable. During a time of closed windows and doors, Reyes urged us to embark on every journey. As I recall him, I am reminded of one of his first stories, "The Dinner," a horror story situated in an everyday setting, in which, at first sight, everything seems normal, anodyne, one might even say a bit saccharine. Between the lines, however, little by little, the reader begins to sense that he is entering an insane, perhaps criminal, world.

That "dinner" must have hit the right spot. Years later, I started writing. Only now do I realize that one of the roots of my narrative lies buried in that story. A large part of what I have done since is little more than a mere set of variations on that story.

My apprenticeship has been the result of an immoderate reading of stories and novels, of my efforts as a translator and the study of some books on facets of the novel written almost always by story-tellers, such as E. M. Forster's classic *Aspects of the Novel*, or the exhaustively prepared *Notebooks of Henry James*, or the fragmentary *Notebook of Anton Chekhov*, as well as a long list of interviews, articles, and essays on the novel by novelists, not to mention, of course, conversations with people from the profession.

These decalogues, enumerations of instructions for use by aspiring young writers, have proven fascinating to me for the mere fact that they allow me to read the authors' work again in an unforeseeable light. The precepts that Chekhov wrote to guide his younger brother who was determined to take up the literary profession are a clear explanation of the poetics that the Russian author had forged. They are not the cause but rather the result of a work in which the author outlined and defined his world and his literary specificity. But will we understand Chekhov's world better because we know those precepts taken from his own professional experience? I think not. In return, the knowledge of the craftsmanship he employed to write his remarkable stories surely intensifies the pleasure of reading them. Knowing those precepts allows us to discover, if not his conceptual world, then surely some secrets of his style, or, rather, the mysteries of his carpentry. Only if we apply as a rule the same precepts to Dostoyevsky, Céline, or Lezama Lima must we disqualify them as storytellers, because both their universe and their methods and purposes are in total opposition to the Russian writer. Indeed, could Horacio Quiroga's decalogue be applied to the work of Joyce, Borges, or Gadda? I am afraid not. For no reason other than they belong to different literary families. In the end, each author has to create his own poetics, lest he be content to be the succubus or the acolyte of a teacher. Each will establish, or perhaps it would be better to say that he will find, the form that his writing demands, since no narrative is possible without the existence of form. And in this way, the hypothetical creator must be guided by his own instincts.

One learns and unlearns at every turn. The novelist must understand that the only reality he is responsible for is his novel, and therein lies his fundamental responsibility. Everything he has lived, his personal conflicts, social preoccupations, his good and bad loves, his readings and, of course, dreams, must come together in it, because the novel is a sponge that will wish to absorb everything. The author will take care to feed and strengthen it, preventing any tendency toward obesity. "A novel is in its broadest definition," Henry James maintained, "a personal, a direct impression of life."

Having quoted this great storyteller, I should admit that I owe some of the crucial lessons about the craft to reading him. I was fortunate enough to translate into Spanish seven of his novels, including one of the most fiendishly difficult to be found in any literature: *What Maisie Knew*. Translating allows one to enter fully into a work, to know its bones, its structure, its silences. James validated for me a trend that was present in my very first stories: a furtive and sinuous approach to a fringe of mystery that is never entirely clear and that allows the reader to choose the solution he believes most fitting.

To achieve this, James adopted a highly effective solution: the removal of the author as an omniscient subject who knows and determines the behavior of his characters and in his place one or, in his most complex novels, multiple "points of view," through which the character tries to arrive at a meaning of some incident he has witnessed. Through this device, the character constructs himself, in an attempt to decipher the universe around him: the real world undergoes a process of deformation upon being filtered through consciousness. We will never know to what extent that narrator (that "point of view") dared to confess in the story, nor what portions he decided to omit, nor the reasons that led to one decision or another.

Similarly, even before reading James, my stories were characterized by their representation of an oblique view of reality. In general, there is a hole in them, an ominous void that is almost never covered. At least not entirely. The structure must be very solid so that the vagueness that interests me does not become chaos. The story must be told and retold from different angles and in it each chapter functions to add new elements to the plot and, at the same time, blur and contradict the schema that the previous elements have established. A kind of Penelope's weave that is continuously done and undone, in which a plot contains the germ of another plot that will in time lead to another, until the moment when the author decides to end his story. It is a literary convention that can be arduous, but is in no way novel. The origin of this literary tradition dates back to *One Thousand and One Nights*. In the Far East, this device has been employed frequently and has produced works that we must inevitably call masterpieces: Cao Xuequin's *Dream of the Red Chamber*, written in China in the eighteenth century, and the short story

"Rashomon," by Ryūnosuke Akutagawa, written in early twenti-eth-century Japan. Its Occidental counterpart is easier to trace. We find it, of course, in the *Quixote*, in *The Canterbury Tales*; it reemerges in the Enlightenment, with amazing energy, in *Jacques the Fatalist and His Master*, by Diderot; in Jan Potocki's *The Manuscript Found in Saragossa*; and in that wonder of wonders, *Tristram Shandy*, by Laurence Sterne. In our century, this type of novel, whose composition has always been associated with Chinese boxes or Russian matryoshka dolls, and which today theorists call *mise en abyme* (placed into abyss), has found a legion of fans. Allow me to cite three remarkable titles: Ford Madox Ford's *The Good Soldier*, Nabokov's *The Real Life of Sebastian Knight*, and *The Garden of Forking Paths* by Jorge Luis Borges.

The writing of my first novel, in the late sixties, coincided with a universal attempt to discredit narrative, a hatred of storytelling. Expressing even a moderate interest in Dickens, to cite just one exam-ple, could be considered a flagrant provocation or a confession of ignorance or provincialism. It was a time of never-ending innovation. Literature, cinema, visual arts, theater, all switched languages with extreme frequency. I was excited about many of these innovations, as was almost every member of my generation. We were convinced that a renovation of form was essential in order to return the novel to the state of health it needed. We applauded the innovations, even the most radical ones; but, in my case, the interest for the new never dimin-ished my passion for plot. Without it, life to me has always seemed diminished. Relating real things and undoing, while at the same time enhancing, their reality has been my calling. Whatever doubt I had vanished when I read Galdós. Even if admitting it in Spain is at times scandalous, he has been my true teacher. In his work, as in that of Goya,

I discovered that the quotidian and the delirious, the tragic and the grotesque, do not have to be different sides of a coin, rather they are able to be a single fully integrated entity.

But, to return to the storyteller's *ars poetica*: Does a single, valid universal principle exist? Golden rules of compulsory application? Does each period add new norms and proscribe others? And yet I still wonder: Is it not true that what is a source of energy for most writers can also be poison for some of them? Are there cases in which a writer, by violating the canon, succeeds in creating masterpieces? Jan Potocki and Jane Austen are contemporaries, but their works seem to illustrate genres that bear no resemblance to each other.

A basic rule, articulated by Gide: "Never take advantage of momentum already gained." Does each book, then, have to start from zero? We have been witnesses to the fall of authors who for years were our idols, whose audacity we admired without reservation; we came to think that their prose and their vision not only renewed narrative language but also modified our perception of existence until, paralyzed, suspicious of our own faculties, we began to discover through one of their books that their language left us cold, that we had become insensitive to their subjugation, only to be convinced in the end that the faculties that should be regarded with suspicion were not ours but those of the formerly idolized writer, whose prose was devoured by a vegetative language from which he could not or did not know how to defend himself, whether out of slapdashness, self-indulgence, or exhaustion; a language that, like a golem, had begun to mark the rules of the game, only to go its own way, to confuse the author, to convert him into a mere amanuensis. Félix de Azúa recalled once a conversation with Eduardo Chillida in which the sculptor told him that in his youth he suddenly felt surprised by the ease with which he carried out his work until, frightened by his extraordinary skill, he forced himself to sculpt with his left hand so he could again feel the tension of the material. It seems clear to me that Gide's warning requires no mechanical change of style, devices, themes, or language. It does not require the writer—in each novel, drama, or poem—to transform himself into someone else. That would be foolish, a masquerade. How do we understand, then, the work of Henry James, Ivy Compton-Burnett, Valle-Inclán, Borges, Saramago, and Gombrowicz, for example, for whom excellence depends on the permanent exacerbation of a personal style? In the end, it is really a matter, I imagine, of preventing language from passing, by sheer inertia, from one book to another and becoming a parody of itself, lulled by the energy of the momentum gained. The only influence that one must defend oneself against is one's own, declares the master of clarity, Bioy Casares. But there, as in everything that has to do with writing, lies the instinct of the writer who will have the last word.

Another definitive rule: never confuse the act of writing with the art of writing. The act of writing does not tend to intensify life, which is the goal of the art of writing. The act of writing will scarcely allow the word to possess more than a single meaning; in the art of writing, a word is by nature polysemantic: it speaks and is silent, reveals and obscures. The act of writing is reliable and predictable, the art of writing never is; it rejoices in delirium, in darkness, in mystery and in disorder, no matter how transparent it may seem. Marguerite Duras: "Writing comes like the wind, it's naked, it's made of ink, it's the thing written, and it passes like nothing else passes in life, nothing more, except life itself."[11]

Writing for me has meant—if I may borrow a phrase from Bakhtin—leaving a personal testimony of the world's constant mutation.

Xalapa, September 1993

---

11 Translated by Mark Polizzotti

HERE COMES THE PARADE!

1980

19 APRIL (ON A FLIGHT FROM SAN FRANCISCO TO MEXICO)
I keep toying with the idea of writing a novel with a detective plot.
Convert the building where I live into a setting with the typical (or
topical) characteristics of a microcosm. I'm thinking about a domi-
nant figure, a kind of monster: a very fat woman who lives with a son
whom she hides. The tenants: people in some way tied to movements
organized thirty or forty years ago by the radical right; also a few
intellectuals whom the others see as rabble; and poor tenants, protected by rent control, whom no one ever sees. And a lonely, maniacal,
and annoying madman named Pedrito…

26 MAY (IN MEXICO)
I had dinner last night with my niece Elena Buganza. She told me
about the thesis she's preparing for her *licenciatura en letras* degree.
As I listened to her, I had an idea that could be the engine of my
novel. Her thesis deals with the work of Bernardo Couto Castillo,
a decadent from the late nineteenth century. A young Mexican aristo-
crat who died at twenty-one, disowned by his family and demonized
by the people of good conscience of the time. I imagine, from what
little I know, he probably died from an excessive use of absinthe

and a violent fit of syphilis. "He enjoyed every vice, even the most perverse," wrote one of his contemporaries. My niece searched for Couto's grave and could not find it. She then located some of his relatives and went to see them in search of information about his life and work. When they heard she was researching him and had already gathered some relatively obscure texts, they grew uneasy and closed the door in her face. They probably feared that details that could once again tarnish the family's reputation would come to light. I am tempted to write a kind of *Aspern Papers*, except, instead of love letters in my novel it would be secrets that compromised the honor of a poet who has gone down in history as a moral example.

1981

9 MAY

...set everything in the late thirties or early forties. I would like this detective novel to also shed light on certain political issues. Unfortunately, the characters I'm thinking about are too parodic and could only serve as incidental figures (Pedrito Balmorán, for example). A clandestine committee has tried a fellow party member in secret and sentenced him to death. Another man, named Martínez (a blackmailer, among other things), is murdered in jail so he can't reveal the details of the trial. Someone had paid Martínez to falsely confess that he was the perpetrator. They had promised him all sorts of things: to prepare his getaway, a substantial reward, etc...but I'm missing something... something related to the Central European Jews who began to arrive in Mexico, fleeing Nazism? Some sort of scam? A marriage of convenience undertaken so a woman could leave Europe? Jealousy, betrayals, vendettas, and all that trove of grisly emotions that complement these topics? I can't figure out how to begin. Everything boils down to the incidental characters, good only for creating atmosphere. The tenants of the building live their life dreaming of a new Cristero uprising and triumph of God on earth...fierce hatreds and rivalries at the core of the rightwing organizations...

1982

11 MAY (PASSING THROUGH MADRID)

As I walked through the city center this morning, I thought obsessively about the building where I live in Mexico, in Plaza Río de Janeiro, and about my hypothetical novel...A character who was nine years old in 1942 returns thirty years later to visit the building where during his childhood a crime was committed that was never solved. He questions several tenants: his Aunt Hedwig, the bookseller Balmorán, the doorman; and thus the plot begins to take shape. An old German woman who never has visitors lives in the building. I'll need to spend a few days locked in the archives...by the end, readers will have learned several things, all more or less trivial, eccentric, but the mystery will not be completely revealed to them.

12 MAY (IN MEXICO)

The story unfolds at the level of masks. The faces will never be seen. The biggest enigma lies in the identity of the protagonists.

12 JUNE

...a novel that isn't a mere *divertimento* but a moral reconstruction of the period…Try to get the microcosm to shed some light on our present. A novel with a more or less hidden moral? No, thank you. Although, at the end of the day, why not take that risk? Attempt a search for the truth, a reflection on the past and its persistence over time. The conclusion is almost topical: the truth, the true truth of the truth, is not likely to be within our reach. We rely only on certain intuitions that allow us to approach it, perhaps to brush against it. Knowing a phenomenon only partially is as if we did not know it at all. However, it is impossible to conform and maintain a passive attitude. An ethical obligation requires us to continue our search. The building in Plaza de Rio de Janeiro becomes a house of Babel.

15 JUNE

…I'm thinking that a theme I tried to develop for several years in a short novel that I never managed to finish (the relationship between a brilliant mother and a timid and unsociable adolescent) will have to be incorporated into this novel. A celebrated hostess holds a dinner for a famous painter and his son who has just returned to Mexico after spending a couple of years or more in a boarding school in the United States.

17 JULY

…another parallel theme: a possessive mother, a possessive son. Widowhood. The mother falls in love again and is eager to remarry. The son sets out to undo the relationship. He embarks on a long trip with his mother through Europe. She begins to deteriorate, succumbs to morphine, becomes a nymphomaniac. Years later, on the skids, they return to Mexico. On the verge of death, she calls him, insults him terribly, and curses him.

1 SEPTEMBER

...the same old story. I abandoned the project about the house in Plaza de Rio de Janeiro to replace it with two stories, two variations of the relationship between mothers and children. I should attempt to summarize all the themes that come to mind into a single plot.

21 SEPTEMBER

Luis Prieto told an amazingly absurd and extraordinarily amusing story last night about a fake Mexican castrato from the nineteenth century that I am planning to develop. A chronicle of the life of the castrato would be the document that saves Pedrito Balmorán and creates panic in a family of whitewashed tombs that fear the revelation of family secrets.

1983

3 JANUARY

Silvia Molina lent me a stack of documents that belonged to her father. They detail the subversive activities of the German colony in Mexico during World War II.

18 NOVEMBER (PRAGUE)

I was officially invited, in my capacity as ambassador rather than writer, to the opening of an exhibition to celebrate the centenary of the birth of Egon Erwin Kisch, the famous interwar journalist. I attended. As I approached a display, I recognized the photo of a house. Of course, it was a house in the Roma neighborhood, located not far from Plaza Rio de Janeiro. Beside it there were photos of Kisch with famous people of the time: Diego Rivera, José Clemente Orozco,

Carlos Chávez, Pablo Neruda, Dolores del Río; but beside them were a hodgepodge of international celebrities of every stripe: Buster Keaton, the wonderful Paulette Goddard, Orson Welles, Prince Drohojowski, the Soviet ambassador, Louis Jouvet, Jules Romains, Anna Seghers, and many other faces. Very elegant people beside intellectuals dressed in proletarian-looking jackets, actors, writers, communist leaders, countesses and princesses, Mexican intellectuals, Hollywood luminaries. A world of highly contrasting shades brought together in Mexico by the war. I can only imagine the degree of confusion such a divine galaxy of stars must have caused in a city as provincial as Mexico was at the time. A non-stop comedy of errors.

19 NOVEMBER
I entered the Café Slavia, sat at a table with a view of the river and the castle, and began to write my novel. I made a rough outline of the first five chapters.

20 NOVEMBER
Last night, I finished the full outline of my novel, and today I started filling in some details and incidents of some chapters. I need to decide the tone, the temperature of the language. But the heavy work, the novel's carpentry, is already there. I made very detailed notes for one of the chapters: the scene in which Martínez, the blackmailer, seeks information about the past of the German Hispanist, Ida Werfel, and her family. Ida tells him about *The Garden of Juan Fernández* by Tirso de Molina, in which no one is who they are believed to be; the blackmailer takes it personally, an oblique reference to his secret activities, and flies into a fit of rage that drives him to the brink of madness...

No one wants to talk about the German woman who lives locked in an apartment that has become a pigsty. "How do you expect me to know who he is? Do you think I'm the phonebook or something?" says Aunt Hedwig gruffly to the protagonist. "I haven't wanted to know anything more about that building since I left it," Delfina Uribe replies. "And you, what right do you have to question me?" Pedrito Balmorán shouts. "With all due respect, my rule is never to interfere in the lives of the tenants," the doorman replies.

19 DECEMBER

Everything is working out so well for me, the novel is moving along so quickly that I fear it's nothing more than an outbreak of graphomania. Tomorrow, I'll start working on the chapter on Delfina Uribe.

25 DECEMBER

The structure is very simple. Gogol used it in *Dead Souls*: a stranger arrives at a place and begins to visit different people one by one to address a particular topic. The detective novel has used it almost from its beginning; many of the Agatha Christie novels are structured this way. Ambler's splendid novel *The Mask of Dimitrios* is the perfect model. In the detective novel, the character who undertakes this journey and convinces people that they must open the door and answer his questions is a police officer or a private detective. Ambler uses a novelist who, if I remember correctly, is also a journalist. This makes his intrusion into private spaces and other people's lives seem normal. I thought my character would be a journalist, then I turned him into a historian who's researching a particular period: the World War as seen from Mexico.

1984

17 FEBRUARY

I spend hours reviewing the volumes of photos by the Casasola brothers in the embassy library. I'm able to see what people wore to the races, to the opera or, simply, to walk down the street. The entire *Who's Who* of the period appears in these books. This allows me to visualize the characters.

17 JUNE (IN MOJÁCAR)

I've been in Mojácar for two weeks. I'm working from morning to night. I think that what breathes life into the novel is kind of cheerful expressionism, if such an expression is possible, resulting from many years of parodic games, improvisations, and a caricatured invention of reality practiced with Luis Prieto and Carlos Monsiváis; but also from certain effects from American movies of the thirties and forties, especially those by Lubitsch, and the later Italian movies, Fellini above all; from the constant reading of plays and their application in the construction of dialogue, as well as certain devices from opera in the creation of staging; the relationship between movement and the grouping of characters (solos, duets, quartets, with or without choruses, etc.) is also operatic. I should also cite the impulse born of a genre that I love, the comedy of errors, those by Tirso and Shakespeare, especially, and in the novel *Our Mutual Friend* by Dickens.

24 JUNE

I don't think there will be the slightest doubt in the reader's mind that the plot revolves around a settling of accounts between the various

Mexican fascist groups during the days immediately following the official declaration of war. The character Briones is a spent cartridge. He's trapped, doomed before the fact. What remains unclear—but the lack of clarity, the gap in the story, seems necessary to me—is his past in Berlin. The death of his first wife, for example, the agreements he reached in Germany, and with whom, before returning to Mexico. Should I allude more openly to his sexual impotence so that the reader will begin to question the ghostly aspect of their married life? What role does the Jewish doctor, whose ex-wife, also Jewish, Briones ends up marrying, play? But these, in my judgment, are matters for another novel.

26 JUNE

My stay in Mojácar and the novel are finished. Its title: *El desfile del amor* (Love's Parade). Day after tomorrow, I'll be in Barcelona to hand it over to Jorge Herralde at Anagrama.[12] From there, I'll fly to Prague where I'll await, terrified, if there is a finding, the jury's verdict.

---

12 Publisher Jorge Herralde is the founder of the prestigious publishing house Editorial Anagrama and namesake of the Herralde Novel Prize, which the novel Pitol references here would win that same year. The prize, which is awarded to an unpublished text and includes publication, has been responsible for launching numerous literary careers. Subsequent winners include Roberto Bolaño, Enrique Vila-Matas, and Juan Villoro. —*Trans.*

CHARMS

As is known, a charm is an object or animal to which supernatural properties are attributed, beneficial to whomever possesses it.

I do not own anything to which I could honestly ascribe the qualities of a charm, much less one that might have protected me throughout my life. Outside of a few pictures and some books, nothing in my house comes from my childhood, adolescence, or my early youth. I have had paintings that I got rid of, not unlike someone who frees himself of a heavy burden, but with very little emotion. I was fortunate during my travels to find some bibliographic gems, and I also ended up getting rid of those. I have lived in many cities, which involves changing residences frequently; only once did I feel regret when leaving one. Perhaps I have enjoyed the kind of instability I was living, and the huckster-like pleasure of getting rid of my things. I only keep letters, but I do not attribute charm status to them.

I would love for Sacho, a dog I worship, to be my charm; unfortunately, he is not. When he walks up to me, I see in his eyes that I am his, the only powerful and absolute charm he has known in his life. I have collected and sometimes bought small stones, amber and jade beads, whose subsequent loss for a few days made me feel vulnerable to the dangers of the world. But such a feeling soon fades. So, I used to believe in their protective power, but not in excess. Where I glimpse a higher power beyond all reason is in reading. If I receive good news while reading a certain book, it will never lose its magnetic power or its expiatory capacity; so, on the eve of a trip, awaiting an important decision or the news of an X-ray, for example, I must necessarily repeat the readings that have already proved their virtues. My four decisively propitiatory books are: Borges's *The Aleph*; *The Duenna* by Richard Sheridan; and *The Court of Carlos IV* and *The Baggage of King Joseph* by Benito Perez Galdós.

Similarly, I have eliminated books whose reading coincided with a piece of devastating news, a serious setback, or the announcement of a necessary surgery. Thus I have lost books that otherwise would have seemed impossible to let go of. In any event, I consider it fortunate that lightning has not struck those writers who are very important to me: Cervantes, Rulfo, Sterne, or Henry James—that is, those without whom it would be torture to live. This adds to the frequent reading of my favorite authors a trembling uncertainty, a chill, an intensity of emotion, in the face of the terrifying fear that something nefarious might happen during their reading—that a fax might arrive unexpectedly, a phone call, a visitor with horrible news—and that I might be forced to say goodbye to them forever.

Xalapa, February 1996

READINGS

THE GREAT THEATER OF THE WORLD

The events described in *The Court of Carlos IV* take place in the year 1807. Galdós, through Gabriel Araceli, the narrator-protagonist of the first series of the *National Episodes*, allows himself to begin the story with an event that transpired two years before: the premiere of Leandro Fernández de Moratín's comedy, *The Maidens' Consent*. Araceli, in fact, acknowledges his participation in the performance that tarnishes the process of personal dignification in which Galdós has consciously and tenaciously implicated him.

The historical event depicted in the Episode involves a palace plot hatched by the Prince of Asturias against his parents, the King and Queen. Delaying this account in order to recreate the rather droll circumstances of a theater performance might seem disproportionate and even incongruous. And, yet, it is not. The novel's architecture requires the initial appearance of a dramatic scene that insinuates the interplay between life—as everyday reality or historical fact—and the theater. The novel thus opens with the premiere of a work that endeavored to change Spanish theater, to free it from the extravagances that plagued it and to introduce, at last, dramatic precepts and a didactic and moral zeal. An effort that, from the beginning, was opposed by old playwrights, actors, and in large part by the audience, who considered a theater based on rules to be a foreign imposition—French, for added insult!—an affront not only to their theatrical tastes and preferences but also to national sentiment. The very idea of subjecting the theater to rules, "the dramatic unities" of place, time and action—catchphrases that few were able to understand and, therefore, were interpreted in the most outlandish ways—was an outrage. The French were different, this was well known. Let them keep their Corneille and Racine and their exacting rules! That Lope de Vega had not allowed himself to be inveigled by such nonsense made him far superior to the foreigners. That the unities came from France made the affront even more visceral. To establish a set of symmetries, Galdós closes *The Court of Carlos IV* with a representation of *Othello* in a palace theater, a rather free Spanish translation of a French variation of Shakespeare's play, a piece absolutely foreign to any of those precepts "obsequiously obeyed" by the Frenchified Moratín. The tale opens and closes framed by two theatrical performances. But there's more. Some of the actors who stage *Othello* are professionals (including one who existed in real life: the great Isidoro Máiquez) who belonged to the renowned company of the Teatro del Príncipe; others are aristocrats who were acting aficionados. There are love affairs between the nobility and members of the theatrical world, scenes of jealousy, intrigue, and heinous acts of revenge that, from beginning to end, imbue this Episode with an intense theatrical coloring. If the actors are performing all along, the members of the court who have temporarily joined them do so even more.

Gabriel Araceli, whom readers met in *Trafalgar*, the first Episode of the series, has undergone visible changes in his attitude and lifestyle.

He has awakened, sharpened his wit, and is much more aware of himself as an individual. The pretensions of the courtly city and, above all, his daily interaction with actors have given him a presence he could have hardly acquired in Vejer, the small Andalusian town where we left him. Araceli believes that he has had an exceptional run of luck; shortly after arriving in Madrid, dogged by hunger and difficulties of an unspecified nature, he manages to enter the service of Pepa González, an actress widely celebrated in Madrid for her talent, wit, and, above all, her beauty. During discreet soirées at his mistress's home, Gabriel attends not only to people of the theater but also to more illustrious personages who, it appears, are unable to find either the happiness or informality that reign in the actors' homes or in other places, to which they sometimes refer, quietly of course, that attract the cream of Madrid's demimonde, where knives are brandished when least expected and singing and dancing are abruptly interrupted, transforming the *tertulia* into a raucous free-for-all.

It is not surprising that because of his connection to theater people and their coterie Gabriel Araceli might at times escape the role assigned to him by Galdós: that of the exemplar of virtues of a ruling class that, out of nowhere, was destined to occupy the space that the nobility had begun to lose. From his youth, Gabriel, whom military honors would soon transform into a member of the new redemptive class, was to represent the ideals of the new society that was taking shape and be the champion of unimpeachable morals. That burden, similar to that which weighed on the "positive hero" of the ideological literature of the twentieth century, tends to diminish in some episodes his verisimilitude as the protagonist, and strips him of the essential inner life necessary to become an entirely convincing character.

But the boundless energy of the social fabric that surrounds him saves him from becoming a mechanical doll. Galdós endows him with keen powers of observation, a facility for establishing relationships between characters and situations, the qualities necessary for the proper development of a novel, apt for enriching its dramatic moments, ennobling the heroic ones, and heightening the joyous ones. All this at the cost of suppressing in large part his life of instinct.

In *The Court of Carlos IV*, Gabriel experiences moments of joyful rebellion against the demiurge. It must not be forgotten that he is in the prime of his life, moves in a social circle free of rigor, and carries himself with great ease in settings where aristocrats, actors, and even less reputable characters are accustomed to exchanging partners. If in the first chapters we find Gabriel chastely in love with a sweet neighbor, a young seamstress, we can also imagine him as the possible future lover of a great lady of the Court, a beautiful countess of exceptional powers at Palace with whom he dreams of repeating that infamous story whose protagonists are the Queen María Luisa de Parma and Manuel Godoy, her minister, whom she plucked out of a barracks and transformed into the most powerful man in the kingdom. Gabriel has become so independent of the fate imposed on him by his creator that, now blinded by the beauty of the supreme Amaranta whose "ideal and stately beauty roused a strange emotion akin to sadness,"[13] as her adolescent lover describes her with happy intuition, he embarks on an adventure that overtakes, disillusions, and humiliates him, but that provides him a unique view of the world from above, of its unprecedented powers and also—alas!—its secret vulnerability.

---

13 Translated by Clara Bell

If *Trafalgar* constitutes an initiation test under the sign of the Epos, *The Court of Carlos IV* will place before our hero another, more difficult, kind of test. Gabriel has penetrated the world of fiction with weapons and heroic deeds; he has yet to discover other scenarios where battles are fought in secret and surreptitiously, battles that possess another dimension and are fraught with traps and unknown risks. Araceli enters a minefield, the same one that members of the royal family and their closest retinue tread.

Gabriel will walk away from this Episode more cautious than from other apparently more dangerous ones, like the heroic military sieges and memorable battles. Here, the plot flows through two parallel channels: a public one—the conspiracy of the Prince of Asturias, the future Fernando VII, to murder his mother and dethrone his father; and a private one—a relationship of love and jealousy, whose threads have been cleverly woven to lead to a crime of passion. The two plots continuously intertwine and support each other. The public one is an affair of State; the private one, which gives the story its true body, functions through a mechanism widely used in Renaissance drama; we find it in several of Shakespeare's comedies, many of Lope's and Calderon's, and almost obsessively in Tirso: Pepilla Isidoro loves González Máiquez, who doesn't even notice her. Máiquez loves the Duchess Lesbia, the Queen's lady in waiting and secret agent of the Prince of Asturias, who despises him. Lesbia loves Don Juan de Mañara, a handsome officer of the King's guard and also agent of the Prince of Asturias, who is deceiving her with a wench from the slums of Madrid. Everyone is jealous of everyone. Two of the characters from the romantic entanglement are already embroiled in the Palace plot. The Countess Amaranta, who neither loves nor is loved by anyone, participates in a scheme to punish Lesbia's disloyalty. The fake knife with which Máiquez, in the role of Othello, will punish the wantonness of Desdemona, played by Lesbia, will be replaced at the last moment by a real one that will be plunged into the heroine's chest. At that moment, Gabriel will act with great courage and race to prevent the crime.

The tone of the Episode is unmistakably Goyaesque. It could not be otherwise. The very title recalls Goya's most celebrated painting, *The Family of Carlos IV*. Goya was the official court painter of the Crown. In that role, he painted a series of portraits of Carlos IV and the Queen María Luisa, of Fernando as Prince of Asturias and as King of Spain, of the rest of the *infantes*, the royal children, the large canvas on which the entire family appears, as well as a remarkable portrait of Godoy. The actor Isidoro Máiquez was also painted by Goya; his portrait hangs today in the Museo del Prado, near the King and Queen and the *infantes*. Amaranta, in a fit of capriciousness and defiance, had Goya paint her nude, which leads us immediately to associate her with *The Nude Maja*. The curtains for the performance of Othello, we are told, were also painted by Goya. The Aragonese painter is present everywhere and at all times.

A powerful and perhaps more troubling referent than the plot itself is represented by the distant, and for the majority of Spaniards, blurry, figure of Napoleon Bonaparte, whose army enters Spain the day a dinner is held at the home of Pepilla González, where comedians and courtiers meet to work out the final details of the performance of *Othello*. No one in the course of the Episode knows for sure what Napoleon proposes upon entering Spain, and each person attempts to reconcile that enigma in the way that best suits their interests.

"Someone who performs or plays a role in theaters is commonly known as a *comediante*," states the first edition of the Dictionary of the Royal Spanish Academy. The *comediante* appears to be someone other than who he in fact is; his function is to portray someone else. One day he pretends to be the king, and the next day he is a laborer, saint, or ship's captain. That ability to pretend, that ability to create ecstasy out of nothing—shipwrecks, love affairs, dethronements—tends sometimes to filter in a perverse way into the *comediante's* personal life. Isidoro Máiquez, for example, during the rehearsals for *Othello*, becomes delirious; jealousy has overtaken him, fueled, among other reasons, by malicious anonymous letters informing him that he has been nothing but a whim to "his Duchess," a common plaything of a refined lady who, incidentally, has replaced him with Don Juan de Mañara, a gentleman in his own right. In the drama's final scene, Máiquez's personality has vanished; he has been entirely transformed into a crazed Moor, a murderer. The version represented differs in some aspects from the original drama. The proof of Desdemona's infidelity is found in an impassioned letter that she has supposedly written to her lover. An anonymous hand has forged her handwriting and signature. Faced with this evidence, Othello can no longer doubt her guilt. The letter seals the couple's fate. Desdemona must inevitably die at the hands of the Moor. A letter in which Lesbia attempts to assuage Mañara's jealousy has fallen into the hands of someone intent on punishing her. She reprimands him for daring to imagine that a woman of her stature might be interested in a ridiculous little comedian. Someone has removed the paper that Othello must read before the prostrate body of Desdemona, replacing it with the letter in which Lesbia ridicules him to reassure Juan de Mañara, and that same someone has replaced the stage dagger with a real knife. The Marquesa's die is cast: she will die that night before her lover's eyes, before those of her ferocious husband, and those of the very distinguished audience made up of the kingdom's great nobility. Only Araceli's timely intervention manages to avert the disaster.

Gabriel will discover from personal experience that the same functions of representation and the same to-and-fro between being and seeming that so unsettles comedians is repeated at Court, only there the reality of being gradually atrophies, while the function of seeming, of pretending, grows disproportionately larger. Court life requires a permanent ability to make believe. Its ceremonies become a never-ending performance that demands more complex dramatic talents and more stylized techniques than those required on the stage. One acts there not only in the performance of protocol, but also in the royal chambers, in the visits that the courtiers pay to each other in their respective palaces, in the theater, the bullfights, in walks in the countryside and, above all, in the passageways where they pretend to be who they are not, when they attend *de ocultis* the dinners of the fashionable comedians and bullfighters of the day, the popular dances and festivals, or even less desirable establishments where it was possible to rub elbows with the picaresque of every stripe that flourished in the slums of Madrid.

Living at the service of comedians or being a page in the palace precincts means participating in a perpetual representation, pretending to perform one activity when, in fact, one performs another. In the first chapter of *The Court of Carlos IV*, the young Araceli describes a heterogeneous list of duties that he must fulfill that constitutes in itself a delightful passage of local color. Among them, there are two that are mere affectation: "To walk out on the square of Santa Ana, pretending to look into the shops, but in reality listening with covert attention to what was being said in the knots that collected there of actors or dancers, and trying to discover what those of la Cruz theatre had to say against those of el Príncipe"; the other: "To call every day at the house of Isidoro Máiquez under pretext of asking him some question with reference to the dresses in the play; but, in reality, to ascertain whether a certain person happened to be with him—whose name I reserve for the present." That is, to feign one interest when the real interest is another, a quite despicable one, I might add; to hear what is being said on the street only to repeat it later to a master; to ask something trivial about a garment when in fact the intention is to discover who is visiting whom, how those being observed carry themselves during the visit, what they talk about. They are of course the activities of an informant, a cop, a spy. Another mandatory activity was "to frequent the gallery of the theatre de la Cruz in order to hiss *The Maidens' Consent*, a play that my mistress held in at least as much aversion as the others by the same author"—a provocative activity that complemented that of being a spy. The role of a page at court was very similar, exalted not only by the majesty of the settings and the rank of the protagonists but also by the cruelty of the measures the page must employ. The Countess Amaranta casts a spell over the callow Andalusian whom she invites to be her servant. She offers him the acquisition of a bright future as long as he becomes her slave. His astonishment will disappear within a few days, as soon as the Countess gives him his first instructions. To begin with, she will place him in another home from where he must inform her of everything that happens. Even if this arrangement shocks him, he will continue to be her page. Confident of the spell she exerts over the boy who was plucked from González's home and carried off to the Escorial, Amaranta launches a far-reaching plan that will solve her problems forever. His role would consist of observing from behind tapestries or curtains, listening behind doors, winning the hearts of the handmaids of the ladies-in-waiting and of the ladies themselves, to obtain secrets of all kinds and become a major power in the Palace. By then, the Countess would secure for him letters patent of nobility; once titled, and with her help, he would enter the Royal Guard. Her power would become extraordinary: "A guardsman has indeed an advantage which princes themselves have not, for while these know nothing beyond the palace they live in—which is the reason why hardly any king governs well—the soldier is equally familiar with the palace and the street, the folks outside as well as those within; and this more general knowledge enables him to make himself useful to all parties and to pull the wires of a vast number of springs. A man who knows what he is about here is more powerful than all the potentates on earth; he can make his influence silently felt to the uttermost ends of the kingdom without its ever being suspected by those who give themselves such airs, calling themselves ministers and councilors."

The fate assigned to Gabriel Araceli, that of becoming one of the future redeemers who would reclaim Spain, who have arisen from almost nothing—or, in his case, from absolutely nothing—prevents him from accepting the career of indignities proposed by the Countess. Again and again, he will place ahead of her and other members of the nobility the obligations that his honor and dignity require, even if at every turn he is met with hurtful and bitter comments in return. Honor and dignity are attributes characteristic of a gentleman, not of an insignificant louse who dares to claim them for himself. However, unwittingly and by chance, Gabriel will continue to find himself in situations that will allow him to hear terrible secrets, compromising not only for certain people but also for the affairs of the Crown; he will learn the contents of letters and messages that could cost very important persons their life and liberty; he will witness scenes concerning the security of the kingdom. It goes without saying that Galdós will not allow his creation to obtain any personal benefit from such secrets.

Many of Gabriel's duties in service to Pepita González were, not surprisingly, closely related to the theater. One, already mentioned, was to campaign against *The Maidens' Consent;* another, "to accompany her to the theatre, where it was my part to hold the sceptre and crown till she came off after the second scene of the second act in *The False Czar of Muscovy* to reappear transformed into a queen, to the utter confusion of Orloff and the magnates who had supposed her to be an itinerant tart-seller." It was also his duty "every afternoon to take a pot of leftover stew, crusts of bread, and other scraps of food to Don Luciano Francisco Comella, a dramatist whose plays until recently had been much celebrated, who was always starving in a house on the Calle de la Berenjena, with his hunchback daughter, who helped him in his dramatic work." Galdós digresses at every turn on theatrical topics, sometimes insignificant, others of greater importance, such as the battle waged by the neoclassicists against the verbal diarrhea and tacky scenery of the theater of the time, a trend led precisely by Comella, the author, among other rubbish, of *All Lost in a Day for a Mad and Blind Love* and *The False Czar of Muscovy*, which had earned Pepita standing ovations in the past. This *astracanada* theater felt threatened by the loathsome dramatic unities postulated by an equally loathsome Moratín. But let us return to the first question: why begin the history of the palace conspiracy with the premiere of *The Maidens' Consent*, which took place two years before?

Miguel de Cervantes scatters throughout the *Quixote* a wide range of authors' names and book titles. This reference is not intended to boast of the author's culture. These cultural references are there because they play a decisive role in the narrative structure: they support the protagonist's motives and the mad ideas; they determine the profile of other characters; and they allow stylized mirror games, such as comparing a work in progress: the very history of the hidalgo of La Mancha, to its fake derivations, such as Avellaneda's apocryphal Quixote. Playing with other books infuses a new style into the art of storytelling and demonstrates the relationship of the novel with the Renaissance culture that surrounds it. Cervantes's eagerness to intertextualize had few successors in Spanish narrative. Galdós is one of the few writers in our language who employed and renewed this device. The war Luciano Comella and his followers wage against Fernández de Moratín is without a doubt the transplantation of a struggle between the old and the new that is beginning to insinuate itself in Spain. The brutal struggle between playwrights is a kind of first call in the debate between a stagnant and incoherent culture and the effort to establish the order and the task of tidying up in every corner of the kingdom. The fact that Moratín's work deals with the education of society, and women in particular, appears as a response to that frenzied court where the majority of its members are not educated at all, and where the only roads available to arrive at a goal are pretense and intrigue.

That exercise of intertextuality may precede the same diegesis of the *Episodes.* The device allows Galdós to avoid sinking into long didactic explanations, the very kind that renders so many of his contemporaries' works unreadable. By listing Pepilla González's readings, her omissions and literary shortcomings, Galdós is able to provide us, for example, with perfect subtlety, the image of her person, more powerfully than would have been possible in a store of pages that contain an infinite number of details about her habits, virtues, and weaknesses. Gabriel Araceli comments—and here we sense again the voice of the former narrator, not that of the page, who could scarcely translate his feelings in such a learned way—that the actress was not known for her good literary taste, among other reasons because whoever approached her always had Ovid and Boccaccio in mind rather than Aristotle. A remarkable way of saying everything, without going into details.

Ortega y Gasset points out in his essay on Goya how decisive the popular veneer was for Spanish culture in the eighteenth century: "In the second half of that century the masses were housed in life forms of their own invention, with an enthusiasm aware of itself and with ineffable delight, without looking sideways at the aristocratic customs in anxious flight toward them. Meanwhile, the upper classes were only happy when they abandoned their own ways, and they became saturated with plebeianism."

Regarding that plebeianism alluded to by Ortega, Carmen Martín Gaite, in *Love Customs in Eighteenth-Century Spain*, studied the changes that took places in Spanish society at the end of the eighteenth century due to the introduction into court life of traditions and customs viewed until then with contempt by people of higher rank. Martín Gaite amply illustrates this desire for debasement to which Ortega alluded.

THE ART OF FLIGHT

We are introduced to a world in which ladies and gentlemen competed to speak, dress, and behave like their maids or footmen, with the relaxation of customs that this implied. Jean-François de Bourgoing, a French traveler in Spain, writes: "There are, among both sexes, persons of distinguished rank, who seek their models among the heroes of the populace, who imitate their dress, manners, and accent, and are flattered when it is said of them, 'He is very like a *majo*.'— 'One would take her for a *maja*.'"[14] And other authors of the time lament that "ladies and even the *señoras* of the highest birth, have been transformed into so many other *majas* in their dress, their conversation, and their manners as to be indistinguishable from that despicable class of people [...] and they have reached such a point in the degradation of their respective graces, lordships, and excellencies that when they have a cigar in their mouths they resemble even more the most vulgar women of this low caste [...]. In general, all those fops eager to practice their *majismo*, to be seen on the Pradera de San Isidro, and learn from their footmen the *jota*, the *guaracha*, the *bolero*, in short, their songs and dances, boasted of courting an actress." Another traveler picks up on the rumors that were spreading through Madrid about the Duchess of Alba, advanced in her desire for unprejudiced modernity: "Several years past," they say, "she had already put aside any appearance of dignity to the point of going out in search of adventure in the public squares, her lack of scruples reaching such a degree that she even counted toreros among her lovers. At midnight, they would gather in the middle of the Prado to have a *tertulia* and play music."

The plebeianization of the aristocracy covers an unfilled spiritual space. It was a means of escape from the ailing morality in use;

---

14 Translated by Maria G. Tomsech

perhaps also a vital response to the apparent backwardness before an enlightened Europe, and, above all, before the greatness of a lost past. That taste for popular customs and expressions becomes the Hispanic embodiment of Volksgeist (the spirit of the people) celebrated by the German Romantics and disseminated at a rapid pace across the rest of Europe. The greatest exponent of that popular spirit in Spanish art was Francisco de Goya. It could be said that if the Volksgeist produced an immense figure in the art of Europe, it was precisely that of Goya. The Spanish artist painted the populace in a thousand ways, as mere ornamentation, with an almost Arcadian tone, in the tapestries for the Royal Palace, as a collective hero in *The Second of May 1808*, as a tragic character in *The Third of May 1808*, as a demonic protagonist in many of his witches' covens, as maker of a thousand disasters in his etchings, and as magnificent representative of the absurd in an extraordinary painting, the absurdity of absurdities, carnival itself—Bakhtin in the raw!—which is that small glory called *Burial of the Sardine*.

The aristocracy assumed *majismo* in an absolutely theatrical way; pretending to be what it was not, making daily rituals a form of spectacle. Living in the theater and dramatizing life to the unthinkable. For many of the characters in *The Court of Carlos IV*, the descent among the rabble is like taking the waters: a powerful source of life. Among them, the Queen María Luisa, no less! And the Duchess Lesbia and Don Juan de Mañara and, on a smaller scale and more in the past, the Countess Amaranta.

If Galdós lingers on Moratín's *The Maidens' Consent*, it is not due to any special appreciation for his prescripts, which he never accepted, but to moral imperatives. For the young liberal writer who undertakes in 1873 the task of fictionalizing a century and a half of Spanish history, that is, after the Prim Revolution and on the eve of the First Republic, educating Spain marks the beginning of regeneration; once placed in this terrain, the education of women seems essential to the efficient running of the country he believed to be on the horizon. *The Maidens' Consent* was one of the first calls to educate young women and a warning against the education in convents, where pretending was considered an ideal standard of social co-existence. Moreover, the implementation of a neoclassical theater with its unities of place, time, and action suddenly made the theater of Luciano Comella obsolete with all its disparate theatrical effects, its booming titles, its historical improbability, and its cheap sentimentality. The collapse of this false, ludicrous ostentation and the return of dignity to theatrical language must have seemed to Galdós like signs that were already pointing to the mature and industrious Spain that he desired.

In fact, this new theater that excited a handful of spectators and terrorized the old guard had a short life in Spain. Alfonso Reyes reminds us that Spanish humanism has always distinguished itself because of its aversion to a strict adherence to convention. Therefore, no great work of art in Spain has been born of narrow precepts. Galdós himself, however much sympathy he might have felt for Moratín and his didactic theater, places in the mouth of Araceli, in passing, a comment that to us seems like an unrepressed sigh of relief. Once again, the speaker is not the young page who was the protagonist of the story but the old Don Gabriel de Araceli who, recalling Moratín's importance during his time, wrote: "No one could deny him the honor of having revived the true spirit of Spanish comedy, and *The Young Maidens' Consent* has always seemed to me a work of great genius in spite of the part I took at the first performance of that play—as the reader may remember," concluding, "He died in 1828, but his letters and papers reveal no trace of his having known the works of Byron, Goethe, or Schiller; he went to his grave believing in Goldoni as the greatest poet of his day." A superb way to dot the i's and cross the t's because, until recently, the stature attributed to the Venetian playwright in Spain was more or less the same as that enjoyed by the brothers Álvarez Quintero.

In Galdós, exercises of intertextuality and meta-fiction complement and constitute each other. In *The Court of Carlos IV*, a complex and almost imperceptible game between Gabriel Araceli, the very young central character, and the same Gabriel sixty-something years later as he is writing his memoirs, takes place. The circumstances viewed through the eyes of the young narrator are recounted with the voice of someone who is living amazing times. On those occasions the space is covered with a bright light and that brightness endows the page's movements with an exceptional agility. Gabriel's complicated maneuvers to dodge the weighty commissions of comedians and aristocrats, and finally, of constables, the speed of his movements, his personal grace, the repetitive game of hide-and-seek that allows him to survive risks, inevitably evoke the quintessential page, the marvelous Cherubino, less Beaumarchais' than Da Ponte's and Mozart's. The author's sporadic interventions, in the voice of the former page turned prosperous octogenarian, exist to correct or broaden assertions made by the young protagonist, if not to inform the reader about events following the period during which the Episode takes place. In 1805, the year in which *The Maidens' Consent* was published, Moratín was a living author, and even lived twenty years more in exile in Bordeaux; the judgment regarding his ignorance of Byron, Goethe, and Schiller constitutes one of the additions of the old Araceli to the past. The young Gabriel would not have been able, for obvious reasons, to make that comment. The use of more or less disguised meta-fictional techniques provide a ripple that animates the story without creating unnecessary difficulties.

In *The Court of Carlos IV*, the war between the dramatic schools is ubiquitous and permanent. The same happens with the *comediantes*; a sworn enmity reigns between those from the theater of Caños de Peral, those from the de la Cruz, and those from the del Príncipe. In the Palace, something worse is taking place: the fight to the death between the supporters of the Crown Prince and those of his royal parents. The majority of the courtiers are loyal to the Prince's cause, while the group favorable to the King and Queen diminishes. The palace residents, both those of the noble floors as well as those on the lower floors, are protagonists of an internal struggle. Intrigue flourishes everywhere; the hatreds are Spanish, that is, frightening; only blood seems to be able to appease them. Not long after this Episode begins we meet Lesbia and Amaranta at the dinner of Pepa González; upon their arrival they pretend to be on good terms, but the allusion to the palace dispute is enough to cause the masks to fall and the hatred to present itself in its fullness.

The genre of the historical novel that Galdós writes often acquires an antiheroic tone. The characters are never the noteworthy protagonists of history, but rather everyday individuals who, for some reason, are positioned at a given time beside the noteworthy and are witness to their misfortunes. Important historical events occupy much less space in these narratives than human conflicts. The established interrelationship between real and fictional characters demands of

Galdós a special novel structure, to which he must have arrived by pure instinct. The architecture of some of the Episodes is superior to that of his thesis novels written during the same period—*Doña Perfecta, Gloria, The Family of León Roch*—in which the stories possess a prefabricated and stiff quality, and where the action is reduced to a succession of almost always predictable scenes. In the majority of the *National Episodes*, the historical event is known only through the reflection projected onto the social swarm. Often that reflection illuminates incidental, almost faceless, characters who in a few sentences lend the requisite accuracy or inaccuracy to, and pass judgment on, the historical event; that participation, however, gives them a momentary face before returning to the shadows. Thanks to that wonderful institution known as the *tertulia*, the uniquely Spanish version of the *salon*, which is as vibrant as or more so than the street, history is reflected every night through a prism of a thousand faces. Everyone expresses and maintains an opinion, unleashes his passions, expresses his truth in a violently biased manner according to his stake in it, until suddenly all that remains of that historical event are words rendered unintelligible from constant rumination, quarter or half-truths, distorted shadows of great figures, faces in chiaroscuro, the suppuration of tumors of a society whose spokesmen have been, in appearance only, selected at random.

In addition to the conspiracy present in *The Court of Carlos IV*, there is another rather blurred event kept in the background: the march of Napoleon's troops into Spanish territory, an event that will condition the ten Episodes of the First Series in which Galdós proposes to give us the terrifying and exciting image of French intervention in Spain and the heroic *reconquista* of its sovereignty won by the Spanish people. Notwithstanding the magnificent epicness of the subject, the author seems to revel in an exaggerated lack of urgency in order to approach any historical record. Only from the twelfth chapter of *The Court* on do we witness Gabriel Araceli enter the Palace—that is, the court of Carlos IV. Throughout all the previous chapters, we have known the exacerbation of popular passion for the Prince, the general repudiation of the King and Queen and the immeasurable hatred for Godoy, the Prince of Peace, Prime Minister of the Kingdom, and favorite of the Queen. Fernando is vested with all conceivable virtues, and the King and Queen with vices and defects in abundance, and Godoy with all the ills of the troubled kingdom. Whether in the royal premises, the palaces of the nobility, or Madrid's most ramshackle cottages, the people yearn for change. Fernando's popularity is able to withstand all attacks. Once the conspiracy is discovered, and the Prince faces a possible death sentence, that popularity is transmuted into worship. After having confessed his participation in the frustrated crime, begged forgiveness from the King and Queen, sworn vows of repentance, and shamefully denounced several of his friends as the true conspirators, no one in Madrid is able to believe the news. In the mind of the people, there can be only two possibilities: either that ignoble confession bears at the bottom a forged signature or, if it is authentic, it must have been extracted from the barrel of a gun pointed at his chest. In this way, Fernando adds to his many honors already won another of overwhelming force: martyrdom. The news of the advance of French troops fills the Madrileños with joy; everyone assumes that Napoleon's intention is to rescue the Prince from the hands of his executioners and place the crown on his brow.

The morning that the news of the military invasion spreads, Araceli has gone out shopping for his mistress. Hans Hinterhäuser notes that the vitality of Galdosian characters crystallizes in not only an aesthetic but also a moral category. Gabriel's morning walk amply demonstrates this. Each of the acquaintances he encounters is convinced—as if having heard it from the most reliable of sources—that Napoleon and his myrmidons are advancing with the purpose of ridding Spain of all its woes. The dialogical carnival takes place, the triumph of heteroglossia; Galdós grants his creatures all the space they require, giving each of them a unique and unmistakable voice to express themselves freely. Both the *National Episodes* and the so-called Contemporary Novels share attributes that Bakhtin identifies in Dostoevsky when coining the terms polyphony and heteroglossia. "A plurality of independent and unmerged voices and consciousnesses, a genuine polyphony of fully valid voices is in fact the chief characteristic of Dostoevsky's novels."[15] The novels of Galdós's early period, written at the same time as the first two series of Episodes, represent, on the other hand, polyphonic negation; the protagonists do not participate of their own will, but rather recite a role dictated by the author. They are divided sharply into black and white, according to their political and religious convictions. The author manipulates them unscrupulously and does not allow them to develop. In the Episodes, however, perhaps because he considers them minor works, mere exercises for teaching national history, the freedom denied in those first "serial novels" is allowed.

If the *tertulia*—whether it takes place in a house, a casino, or a café—is the perfect venue for polyphonic flow to occur completely, the other is the street. Let us return to Gabriel's shopping excursion:

15 Translated by Caryl Emerson

an acquaintance of his confides to him that Napoleon has undertaken the conquest of Portugal to then give it to Spain, a country he loves, and, above all, to rid Spain of Godoy, "an impostor,
insolent, lustful, deceitful, and designing." A priest is sure that
Napoleon has taken this step to punish the excesses of Godoy against
the Church, and concludes that he will place the Prince of Asturias
on the throne to restore abused ecclesiastical rights in the Kingdom;
the playwright Luciano Francisco Comella, the unrivaled enemy of
any dramatic precept, swears that Napoleon is coming to do away with
Godoy, who could be forgiven for all his sins but never his protection
of bad poets, giving short shrift to good, national poets, Spaniards
like him, who did not accept that mishmash of ridiculous foreign
precepts with which Moratín and other gaiter-clad poetasters tried
to trick simpletons. Everyone vents his spleen. They agree on two
points: one, that Godoy was corrupt, wasteful, immoral, an influence
peddler, polygamist, enemy of the Church who, moreover, aspired
to sit on the throne of the kings of Spain; and, the other, that Spain
would only be happy and recover its past grandeur when the *infante*
Fernando took the crown. Gabriel only found one person, a modest
knife-grinder, who despised the delusions of the others. Neither the
King and Queen nor the Prince deserved his trust. "Napoleon," he
said, "would invade the kingdom, get rid of the parents and the son,
and put one of his relatives on the throne, as he had done in the
other countries he had conquered," words that produce in the page
the effect of an ice water bath. The drunkenness produced by the
collective rumor seemed to vanish.

As Amaranta's servant, who lodges at the Escorial, Gabriel witnesses
an extraordinary event. The day of his arrival he wanders the corridors

near his mistress's apartments in the interior of the Palace. He sees there an imposing procession returning the Prince to his room as a prisoner. The sepulchral chiaroscuro of that scene again evokes Goya.

Gabriel spends only three or four days in the Escorial—long enough to reveal to him part of the rich variety of human baseness, and for him to comprehend the foul air and minefield that are part and parcel of living off the royal family. His experience in Madrid had accustomed the young protagonist to comedians—their habits, their whims, and their weaknesses. He need only step foot in the Palace in order to witness scenes that exceed in theatricality those previously enjoyed in the theater. Except that the monarchs represented by Isidoro Máiquez seem much more dignified and majestic to him than the one who wears the true crown. The flesh and blood king turns out to be "of middle stature, thick-set with a small face and high color, and devoid of any single feature which could suggest a distinction imprinted by Nature on his physiognomy between a king of blue blood and a respectable grocer."

The scene in which Gabriel sees him for the first time constitutes the novel's climactic moment: the Crown Prince is being led by his father through a dark corridor dimly lit by a single candlestick. Accompanying the King and the Prince are palace guards. The conspiracy has been uncovered: Fernando has just given a statement and is led to his quarters, where he will remain from then on as a prisoner. "His anxious, gloomy face revealed the bitterness in his soul." A palace purge has followed the arrest of the Prince. No one feels safe in the royal premises, neither gentlemen nor ladies of the court, neither officers nor servants. Gabriel witnessed several spectacular arrests and senses fear and confusion in both courtiers

THE ART OF FLIGHT

and servants. Everything becomes fiction, pure theater; impure theater. The edifice of the State is about to collapse, but the King, as if he were aware of nothing, entertains himself in the hunt from morning to night at the royal reserves. No member of the family seemed to serve any purpose: a proclivity for laziness and a widely cultivated ignorance render them incapable of reacting to the storm that is brewing. Palace residents move incoherently, stunned by the Prince's confession and his betrayal. His only hope lies in the arrival of the French army, the resulting liberation of the Prince and his ascent to the throne. Hidden involuntarily behind a tapestry, Gabriel overhears a conversation between Amaranta and Queen María Luisa. The Queen implores her loyal maid to intervene with the Minister of Mercy and Justice so that Lesbia is not questioned. She knows too many secrets; she may implicate her. She may have kept letters and objects that can be presented as evidence. Her appearance in the case was to be avoided by all means necessary. Having forgotten briefly about the danger, they speak glibly about past trysts and the distribution of governmental posts or ecclesiastical benefices and sinecures. The Queen wants Godoy to grant a bishop's miter to the uncle of her youngest son's wet nurse; he is opposed for petty reasons, simply because the aforementioned uncle has been a contrabandist and is semiliterate. But she is going to pressure Godoy—she says boasting of her powers—to force him to sign the appointment; otherwise, the crown will refuse to ratify the secret treaty with France that would grant her favorite sovereignty over the Algarves, which the French have promised after they occupy and divide Portugal. Look, if you do not make Gregorilla's uncle a Bishop, we will not ratify the treaty, and you will never be King of the Algarves! Only a Queen could say such things.

A complex episode in the history of Spain plays out in the house of Carlos IV: a palace revolt, a frustrated parricide, Napoleonic troops advancing on national territory; the secret treaties with Napoleon have not been ratified. Danger lurks everywhere. Life at Court at times hangs in the balance. But in the den of the Grandees of Spain nothing seems to achieve greatness. The Queen amuses herself rambling about her love affairs, the hatred she feels for those who "slander" her, the machinations she must contrive to block the path of some ladies and gentlemen who support her son's cause, and the negotiations with her favorite. Her concept of justice slithers along the ground; the great qualities she recognizes in Caballero, the Minister of Mercy and Justice, her friend and ally, lie in his ability to conceal her indiscretions. "He is our great friend. Ever since he found a means of accusing and sending to prison the sentry and the civilian who recognized us when we went in masks to the fête of Santiago, I am greatly in his debt. Caballero does nothing but what we tell him; he is capable of making Lords of Appeal out of markers from the bullring if we ordered it. He is a capital fellow and does his duty with the docility that becomes a true minister. The poor man takes great interest in the welfare of the country." No heroics, no true agony can thrive in this world of frightened puppets, besotted and whimpering, lacking the slightest notion of State; the welfare of the kingdom, her Majesty believes, lies in incarcerating those who have discovered her presence in an inconvenient place, and in an obedient minister, a simple accomplice, who promptly obeys her wishes.

Gabriel contemplates the scene exactly as he might follow a performance from a box at the Teatro del Príncipe; because in *The Court of Carlos IV* the theater as world and the world as theater appear to be

THE ART OF FLIGHT

one and the same. Palace life is for him so dramatic, so theatricalized, that the boundaries between the real and the fictional, the realistic and the unreal, seem to constantly blend together. Situations that could be tragic with other characters the closer they get to the circle of Carlos IV and his favorites are highly ribald. The mechanism is one of farce with piquant details. The Queen is one of the targets at which they aim; popular fury against her is unanimous—for being a libertine, predatory, a fool, ridiculous, ugly. In that theater where Gabriel has appeared, the comments he overhears accentuate the comedic toy-like character that the royal family represents. A kitchen assistant reveals to him that the Queen's teeth are false, and she has to remove them to eat, and she doesn't allow anyone to see. "'You see,' the scullion went on, 'they are quite right in accusing the Queen of deceiving the people and trying to persuade them to believe the thing that is not. How can she expect her subjects to love a sovereign who wears other people's teeth?'"

The only mechanism that seems to sustain him and lend an appearance of life to that rusty building is intrigue. There is no one in Court who does not scheme, from the monarchs to their grooms. And this activity generates a vitality, fictitious perhaps, but effective. Gabriel discovers the strength of this practice by observing the machinations of his protector: "Amaranta was not merely a cunning and intriguing woman; she was intrigue incarnate; she was the very demon of palaces—that terrible spirit which makes history, with all her sense and dignity seem sometimes the genius of mystification and mistress of falsehood—that terrible spirit which has brought confusion on our race and made nations enemies—debasing monarchies and republics alike, and despotic governments no less than free ones.

She was the incarnation of that hidden machinery, of which the outer world knows nothing, but which reaches from the gates of a Palace to the King's chambers, and on whose springs, worked by a hundred hands, depend honors, dignities, nay, life itself; the noble blood of armies, and the glory of nations. Greed, bribery, injustice, simony, arbitrary and licentious authority…"

In this world where dignity and greatness are mere appearances, the desire to be someone grows stronger in Gabriel. They may scoff at his aspirations for rank and honor, but no one will stop him. Gabriel senses that he and those like him who were born and raised in the midst of the harshest reality will eventually survive the disaster. It will be they who steer the ship we see on the verge of capsizing. Galdós seems to give his hero wings in order to soar. Forty years later, when he writes the final Episodes, his vision will be more skeptical, but, at the same time, more certain.

Galdós anticipates a device that Franz Werfel will employ successfully in this century in *Juarez and Maximilian*, a play in which, from beginning to end, he was able to make the presence of the Mexican hero felt without his ever appearing on the scene. In each of the chapters of *The Court of Carlos IV* the name of the most powerful man in Spain is mentioned; he is damned and cursed forever; we know the places he visits, the comments he makes, when he arrives to the Palace, and even what he eats, but he never appears. He is an invisible man who for many years has pulled, at his discretion and pleasure, the strings of the kingdom only to become ensnared in the tangled web of his own making. His fate, like that of the King and Queen, like that of the Spain we visited, is sealed. The curtain is about to fall. Other dramas, comedies, and farces will be performed. Other characters will be the protagonists. Another chorus, riotous, monstrous and generous, naive and cunning, clueless, intuitive, manipulated, mean and tender, is about to enter the stage. Forever a giant. The Spanish people! In the Episodes that follow, their presence will be definitive.

Xalapa, September 1994

OUR CONTEMPORARY CHEKHOV

Cyril Connolly asserts that the writer must aspire to write a work of genius. Otherwise, he is lost. This preemptory requirement is, of course, stimulating, a crack of the whip to banish idleness, conformity, the temptation of easiness. But it must arrive when the time is right if he does not want to herd the sheep toward the wolf. Whosoever seeks his soul will lose it, say the Gospels. Did the young Joyce know as he was struggling with the *Dubliners* that *Ulysses* lay in his future? Were Mann and Kafka aware of what destiny held for them when they were writing their first stories? Did the young Cervantes, when writing his first lines of verse, which were presumably mediocre, imagine himself as the immortal author of the Spanish language? It occurs to me that one could interpret Connolly's assertion in a less dramatic way: Every writer should from the beginning remain faithful to his potential and try to refine it; have the greatest respect for language, keep it alive, update it if possible; not make concessions to anyone, least of all to power or to trends; and contemplate in his work the boldest challenges it is possible to conceive. At least that was the way Chekhov came to be the great writer he is. He wrote at first, when he noticed his facility for inventing stories, to earn money to support his family;

it took a few years to discover that being a writer required more than relating a funny anecdote or a dramatic episode. Daily practice made him aware of the possibilities of the craft. He was always faithful to his intuition, exceptionally demanding of himself, indifferent to the judgment of others, alien to any temptation of power, to all forms of excess or falsehood, and indefatigable in the pursuit of a personal narrative method. As a result, he bequeathed to humanity a handful of brilliant works.

The Seagull marks the transformation of the contemporary theater. This is a beautiful and moving work that no one was able to understand in its first performances. It breaks sharply with Russian tradition. And not just with Russian tradition; today's theater, especially the Anglo-Saxon, is still in its debt. In the play, which is set at the end of the nineteenth century, there is a young poet, Treplieff, who does his utmost to create a new literary language; Treplieff belongs to the symbolist literary school. Chekhov makes use of the classical device of theater within theater, and includes in *The Seagull* the performance of a monologue by Treplieff, a verbal delirium, a distortion that is not a recreation but a parody of symbolist language. If Chekhov's sympathy for the young poet and his plight are evident from the beginning to the end of the work, it is also true that his literary activity is treated with a slight disdain. A fragment of the monologue is included in the middle of the first act of *The Seagull*. A beautiful and aspiring actress, who embodies the "Spirit of the Universe," delights in informing us that all living beings have been extinct for several thousand years and that the earth has not given birth to any new species. The Spirit of the Universe opens her mouth only every one hundred years to reveal the relentless struggle waged for centuries against the Devil, the King of Matter. She is convinced that the day will come when she will be able to defeat him. "After a fierce and obstinate battle," the Spirit exclaims, "that could last many millennia, I will conquer the source of the Forces of Matter. Matter and Spirit will merge in glorious harmony, the earth will populate itself again, and the Kingdom of Universal Freedom will be born." The monologue, as the reader has probably noticed, is tedious, naïve, and prosy. The constant use of abstractions, the contempt for real people and their trivial problems, the search for infinity, all correspond to Chekhov's notion of symbolist literature. It is well known that he detested romanticism and distrusted the new school that was beginning to flourish in Russia. He saw symbolists as a new incarnation of the romantics. The symbolists never forgave Chekhov for that parody. He was considered an insignificant writer of local customs. He, however, considered himself a realist. Words like "realism" and "realist" are often discredited today; they are applied cautiously and rather derisively, and leave a sense of imprecision and exude an odor of vulgarity. In a conversation with Serena Vitale, Viktor Shklovsky declared shortly before he died: "The truth is I have never been able to understand what the term realism means, and I'm not talking just about socialist realism, just plain realism. It's a useless designation that means nothing in literature!"

To be clear, when Chekhov defined himself as a realist writer, he did so with the same calm conviction with which Tolstoy and Dostoevsky accepted the term. For them and their contemporaries, the adjective had a precise meaning. Chekhov would undoubtedly be surprised to learn that there is not a single major essay today that does not linger on his work's intense symbolic charge. *The Seagull,* where he parodied that current, is perhaps the most symbolist—from the very title!—of his dramas.

Even if Chekhov considered his literature to belong to the Russian realist tradition, he was aware of the fundamental differences between his work and that of his predecessors and contemporaries. His quests and intentions could not have been more dissimilar. The epic breath of Tolstoy, the spiritual exaltation of Dostoevsky, and the pathos of Andreyev were viscerally foreign to him. His work marks not only the end of a literary period; it also brings to a close a historic world. He is, as Vittorio Strada has accurately observed, a transitional writer situated between two worlds. Chekhov's originality was disconcerting to his contemporaries and, during his early period, truly incomprehensible. "Even today," the Italian critic adds, "he remains the most *difficult* writer in Russian literature, because under a maximum of apparent transparency lies hidden a core that resists all critical formulations."

One of the modes of Chekhovian narrative is its fragmentation, sometimes its pulverization. This is not capricious, rather a formal response to one of his fundamental concerns. The world of Chekhov seems to turn on a single axis: lack of communication. The breakdown in communication occurs especially among the most sensitive and generous people, and affects the most delicate relationships: lovers, friends, parents, and children. Little by little, the characters lose their voice, they become frozen by their words, and when they are forced to speak they coagulate language, infect it, so what could be a celebration of reconciliation becomes a duel of enemies or, worse still, a contemptuous indifference.

In 1888, with "The Steppe," Chekhov initiated a new form of writing whose originality seems to have gone unnoticed, at least at the time. For eight years he had written stories and novels. The world in "The Steppe" is seen through a child's eyes, but the language is not the language of childhood, rather it struggles to reach other levels. The challenge was more demanding than it seemed at first sight. Chekhov was not content to follow the child's gaze and translate in perfect language his discoveries, passions, fears; he proposed something more complex: to fuse his own view of the universe with the limited perceptions of a child protagonist. Hence a new poetics was born. The perceptions of the child, Yegorushka, constitute the main body of the story, but the refined descriptions of nature, the digressions and reflections on it could scarcely be attributed to him. The story corresponds to a child's gaze, but it is written in a style not always accessible to that gaze.

"Chekhov," says Dmitry Merezhkovsky, "does not contemplate nature only from an aesthetic point of view, even if all of his works contain a multitude of tiny, elegant brushstrokes that document the subtlety of his powers of observation. Like every true poet, he feels a profound affection for nature, an instinctive understanding of his unconscious life. He not only admires it from a distance like a serene and observant artist, but he also absorbs it fully as a man and leaves his indelible mark on all his ideas and feelings." In "The Steppe" the description of nature and the reflections on it are Chekhov's; the perception of human events belong to the child protagonist.

It is the retelling of a child's first steps through the world. As he travels across the steppe he comes to know the unpredictable world of adults and the no less disturbing world of nature. He confronts dangers from which, in the end, he will emerge *invictus*. His experience possesses all the features of an initiatory rite. For the author, it is a question of a journey as well as a challenge. It is a journey toward a new narrative form. Like the steppe, the story lacks fixed boundaries at the beginning and the end.

There appears in the story a character destined to grow in importance in the Chekhovian universe. He lacks any appealing quality. Neither Gogol nor Turgenev, Tolstoy nor Dostoevsky could portray him because he did not exist during their lifetime. He is an entrepreneur, the representative of the new capitalism that is beginning to take shape in Russia. That character's name in "The Steppe" is Varlamov; Varlamov, not unlike the representatives of the new Russian intelligentsia—Stanislavsky, Diaghilev, and Chekhov himself—was probably the son or grandson of serfs. To Chekhov these energetic and active men who were beginning to lead the world were necessary but also deeply odious. Yegorushka hears about Varlamov from every character he encounters along his journey across the steppe. He is in charge. However, when he finally sees him more than halfway through the novel he is surprised by his appearance. He expected to see a kind of tsar but what he finds is an insignificant man in a white cap and plain corduroy suit. He's the "short, gray, large-booted little man on the ugly nag who was talking to peasants at an hour when all decent people are still abed."[16] Twice he sees him use the whip: once to beat Jewish innkeepers; a second time to whip a character that was unable to give him accurate information. Such is his way of communicating with the world: his language. It does not escape Yegorushka that however insignificant he may look there was a sense of strength and control over his surroundings in everything about him, even in the way he held the whip.

16 Translated by Ronald Hingley

Varlamov's fists decide the fate of all those who inhabit or travel the steppe. He exists on the same level as, if not above, nature. During a march in a storm at night, Yegorushka, half-asleep, is able to see, through the flashes of lightning, his fellow travelers. The image transmitted to us is like that of Breughel's blind men. The old men lean on each other, one's face is deformed due to chronic swelling in his jaw, another drags his swollen feet; another, ahead of them, like a sleepwalker, a former cantor who has lost voice, trudges along. Covered in coarse straw mats, they crawl beside the wagons. These monstrous figures, nature's castoffs, are the future portrait of what the handsome, strapping young men, newcomers to the trade, walking behind them, will become.

As a rule, the first paragraph of a Chekhov story gives us the essential data and tone of the story. We should not expect major surprises in the story, rather a mere germination of a seed that is already found in the overture. On the first page of "The Name-Day Party," we learn that Olga Mikhailovna is pregnant, that she lives in a provincial mansion surrounded by vast gardens where, on that day, her husband's Saint's Day is being celebrated, and that the celebration has fatigued and irritated her. Everything suggests that the story will be told from her point of view. We also learn that she does not live in harmony with the world around her. She has just been served an eight-course meal, and the endless clamor that accompanied it has exhausted her to the point of fainting. We have the feeling that the society around her irritates her more than what could be considered natural. There appears in her reflections a tension that foreshadows hysteria and foretells a dramatic denouement. That tension is expressed within the dichotomy that always interested Chekhov: the confrontation between society and nature; the former represented by the behavior of the party guests, the latter by the son the woman carries in her womb. Olga Mikhailovna flees the party in the first paragraph to hide momentarily in a garden path where amid the smell of freshly cut hay and honey and the buzzing of bees she surrenders herself to the emotions of the tiny being she carries inside her womb so that they may take complete control over her. But this *raptio* in the middle of nature lasts only momentarily. Society prevails, and that place in her thoughts that was to be occupied by the child is invaded by a feeling of guilt for having abandoned her guests and by a marital quarrel, which is inevitable in all of Chekhov's stories. Her husband has just railed against some recent reforms: trial by jury, freedom of the press, and the education of women—three victories won by liberal society over the autocracy. She disagrees with her husband's position just to annoy him. And this fact brings us closer to the real source of her problems. The dilemma between nature and society finds a viable channel to express itself: the naked opposition between man and woman. Overcome by jealousy, the protagonist only notices her husband's defects and surely magnifies them. Piotr Dmitrich's affectation awakens a morbid hatred in her. But, is she as real a character as she seems? Does she truly live the enlightened ideas that she proclaims? Or does she merely take advantage of some abstract concepts, at moments such as this, in order to feel superior to her husband? Possibly. The fact is that we see something cold and possessive in her agitation, a blind desire to take control of men that renders her odious to us. Both are fed up with the party that began in the morning and will last until midnight. The drama unfolds throughout the seemingly never-ending hours that transpire during the festivities. The inability to speak, to communicate, begins to take control of her, until she can no longer withstand the pressure inside, and it spills out in a fit of near-madness. Resentment, spite, and rage triumph. The ending is tragic. Society prevails in the worst possible way over nature, the biological instinct. The couple, who during the party have played a complicated game of masquerade, end up destroying the unborn life. The original, the important, the essentially Chekhovian, is constituted by the construction of the story through a storm of details, almost all apparently trivial. A single act, two or three words spoken in passing, is enough to recreate an atmosphere and suggest a past. The trivial suddenly becomes important, significant.

When in "Peasants," Nikolai Tchikildyeev, sick and despondent, arrives to his birthplace, he finds a dark, dirty, and miserable place that in no way corresponds to his nostalgia, where life in the village seemed radiant, beautiful, and tender. The initial silence is broken when his little daughter calls a cat and another girl, only eight years, the only human who receives them, exclaims:

"He can't hear. He's deaf. They gave him a beating."

Everything has already been said! The blows that have burst the cat's ear are sufficient to mark the space where Nikolai Tchikildyeev has arrived, and how bitter his days will be before death rescues him. The universe of cruelty is the same in a rustic peasant hut as in the opulent houses of the new bourgeoisie, like the one the protagonist inhabits in "A Woman's Kingdom," or the one belonging to the new rising class of merchants that appears in that extraordinary story, horror among horrors, titled "In the Ravine." If a moral message can be inferred from the Chekhovian characters it is to resist succumbing to the mercilessness and vulgarity distilled by the domestic tyrants who populate the netherworlds where they are trapped. Confronting them is next to impossible. But we must resist, suffer, not yield, work, nor allow ourselves to be pulled under. If they achieve this, they will have won.

In a famous essay on Chekhov, written a few months before his death, Thomas Mann points out: "If references are to be made and praises bestowed, then I must certainly mention 'A Tedious Tale,' for it is my favorite among all Chekhov's stories, an outstandingly fascinating work which for gentleness, sadness, and strangeness has no equal in the literary world."[17] This is a story that can be read from several perspectives, that remains open to interpretation by the reader, and that despite the warmth and pity that the author shows toward his creatures is but the agonizing portrait of a downfall. An old professor, the protagonist, discovers at the end of his days that no matter how noble his efforts to achieve something in life may have seemed, deep down his life has been meaningless; it differs in no way from that of Tolstoy's insensitive Ivan Ilych. And as for the simplest question—"What is to be done?"—with which his young pupil, the only person in the world in whom he has taken any interest, confronts him, he cannot (or will not) but answer, "I don't know, Katya. Upon my honor, I don't know!"

As Chekhov's health failed and the end was looming, his social ideas began to radicalize. He signed documents and protests, expressed solidarity with persecuted students; he distanced himself from Suvorin, his editor, his Maecenas, and until then his confidant and closest friend. In a particularly severe letter ending their relationship, he writes: "Indifference is a paralysis of the soul, a premature death."

From a young age he was an admirer of Comte, a committed positivist.

---

17 From "The Stature of Anton Chekhov" by Thomas Mann.

He once wrote, referring to the Gospel teachings of Tolstoy, that the peasant is turned into a compendium of all virtues: "Tolstoy's morality no longer moves me. I don't find it sympathetic deep inside my heart. Peasant blood runs in my veins. Don't talk to me about the virtue of *muzhiks*! I have believed in progress since I was very young. Objective reflections and my sense of justice tell me that in electricity and in steam there is more love for man than in chastity, fasting, and denial of the flesh."

However, his faith in reason, science, and progress did not stop—because his writing was a pure exercise in freedom—some of his stories from adopting an almost evangelical tone. In one of his last short stories, "In the Ravine," evil and usury are assimilated into a lie, and the only nobility is connected to suffering, the rhythms of nature, the earth, manual labor, with religiosity as intense as that of the late Tolstoy that he disliked so much. The only difference is that in Chekhov, the preacher disappears and only the writing remains. In a letter he writes: "Pharisaism, stupidity and despotism reign not in merchants' houses and prisons alone. I see them in science, in literature, in the younger generation. [...] That is why I have no preference either for gendarmes, or for butchers, or for scientists, or for writers, or for the younger generation. I regard trade-marks and labels as a superstition. My holy of holies is the human body, health, intelligence, talent, inspiration, love, and the most absolute freedom—freedom from violence and lying, whatever forms they may take. This is the programme I would follow if I were a great artist."[18] In his narratives and plays, these clear concepts would be transformed into a storm of details, would fragment, become dust, ashes, unfinished sketches,

---

18 Translated by Constance Garnett

apathy, vague intonations. Paradoxically, this apparent insignificance would infuse his work with meaning and value. Perhaps that is what allows us to read him as a contemporary.

Xalapa, August 1993

ŠVEJK[19]

In the opening scene of *The Good Soldier Švejk*, the author, Jaroslav Hašek, places his protagonist at the very center of history: of Bohemia, his country, of the Austro-Hungarian Empire, of Europe, and of the world. In Sarajevo, Švejk is told that the heir to the imperial throne has just been assassinated. In the subsequent episodes of Hašek's antiheroic tale, history will gradually lose its gifts and privileges, it will fade into a distorted backdrop against which a series of disproportionate and grotesque actions unfolds, whose protagonists are the poor soldier who gives the title its name, his friends and tavern mates, and his comrades in arms, all of whom lack any aspiration to grandeur, prestige, or glory. And, too, as the story progresses, a more abstract plot takes shape: the absurdity that governs and weaves the infinite network of relationships created by power within society and manipulated from above, and, ultimately, the neglect of an insignificant man, who in novels is but an infinitesimal part of a crowd, an easily interchangeable subordinate,

---

19 The surname Švejk appears in various English translations and editions as Schweik, Schwejk, and Švejk. The quotes that appear here have been taken from Paul Selver's 1930 translation for Doubleday & Co, which uses the Germanized spelling Schweik. Selver's translation was later reissued by Penguin Classics using the Czech spelling Švejk, which I have chosen to replicate. All other aspects of the translation remain the same. — *Trans.*

committed, almost always, to being unaware of his neglect. *The Good Soldier Švejk* illustrates how this candid and irreducibly anarchic being, the protagonist, suddenly sees himself trapped by a seemingly perfect machine, and describes further the tools of wit that a homunculus is capable of employing to avoid being destroyed by mechanisms that he will never succeed in or be interested in understanding.

This character, always surprised but never intimidated, who ambles through a labyrinth of bridges and corridors, courts and galleries, until arriving at the front lines, navigates various court proceedings as enigmatic as those brought against Mr. K., his neighbor in Prague. Neglect and lack of pretexts, rather than reduce this Bohemian Sancho, have given him a freedom that the sedentary man would be unable to conceive of. Trapped in a seemingly impregnable and treacherous prison and administrative world, Švejk will have no choice but to topple it or cause it to explode. Because the Švejks of the world, men with doltish faces, are the perfect gravediggers of any empire. Dogged and guileless, they are destined to be implacable moles, cheerful and voracious termites, and time bombs ready to demolish any system considered to be monolithic, rigorous, and univocal. They have as their golem another of the illustrious characters of Prague: the vitality of the imprecise and the unfinished. They are unpleasant, they are vulgar, and above all, they are indestructible. Like cockroaches, they will manage to survive any disaster.

In the opening paragraph of Hašek's novel, Mrs. Müller, a charwoman at a squalid rooming house, announces to her tenant, Švejk, a hawker of dogs: "So they've killed our Ferdinand!"[20] The action takes place in Prague. The author makes clear immediately that an army

20 Translated by Paul Selver

medical board has certified our protagonist an "obvious imbecile." They're talking about none other than the Archduke Ferdinand of Habsburg, the heir to the Empire's throne. From that moment on, a dialogue of the deaf takes place between heraldry and ordinariness at ground level. Mrs. Müller will settle on the highest branches of the ruling dynasty; her tenant, on much more villainous levels. Of course, Švejk will triumph, and although the novel endeavors to address the decline and fall of an empire, it will forever be, from the beginning to end, a chronicle of disorderly factions, those most contemptuous of perfection that society embodies. Hašek's novel is a chronicle that revels in its vulgarity, in the absence of virtues, in bodily filth, and, in due time, in scatophilia.

Švejk, all the while rubbing his knees with an anti-rheumatic liniment, asks the question that anyone would think to ask upon hearing the Christian name of someone who has been killed: "Which Ferdinand, Mrs. Müller?" adding, before the interlocutor can answer, that he only knew two Ferdinands, one the delivery boy of the chemist Prusa, who had once drunk a bottle of hair lotion by mistake, and the other Ferdinand Kokoška, who collected dog waste from the streets. He concludes, "They wouldn't be any great loss, either of 'em."

Thus, from the beginning, an irrepressible and bawdy verbal stream flows from the protagonist's mouth. Švejk's speech recalls those drunken, incoherent, and unhinged tirades heard in taverns in the wee hours of the morning. After hearing that the assassination involved a member of the imperial family, he comments that a customer at the pub had told him not long ago that someday all the emperors in the world would be brought down, which forced the tavern owner to have him arrested, but the bloke landed a punch on the landlord and two on the policeman. He adds that they then took him away in a drunk cart until he returned to his senses, and while the dizzied reader is unable to grasp what the rain of punches was all about—who gives them or who receives them or why they happened in the first place—Švejk returns suddenly to the death of the Crown Prince, without a doubt the most commented upon incident at the time in every corner of the Empire. But the manner in which he explains his reflections is extremely chaotic: "Yes, Mrs. Müller, there's queer things going on nowadays; that there is. That's another loss to Austria. When I was in the army there was a private who shot a captain. He loaded his rifle and went into the orderly room. They told him to clear out, but he kept on saying that he must speak to the captain. Well the captain came along and gave him a dose of C.B. Then he took his rifle and scored a fair bull's eye. The bullet went right through the captain and when it came out the other side, it did some damage in the orderly room, in the bargain. It smashed a bottle of ink and the ink got spilled all over some regiment records." Like us, the readers, Mrs. Müller is completely lost. She ponders everything for a moment, trying to understand the story, then, unwisely, asks her tenant the fate of the soldier. Švejk's response is instantaneous: "'He hanged himself with a pair of braces,' said Švejk, brushing his bowler hat. 'And they wasn't even his. He borrowed them from a jailer, making out that his trousers were coming down. You can't blame him for not waiting till they shot him. You know, Mrs. Müller, it's enough to turn anyone's head, being in a fix like that. The jailer lost his rank and got six months as well. But he didn't serve his time. He ran away to Switzerland and now he does a bit of preaching for some church or other. There ain't many honest people about nowadays, Mrs. Müller.'" And soon after these longwinded and unnecessary circumlocutions, he returns to the topic: "'I expect that the Archduke was taken in by the man who shot him. He saw a chap standing there and thought: Now there's a decent fellow, cheering me and all. And then the chap did him in.'"

In that inornate beginning, overwhelmed by the character's verbal incontinence, we glimpse Hašek's narrative intention: to degrade history, History in uppercase, until it becomes a trivial series of foolish tales. The assassination of the heir to the Austrian throne constitutes one of the most consequential events in our century. The shot that ended the life of the Archduke marked the beginning of the First World War, an event that would change Europe's political landscape and, in the medium or long term, the world. The collapse of the empire would give rise to a new series of nation states. Bohemia, the country where Švejk lived, would unite with Slovakia to form the Republic of Czechoslovakia. Inside Russia, the other great empire of Continental Europe, a transformation of the social, political, and economic structures would take place that would introduce others that until then had been regarded with the conflicting emotions of loathing and hope. Utopia was becoming a reality. Borders everywhere would change. There would be a new distribution of colonial territories and spheres of influence. For Švejk, the assassination of Ferdinand of Habsburg is reduced to the level of the death of the druggist Prusa's delivery boy, that idiot who accidentally ingested a hair lotion, that of Kokoška, the collector of dog excrement on the streets of Prague, or the soldier who hanged himself with the jailer's suspenders. The episodes of greater historical significance are trivialized upon being compared with the most anodyne human detritus. Hereafter, this device will become one of the hallmarks of the best contemporary Czech narrative. The tone of the Švejk's soliloquies resembles the delirium of those drunkards who remember everything only to confuse everything. Hašek's world is a world upside down, where the mechanisms of power are confused with carnival and where plot and language constitute a marked unity with a Rabelaisian seal.

Angelo María Ripellino believes that *The Good Soldier Švejk* belongs to the tradition of Habsburgian literature. "Even if it does so with harshness and bitterness and without a minimum of sympathy, the book expresses the agony of the Empire, the *Finis Austriae*, the twilight of Kakania, of that—as Musil said—misunderstood and now non-existent nation that was in so many ways an unappreciated model." Hašek's book, in fact, does not reveal any sympathy for this world or any of its myths. He does not delight in ironizing the extreme complexity of a culture in the process of growing dark as Musil does in *The Man Without Qualities*, or in the heroic military exploits regarded for centuries as the most valuable foundation of that dual monarchy—royal and imperial—as occurs in the novels of Lerner-Holenia, or in the bitter and melancholy memory of its gradual dissolution, as in Joseph Roth's *Radetzky March*, or the delusional pathos with which Andrzej Kuśniewicz, one of the great chroniclers of that collapse, a Pole born in Galicia, one of the eastern regions of the Empire, who, in *The King of the Two Sicilies* and *Lesson in a Dead Language*, describes the death rattle of the final agony. Hašek doesn't feel the slightest nostalgia for that defeated world on the verge of extinction. The information we have about the character testifies to his disdain for everything related to that political entity, its culture, its customs, its religion. Above all, he detested the judicial and administrative mechanisms in whose labyrinth Švejk, just like the characters of Kafka, his contemporaries, stumble endlessly, as an example that no one, no matter where he was, could permanently escape its tentacles.

Humor abounds in Hašek's account: a malignant, barracks humor that emerges more from the belly than the intellect, more characteristic of popular culture than of the refined strata of Bohemian society. Hašek's laughter comes from the earth and never manages—because neither does he try—to climb upward. A humor centered, to use Bakhtin's words, on the movements of the belly and the bum. According to the Russian thinker, popular humor has a spring, dawn, and morning character par excellence: "More precisely, *folk grotesque reflects* the very moment when light replaces darkness, night-morning, winter-spring."

If the humor that permeates and becomes a foundation of the narrative has this luminous character in the early chapters, where Švejk still remains far from the front, in the last chapters, as the good soldier sinks into battlefields, he changes and connects, even if only in some aspects, with the Romantic root, always present in the Germanic world, where the absence of the solar element is a condition and is the only light capable of penetrating the darkness. The most powerful aspect of German Expressionism was nourished by this violent, blasphemous, and derogatory foundation. Hašek's world at one point coincides with the vision of George Grosz, Otto Dix, and the early Kokoschka. His tone, says Wolfgang Kayser, "is sinister, dreadful, and distressing." During Švejk's journey, the cheerful and luminous tone at the beginning will gradually change signs, and by the time he arrives on the battlefield, it will become fecal. The soldiers march, defecate, kill, defecate again, and, in the end, die, sometimes in the very act of defecating. The war appears as a stage swept by the harshest winds, or reduced to a sordid, drunken brawl like those that might take place at any beer hall in Prague. The adventures and reflections of the delusional character who is Švejk, the dog merchant turned soldier, are resolved through an alchemical pass from dread to laughter. "Fear," and here I return to Bakhtin, "is the extreme expression of narrow-minded and stupid seriousness, which is defeated by laughter." Alexander Herzen underscores the revolutionary character of laughter: "No one laughs in church, at court, on parade, before the head of their department, a police officer, or the German boss. House serfs have no right to smile in the presence of their masters, only equals can laugh among themselves. [...] To cause men to smile at the god Apis is to deprive him of his holy status and turn him into a common bull."[21] And Victor Hugo adds that the great geniuses of literature distinguish themselves by committing to that which the mediocre avoid: excess and disproportion. Hašek revels in these: Švejk is the embodiment of an absence of limits.

Every era mocks certain subjects that were venerated in the past. Shakespeare laughs at the notion of the heroism contained in the Homeric poems, demolishes *epos*, and treats the subject as if the immense movement of troops from every corner of the Hellas to the walls of Troy, and the incessant battles where dying meant an act of obedience to the commands of the gods, were nothing more than a frivolous byplay that illustrated the marital conflict between a whore and a cuckold, as attested by the characters of *Troilus and Cressida*, as splendid as contemptible, the Greek Thersites and the Trojan Pandarus, whose commentaries on war and its leaders are noteworthy for their sarcasm. A very black humor runs through all tragedy.

21 Translated by Katherine Parthé

There seems to be an insurmountable rupture between this kind of humor and laughter. The same occurs in the fables of Swift, the work of Beckett, in all of the theater of the absurd. A frozen grimace accompanies their reading. Hašek's humor is similar. Comparing in the first lines of his novel the most prized offshoot of the Habsburgian dynasty to a collector of street droppings reveals his intention. A few lines suffice to demystify Olympus. The divine Apis suddenly becomes a tame ox.

During the entire course of Švejk's hazy slog, we never stumble upon anyone who possesses the stuff from which heroes, poets, or saints are made. The vast humanity that inhabits the pages of the novel—the officers who lead the military operations as well as the anonymous starving and drunken multitude that marches toward death—is not characterized by its epic spirit. The world of war is reduced to inarticulate cries, swearing, arrests and corporal punishment, deprivation of every kind, stupidity, robbery, incessant transit from one court to another, from prison to a military commission, from the hospital to the madhouse, from the ward to the battlefield. Amid the roar can be heard Švejk's indefatigable mumbling. And how reasonable that voice unexpectedly begins to seem to us as it attempts to superimpose itself onto chaos! In a world that has lost all reason Švejk's incongruent memories, the thousand absurd anecdotes that he reels off in excruciating detail with unrelenting logorrhea seem to border almost on sanity.

The author maintains an attitude of permanent ambiguity toward his creation. Is Švejk, "officially weak-minded—a chronic case," as he likes to introduce himself, truly mentally retarded, or is he a clever impostor, a sly rogue who manages to fool the authorities all the time?

His greatest blunders are always accompanied by an angelic look and an expression of absolute purity. The doubt is never resolved. One of Hašek's great successes is to never reveal to the reader exactly who Švejk is.

Švejk renders candid testimony of every stop along his judicial odyssey. "Nowadays" he says, "it's great fun being run in. There's no quartering or anything of that kind. We've got a mattress, we've got a table, we've got a seat, we ain't packed together like sardines, we'll get soup, they'll give us bread, they'll bring a pitcher or water, there's a closet right under our noses. It all shows you what progress there's been."

In an edition of the *Corriere della Sera* from the end of 1987, I read a story about the political perspectives that were visible at that time in Czechoslovakia; the Italian correspondent gathered opinions from writers and artists. Significant changes were beginning to take place in Eastern Europe. Unexpectedly, warm winds were blowing from Russia that seemed to announce that the end of a hibernation that had extended far too long. The *Corriere* article was titled: "In Prague the soldier Švejk still prevails." One of the interviewees, whom the Italian journalist referred to by first name only, Ludvik, commented: "The country is rife with Švejkism: it's a great literary creation, but from a moral point of view, it's a catastrophe. Czechoslovakia is full of Švejks: hypocrites, opportunists, incompetents. Conformity and concealment know no bounds." At that time, it was impossible for intellectuals like Ludvik to know if the official lie was exposed, strengthened, and laid bare, precisely because of the work, whether conscious or unconscious, of Švejkism. A falsehood published in the press received so much praise, acceptance, and exaggerated approval by an entire army of complacent Švejks, expressed in a tone that never rid itself of a vague taste of parody that, by contrast, was suggestive of a lie. The official statement, which was repeated with exaggerated emphasis by insane voices, was transformed immediately into a caricature. In the world of the Švejks nonsense is exemplary, an achievement of modern times. Error is extolled as a virtue. Servile adjectivization can reach aberrant levels. Švejk, for example, thinks that a prison system is exemplary because the toilets are placed under the inmates' noses.

If prison was for Švejk a sign of obvious moral progress, the madhouse then seems to him like a perfect replica of Eden. The protagonist is tireless when singing the magnificence of these tiny paradises. "I'm blowed if I can make out why lunatics kick up such a fuss about being kept there. They can crawl about stark naked on the floor, or caterwaul like jackals, or rave and bite. If you was to do anything like that in the open street, it'd make people stare, but in the asylum it's just taken as a matter of course. Why, the amount of liberty there is something that even the socialists have never dreamt of. The inmates can pass themselves off as God Almighty or the Virgin Mary or the Pope or the King of England or our Emperor or St. Vaclav, although the one who did him was properly stripped and tied up in solitary confinement. [...] I tell you, the life there was a fair treat. You can bawl, or yelp, or sing, or blub, or moo, or boo, or jump, say your prayers or turn somersaults, or walk on all fours, or hop about on one foot, or run round in a circle, or dance, or skip, or squat on your haunches all day long, and climb up the walls. Nobody comes up to you and says: 'You mustn't do this, you mustn't do that, you ought to be ashamed of yourself, call yourself civilized?' I liked being in the asylum, I can tell you, and while I was there I had the time of my life."

To Švejk, the only access to utopia, then, is found in the world of the insane.

As his adventures go by, the protagonist's heavenly innocence begins to disappear; everything around him seems to grow tense. A foul stench of excrement permeates his surroundings with increasing intensity.

If in the first part of the novel an occasional scatological allusion helps to create one of those festive atmospheres derived from the old medieval and Renaissance tradition where feces, as Bakhtin shows, were always "a wellbeing of body and spirit," what is certain is that as the protagonist approaches the front, this element of laughter wrinkles and blackens. The space of hardships that Švejk moves through is transformed into a spectral field whose elements are mud, feces, and blood. Švejk, a rough and incomplete being, an embryonic golem, moves with a somnambulistic step into a landscape populated by latrines. The bodies constantly return their constitutive matter to the ground. Critics attribute such importance to latrines as if the final victory depended on them. The front is transformed into an area of corporal expulsion, where one speaks only of urinals, enemas, diarrhea, suppositories, stained underwear, and fecal stench. More than the military element, Ripellino points out, war is to Hašek a continuous defecation, a bodily act and a diarrheal mud. "Immersed in the filth of the war, the Hapsburg Empire is revealed as an excremental entity, a foul-smelling region of dirty underwear, of enemas and suppositories."

In short: an Empire drowning in its own excrement.

Švejk, the forced pilgrim, begins to shed his friendly bonhomie and resemble a tragic character. He is unable to do it completely because his memory serves as a counterweight that establishes the necessary stability. The world that Švejk recalls is capable of reducing the brutality of war to a mere escalation of the absurd. His voice, despite the incongruity of his speech, continues to be a human voice, and reminds us that until recently men were bound by bonds different to those that the army establishes, ties that were created by mutual sympathies; they were men in the middle of men, not anonymous sleepwalkers with military step.

The story of Švejk reveals and summarizes the anarchy and lyricism of Prague's demimonde. Like the characters of Boccaccio, Rabelais, and Jarry, from whom he descends, the protagonist remains in perpetual motion. The novel gives off a certain stench of urine, of the den of miscreants, of poorly digested alcohol. Throughout his ordeal, Švejk keeps moving, not to mention talking. He has no regrets, he doesn't swear, he simply tries to ignore what happens around him; he doesn't read books, he barely manages to thumb through a newspaper. His wisdom comes from purely personal experiences, from recounting the actions of the many people upon whom he's stumbled during his life. Through the river of anecdotes that slows the narrative action (but whose appearance in itself is already the novel), foolishness unpunished, the total absurdity upon which all human destinies depend, is manifested. Sometimes these small tales interpolated within the plot are very simple, which does not subtract from their efficacy: "But such is human existence," says Švejk. "Man goes around making mistakes and only death stops him. That's what happened one night to the man who found a rabid dog, frozen half to death; he took it to his room and put it in the bed where he slept with his wife. As soon as the dog came into heat, it began to bite the entire family, ripping the youngest child, who slept in the crib, to pieces and devouring him." As in Kafka, life reveals itself as a mere transit through different proceedings of an endless trial. But what anguish and heaviness there is in the author of *The Trial*, in Hašek it is resolved in a cruelty that on the surface always seems to end in a joke. Other times, his digressions disguise an abstraction that intensifies the absurdity of the story, especially those related to the administration of justice: "'Oh, don't you worry,' said Švejk. 'You'll be all right in the end, just like Janetchek at Pilsen. He was a gipsy, and in 1879 they were going to hang him for robbery and murder. But he didn't worry and he kept saying that he'd be all right in the end. And so he was. Because at the last moment they couldn't hang him, because it was the Emperor's birthday. So they didn't hang him till the next day, when the Emperor's birthday was all over. But he was in luck's way again, because on the day after he was reprieved and there was going to be another trial, on account of some new evidence that showed it was another fellow named Janetchek who'd done it. So they had to dig him up out of the prison cemetery and give him another, proper burial in the Catholic cemetery at Pilsen, and then it turned out that he wasn't a Catholic at all, but an evangelical.'"

Czech critics strenuously ignored Hašek's work for several years. They found the popular vulgarity of the stories of Švejk repellent. But the success of the work abroad changed its destiny. Once again, the generous hand of Max Brod decided the fate of a creator. Just as he had done with Kafka, whose novels he published against the express instructions of the author, or with Leos Janacek, whose libretti he translated into German so that his operas could be sung outside of Czechoslovakia, when the moment was right, he also threw in with Hašek. He translated *The Good Soldier Švejk* into German, and published the first major critical text on the book.

The novel was read voraciously in Austria and Germany. The memory of the recently lived war allowed very different audiences to crystallize in this book their rejection of a disastrous period. One did not have to wait long for its fame to begin to permeate the literary circles of the new Czechoslovakian Republic, reluctant to accept this novel of life in the barracks. Over the years, paradoxically, Hašek's book became the first contemporary classic in the Czech language, and Švejk one of the country's emblematic figures.

Mexico City, December 1991

BOROLA AGAINST THE WORLD

I'm rereading materials for a book I'm endeavoring to write. It is meant to be a record of my journey—the history of a still-unfinished education. As I read, I find leftovers of snobbishness I thought I had rid myself of: among others, the tendency to quote visibly famous readings. It is not a question of invention or forgery, in no way am I interested in pretending to be a reader that I am not; it's just that I have excluded other more "plebeian" books or, shall we say, more "ordinary" ones, which have been tremendously important in my life.

I have always resisted consuming books that are trendy or fashionable. My map of readings has been drawn more or less at random, by fate, temperament, and very much by hedonism. I am fascinated by the eccentrics. For over forty years I have been an avid reader of the novels of Ronald Firbank, when in England his audience was all but non-existent; also of the esoteric novels of H. Myers, which only a tiny handful of faithful have approached. I wrote about Flann O'Brien when the readers of *At Swim-Two-Birds* numbered scarcely a few dozen—all willing to die for that exceptional book.

I try to watch myself, to be careful not to manufacture tastes, fence myself in. I could cite impressive titles; swear that each one is a bedside book. I would be lying. On a trip to New York, a thousand years ago, a female friend pressured me to acquire the six volumes of *The Tale of Genji*, written by Lady Murasaki in the tenth century and translated into English by the eminent Arthur Waley. My friend claimed to be sure that when I returned to Mexico I would devour them immediately, that those books written ten centuries ago had been patiently awaiting me; she did not say that they would come to influence my literature because at that time I did not have the slightest idea that one day I would begin to write. The influence did not happen, for the simple reason that even today there are still books with uncut pages in my small Japanese section. I have not read the *Alexiad* by Anna Comnena, which I found in a magnificent secondhand bookshop next door to the Hotel Metropol in Moscow—an edition in perfect condition, translated into English by Elizabeth Dawes. The manager of the bookshop lectured me on the work, to which he always referred as "the golden rose of Byzantine letters." He assured me, among other things, that it was one of Bakhtin's passions. I have leafed through it once, but so far have not found the energy to go any further. Anyway, as long as I am confessing, I will state that I have not even read Schopenhauer's *Parerga and Paralipomena,* a book that changed the lives of Borges, Mann, and many other famous writers. At this point, it is possible that I will never get to it, but on the other hand, I am certain that I will still reread several of Dickens's, an author who in my youth caused more than a few select spirits to wrinkle their nose.

Reading is a secret game of approximations and distances. It is also a lottery. One arrives at a book by unusual means; one stumbles upon an author by apparent coincidence only to never be able to stop reading him. I have quoted in articles, in interviews, in the body of my own novels several writers to whom I consider myself indebted, but never, as far as I can remember, did I mention one of my principal sources. Recently, while writing some notes on Carlos Monsiváis, I found in his anthology of chronicles some pages dedicated to Gabriel Vargas. Stumbling upon the image of Borola, seeing her, nearly naked, shake her long-legged body, marked a beautiful reunion. She sang and danced to her battle hymn:

> I move my hips a lot.
> I shake them when I walk.
> Why do you give up on me?
> I can't help it, you see...
> Doing *cucuchí, cucuchí...*
> Doing *cucuchí, cucuchí...*

I move cautiously, doing arabesques, as if afraid to arrive at this obligatory confession: My debt to Gabriel Vargas is immense. My sense of parody, my play with the absurd, come from him and not, as I would like to be able to boast, from Gogol or Gombrowicz. Who is Gabriel Vargas? you might ask. Well, he is a fabulous cartoonist, one of whose comic strips, perhaps the most famous, was called *La familia Burrón.*

In mid-1953, after spending a few months in Venezuela, upon returning to university, I ran into two dear friends, Alicia Osorio and Luis Prieto. They greeted me with all the warmth in the world, only to start talking seconds later about Borola, Reginito, Cristeta, and Ruperto, and laughing hysterically as they celebrated the hijinks of those zany characters. Every time I tried to interject into the conversation some incident from the trip, my stops in Havana and Curaçao, the season in Caracas and, above all, stories from the sea-crossing on the *Francesco Morosini* and the *Andrea Gritti*, my first boats, they appeared to be listening to me, but at the first pause, they'd return to the world of Borola. The next day, Luis brought to school the latest issue of *La familia Burrón*. From that day on, I was a devoted reader for many years.

Occasionally Luis Prieto, Monsiváis, and I would run into each other at dinner at the homes of mutual friends, and on more than one occasion at the gatherings we unleashed torrents of laughter as we discussed one of the comic strip's new episodes. Nothing mattered to us outside of whatever was happening to Borola Burrón. Our more tolerant friends, when they realized the waters we were swimming in, treated us like victims of late measles from which we would eventually recover. But there were those who took Borola's circumstances personally, as if her horrifying stories penetrated hidden parts of their being; they began to behave with exaggerated Proustian refinement; they cooed like doves about Vermeer, Palladio, the china they had inherited from *grand-maman*, their first summer on the Côte d'Azur. They switched from Spanish to French in the middle of brilliant and witty phrases, as if every gesture, every word, functioned to maintain as much distance as possible between them and the tenement-patio where the Burróns lived. They were annoyed by the specter of a Mexico that they did not wish to acknowledge—a radiant, barbaric, innocent, and grotesque Mexico that they could not accept, with a much more vibrant language than the foppish grisaille in which they communicated. Distancing oneself from that world meant not remembering the aunt who ran away with a nobody and ended up working in a French dry cleaners, a very respectable business, certainly, even elegant, but a dry cleaners nonetheless; or the grandfather's rambling deathbed confession about the origin of his fortune, which, in the end, could be the product of senility, but for a long time troubled the family. Someone else might recall the uncle who showed up once or twice a year with grease spots on his tie or lapels. And then begin to talk again, now in a shrill voice, about Vermeer, the moment when Swann first entered the Guermantes's house, César Frank's sonata, and other niceties.

Luis Prieto and I visited Don Alfonso Reyes every other week. One day, either by chance or by choice, the conversation turned to Gabriel Vargas and his comic strip; he applauded the appeal of its popular speech and extraordinary melodic styling. When we repeated it, no one believed it.

We were blaspheming! When he said the same thing later in a newspaper interview, some must have thought that, like the aforementioned grandfather, our polygraph was doddering.

The Vargas comic strip recreated the prevailing melting pot of Mexico City and its immense mid-century social mobility. *La familia Burrón* was organized around a married couple: Don Regino Burrón, the sole proprietor and operator of *El Rizo de Oro*, a beauty salon in a poor neighborhood, and his wife Borola Tacuche, who lives a life of eternal conflict. Don Regino is a paragon of modest virtues—wisdom, honesty, thrift—but is also the most perfect expression of ennui and lack of imagination. Borola, on the other hand, represents anarchy, abuse, cheating, excess, and at the same time imagination, fantasy, risk, insubordination, and, above all, the unfathomable possibilities of the joy of living. Determined to conquer the world, to make it to the top, she takes everything on: business, politics, and entertainment. She fails at everything. She returns defeated from each experience to her lair, the cacophonous courtyard from which apparently it is impossible to escape. But at the very moment she returns to her faithful Reginito's side to apologize for her shenanigans and to swear never to return to her old ways, she's already plotting a new adventure even more outrageous than the last. The secondary characters, the other family members, move in opposing circles. There's *tía* Cristeta, the millionairess who lives with Marcel, her pet alligator with which she takes a plunge every morning in a pool of champagne; and there's Borola's brother, Ruperto, a hapless gangster and perpetual fugitive from justice whose face we never see. The main couple is only able to reconcile for a time: revolt and submission do not a happy marriage make. The world outside this courtyard of destitute houses is governed and sustained by corruption and arrogance: corrupt police, corrupt inspectors, corrupt judges, and corrupt bureaucrats. I imagine that the vast majority of readers, myself included, sided with Borola, for whom all the recriminations, sermons, moralizing, and advice go in one ear and out the other. The effect is the same as that produced by many of the English novels that scrutinize Victorian morality. Who does not prefer the unscrupulous Becky Sharp over the whitewashed tombs who inhabit *Vanity Fair*? Who among us who has read *Treasure Island* at the appropriate age does not prefer Long John Silver, the ruthless and seductive pirate, to the solemn gentlemen who advise Jim Hawkins in his business and who, let us not forget, will share in the coveted treasure on which the novel is based?

In a world of insufferable yuppies, the name Borola is an anachronism. Recalling her sends me back to a vibrant time and a place now gone.

Xalapa, February 1996

TWO WEEKS WITH THOMAS MANN

For Juan Villoro

13 JANUARY 1995

I returned to Mann's diaries; the first volume. They comprise two different periods: the years 1918–21 and 1933–37. I was only familiar with the Spanish edition, a selection focused above all on his personal affairs, where is evidenced an attempt to discover the dark aspects—and secret areas—of the author's life, which were already a source of scandal in Germany when the diaries appeared. The English version emphasizes, on the other hand, Mann's political tribulations and moral dilemmas during those two especially troubling periods of his life. I read one edition and then the other, following a strict chronological order. This arrangement allows me a completely new reading, much richer than the partial reading I had done in Lanzarote when the Spanish version appeared. The first period comprises the end of the war in 1914, the defeat and sanctions imposed by the Allies. Mann had just published *Reflections of an Unpolitical Man*, a book in praise of Prussia, of drunken nationalism. By that time Mann was a celebrated writer whose life seemed to be collapsing around him. The German defeat stuns him. His hatred for a "French-style" democracy is brutal, and he renews the conflict with his brother Heinrich, the democrat and, therefore, the victor. His scorn for the concept of democracy leads him to make unimaginable leaps, completely unexpected and incompatible with his world for the purpose of hitting his target. On 24 March, 1919, at a moment of extreme agitation, he writes: "Rejection of the peace terms by Germany! Revolt against the bourgeois windbags. Let us have a national uprising now that we have been worn to shreds by the lying claptrap of that gang—and in the form of communism, for all I care; a new August 1, 1914! I can see myself running out into the street and shouting, 'Down with lying Western democracy! Hurrah for Germany and Russia!'"[22] This represents, of course, a momentary outburst. It is natural that he would not be attracted to the Bavarian Soviet Republic; it celebrates Heinrich, his enemy brother, excessively; what's more, its tinge is too plebeian and Judaizing (Katia, his wife, is Jewish, but because she belongs to a very rich family it is as if she were not). The notebooks that contain this portion of the diaries were saved by chance. Mann used them to recreate the period's atmosphere while he was writing *Doctor Faustus*. Fortunately, he did not include them among the other notebooks that were burned during his stay in California. As it turns out, he did not want to leave any testament in his diaries of his behavior before 1933, the year in which his political exile began. I read this portion of his diaries with astonishment, lamenting that there no longer existed a bridge that connected this moment to the beginning of the author's conversion to the abominable cause of which he later became an apostle: democracy.

The diaries from both periods have something in common. In them we find the author in total defeat, lacking *terra firma* on which to stand. They are writings filled with turmoil and anger, with confusion,

---

22 Translated by Richard and Clara Winston

humiliation, and outbursts of irrational violence, physical and nervous illness. Mann is one of the authors whom I've read obsessively since adolescence. Calvino, in his *Six Memos for the Next Millennium*, considers *The Magic Mountain* to be the book key to understanding our century, because it contains the issues and problems that continue to concern us today. *The Magic...* is for me the most difficult test to which the spirit can be subjected, the very camera with which to reproduce the spectrum of a way of thinking. The fool will lose himself in the folds of its prose and will believe that its thousand pages contain a degree of foolishness comparable only to his own. There will also be those who approach the work with priestly veneration and will be, in spite of whatever they may think, the least apt to understand the book. Their fatuous severity will prohibit them from understanding Mann, a fundamentally parodic writer; a thinker, yes, but one who subjected thought to the corrosive acid of relentless irony.

24 JANUARY

A little over thirty years ago I met the great Polish writer Jerzy Andrzejewski. We met for the first time in Warsaw in a café in the Hotel Bristol to resolve some doubts that had arisen in my work. I was translating *The Gates of Paradise* at the request of Joaquín Díez-Canedo. I had the impression that the author did not care if the translation was good or bad. It seemed strange to him that his novel, which related an obscure medieval episode—the fantastical children's crusade that marched toward Jerusalem to rescue the Holy Sepulcher from impious hands—would interest anyone in Mexico. He dealt quickly with the questions relevant to the book, and we then began to talk about other topics. He asked me about my professional experience. I listed among my translations Conrad's *Heart of Darkness*. He seemed to perk up. He told me that the writers who most interested him were Joseph Conrad and Thomas Mann. Before the war, in his youth, he had become excited by a few French Catholic novelists, but the brutal experiences—the occupation, the destruction of Warsaw, everything that happened afterward—had erased that enthusiasm. He did not deny that Mauriac could be a competent storyteller, but thought his sermonizing was petty. Conrad and Mann had become giants for him during those dreadful years. Only the person who had read *Doctor Faustus* could understand the devastation to the soul caused by the German occupation. When he realized that I was able to speak with ease about those authors, Andrzejewski's attitude changed. We went over the translation again, and he clarified a few things for me. And then he continued to talk about Conrad and Mann.

26 JANUARY

Kundera on *The Magic Mountain*: "Thus a vast *background* is meticulously depicted before which are played out Hans Castorp's fate and the ideological duel between two consumptives: Settembrini and Naphta: the one a Freemason and democrat, the other a Jesuit and autocrat, both of them incurably ill. Mann's tranquil irony relativizes these two learned men's truths; their dispute has no winner. But the novel's irony goes further and reaches its pinnacle in the scene where, each surrounded by his little audience and intoxicated by his own implacable logic, they both push their arguments to the extreme so that no one can any longer tell who stands for progress and who for tradition, who for reason and who for the irrational, who for the spirit and who for the body. Over several pages we witness an enormous confusion where words lose their meaning, and the debate is all the more violent because the positions are interchangeable."[23]

27 JANUARY

Reading Thomas Mann's diaries, his memories of his children, of his wife, at times produces an uncomfortable feeling: there is too much intensity in the family drama, excessive complexities, the more evasive the account becomes the more shadows it casts; each fissure, each silence, seems to conceal a torture, an upheaval. One has a feeling of scrutinizing characters through a keyhole. We see only a part of the action; everything else remains in the shadows. It embarrasses us to be pilfering through other people's lives and at the same time we cannot help but do it. A few months ago I experienced the same feeling of sneaking into a world where I was not invited when I visited the residence where Mann lived for a little over a decade in Pacific Palisades, a neighborhood of Los Angeles, with Efraín Kristal, a close friend and expert on Mann. We took advantage of the goodwill of the army of Mexican gardeners who were pruning the trees near the garden; our common language served as our password. Strolling the lawns, being on the terrace I had seen so many times in photographs where Mann usually took coffee with his family and a handful of privileged visitors, seeing the grove that surrounded the house with such grandeur that one can only classify it as Wagnerian, overwhelmed me with emotion. I imagined the wonder that the son of the North must have experienced each time he arrived home and happened upon a landscape comparable only to the beginning of creation, which he

23 Translated by Linda Asher

had glimpsed during his childhood in the albums or stories of his Brazilian mother. In that house Mann finished the last volume of *Joseph and His Brothers*; it was there that he conceived, wrote, suffered, and finished *Doctor Faustus*.

29 JANUARY

During the day, I did nothing but read Mann's diaries. His exile in Switzerland, the nervous crises that cause him to fear that he had plunged into madness. His comparison of the image of Germany and Germanness prevalent in the first section of the diaries (1918–21) and the second (1933–37) is rather interesting. On the 23rd of March of 1933, having just gone into exile, he writes: "At breakfast one of these necessarily unresolved talks with Katia about Germany and the terrifying side of its character." The fact that Germany feigns possessing a different (and superior) fate than the rest of the world becomes an obsession for Mann. Already in the first section of the diaries he had written: "I am surprised to see that Jakob Schaffner had written that 'the German people in the depth of their soul believe that its peculiarity in the world will never be understood or permitted; the German nation must exist in opposition to the world or it must cease to exist.' This is exactly what I maintain in my *Reflections*, even though I express it differently." This character of uniqueness defended in 1918 changes direction radically during his years of exile: "But this is the only nation in Europe that does not fear and abhor war; rather it deifies it," he writes on 7 September, 1933. "Wretched, isolated, demented people, misled by a wild, stupid band of adventurers, whom they take for mythic heroes," he notes on October 14 of the same year. "Rychner [...] speaks of the isolation of Germany and her painful preoccupation with herself. For an analysis of this aspect of Germany, always out for different things from what the world needs, see Nietzsche," he opines seven days later on October 21. That preoccupation, that rejection of the notion of a different fate for Germany, which he had so exalted in the past, will permeate Mann's writing until his death. Germany's loneliness in the world! The world's inability to understand Germany! On January 11, 1934 he notes: "During our stroll at sunset I thought again about the novel about Faust. Such a symbol of the freedom of the character and fate of Europe will be, perhaps, not only happier but also more correct and adequate than an oratorical and condemnatory confession about the present."[24] Years later, he would add: "In the moving admiration of Leonard Frank [toward the first chapters of *Doctor Faustus*] I sensed a kind of warning, of avoiding contributing with my novel the creation of a new German myth, praising the demonic character in Germans."

30 JANUARY

To understand the range of elements that bubble in Mann's Faustian cauldron, one only need look at the fragments of the diary that Mann incorporates in *The Story of a Novel*, the account of how he wrote *Doctor Faustus*. The vigor and curiosity of the old writer in exile are worthy of a titan. Those pages are testimony to the complexity of his endeavor. The annotations correspond to different orders: geographic, political, theological, medical, historical, musical, in addition to references to the political news of the day and to the tribulations and joys of family life and of his intimate group of friends: "Read an excellent article in *The Nation*, a piece by Henry James on Dickens.

---

24 This entry is missing from the English translation. —*Trans.*

[...] Written in 1864 at the age of twenty-two. Amazing! Is there anything like it in Germany? The critical writings of the West are far superior... Extensive reading of Niebuhr's book, *The Nature and Destiny of Man*... Till after midnight reading in its entirety Stifter's wonderful *Rock Crystal*. [...] The coal miner strike, serious crisis. Government takeover of the mines. Troops to protect those willing to work—which will be few...Read some curious things on the inglorious defeat of the Germans in Africa. Nothing of Nazi fanaticism's 'to the last drop of blood...' Talking in the evening with Bruno Frank on the new strike wave here and the administration's responsibility for it. Concern about the North American home front... Heaviest bombing of Dortmund, with more than a thousand planes. All Europe in invasion fever. Preparations of the French underground organization. Announcement of the general strike. The garrisons in Norway are instructed to fight 'to the last man'—which never happens. In Africa 200,000 prisoners were taken. Superiority of materiel in quantity and quality explains the victory...Expectation of the invasion of Italy. Undertakings against Sardinia and Sicily are in the offing...In the evening read *Love's Labour's Lost*. The Shakespeare is pertinent. It falls within the magic circle—while around it sounds the uproar of the world. Supper with the Werfels and the Franks. Conversation on Nietzsche and the pity he arouses—for his and for more general desperation. Meetings with Schoenberg and Stravinsky planned...Calculations of time and age relationships in the novel, vital statistics and names...On Riemenschneider and his time. Purchases. Volbach's *Instrumentenkunde* [a handbook on musical instruments]. Notes concerning Leverkühn as musician. His given name to be Anselm, Andreas, or Adrian. Notes on Fascist ideology of the period.

Gathering at the Werfels with the Schoenbergs. Pumped S. a great deal on music and the life of a composer. To my deep pleasure, he himself insists that we all must get together more often....On May 23, 1943, a Sunday morning little more than two months after I had fetched out that old notebook, and also the date on which I had my narrator, Serenus Zeitblom, set to work, I began writing *Doctor Faustus*."[25]

1 February
Juan García Ponce published in 1972 an exceptional essay on Mann's work: *Thomas Mann Alive*. It was published by Era. It is inexplicable to me that it has not been reissued. A book that critics, aspiring critics, everyone should study closely.

2 February
Mann's anger is fierce, visceral, Olympian. He unleashes on a general target: Western democracies—particularly the French—during the first period; and Nazism during the second. He also returns to another topic in particular: the intellectuals who support these movements. During his exile he believes that the entire non-rationalist philosophical tradition is responsible for the tragedy Germany is experiencing. Even Bergson is accused of being a precursor of the Nazi model. Everything that sustains Mann's work—instinct, the irrational, myth—ends up being frantically condemned by him in moments of desperation. Kundera says: "There is a fundamental difference in the way philosophers and novelists think. People talk about Chekhov's philosophy, or Kafka's or Musil's, and so on. But just try to draw a coherent philosophy out of their writings! Even when they

25 Translated by Richard and Clara Winston

express their ideas directly, in their notebooks, the ideas are intellectual exercises, paradox games, improvisations, rather than statements of thought…"[26] Indeed, there is an ongoing discussion in Mann's great books—with others, with who he has been, and with who he is when he writes in his diary—but the novelist's instinct transforms it, gives it another dimension, confers on it a different meaning. In a single diary entry he can state one idea and end up sustaining its opposite. All of this material, by the time it reaches the novel, will come out of chaos, will be coherent and cease being formless without losing the intensity it had in real life, that is, in the diaries.

3 FEBRUARY

All throughout the day I did nothing but read Mann's diaries and take notes. Afterward, I read the autobiography of Klaus, his son, to compare each one's version on certain episodes. I did not finish reading until after three a.m. Despite being tired, I was not able to fall asleep right away, so I took a higher dose of Lexotan than normal. The plot woven between their two lives overwhelmed me with sadness. The young Klaus's thrilling ascent and his unhappy decline, his fragility, and the maddening upheaval of history are the elements of the story. The relationship between Klaus and his father is marked by darkness, bursts of passion, and distance. They seek and at the same time establish their distances. The son's autobiography outlines his initial triumphs and his final anguish. The victories were short-lived; anguish, on the other hand, accompanied him for years. Let us consider Klaus's diaries: "October 24, 1942: Terrible sadness. I want to die. October 25: I want to die. October 26: I want to die. How long will I be able to hold out?

---

26 Translated by Linda Asher

October 27: I want to die. I want to die. I want to die. Death seems the ideal solution. I would like to die. Life is unbearable for me. I have no desire to live. I want to die." Five years later he would commit suicide after several failed attempts. In his diary, Thomas Mann embodies Settembrini, but also Naphtha. Sometimes both at the same time. What is remarkable is that he seems not to notice except in a chance moment, like when he reads the following words in an essay by Gide: "While in the war of 1914 the best of French thinkers fought alongside France, the best German thinkers rebelled against Prussia..." Mann is surprised, as if this included him, but not entirely. "That I have attempted, in *Reflections,* to contribute to and fight in favor of Prussianism is something that will remain ambiguous and strange, like an odd paradox." Gombrowicz commented that his mother claimed a number of virtues, firmly convinced that she possessed them in full, when the truth was that in real life she possessed defects that were antagonistic to those virtues. Mann often speaks of his modesty, his life as a recluse, his exclusion from the world, when in fact his life constitutes a daily and ongoing relationship with fame. The slightest sense of failure is unbearable for him; it causes him to become ill. Photos from his exile in Switzerland bear witness to the everyday drama. His face, like all his faces, possesses something demented, distraught; they are faces of vampires, of possessed men. They are marked by insecurity. Years later in California, restoration, embellishment, and supreme elegance will all be regained. His work discipline is exemplary, admirable, and heroic throughout his life. Knowing that he is the owner of a word that others are anxiously awaiting—a single word to awaken or reassure his flock—gives him in due course a sense of continuity.

4 FEBRUARY

His admiration for Kafka is constantly growing. In April 1935, Mann writes, "I resumed reading Kafka's *Metamorphosis*. I would dare say that Kafka's legacy represents the most brilliant German prose written in the past decades. Is there anything in German that is not mere provincialism alongside him?"

5 FEBRUARY

Mann's characters embody the greatness of our species: Joseph, Jacob, biblical heroes; Goethe; a medieval pope who becomes a saint; Adrian Leverkühn, a composer who transforms contemporary music. They are all eagles who soar in the highest heaven. Kafka's, on the other hand, barely have names, some only receive an initial. They move through streets as oppressive as the sewer drains. They move like moles, puppets, sleepwalkers. Mann is the subject of tributes attended by heads of state, crowned heads, hundreds of prestigious guests. Kafka meets with a few close friends in café Arco, a modest locale in Prague. The thought that someone might host a banquet in his honor could only occur to him in a fever-induced dream. Mann! Kafka! Everything between them would seem to belong to different worlds. But in the world of great literature profound coincidences are often recorded. Those differences that the idle and foolish delight in pointing out are almost always superficial. Art, when it is worthy of receiving that name, is a testament to having reached its ultimate limit, of reaching resolutely the goal that bears the sign of the extreme. Mann *dixit*.

Xalapa, February 1995

THE GATES OF PARADISE

For Carlos Monsiváis

Jorge Luis Borges writes in a preface to Marcel Schwob's *The Children's Crusade*: "At the beginning of the twelfth century, two expeditions of children departed Germany and France. They thought they could cross the sea unharmed. Did not the words of the Gospel authorize and protect them? 'Let the children come unto me and forbid them not' (Luke 18:16). Had not the Lord declared faith is enough to move a mountain (Matthew 17:20)? Hopeful, ignorant, happy, they set out to the ports of the South. The foretold miracle did not happen. God allowed the French column to be kidnapped by slave traders and sold in Egypt; the German one became lost and disappeared, devoured by barbaric geography and (it is surmised) by plagues."

Borges cites, as a precursor of the narrative form chosen by Schwob, *The Ring and the Book*, by Robert Browning, "a long narrative poem that reveals through twelve monologues the intricate history of a crime, from the point of view of the murderer, his victim, the witnesses, the defense attorney, the prosecutor, the judge, even Robert Browning," a device widely used before and after by the English novel. I could immediately cite an extensive list of titles employing the same analytical method, where the reader looks over a series of monologues in his eagerness to elucidate a specific mystery. The cast of characters includes some who are directly implicated in that mystery, not necessarily involving a criminal act (it can refer to an obscure relationship, a hard to explain friendship, the secret rites of a religious sect, many other activities). Wilkie Collins ingeniously employed that architecture in *The Moonstone* and created a canon from which the majority of this century's detective novels draw. The characters that produce these particular versions can be reliable, uncertain, or unreliable; the first utilize all their resources in an attempt to arrive at the truth; the others persist in corrupting, impeding, and distorting that process. Ultimately, in good or bad faith, every witness is in some way unreliable. Even the most upright, scrupulous one ends up contaminating his version with his own emotional baggage, his philias and phobias, or simply because he occupies a specific position relative to the incident about which he must give witness. Consider Emily Brontë and *Wuthering Heights*, where even the well-intentioned characters, even when attempting to explain it, assist in confusing an already too intricate story. Closer to our time, these suspicious truths, oblique and conjectural, become more obscure due to the complexity of modern narrative forms. In Akutagawa's *Rashomon*, Faulkner's *The Sound and the Fury*, and Juan Rulfo's *Pedro Páramo* the reader is forced to continually reconstruct a plot that is constantly changing, in which the apparent certainties that any of the protagonists allows you to anticipate are partially or completely invalidated by the testimony of the next.

In *The Children's Crusade*, that perfect hallucination by Marcel Schwob, each monologue is followed by a more intense and disturbing one: they are the voices of those who make up the long column marching toward the liberation of the Holy Sepulcher, and also those of some characters related to it in one way or another. We hear the voice of popes, lesser clergy, and merchants, of children, and a leper. From this disharmony a song of innocence is born, at the same time one of its counterpoints insinuates a suspicion of that innocence. It is a story that contradicts at every moment its unassuming appearance. The language is stripped of any hint of opulence, any desire for ornamentation, in search of an essential nakedness, without damaging at any moment its extreme elegance. The sudden appearance of blind and mute children, of leprous witnesses, in this march that takes place amid pious songs, assimilates the cruelty of the world and its sacred character into a single vision. The leper's monologue is perhaps the most fantastic prize that reading has ever given me. I have read this wonderful story by Schwob countless times, and when I arrive at the leper's words, I am as amazed and moved as intensely as the first time. The mystery encapsulated in those two pages occurs, I imagine, by the brush of the monstrous and redemption, or of abjection and grace. This is undoubtedly the result of a process of verbal alchemy, a symbolist vision awash in astrological flourishes. It is well known that Schwob was a symbolist writer, but he was also a theosophist. The essential material of *The Children's Crusade* seems to have been collected and amassed in a secret path between the twenty-two paths that lead to the *Tree of Life*.

In 1959 a contemporary version of *The Children's Crusade* was published in Poland. Its author, Jerzy Andrzejewski, a stranger to the symbolist aesthetic as well as to any theosophical temptation, managed to create with this ancient topic a monologue of extreme tension whose linguistic core is even more impenetrable than that of Schwob's story. The publication of this novel represented a challenge at the time.

The refined stylization of form, his stubborn refusal to make concessions to the reader, was the clearest expression of rejection of
the official aesthetic. And although it is true that Andrzejewski had
not previously succumbed to the inanities of socialist realism, such
a departure stunned the Polish intellectual community, not to mention the censors and Party ideologues. Moreover, the intense homo-
erotic current that sustains the novel angered many sectors, both
Party officials and conservatives. Two years earlier, in 1957, another
of his novels, *The Inquisitors*, had provoked heated debate. It was
a bold invective against Stalinist terror and intimidation. Thereafter,
Andrzejewski became an uncomfortable presence for many Poles.
He did not seek to flatter the government or the Church. His courage seemed suicidal, the proof of which was not only these novels
but also his many outbursts, both public and private, his statements,
and the documents that carried his signature.

I lived in Warsaw from 1963 to 1966, a surprising period in many
ways. A few years earlier, in 1956 in Moscow, during the famous
20ᵗʰ Congress of the Communist Party, an incredible document was
read condemning Stalin's crimes, which in Poland translated into
a spring that lasted several years. Beginning in 1957, censorship began
to yield ground; Witold Gombrowicz's novels were able to be published, as well as "difficult" works by authors from within, the aforementioned novels by Andrzejewski, and Kazimierz Brandys's *Mother of
the Kings*, Leszek Kolakowski's *The Key to Heaven*, and *Shakespeare Our
Contemporary* by Jan Kott, which would have caused serious problems
for the author had it circulated a few years earlier. During that time,
a prewar avant-garde repertoire reappeared in the theater, especially
Witkiewicz's dramas of the grotesque; the contemporary works by

Slawomir Mrozek also premiered. Bruno Schulz's work was published again, and included in the index of socialist realism. There was a lot of experimentalism and energy in the theater, cinema, music, and, to a certain extent, in literature. Before I left Poland, the situation was beginning to change—for the worse, of course, and the spaces that had been gained were gradually closed.

Shortly after I settled in Warsaw, I received a copy of an Italian translation of *The Inquisitors*. I read it immediately. It seemed unimaginable that in an Eastern European country something like it could be published. The story was set in fifteenth-century Spain, the central character was Torquemada, and the setting was the tribunals of the Holy Inquisition. There was something shocking about reading that book at that time. Its similarity to the mechanisms, to the methods, and even to the language of the repressive organs of the immediate past was astounding. A theatrical version, directed by Andrzejewski himself, attracted crowds that remained in the theater, breathless, as if they were attending a mystical session or an exorcism. The Poles recognized the cruelty of the times they had endured—the destitution, the unscrupulousness, the surveillance, and the inhuman punishments—everything attenuated by the belief that the end justifies any kind of means. And that end was sublime, delusional, and redemptive: the establishment of the Kingdom of God on Earth, no less! The audience recognized its executioners in the play, they heard a language similar to one they had been subjected to, but at the same time they were obligated to recognize the personal role they had played in one way or another in the cruel masquerade. It was obviously the work of a moralist; the theatrical version had the steely character found in the morality plays of English medieval drama used to reinforce catechization, not unlike Spain's *autos sacramentales*. The difference between *The Inquisitors* and its contemporaries, the moralizing and didactic works of socialist realism, was vast; Andrzejewski's literary mastery was undeniable, thanks to which the abstract character that the subject demanded did not come off as hollow sermonizing. The reader and viewer received the balm they needed because, despite the discursive tone, a feeling of mercy emanated from the work, not only toward the offended and humiliated but also and especially toward men who in their youth had joined, with passion and absolute faith, a cause in which they believed, only to discover years later that instead of serving God they had become followers of the devil. Their lives shattered suddenly into bits of ash and rubble. Their commitment and zeal had only served the forces of evil. As they lost their faith they also saw themselves stripped of all dignity and self-respect, yet they refused to allow society to treat them like dung.

Around that time, I read Ryszard Matuszewski's *Profiles of Contemporary Polish Artists* to familiarize myself with contemporary Polish literature; a purely informative book, not dogmatic, but yes, as far as I remember, too cautious—one of those phlegmatic literary panoramas, a bit bland and sparing in terms of ideas—but decidedly useful. I searched for Andrzejewski's biographical sketch. Matuszewski profiled the young Catholic pre-war intellectual and follower of Jacques Maritain; he spoke of the success of his first novel, *Mode of the Heart*, of the presence in the work of echoes of Joseph Conrad and two French Catholic writers, François Mauriac and Georges Bernanos. He also spoke of Andrzejewski's activity in the resistance during the period of occupation, of his distancing from the right-wing groups he had frequented in the past, until arriving at the discovery, once

Poland was liberated, of a devastated, amorphous, and lost, but at the same time hopeful, society, which he described in his first major novel, *Ashes and Diamonds* (1948), in which he treated with evenhandedness the men of the new regime as well as the desperate youth who shed their blood and others' on the altar of a dead Poland, of exhausted values, of the former marshals. Matuszewski referred to Andrzejewski as a new type of Polish writer: a moralist. The profile ended there; it did not treat the novelist's new works: *The Inquisitors* and *The Gate of Paradise*; I do not know, nor do I now have means to verify, if it was because the *Profiles* were published before the appearance of those novels, or if out of caution, or fear of unpleasant consequences, he might have preferred not to comment on those books that seemed to give off a strong odor of sulfur.

So when I arrived in Poland Andrzejewski's celebrity had already been established. To his enthusiasts he represented the moral con-sciousness of the nation, a lone voice in the midst of a multitude of opportunists, of triflers or imbeciles, and during the years I lived in the country I was witness to infinite, never-ending, and violent arguments about his personality, his opinions, and his life. Filmmakers, young writers, and university students all revered him. The dogmatists, people of reason, those on the left as well as the right, condemned him. The former were proud of his clarity, his literary talent, his consistency, and, above all, his courage—a superlative quality in Poland; the latter, the representatives of order, Catholics or Communists, abhorred him. He was the worst possible example for Polish youth; the sordidness of his life, the places and people he frequented would have—they argued—led him many years before, in a truly respectable country, to prison. That this arrogant pervert—friend of Jews, perhaps Jewish himself by some branch of the family—dared speak about public morality made them tremble with rage. I lived for a long period of time at the Hotel Bristol in the center of Warsaw where there was a small café-bar whose atmosphere could be dazzling. There I was able to see up close Marlene Dietrich, Jacques Brel, Peter Brook, Arthur Rubinstein, Claudio Arrau, Giorgio Strehler, Ella Fitzgerald, and Luchino Visconti. These colorful and illustrious guests stayed in the Bristol when they came to Warsaw; the locale was also frequented by Polish writers and artists. They would have had to chain me in my room to stop me from showing up there every evening. On several occasions, I saw Andrzejewski in conversation with Andrzej Wajda, the director who had adapted his novel *Ashes and Diamonds* into an extraordinary film. They were working, it seemed, on a new script; they read, drank vodka, and argued endlessly. Eventually, they were joined by so many famous actresses and actors that their table became the café's center of attention.

I do not recall who introduced us, but I do remember at our first meeting he spoke specifically of Dostoevsky's *Crime and Punishment*. He said, dismissively and shrugging his shoulders, that the Poles would never be able to understand Dostoevsky. They tried to approach him from only a religious perspective. They had turned Romano Guardini's book into a primer from which they were afraid to stray. Reading Dostoevsky was for them a form of prayer. "If someone were to tell them that what was truly important was to pay attention to the struggle in any of its chapters between instinct and reason and the feeling of victory and defeat that the contenders shared after the fight, my countrymen would be dumbfounded, because that's not how it is written in their prayer book. All they care about is that, you know, prayer—not just the Catholics, the Communists too," and he shrugged his shoulders again as if trying to rid himself of a heavy burden, while the shadow of a flash of lightning passed through his eyes. On another occasion, I heard him comment that of the Hispano-American authors translated into Polish, which were then still very few, the only one that interested him was Carpentier. Not *The Lost Steps*, he clarified, where the opulence of language and the masterful architecture was wasted on an insignificant topic: the futile search for the sources of creation and the attempt to find them in their most primitive veins—the forest—as opposed to the elements developed over centuries by thought. Stravinsky had already done that at the beginning of the century. The opposition seemed obsolete to him. "Only the most primitive Polish nationalists could hold such nonsense. For them folklore is the greatest gift that mankind has received from the gods." *Explosion in the Cathedral* was another matter. "Anyone who lived through the German occupation and the hardest chapter of the totalitarian state could read that book as if the story of betrayed ideals were part of his own experience. When I got to the last paragraph I returned to the beginning to reread that exceptional book." He declared that in literature he only appreciated real challenges and the search for great form, and that in Poland novelists had become so lazy and demoralized that nobody dared to undertake such an ambitious effort as Carpentier had in that book. Someone mentioned then a recent novel by Jarosław Iwaszkiewicz, and asked with feigned innocence if it was not perhaps the equivalent he was looking for. Andrzejewski again shrugged his shoulders, cast a burning look, smiled sarcastically, and said something in slang that I did not understand but that provoked a perverse laugh from all those present.

By then, I had already read *The Gates of Paradise* and recommended the book to several Spanish-language publishers. One day a contract arrived with instructions to give it to the author for his signature. I phoned him and we met at noon at the Bristol's café—a neutral time, devoid of *tertulias* or extravagant characters. It seemed to surprise him that one of his novels—and particularly that one!—was going to be published in Mexico, a country he did not know except for a few characters and episodes from the revolution and those from the movies. It was the first time I talked to him alone. He received my enthusiastic comments about his novel with skepticism, as if it were a joke he had to tolerate. He lashed out incessantly at the limitations of the Poles, but at the same time—and to my surprise—he related the value of every literary work to the circumstances of his country, its historical tragedies, its bloody past and mediocre present, which seemed to me to be a more sophisticated and slightly comical form of nationalism. When he was convinced that I knew the authors, that I had translated Conrad, and that I was obsessed with Mann, everything changed. During the following weeks we meet four or five times to solve some problems of translation; during our short breaks, I asked him about Polish writers. Usually, when I mentioned the name of an author he would make a gesture with his hand as if shooing a fly and mutter: "His brain is smaller than a flea's," or "Let's not waste time talking about that idiot." He respected Bruno Schulz greatly. It is strange, but I cannot recall a single opinion about Gombrowicz, whom out of necessity we must have talked about. Although at midday we talked about literature, when I met him later in a nightclub on Foksal Street, the subject was completely different. Even in lighthearted moments he was stern, even theoretical.

What I know is that during our daytime sessions, as well as our informal evening encounters, he always erected an invisible wall around the table, seemingly by his own choice, beyond which the world ceased to exist.

After translating *The Gates of Paradise*, someone handed me Czeslaw Milosz's *The Captive Mind*. When I finished reading it, I had the feeling that someone had just given me an inexplicable beating. I found it inconceivable that the exiled poet had been able to incorporate into his book such a hurtful and offensive biography of a writer whom the best Poles considered a paradigm of national dignity. The fact that Milosz would begin this text by recounting an intimate childhood friendship, almost a brotherhood, and would recount some of the most heinous moments shared during the German occupation, as well as after, seemed to make the insult more powerful. It was like someone's boasting of having stabbed someone in the back, only later to reveal flippantly that the dead man was his own brother. *The Captive Mind* appeared in the U.S. in 1951 during the harshest moments of the Cold War, and, as always with a political book written with honesty, it irritated both the left and right. It was in no way a mere political pamphlet but an autobiographical account that included an infinite number of nuances, that tried to explain to the foreign reader the complex knot of passions and experiences that made the history of his country something very different from that of other European nations. It was not about a world of absolute good and evil but the result of circumstances inherited over centuries, a feverish world, strained by history. When Milosz received the Nobel Prize, he made one of his first trips to Poland after a thirty-year absence. There was an emotionally charged event during which the poet read his work. In the front row sat Andrzejewski. They were, apparently, no longer enemy brothers.

Shortly before beginning these pages, I reread *The Captive Mind* and found it remarkable; the immense changes in Poland, unthinkable during the period in which Milosz wrote, put many things into perspective and clarified others. There is a passion evident in the book not too different from that experienced during a civil war: discovering that a brother has gone to the opposing camp is an affront that cannot be forgiven, the wound that takes longest to heal, many threads become entangled at once, very delicate tapestries move in an unpredictable way, stage by stage, the brother's past conduct is examined, and in each of them grounds for reproof are found, an unbearable tension is reached until a trigger, any trigger, produces the explosion. Milosz alludes repeatedly to the extraordinary pride and unbearable arrogance with which Andrzejewski carried himself; he recognizes his almost suicidal activity and value of his work during the darkest years of the German occupation, but forever regrets the major role such activity disguised; he even goes so far as to reproach him for being so perfect during the terrible years when life was constantly at stake. He finds that same organizational drive, that is, leadership, during the period of Communist militancy. He minimizes the quality of *Ashes and Diamonds*, which he points to as a sample of ideological literature, about which he is mistaken.

Surely Andrzejewski must have been insufferable, both in his role as Catholic intellectual and as well as that of Communist writer. We now know that these events are only a fragment of a longer history that was far from being finished when *The Captive Mind* appeared. Everything that followed exacted a heavy price. Renouncing with a minute handful of writers his membership in the Communist Party in protest of the Russian military occupation in Hungary in 1956 was not a joking matter. A decision of that caliber in a country where the Party was in power, and doing so during those years, had something of the unreal and much of the truly heroic about it. One left the Party by death or expulsion, and it is well known what was meant by expulsion. Writing and publishing the literature that Andrzejewski produced thereafter also exacted an enormous toll. It is possible that his personal liberation, and his decision not to make concessions, was based on the fiendish pride that was the most visible characteristic of his personality. Perhaps, deep down, driven by some earlier religious zeal, he would have liked to have been a martyr and to have died as such. He did not. He managed instead to leave behind perfect pages, of which *The Gates of Paradise* is perhaps the clearest proof.

When the Polish author spoke in the Bristol's café of the great literary challenges and the desire to achieve the greatest possible form as a maximum virtue, I thought of *The Gates of Paradise*. The difficulties involved were immense. To begin with, the novel consists of only two single sentences, the first consisting of one hundred and fifty pages; the other, just five words.

And in that first never-ending sentence weaves a complex and dark story in which, unhindered by a single period to fragment it, the confessions of the five adolescents who lead this illusory crusade become intermingled, a crusade that will never succeed in reaching the gates of Jerusalem and that will not even get close to them. It has been thirty years since I translated this enigmatic book whose center seems to shift at every moment. I was afraid that it had aged. Not so, its poetics has weathered time perfectly, and its meaning, in spite of how explicit its confessions seem, seems even more secretive now.

We come to know in great detail the love story of each of the adolescents who appear partially and piecemeal during the general confession by an insistent iterative exercise. We come to know the dramas that darken their lives, but could that be the goal of the story? Or did the author simply create a particularly refined style and a purely formal architecture for the pleasure of experiencing new narrative processes? Those questions distract us in order to keep the novel's very center hidden and wrapped in armor, to the point of preventing us from knowing with absolute certainly in which section it is located.

Four adolescents from the village of Cloyes march toward Jerusalem to deliver the Holy Sepulcher from the hands of the infidels: Maud, the daughter of a blacksmith; Robert, the miller's son; Blanche, the daughter of a carpenter; and Jacques, a shepherd who does not know who his parents are. Accompanying them is Alexis Melissen, a Byzantine Greek, Count of Chartres and Blois, titles he inherited from his late adoptive father. Everything begins when the shepherd Jacques ventures down to the village square one night, as if suffering hallucinations, and interrupts a feast with these words:

"The Lord God Almighty has revealed to me that because of the blindness and cowardice of kings, princes and knights, it is fitting that the children of Christ should go, for the love of God, unto the relief of the city of Jerusalem that is fallen into the hands of the infidel Turk, God the all-powerful has chosen ye, for the confident faith and innocence of children, greater than all the powers on land and sea, are able to accomplish the most holy miracles, therefore possess your hearts with pity, for the Holy Land and for the desolate sepulchre and tomb of Jesus…" [27]

---

27 Translated by James Kirkup

In *The Children's Crusade* Schwob presents in succession the children's monologues, as well as those of some characters who participated in this unprecedented enterprise. Andrzejewski, on the other hand, strives for simultaneity. In the endlessly interwoven opening sentence, the author integrates the stories of the four crusaders from Cloyes with that of Alexis Melissen, who voluntarily joins the group of modest artisans who heed the divine call. The exercise of confession sets the tale in motion. A unique receptacle has been created into which the information extracted from their confessions, as well as the self-confession of the old priest, flows and is collected. The call to the crusade is submerged in a complex tapestry of passions: loves of gleaming purity alongside others born of bloodshed, nourished by it, hidden beneath ominous burdens. Every character, both chaste and lascivious, has learned that suffering is the shadow of all love, that love divides into love and suffering, and that this will be one of the musical lines that will run throughout the book. The words of each of the children are echoed by those of the others; each confession modifies, expands, or clarifies those of their companions. A system of constant reiterations links the diverse monologues in the mind of the confessor, which provides the illusion of simultaneity. The long-awaited *multum in parvo* of the epigrammatic poets is achieved here through excess, fragmentation, and verbal interaction.

The novel begins with a cruel dream, filled with horrors and terrifying omens. The old priest dreams of two adolescents who move with great difficulty through an implacable desert. One of them falls prostrate on the sand; before dying, his moribund lips emit an exhortation to the other to continue the journey until he reaches Jerusalem's immense Gates of Paradise and carry out the magnificent task that has been entrusted to him: the liberation of the Sepulcher of Christ. The other, even weaker and more defenseless, continues the march at a faltering pace, feeling the empty air with his hands, as if he were about to touch with them, the long-awaited walls. Suddenly, he turns his face toward the priest and sees his empty eyes, eyes that will never behold the towers or the walls of the holy city. At that moment, the priest discovers with horror that the martyred face is that of the enlightened leader Jacques de Cloyes. The revelation terrifies him. It is necessary to find the source of the evil dream to understand its meaning. He decides to undertake a general confession, to probe the children's souls, to discover whether one harbors a dark sin, and, of course, to absolve it. At the end of the third day the general confession will end with that of the five children of Cloyes, the first to begin the march. The priest is determined to forgive everything. Nothing will stop the crusade. His long life as confessor has taught him that the desire for faith can also be born from suffering, misfortune, and destruction, and that the same poisoned sources are capable of generating a miracle. And that miracle can be none other than the rescue of the Sepulcher of Christ. He will be present at the supreme moment. He senses that his death is near, but that death will attain a greatness that his life has never known. Assisting in the mission undertaken by the children, entering with them into Jerusalem, prostrate at the finally-liberated tomb of the Lord, will endow his existence with the highest meaning to which it is possible to aspire.

As the confession progresses a moral conflict begins to loom, which the author was unable to do without and which functions as the strongest pillar of the story; without that ethical reflection the novel would still be amazing, but would run the risk of suffering from a decorative and archaeological saturation, as is the case with Flaubert's *Salammbô*, which would be entirely foreign to his intentions. Those battles between instinct, faith, and reason that Andrzejewski considered essential in the work of Dostoevsky are also present in his account and confer on them a modernity that could render incidental the fact that the action transpires in the early twelfth century.

"It's no use," Alexis Melissen confesses, attributing these thoughts to his adopted father, "all is vain apart from shame and prejudice, the satisfaction of the senses does not still desire and lust, for as soon as one desire is satisfied a hundred others awaken even more imperiously actions born of the purest desires end in remorse and infamy and perhaps there are no pure desires, the need for violence and cruelty takes possession of man's nature, he flees from it in a trembling and shame-filled solitude, then, drawn back once more into the ravening pack, driven by folly and the furies of physical strength, again he goes murdering and violating right and left until the moment of awakening arrives and then man finds himself once more alone in his solitude but because of the criminal gravity of his folly even more solitary than before and in that absolute solitude, in the prison of his flesh and spirit, he searches desperately and in vain for some way out, but there is no way out, he snatches blindly and vainly at what appear to be promises of salvation, but he can forget himself only in violence, a violence bereft of illusions, naked and black as hatred…"

The fatality with which man is drawn to crime, as if it were his only possible destiny, finds in that abstract struggle (like that contained in the mystery plays) the grace, the redemption, or the reason to save him. The search for good is as present in man as his instinct toward evil. The confessor knows this well: "No man could be evil all this life, and it can happen that when he has lost all hopes and all illusions a man kills this man in him and voluntarily takes his own life in a second of time and yet still goes on living, but in order to kill within him the need for love and the need for hope he has to live through many long, painful years, like a drowning man grasping at air, seizing a handful of water, now when the man in him is still not entirely dead and still walks the somber haunts of evil, if there be even the feeblest glimmer of good, of yearning for good in him, the man will crouch over that little wavering flame in order to delude himself in moments of solitude that what he sees there then, uncertain and weak, could still, with a favorable wind, be transformed into an immense blaze."

The ending is terrible. The last confessant, Jacques de Cloyes, who was thought to be illuminated by the grace of God, cannot be absolved. What the child believes to be an illumination in fact is not. The confessor understands that he must stop the march of madness, of innocence, of passions, and of lies. He also understands that his initial dream, that of a blind youth with hands groping the air while another dies in the desert was a premonition; that if he does not stop the thousands of children, they will perish along the way, and that he, poor and old, will not be granted the grace to reach Jerusalem with them, that he will not be witness to the liberation of the Holy Sepulcher. He stops and cries out in the middle of the night in an attempt to stop the children, but to no avail. Plunged into darkness, strengthened by their chants, the children will continue the march. Their voices will drown the words of the only man who has managed to understand the reason. And the heavy arm of a cross will knock him down, and the children will pass over his dying body as over a mere rough spot on the ground, and one after another will walk on him until his entire body is sunken into the mire.

Is the story perhaps a metaphor that draws us closer to events that occurred in a recent past? Will this march that progresses blindly amid chants and canopies and crosses toward an impossible end that rejects reason serve as an allusion to the permanent trepidation that has shaken our century, where the status of some words has led to nothing but unrest, cruelty, and madness? It is evident that God has not inspired the crusade. The illuminated pastor, in the constant transfer of passions that the novel records, wants to become someone else, to save his soul and free it from terrible guilt. Only chance, that night when Jacques de Cloyes went out into the square, interrupted a party, and implored the children to deliver the Holy Sepulcher, could prevent him from being branded insane. A moment was enough to save him, the acceptance of a girl who loves him, and then that of the boy who loves that girl, and so on to infinity. From that moment, once again, the energy of error showed its efficacy. Thousands of children abandoned their homes, traveled the roads of Europe, adding their voices and steps to a cause already lost.

The human and the sacred, the rational and the oneiric, the individual and the herd, love without hope and the assault of the body, the shadow of a dark present and the haziness of a time lost in the dawn of the twelfth century, an ancient history difficult to verify and an uncertain hope in the future—all will be added to Andrzejewski's tireless sentence (that syntax that now seems familiar because great novelists have employed and even exaggerated in recent years, but in 1957, when *The Gates of Paradise* appeared, it was absolutely unheard of) and will help transform it into the masterpiece that it undoubtedly is.

Xalapa, November 1995

OUR ULYSSES

I must have been eleven or twelve when I first heard the name José Vasconcelos mentioned. Once, while on holiday in Mexico City, where one of my aunts on my father's side lived, I picked up a book someone had left on a chair and glanced at it absentmindedly. It was Vasconcelos's *The Storm*. I was turning the pages mechanically, almost by inertia, more or less disinterested, when my aunt appeared—she had generously provided me with the canonical readings that corresponded to my changes in age: fairytales, Verne, London, Stevenson, Dickens; I think during the period in reference we had made it to Tolstoy. She seemed surprised to see that particular book in my hands. Without giving the matter too much importance, she casually suggested that I read something else; the book dealt with issues that were too complex—she told me—and since I did not know enough about the history of Mexico, I would only be bored. I thanked her for her advice. At home they had tried to interest me in the voluminous encyclopedia of Mexican history, *México a través de los siglos*, where from the opening statement of purpose I felt lost. Everything would have remained there had my aunt that night during dinner not mentioned the incident, adding some mysterious reference to my precociousness.

She commented that she had found me absorbed in one of the more lurid passages of the book, which, if true, had occurred unbeknownst to me. That comment led to a heated discussion. A doctor who was an intimate family friend vociferously expressed his admiration for the Maestro and his revulsion for the immoral manner in which the country had repaid his efforts. His books claimed not one but many truths that no one in Mexico had had the courage to utter, adding that, unlike so many hypocrites and prigs, he was not appalled that the Maestro—for years when anyone mentioned Vasconcelos's name, they placed before it the word "Maestro," a term that instantly added a patina of greatness and martyrdom—had described his passions in such a stark fashion. The Maestro could allow himself the luxury of talking about his lovers and about any other matter he damn well pleased. "Read it," he told me, "don't allow them to keep anything from you; read it, it'll do you good. You'll find out what it means to be a real man in the midst of a bunch of lackeys and cowards." Later, the conversation became even livelier with anecdotes about the personage—his past, his women, his presidential campaign, his defeat, and his faith in Mexico—whom the nation had failed to appreciate.

After returning from the holidays, I found at our house *Creole Ulysses* and *The Storm*. Works, I suppose, that appeared obligatorily on the bookshelves of every enlightened middle-class family in Mexico. I mentioned the lively discussion that took place in Mexico City, and to my surprise, my uncle (my guardian) did not find it amusing. The very mention of Vasconcelos immediately imposed a tone of sober respect. He confirmed Vasconcelos's extraordinary worth, the admiration he deserved, and added that, in fact, I was not yet old enough to read these books, the memoir *The Storm* in particular, which dealt with personal issues about which it made no sense for me to know. Naturally, I concluded that these issues were the Maestro's "women." My grandmother spent much of her time buried in novels. She did not share my uncle's notion of progressive readings in relation to my age; all of her books were at my disposal. If I had been allowed to read Zola's *Nana* and, on the other hand, was not allowed to go near the pages of *The Storm*, it must mean they contained truly apocalyptic scenes. Perhaps it was a book similar to those written by Peral or "El Caballero Audaz," two of the most vulgar pornographers of the time, whom a classmate of mine had discovered in his older brother's bedroom, and whom we read in secret, more bewildered than excited.

Just three or four years later, as a student in preparatory, I was able to devour—with passion and astonishment—those first two autobiographical volumes; later in university, I continued with the remaining two, but I did so then with waning interest and too often defeated by exasperation and displeasure. Nowhere did I stumble upon the risqué scenes I expected. The figure of Vasconcelos was already well known to me; I had read and heard none too enthusiastic comments about him, some brutal, some apathetic; all of them iconoclastic. For example, he was no longer called Maestro, unless the word was accompanied by a sarcastic tone of irony or scorn.

After reading *Creole Ulysses* and *The Storm* I felt electrified by the energy of the prose. Reading was becoming an extraordinarily sensual experience. Vasconcelos, at his best, is a writer of the senses. Voluptuousness penetrates his language. I saw images, yes, but I also shared the tastes of desserts and delicacies, I sensed an array of aromas, from the sweat of the horses of troops on the move to the perfume of the opulent women evoked in certain passages. I suppose had I read

Mme. Blavatsky during that eager period of initiations I would not
have fallen into such deep trances. I recognized the character's heroic
spirit but, fortunately, he was a hero who refused to allow himself to
be transformed into a statue. I often became lost in the details. I knew
the revolutionary period only in broad terms, and the frantic sequence
of events and characters made me dizzy. The story of his passionate,
tumultuous, and ill-fated love for a woman named Adriana did not
seem at all unusual to me; I had often read similar things in novels and
had seen worse in the movies, to the extent that I thought that it was
completely normal, commonplace, something that awaited every man
upon reaching a certain age. It seemed inconceivable to me that some
readers would be scandalized by certain passages of his life because,
of course, at the time I did not understand, and I only managed to
during a later reading, to what extent the personal story recounted
by Vasconcelos violated the traditional notion of Mexican respect-
ability: that a man of his rank openly spoke out against marriage; that
he opposed marriage as an institution; that he reveled in his wife's
insufferable nature and preferred to live for many years in the company of a woman who at every turn encouraged excesses of elation,
passion, contempt, hatred, and even disgust, aware that the woman was
cheating on him—at times with very close friends—and who, aware
of her infidelities, would attempt to make her return to him, pleading
and threatening, and that after insulting her would reassure her, prepare
her food, and wash her clothes; who in his youth had been in love
with a girl from the underworld and had accepted money from her to
finance his carousing and drunkenness; and finally, distraught by the
insolence of such whores would, like a madman, track them down in
taverns and inns and then beg for their forgiveness: one could watch

all these things on screen or read about them quietly in a novel of any nationality and time; but that a Mexican man, a gentleman who was also a *macho*, would live it—which, although sad and regrettable, was little more than personal tragedy—and confess it, especially in print. The fact that the person sharing such unfortunate intimacies, his darkest moments, with the world was a man who had known the smell of gunpowder up close and held important public positions and was recognized by the youth of the continent as the *Teacher of America*, represented a transgression of customs that was difficult to forgive. Societal pressure eventually triumphed. In the last edition of his *Memoirs*, published during his lifetime by a Catholic publisher, Vasconcelos suppressed those passages. Families could once again sleep peacefully.

As an adolescent, reading all of that meant nothing; it did not exist. What is astonishing, however, was sharing in some way the fate of an exceptional man and his capacity for adventure; a man born not to obey orders of which his conscience would not have approved in advance; who had known prison, poverty, victory; who had participated in conspiracies and uprisings; a man able to relate the accomplishments and vicissitudes of his political activity with the same intense mystical aura with which he spoke of his philosophical discoveries and amorous exploits.

I was excited to learn, for example, that Vasconcelos had crossed most of the country on horseback, accompanied by a small band of loyalists and his mistress, Adriana—a woman who on that occasion was worse than the most destructive plague imaginable—venturing for days and days along the riskiest trails of the Sierra Madre, fleeing his enemies, constantly at risk of being ambushed, until finally crossing the Rio Grande and knowing that for the time being his life was safe; only to then find him almost immediately in the library of San Antonio, Texas, gathering materials for his *Aesthetics*; and a few weeks later in Paris, attending the historic premiere of Stravinsky's *The Rite of Spring*. Such was his life, and it was prodigious; that one day he would be conspiring for or against Pancho Villa, and in the next chapter studying Pythagoras or Plotinus in New York, or touring the Metropolitan Museum after diligently reviewing Burckhardt to better understand the painters of the Italian Renaissance. The upheavals in Mexico and his visions of the wider world alternate and overlap constantly. Sexual passion, intellectual desire, and a resolve to transform the country through spirit are the constants of the young Vasconcelos. Another, which spans everything, is the notion of "Glory," which he considers inherent to his person; he senses it from childhood, develops it in his youth, and defends it by any means necessary in the moments following the disaster.

That first reading, of course, was incomplete, and could not be otherwise. But it left me with the impression of having come into contact with a man of surprising originality and multiple visions. Further readings have refined, stylized, or altered that view. I do not share the majority of the opinions that Vasconcelos sustains; despite that, however, my astonishment, admiration, and recognition of his courage to confront the world and, above all, his refusal to follow the herd, still remain.

In 1956, at the request of the editor Rafael Giménez Siles, I visited Vasconcelos on two occasions at the National Library, the *Biblioteca México*, to clarify some doubts that arose while correcting the proofs of the first volume of his *Collected Works*, which were being prepared by one of the many publishing houses belonging to Don Rafael.

He had put me in charge of the first volume. The purpose of the visits, if I remember correctly, was to standardize the spelling of some names that the author employed arbitrarily. On both occasions, he received me in his office, in the company of the ambassador of the Dominican Republic. Vasconcelos had become in his final years a very pleasant man, always smiling, but at the same time very distant. He seemed not to take interest in the fate of that edition that would finally bring together all his books, some having been out of circulation for thirty or forty years. I stressed the desirability of standardizing the different ways he had written some geographical or biographical names and, above all, the various spellings of Russian and Asian names, sometimes copied from a French or English transcription, as well as obvious misprints in the original editions. He asked me to leave him the proofs and the list of possible corrections and return a few days later to pick them up. I went to see him a second time and again found him talking with the same diplomat. He apologized for not being able to review the papers. He then began to review the proofs with me, as well as the list that the proofreader had sent. With each of the items he would pause thoughtfully for a moment, continue his interrupted conversation with Trujillo's ambassador, and finally give his opinion; after five or six consultations of a relatively long list, he said there was no point in worrying about such minutiae, that the publisher should decide for him, that he had full confidence in Giménez Siles, and when it was all said and done the only thing that mattered were his thoughts and not such insignificant trivialities.

I had long since ceased to admire him. His articles in the press were dreadful. His defense of Francoism, of the totalitarian regimes in Latin America, his sympathies with the most reactionary sectors within the country, his raging anti-indigenism, his anti-Semitism, his disdain for modern literature—all preached in a tiresome and humorless way—turned their reading into a tedious enterprise. His philosophical books, of which he had long boasted, no longer interested anyone; his books on the history of Mexico no longer convinced anyone but the most intractable conservatives. His stories and literary meditations had aged. The youth had turned their back on him, and even his memoirs had paid a heavy price. None of this seemed to discourage him. On the contrary, he enjoyed the fight. If for a quarter century he had continuously said that Mexico was a debased nation and that all the revolutionary governments after Madero had been made up of thieves and scoundrels, he accepted as acknowledgment of his integrity the insults that the nation and the handful of crooks and incompetents hurled at his person. He seemed to be aware of the role he played: even if Mexican society no longer supported him and rejoiced in his downfall, even if it turned its back when he was ready to redeem it, even if politicians and their followers regarded him as a clown (a term that seemed to offend him more than any other, having said so many times, he continued to behave as he liked, in order to show what the politicians had managed to do to the country and even to him. If the world had grown debased and unhinged, if reason had lost its way, he would play a role commensurate with the circumstances. The real culprit was not the individual but the machinery of corruption manufactured by the governments that betrayed the Revolution.

To understand *Creole Ulysses* and his other memoirs it is worth recalling certain events. Vasconcelos begins to write his first volume in 1931, two years after his defeat in the presidential elections. He never recognized the official results. During the campaign he and his supporters were repeatedly harassed and ridiculed. Some Vasconcelists were killed, many others imprisoned. José Vasconcelos had been, at home and abroad, the great symbol of the revolution: educator of the nation, literary apostle, thinker, and, most importantly, the creator of an authentic and extraordinary cultural renaissance in the country, an effort in which all his gifts and prestige came together. Even now, our debt to the period of cultural renewal initiated by him seventy ago years is still immense. Universal education and textbook distribution became national causes during that period. They were christened "the years of the eagle" by Claude Fell in an excellent book on the period, borrowing an exhortation that Vasconcelos himself used with teachers. Although immense, it was the only triumph of his political life. The three times he ran for elected office he was defeated. First, as a potential candidate for a deputy position during the period of Francisco Madero; then in 1924, following his brilliant tenure in the Secretariat of Public Education, as candidate for governor of Oaxaca; and finally in 1929 as candidate for the presidency of the Republic. The rest is known by everyone: long years of exile, vain attempts to maintain a political presence in Mexico from abroad, long stays in Spain, speaking tours in South America, an invitation to the United States where several universities opened their doors to him. Gradually, active politics began to take a backseat, and the void left by that pursuit was filled by what he considered his essential vocation: philosophy. During this period, while working on his *Aesthetics*, he also wrote his autobiographical books to which he attributed a rather utilitarian character and in which he defended himself against the smear campaign orchestrated by his detractors; at the same time he went on the offensive and began to war ferociously against his enemies, old and new—those who had suddenly become turncoats. In his zeal to disparage his detractors he committed more than one injustice, sometimes by mere whim, or out of personal disagreement—and even over aesthetic disagreements.

The years of disillusionment, frustration, and resentment following the electoral defeat of 1929 play a major role in the development and content of the narrative about his life he would soon undertake. Upon leaving Mexico he discovered that his intellectual stature lacked the dimension he attributed to it, deluded by the arrogant conviction of his greatness, the blind devotion that his disciples and closest collaborators rendered, and, also, by the praise of some foreign intellectuals who had been invited to Mexico during his term as secretary.

Dialogue was not his forte, it never had been. One of the few childhood friends who dared to address him during the height of his career with the same familiarity as years before, during the period of the legendary meetings of the Mexican Youth Athenaeum, was Alfonso Reyes, who in a short period of particularly active correspondence offered the following advice: "…as I am in conversation with you, I am rereading some of your things, as I want to absorb everything you have published all at once, before continuing with my Hindustani studies. I must make two caveats that my experience as a reader demands: first, try to be clearer in defining your philosophical ideas; sometimes you only say half of what you should. Rise above yourself: read yourself objectively, do not allow yourself to become bogged down or consumed by the course of your feelings. To write you must think with your hand also, not just your head and heart. Second, put your ideas in successive order: do not insert one into another. You have paragraphs that are confusing by dint of addressing completely different things, and that do not even seem to be written seriously. One thing is the vital order of ideas, the order in which they are generated in every mind (which is only of interest to the psychologist and his experiments), and another is the literary order of ideas: which should be used, like a language or common denominator, when what we want is to communicate with others." Following this direct and cordial advice communicated in a letter of May 25, 1921, the tone of their correspondence continues to cool over a period of years to the mere exchange of formal, friendly cards.

While in exile, Vasconcelos visits José Ortega y Gasset in Spain, who received him and some close disciples in his office. Shortly before his death, Vasconcelos expressed disappointment at the meeting: "He did not make a good impression on me, nor I on him." There could be no dialogue: the Mexican's philosophical tools—a composite of vitalism, irrational energy, Bergson, Hinduism, Schopenhauer, refutations of Nietzsche, messianism, Dionysian exaltation—all nineteenth-century concepts, at time taken from second-rate treatises—in no way reconciled with the philosophical discourse that Ortega had resolved to introduce in Spain through the journal *Revista de Occidente*. In Buenos Aires, one of his former strongholds, he was considered by modern writers to be a completely dispensable figure, an eccentric character, irascible and obsolete. His old liberal and socialist friends no longer interested him, and the group from the journal *Sur*, where his companions from the Athenaeum, Reyes, and Henríquez Ureña, were like fish in water, represented for him the caste of literati "preoccupied with the trivialities of style," which he hated. He began touring the world, like a ghost, and that wandering deeply colors the emotional and conceptual content of his memoirs.

The more distant *Creole Ulysses* is from the present, the more imbued it becomes with a brilliance, a passion, and an innocence that do not appear in subsequent volumes. It is, from beginning to end, the account of a sentimental education and a chronicle of numerous initiatory experiences. It is the transcription of the astonished gaze of a child who engages in the task of becoming acquainted with and recognizing the world; a task that is renewed in each of the character's biological changes. The world is real, there is no doubt; what differs, and therein lies one of the largest enigmas of this formidable book, are the perceptions that the author attributes to the character: the child, the adolescent, the young student, the successful professional, and, later, the revolutionary he was before writing the book. Not only do the opinions disagree, they are often radically different from those he sustained in letters, books, speeches, and interviews before 1929.

The only explanation that comes to mind is that *Creole Ulysses* belongs to a different genre than the other three books that make up his so-called *Memoirs*. Is it really an autobiography? *Creole Ulysses* is usually included in collections of "novels of the Revolution," while in literary histories it is placed in the same section with Luis Martín Guzmán's *Shadow of the Caudillo* and Maríano Azuela's *The Underdogs*. Historians of literature and critics are right. *Creole Ulysses* can be a novel whose protagonist is called José Vasconcelos, just as the main character in *In Search of Lost Time* is called Marcel. Both authors fictionalize their circumstances, their setting; they linger on their love for their mother and on other loves; they narrate their initiation into an aesthetic universe, their passion for Bergson and a thousand other situations. If they had met, they would not have had anything to do with each other; on the contrary, it is much more likely that they would have despised each other. And even though they never met, Vasconcelos was viscerally repulsed by Proust the figure and his style. Just as *Swann's Way* is a work of fiction closely linked to Proust's real life—a life that is filtered, distorted, created with liberties that characterize the novelistic creation, which the historian or mem-oirist cannot take—in *Creole Ulysses* the Mexican author fashions and recreates at his discretion a series of events he has lived. The character José Vasconcelos inherits from the author José Vasconcelos his temperament and messianic vision, as well as many other coinci-dences: date of birth; parents and siblings; travels around the country and to cities of the world; an insufferable wife; and a mistress named Adriana who drives him mad daily; his studies and mutual friends; and the same revolution in which author and protagonist do battle and triumph and are ultimately defeated. The objective circumstances may be identical, but the novelist can afford to breathe into his crea-ture feelings, emotions, ideas, philias, and phobias that are radically different from his own. This is what the novel is for! Under the guise of establishing the novelistic nature of his character, Vasconcelos makes him proffer opinions that he, the author, did not sustain during the time in which he situates them. To accomplish this, "he develops a theory of social resentment that he applies to his earliest memories," as the Argentine Noé Jitrik points out.

If anything gives unity to the account, it is the process of con-structing a will and the incessant exercise of that will in shaping a destiny. "Will can move mountains" is the motto of Ibsen's Peer Gynt, a character with whom Vasconcelos identifies on more than one occa-sion. They are wedded by the use of a superhuman power to forge their destiny. Both conceive of themselves as creators of a personal future outside the normal where even chance is a product of energy itself. "The art of bravery in act, is this: to stand with choice-free foot amid the treacherous snares of life."[28] That statement by Gynt seems to govern the entire existence of our Ulysses, and he employs it consciously in the organization of his memories.

Like characters in Stendhal—an author whom he loathed with the same intensity with which he despised Proust, Flaubert, and Mallarmé—Vasconcelos knew, very early, that will is all that is opposed to reality no matter how steely and impenetrable the latter may be. And he builds his life around this conviction. If reality conquers him, his will ignores the defeat. The result: an unpredictable personality even for himself. He never imagined, for example, that his autobiographical books would, from the moment they appeared, reduce the rest of his work to nothing. His *Aesthetics* comes out the same year as *Creole Ulysses*. He is convinced that this treatise is the culmination of his philosophical thought. He places all this faith in it and not in *Ulysses*. However, the autobiography rendered dead that collection of reflections on art and nature. It could not be otherwise: an egotist of such dimensions could only capture all of his powers in the story of his life.

"Vasconcelos's biography," writes Jorge Cuesta in an article published shortly after the appearance of *Ulysses*, "is the biography of his ideas. This man has had ideas that *live*, ideas that love, suffer, enjoy, feel, hate, and become inebriated; those ideas that only *think* are indifferent and even odious. *Creole Ulysses* is, for this reason, the book in which Vasconcelos's philosophy discovers its genuine, authentic expression. Those books in which he has expounded it in a purely doctrinal mode are almost unreadable." And then he adds: "As inconsistent,

---

28 Translated by William and Charles Archer

as poor, and as confused as his doctrine is when it is viewed as *thinking*, it is even more vigorous, impressive, and fascinating when viewed as *living*."

In the first preface to *Creole Ulysses,* the author not only explains the reasons for the title but also introduces a theme that will become a constant throughout the tetralogy, eventually constituting an axis and assuming an obsession in all his latter endeavors: *criollismo* as the Mexican nation's only possible zone of regeneration. "The title that has been given to the whole work is explained by its content. A destiny that soars like a comet, blazing across the sky, before burning out during long periods of darkness, and the turbulent atmosphere of present-day Mexico justifies the analogy with the classical *Odyssey.* As for the adjective *criollo,* I chose it as a symbol of the defeated ideal within our homeland...*Criollismo,* that is, culture of a Hispanic type, in its ardent and unequal struggle against a counterfeit *indigenismo* and an Anglo-Saxonism that dresses up in the rouge of the most deficient civilization known to history; those are the elements that have waged battle in the soul of this *Creole Ulysses,* as in that of each of his countrymen."

Creole Ulysses reflects the character's life from his birth until the military coup of Victoriano Huerta, and Vasconcelos's preparations to participate once again in revolutionary action. This is the story of a long march toward his personal depths; it begins with the immediately postnatal state from which emerge his oldest memories, wrapped "in a caressing and melodious feeling, a physical extension, a section barely cut off from a warm, protective, almost divine presence. The voice of my beloved mother guided my thoughts, determined my impulses. One might say I was tied to her by an invisible and voluntary umbilical cord that lasted for many years after the rupture of the physiological bond," until the moment of affirmation of an independent personality. The rupture of the aforementioned cord took longer than necessary to occur, which comprises almost all of the book's pages. They were years marked by his love for his mother and despair for her loss; then by the temptation of the flesh and the subsequent feeling of condemnation, of abjection, of horror of the body and atonement mitigated only by the certainty that "glory" awaited him in a still imprecise future; years marked also by the astonishing discovering of his own country during his travels and also by his participation in political life, which causes him to discover the weight of the Porfirian dictatorship and the paths to fight and defeat it. All this is but a glimpse, the preamble to the apotheosis to which he would later arrive. Apotheosis in action and in thought. And also of the flesh.

All these things and more nourish this first volume, a suggested point of departure and waiting period before the arrival of the fatal revelation that he will seek to develop and demonstrate obsessively at the end of his memoirs and will not abandon for the rest of his life: the bitter conviction that Mexico is a vile and irredeemable country. Between the two options proposed by Sarmiento for our continent, Vasconcelos had wagered with all the strength he could muster in favor of civilization and against barbarism. He had believed in a ferocious, delirious, and messianic way that a person's will, his own in particular, could move not only well-worn mountains but also souls—an enterprise that was much more difficult and complex than expected. He fought to become the Quetzalcoatl that would defeat forever Huitzilopochtli, the eagle that in the end would finally devour the snake. Of course, he failed.

Upon remembering the past fifty years later, the recent political defeat behind him, we find that Ulysses, the child, is already aware that the nation has two enemies, one external—the Yankees—another internal: the Indians. His first memories are situated in Sasabe, scarcely more than a hamlet, an enclave in the Sonora desert, a border post with the United States, where life passes by in perpetual fear; whether of the Americans, who appear out of nowhere to lower the Mexican flag and raise the Stars and Stripes, forcing the Mexicans to retreat and accept the imposition of a new boundary line; or of the Apaches who show up from time to time to loot and destroy the few villages in the region. Later he will glimpse his only salvation, port, and hope when he comes into contact with the mainland, where the Hispanic presence becomes visible.

After recalling his adolescence in Campeche, he notes: "In the beautiful tropical garden the band still brought together families for open-air concerts, but the beautiful girls of languid carriage, light complexion, and black eyes became increasingly rare. The beautiful, sensual caste yielded to the crude natives of the interior who in hushed groups listened to the concerts from a distance as if waiting for the moment to occupy the homes that the whites abandoned." In the Vasconcelos universe, the Indian is everywhere, lying in wait at all times. He is just around the house, in the garden weeds, under rocks, shape-shifted into a vine, water, thunder. He is backwardness, the embodiment of brutal gods, cunning patience, evil calculation, lightning and punishment. "Within Durango and the main district centers," he writes later, "the population is *criolla*, but it barely leaves the city limits; the Indian lives in conditions similar to those known in the times of Aztecs. It is for want of spirit and organization that the Indian continues in its backwardness." The tone becomes almost frantic in the last volumes. When evoking the archaeological discoveries made in Uxmal and Chichén Itzá when he was Secretary of Public Education, he will say years later: "As the digger's pick advances, there appear year after year new wonders: but everything is uniformly barbaric, cruel, and grotesque. No sense of beauty; the decoration is nothing more than simple paleographic work. Since they had no efficient alphabet they used drawing and relief as language, which distorts and delays the possibility of a disinterested musical development, which is the essence of art; utilitarian decor that, as such, elicits no aesthetic emotion, only the astonishment of their guesswork and the aberrations of the human soul." He came to detest archaeologists and scholars of pre-Hispanic cultures of any kind. "Petty scoundrels" at the service of Yankee interests to reduce the footprint of European culture on the continent, the fruit of an abhorrent *mestizaje*, the result of mixing of two detestable races: Indian and Jewish.

"In Veracruz and Campeche the vigor of the race had become so weak that it allowed Indians and Blacks to become part of Europe's vitality," he states, and evoking a trip to Oaxaca and the visit he pays to two elderly sisters of his mother, he was distressed by "the plight of those old ladies, the vestiges of a generation exhausted by their own creative effort and ultimately defeated by the harsh environment, absorbed by markedly inferior races." In the decline of those old women, he sees "all the drama of the defeat of the white man of Spanish race, replaced gradually by the mestizo and threatened by the return of the Indian."

This is too much, I know. However, Vasconcelos never uttered these outrages during the time in which he situates his autobiographical novel. His work offers us the greatest proof. In 1920, in *Hindustani Studies*, he states categorically that only mestizo races were capable of great creations; in 1925, in *The Cosmic Race*, he glimpsed the future of humanity in the emergence of *mestizaje* that was shaping Latin America. This region of the world was the custodian of a new spiritual energy, which renewed ancient myths and recreated the Dionysian spirit. In 1926, in *Indology*, he makes a confession that refutes the racial resentment that, little by little, grew increasingly more virulent. "Unfortunately," he said, "I have no black blood, but I possesses a small portion of indigenous blood, and it is to it that I believe I owe a greater sensitivity than that of the majority of whites; I have the seed of a culture that was already brilliant when Europe was still barbaric."

Creole Ulysses is also the record of an initiation into the world of culture, of the handling of ideas, of a spiritual journey, in short, of a path to the stars. If on other subjects his pronouncements were at times retroactive and he made them appear valid at a time when they were not, there was one on which his thought was always consistent: his contempt for what he considered unnecessary stylistic frills. He explains at the beginning of *Ulysses* that after learning to read, the only thing that interested him was content, not form. This statement will become an irrefutable principle, strengthened by the certainty that his fate would infallibly lead him to glory. "At ten years old, I felt alone and unique and called to lead...A certain disposition of my temperament and the habit of translating since childhood has left me with this indifference and lack of talent for form."

Regarding his membership in the group of intellectuals who formed the Youth Athenaeum (Antonio Caso, Alfonso Reyes, Luis Martín Guzmán, Pedro Henríquez Ureña, and Julio Torri, among others), he has serious reservations: "For my part I never valued knowledge for knowledge's sake. On the contrary: knowledge as a means to reach the supreme essence; morality as a ladder for glory, without empty stoicism, such were my standards, and they were firmly directed toward the conquest of happiness. There was no cult of worship for that which is half or in-between; all my vehemence was directed toward the conquest of what is essential and absolute [...] My colleagues read, cited, compared for the mere love of knowing, I selfishly peered into all knowledge, all information, material useful for organizing a theory of being in its entirety. Using a botanical term much in vogue in our country, I took for criticism only what it could contribute to the *eclosion* of my personality. I myself was the sprout immersed in the elements and eager to flower." A credo that is equivalent to carrying with arrogant pleasure a heavy stone tied around one's neck. The limitations of some philosophical texts come from this permanent blindness in which he took pride. There is never in him a disinterested, contemplative attitude toward language, nor toward ideas. Nor is there emotion or surprise for literary achievement. Rather there is something akin to outrage in his contempt for form, in the non-recognition of the intrinsic value of word or thought, but instead a manifest calling to utilize any element that will allow him to attain power, salvation, and glory. "Due to the contagion of the literary-esque environment, I took on the thankless task of writing descriptions of each of these dances [those of Isadora Duncan]. I read these pieces in the Athenaeum, and they were poor and faulty in style. They did not reveal what I had wanted to put into words. No literature would have sufficed for an essay into which I poured the echoes of the Cosmos. Someone assured me:

'Your subject would require the style of Mallarmé.' It is impossible to convince them that a Pater, a Mallarmé, interpreters of decadence, cannot bear the weight of a new, vigorous, and complete vision of the world. I did not lack style, rather accuracy, and clarity of concept. My concept was so great that when it unfolded it created its own style, built its own architecture. In turn, I thought: my literary colleagues will one day say that Pythagoras's writings need to be retouched by a Flaubert [...] Many of them were the precursors of those who today disdain Balzac for his neglect of form yet support the follies of Gide or Proust, which proves that the professionals of style eternally ignore the brilliance of messages that contain spirit."

Vasconcelos is enamored of his shortcomings; he is obsessed by them. This personality type by nature imposes its ideas on others. However, they in no way hinder him from accomplishing the cultural program that he outlined and undertook when he was appointed Secretary of Education. A program that, plainly speaking, can be described as titanic. For this period of wonders alone, his name deserves to go down in history. To discredit him, some within the United States press and all of the conservatives in Mexico accused him of a Soviet-style educational and cultural program with Bolshevik intentions. The brilliant educational reform and cultural renaissance that he began always were, at the time and for many years after, plagued by misunderstanding, undermined by suspicion, envy, and the mistrust of his inferiors. Nevertheless, his energy prevailed. To achieve his goals, he surrounded himself with the most talented writers in the country, not only those committed to his educational ideals but also those devoted to the cult of form, as well as musicians, painters, and architects of all ages and movements, even those who admitted to not understanding, or who openly did not share them. In this regard, he was absolutely ecumenical. During his tenure, almost every writer who formed our literary avant-garde debuted; and the first murals—to the horror of people of reason, the "culturally Hispanized"—were painted. He called on all artists to collaborate with him, without turning them into bureaucrats. And that in itself was a miracle.

Much has been written on Vasconcelos's educational and cultural crusade. It will suffice to quote a few lines of Daniel Cosio Villegas, an intellectual known for his skepticism and even a certain coldness toward his peers: "So, yes, there was an evangelical zeal to teach others to read and write: then, yes, every Mexican felt in his heart of hearts that the educational effort was as urgent as quenching thirst or appeasing hunger. They then began the great murals, monuments that aspired to depict for centuries the country's anguish, its problems, and its hopes. There was a faith in the book, and in the book of eternal quality…"

Creole Ulysses covers the first thirty-three years of the author's life. It closes with the murder of Francisco Madero. For many years his relationship with women and with ideas had been contentious and incomplete. But it was much more difficult for him to live without them. His dealings with the former were stained with subsequent feelings of abjection. His relationship with ideas had been until then merely a necessary catalyst for getting rid of the positivist thought that permeated the era. It seemed that everything he had lived—from his childhood to the end of his university studies—was waiting for something to unify him. Harmony would only come to him through the Revolution: his support for Madero; his activity during the anti-reelection campaign; victory over the *Porfiriato*; the dawn of a new Mexico; and, in the end, the first defeat. This period of political activity reaches in the book a brilliance, a mythical aura unrivaled in our literature. Here, the long awaited harmony is glimpsed. All the threads lead toward the unity of being: the triumph of the flesh—free now of anguish and recrimination—political success; the cosmic link. "As surprising as he has been and continues to be," Cuesta says, "and as incomprehensible the causes that motivate him are, Vasconcelos's thought is so intimately linked to the revolutionary movement that it is impossible to consider one separate from the other."

Thirty-five years have passed since the death of our Ulysses. By the end of his life, he was a mere shadow of himself. There remains little trace of his philosophical thought; his battles, his fury, his contradictions, and his unpredictable changes of allegiances have ceased to stir passions. Of him there remains, above all, a testament of insubordination. The example of an individuality that refused to submit to any rule imposed from without. There remains the splendid faith of an apostle who saw salvation in the spirit and who turned the book into his favorite instrument. There remains the splendor of his prose, which illuminates all of *Creole Ulysses* and many other fragments in the other memoirs. There remains the image of a man who, wanting to save everything, becomes lost completely. There remains the memory of his redemptive power. And for all this, in a world where submission is the rule, we will never be able to thank him enough.

Xalapa, July 1994

PEREIRA DECLARES

Writing about Antonio Tabucchi has always placed me on the threshold of the impossible. Dazzled by his writing, my greatest temptation is to reproduce it abundantly, to fill pages with his quotations, find a common thread, and deploy them in an order best for sharing with the reader the pleasure of reading him. His prose is hard to imitate; it possesses its own melody, an emotional tension moderated by intelligence. His writing is conjectural and at the same time precise. In his novel *Requiem: A Hallucination*, a ghostly Pessoa pleads with the narrator: "*Please*, don't abandon me to all these people who are so certain about everything, they're dreadful."[29]

Misunderstandings, ambiguities, grey areas, false evidence, imagined realities, and dreams mottled by a terrible reality, the search for what we already know is lost, backward games, voices from the gates of hell—these are elements that we often find in Antonio Tabucchi's world. Another one: a perfect elegance born of simplicity. Tabucchi's elegance is like melancholy, always clinging to the shadow of the story, or buried in the subsoil of language.

---

29 Translated by Margaret Jull Costa

Tabucchi declares that he aspires to write for a reader who expects neither solutions nor words of consolation but rather questions. The presumed reader should be willing to be visited, to host the imponderable, to modify mental categories, lifestyles, to introduce new ways of approaching the human condition: to force destiny rather than be condemned to an early requiem.

In a lecture delivered in Tenerife in 1991, entitled "The Twentieth Century, Balance and Perspectives," Tabucchi asserts: "A writer who knows everything, who is already familiar with everything should not publish a book. The only certainty that I have is that everything is relative, that there is another side to everything. It is, above all, this area where I like to investigate, where nothing is immediately visible." And later: "The man given to us by the literature of our time is a solitary and broken man, a man who is alone but no longer knows himself and has become unrecognizable [...] One must reclaim the right to dream. This may seem, at first, like an insignificant right. But, upon further reflection, it will seem like a great prerogative. The man who is still able to nourish illusions is a free man."

And that brings us to Pereira and what he declares in the novel that bears his name. Tabucchi takes risks that few authors are willing to take. *Pereira Declares* is, among other things, a political novel, which in itself will cause some to furrow their brow. It narrates events that occurred in Lisbon during the span of a month, between late July to late August 1938, a period during which the Salazar regime strengthens its totalitarianism and locks Portugal away in a seamless dictatorship that will last thirty-five cruel years. It is, indeed, a political novel, but different in every way from the ideological narrative of socialist realism. The only thing that Tabucchi's novel shares with stories of an ideological character is its parabolic nature. And this is perhaps the source of its greatest challenge. Every character that participates in an apologue exemplifies a virtue or a vice that will ultimately be unmasked and punished or rewarded; all of their words and actions are predetermined in general terms to achieve this purpose. However, in order to be novelistically valid, it must have its own breath, assume those virtues or defects as an individual expression, otherwise the language will always give off a whiff of pamphleteering.

Pereira, the protagonist of Tabucchi's novel, like Ariel from *The Tempest*, is built of "such stuff as dreams are made on." However, as he fulfills his destiny he becomes imbued with reality, a tragic reality. In the end, we find him transformed into an extraordinarily animated character, one of the most lovable of contemporary narrative. He enjoys the double privilege of maintaining his individuality and of becoming a symbol.

Who, then, is Pereira, what does he do, what problems does he face? Well, he is an old journalist, an infernally fat widower, plagued with ailments, whom doctors have given only a few years to live. Not long ago, he began to edit the weekly literary page of a second-rate evening paper. He becomes obsessed, almost maniacally, with obituaries. Several things could explain this phenomenon, perhaps because his father was the owner of a funeral home called La Dolorosa, or that his wife suffered from tuberculosis during their entire marriage, to which she eventually succumbed, or the conviction that his heart problems would lead him to an early grave. But, too, because during the radiant summer of 1938, he began to sense that Lisbon reeked of death, that all of Europe reeked of death. Pereira is Catholic. The immortality of the soul and the resurrection of the flesh are topics on which he meditates incessantly. The first illuminates him; the second terrifies him. Imagining that the vast quantity of fat that smothers him will be resurrected makes him dizzy. Pereira, plain and simple, is a good man, immersed in a world that he finds increasingly more disgusting. His cult of death leads him to create an obituary column for the literary page he edits, to prepare in advance the obituaries of writers whom he admires; but, for some reason, he refuses to be the one to write them. To this end, he contacts a young man, who has recently graduated university, from the Faculty of Philosophy, Francisco Monteiro Rossi, whose essay precisely on the subject of death he has just read.

Pereira Declares at times sends me to one of the author's earlier novels, which I revere: *The Edge of the Horizon*. At first glance they might seem like opposites. An old Pereira moves under Lisbon's radiant blue sky. Spino, the protagonist of *The Edge of the Horizon*, on the other hand, carries out his investigations under a hazy sky in a city steeped in humidity and darkness. Pereira's search ends with the discovery of personal freedom, the performance of an act of protest, which at the time disguises a heroic quality: by revealing himself he discovers the society that surrounds him. Spino, however, isolates himself little by little from society as if trying to suppress a metaphysical sign. How, then, are these stories alike? On the one hand, the theme of death is always present in both. Pereira imagines a collection of obituaries at the service of his cultural page. Death and eventual resurrection are his obsessions. Spino works in a hospital morgue, he is in constant contact with corpses. In both novels, personal identity is the underlying theme. In both, the result is the same: each of the characters marches toward the revelation of a destiny that is incubating inside him.

Upon meeting with the young Monteiro Rossi and his girlfriend,

Pereira's *via crucis* and final resurrection begin. "He asked himself: Am I living in another world? And he was struck by the odd notion that perhaps he was not alive at all, it was as if he were dead."[30] The journalist, however, is predestined to remain alive, even if each of his meetings with the young couple leads him to difficult situations, to truly atrocious moments. And perhaps therein lies the most difficult challenge that Tabucchi has assumed: to not introduce a young communist in the thirties as a cruel and callous sectarian, which today is usually considered mandatory. The young Monteiro Rossi and his friends are communists, yes, and are aware of the need to strengthen the International Brigades fighting in the Spanish Civil War, among other things, because Franco's victory would mean the continuation of the Salazar dictatorship in Portugal. He knows nothing about the purges in Moscow and, if anyone had spoken to him about them, he would think it was a lie invented by fascist propaganda, or the punishment of a group of traitors who committed crimes before being executed. The same thing Kio would have thought, the character from Malraux's *The Human Condition*, one of the most beloved heroes during my youth, whose death moved me as if it he had been one of my closest friends. In this way, Tabucchi shatters a rigid form of contemporary "politically correct thought," that of turning any communist militants living during the years of the Soviet purges into monsters of abjection, into active accomplices in the crimes of Stalin, and into builders of the extermination camps. That would be like condemning Walter Benjamin, Picasso, Tibor Déry, and hundreds of intellectuals who believed in the possibility of changing the world. The young hero of *Pereira Declares* could be one of them. Not long ago,

---

30 Translated by Patrick Creagh

Jérôme Garcin reported that during a conversation with Julien Gracq this remarkable writer above suspicion had addressed the situation in the thirties: "The Revolution was a job and an article of faith. He was a communist then and was active in the *Confédération générale du travail* (the CGT). He didn't miss a single meeting [...] He remembers with amusement almost being discharged in 1938 for being the only teacher at the Lycée de Quimper to participate in a banned strike. He continues to evoke that period of collection drives, of meetings and illusions during which he headed a section and delivered the Party word to the trawlers of Douarnenez, to the tuna boats of Concarneau, and to the lobster boats of Guilvinec, in cafés where the *chouchen* inflamed the minds of the seaman. Gracq surrendered his card in 1939, when the German-Soviet pact was announced. Did he get out in time? No, he retorts, it was already too late. From the first trials in Moscow, he says in retrospect, I should have made a clean break. But he adds he would have been deprived of the beautiful moments of fraternity in the secret and harsh Finistère, where he learned about a universe at once pure and Manichean."

Censorship, distrust of his newspaper, and police surveillance barrel down on Pereira. It seems the meeting with the young couple who write delusional and unprintable obituaries was a curse for the old and infirm journalist, who becomes increasingly more engaged with the "pure and Manichean" world to which his protégés belong. In the end, he will become another man. His obstacles to survival will surely become greater, but he will have the certainty of having saved his soul. His victory will be immense. The only obituary he manages to write is that of the young Monteiro Rossi. It will also be the most beautiful page of the novel.

We do not know to whom Pereira is speaking, to whom he *declares* what happened during that terrible summer of 1938. Perhaps he shares his testimony with fellow exiles, one of them the novel's supposed author, who glosses, details, and shades everything the journalist declares in order to transmit it later to the reader, who in fact becomes the true recipient of the testimony. The method is perfect. It allows both proximity and distance. And those two words: "Pereira Declares"—repeated throughout the novel—work as a refrain that accentuates the melody of perfect prose.

Xalapa, July 1995

ENDING

JOURNEY TO CHIAPAS

I. THE BEGINNINGS

2 JANUARY 1994

Ominous headlines appear in today's newspapers: "Revolution breaks out in Chiapas. San Cristóbal de Las Casas and three cities fall into the hands of rebels." A friend, who as a rule is very well informed, phoned me this morning to wish me a happy New Year. She answered my questions and told me that the situation had returned to normal, but that there had been wide-scale fighting and several deaths. Yesterday I went to my cousins' for New Year's dinner. Some of those in attendance expressed enthusiasm for the North American Free Trade Agreement, which was coming into force. We would soon be like the United States and Canada. Well, not the country, it would still have to wait a while, they clarified; but everyone present agreed it would be a good thing for us. Someone claimed to have heard on a radio newscast something about the occupation of some cities in Chiapas. No one took it seriously. They tell him he must not have understood correctly. Some fanatical opposition groups have begun storming the city halls in some villages, only to abandon them after four or five days of anarchy...In fact, my friend in the know told me that the army had to intervene to liberate the occupied towns. She was sure that it was an act of revenge against the president.

Someone had pledged to ruin the day that the Free Trade Agreement went into effect. Without a doubt we would find out who was responsible for the disturbance. Newspapers, for their part, are saying that someone incited the Chiapanec indigenous communities to revolt. But no one knows for sure who that someone is who is capable of ruining the President of the Republic's day and making the Indians revolt. It seems to me that right now anyone who wanted to could organize uprisings in different parts of the country, because there is extreme poverty, and people in the countryside are desperate. As incredible as it may seem, the insurgents said they would advance on Mexico City and would not give up until they overthrew the government. They would not settle for being the protagonists of a regional insurrection.

4 JANUARY

What days! The rebellion in Chiapas has everyone on end. Contrary to what was said, it hasn't been defeated. I watch television and everything seems unreal and quite terrifying...I'm exhausted, overwhelmed, in a foul mood...I'm almost certain this year will be horrible. The worst thing that could happen to Mexico would be the birth of a Shining Path. During a television newscast they said the leader of the guerrilla movement is twenty-four and speaks four languages. Surely some new information will come out soon. But how were these people militarily trained? That will also be made public soon, they say. I feel like going to live in Italy or Spain. Portugal. The Salinas era will wind down this year. But it will leave a lasting wound on the country.

5 JANUARY

Farewell dinner for John and Deborah, who will be spending a few months at Yale. The topic, like it or not, was the uprising in Chiapas. Later I went by Rodrigo's house and the conversation was the same; then Braulio visited me at the hotel and went on about how complex the situation is. I went up to my room, turned on the television, and listened to the spokeswoman for the Secretariat of the Interior, Socorro Díaz, read a document on the insurgency's structure: military training, weapons, recruiting, etc. It is incomprehensible that the authorities were not aware of these preparations. Either the guerrillas were protected by a powerful sector inside the government or had the full support of the indigenous communities who allowed them to create this army, or both. Everything seems to be in Chinese.

8 JANUARY

The fighting continues, and there were some terrorist acts in different parts of the country. No significant damage. Instead, they seemed intent on showing that danger lurks everywhere all the time. The television reports produced by the government, as usual, are very clumsy; they're attempting to deny the main problem: the extreme poverty and contempt to which the indigenous population has been subjected. How did the government not know that something on this scale was going on? Army shelling continues near San Cristóbal in areas largely populated by Indians. There are constant marches for peace and for cessation of the shelling in Mexico City. I ask myself again: Did the army not notice anything during the year that, according to the Interior Secretariat, the preparations were underway? Or the secret service of the various police forces? Or the much-trumpeted military intelligence? Was the information intercepted, or was it received and then dismissed because of the leadership's eagerness to reach the inflationary target? I stood in a long line at a newsstand today to buy *La Jornada* and *El Financiero*. I wasn't able to work this weekend.

11 JANUARY

So far this month my life has been a bundle of nerves. A friend from Mexico City just called me. She was hysterical, bordering on delirious. There was something truly irrational about her excitement. The revolution was beginning to save the country from its sins and would deliver it from the many evils that afflict it! She spoke as if the guerrillas had already taken the National Palace. When I hung up the phone, I felt compelled to examine my conscience. I continue to be encouraged by the revolutionary uprising in Chiapas because it lays bare the official lie that had been nagging at me and many others. But that feeling of encouragement goes away as I think about the victims who will die: Indians and Indian children, whose constant presence on television has begun to haunt me, as well as the fear that the country is going to hell, terrorized by a group that could well prove to be (we know nothing about its leader or its members) a variation of the Shining Path. A unilateral ceasefire was declared yesterday. I was relieved to hear that Camacho Solís had agreed to attempt to broker a peace settlement. If he is successful, he will become a giant. A giant in a world of midgets who govern our country. My hate, my contempt for the whole lot of arrogant scum who have constantly boasted of their so-called macroeconomic successes, has grown more intense and more radical. What an immense waste of money and effort on that solemn buffoonery that was Solidarity, for example! Today we saw a new image of Salinas on television. He no longer looks like the President of the Century but a tiny man with shifty eyes and a look of defeat: the man who for five years has misled the nation and deluded himself into believing that he was Caesar is forced—by grace of a group of Indians whose miserable existence he denied—to look into a mirror that reflects his true dimensions. I'm reminded of Tosca's words as she stands over Scarpia's corpse: "*E avanti a lui tremava tutta Roma!*" All Rome trembled before him! The only thing we can hope for is that these ten ultra-enigmatic days we have lived not be forgotten, that they serve as a lesson, that they initiate a period of national reflection, that our leaders wake up to reality, that they realize how far we are, because of them, from the First World in which they believed they were already living.

13 JANUARY

Today in *La Jornada* there appeared an open letter explaining the Jesuits' position on the Chiapas conflict. I find it surprising. Among other things, it says:

> Violence that causes loss of human life goes against the will of the God in whom we believe. However, violence in Chiapas did not begin with the armed uprising on the first day of last January. A secular history of plunder, abuses, marginalization, and murders has made victims of the poor inhabitants of that state, particularly the indigenous. This is, perhaps, the origin of the indigenous groups' desperation that manifests itself now in armed counter-violence. So our rejection of violence, if it is to be just, must tend to its roots. The first and fundamental violence to be condemned is the structural-social-economic-political-cultural violence of which the ethnic groups

and popular sectors of Chiapas and much of the national territory have been victims. Not to acknowledge this would be to avoid the state of things that have led to the current confrontation.

And later:

> We believe that the events in Chiapas are a wakeup call for the entire national consciousness and an invitation to reflect on the risks of continuing a modernizing policy that benefits the ruling elite while marginalizing the country's popular majorities. They are also a call for the government to take seriously the path to democracy.

> Let us therefore acknowledge that the problem is essentially social and political, although it has now been expressed through violence due to the absence of legal channels. For this reason, a military solution would leave untouched the root causes and not lay the foundations for progress toward an enduring harmony and peace in that state. Paths of dialogue and of real agreement on acceptable terms for the parties involved must be opened.

And it concluded:

> Consistent with the above, we demand that:
> THE GOVERNMENT OF THE REPUBLIC, in accordance with the political measures recently taken, establish an immediate

ceasefire and lift the de facto state of siege that it has imposed on some two thousand indigenous communities of Chiapas.

We believe that at this time a political will is urgently needed to initiate means by which to place the Federal Electoral Institute (IFE) in the hands of the civil society.

THE ZAPATISTA ARMY OF NATIONAL LIBERATION take a clear and flexible position in favor of a dialogue of reconciliation with the aim of achieving the necessary changes that led it to the decision to take up arms.

ALL BELIEVERS, as part of the Church in Mexico, undertake the self-examination necessary to be more attentive to the suffering of our people, to be companions to them and find, with them, effective paths to achieve the justice they deserve as children of God.

ALL MEXICANS open their consciousness to overcoming the racism within us and accept the indigenous as brothers, children of the same Father, and as members of the national community, with equal dignity and rights.

SIGNED: José Morales Orozco, S. J. Provincial

This is perhaps the most surprising and most serious thing published during these hysteria-filled days: the violence was not committed by insurrectionary indigenous peoples, rather by those who have exploited them for five hundred years. Right, then, is on the side of the indigenous groups, whom despair has compelled to manifest themselves in armed counter-violence. The letter serves as a brake on the unbridled racism that has begun to spread. Recently, one hears unbelievable things said against the Indians; sometimes the most violent are spoken by people whose faces are marked with indigenous features. They are relentless. They advocate for extermination. I suppose they believe at that moment their listeners are seeing them in a different light: blue eyes and Viking hair.

15 JANUARY

In Cuernavaca, at the home of an industrialist friend and former classmate at university. For a while we talked about nothing in particular until someone mentioned the name of the president. My host almost jumped out of his chair. He got up from the table and began to pace the room, violently cursing him. He spoke of the murder of his servant, the slaughter of his mares, of his obsession with power, of his arrogance, and the problems of misgovernment we owe to him… I was dumbfounded. So the hatred toward him and the current group in power has taken root in the different strata of society! In some cases, and this may be one of them, it's probably a matter of interests…

16 JANUARY

Another day without being able to focus on my work! I have done nothing but read newspapers. Hours and hours of consternation. I seem to understand the situation less and less. I've read all kinds of editorials. I went through some excellent parodies by Carlos Monsiváis, his incisive criticism of José Córdoba and his disciple Salinas in

El Financiero, and the visceral feelings of some journalists from other newspapers who seem almost to be calling for the final solution for the Indians, the guerrillas, and their handlers; the latter, according to one of them, are headquartered in the UNAM and the state of Michoacán, where they are devising new plots against the nation and other evil deeds and things of that sort. I was dizzy and very exhausted. I still do not understand much. Who encourages and supports rebellion? The Church in Chiapas expresses support for the indigenous...The Pope himself has declared himself in favor of peace and relief for the extreme poverty in which the Chiapas Indians are living.

18 JANUARY

It looks like things are on a good and fast track. The government has declared an amnesty and the rebel army is beginning to send signals that they could initiate contact and later negotiations. Monsiváis says that the Zapatista positions are quite realistic. Perhaps we'll be at peace again soon. What will happen next? Will Colosio continue his electoral campaign? Will the many questions that have been posed be answered? I find it impossible to think about anything else.

19 JANUARY

...Since the first of January, I've not been able to do anything except read newspapers, watch the news, and talk about Chiapas.

21 JANUARY

I'm copying a communiqué by the Subcomandante Insurgente Marcos that has been discussed widely today. It has impressed me more than any of his other statements:

Until today, 18 January 1994, the only thing we've heard about
is the federal government's formal offer to pardon our troops.
Why do we need to be pardoned? What are they going to
pardon us for? For not dying of hunger? For not accepting our
misery in silence? For not accepting with humility the enormous historical burden of contempt and abandonment? For
having risen up in arms after finding all other paths closed?
For not having heeded the Chiapas penal code, one of the
most absurd and repressive in memory? For having shown the
rest of the country and the whole world that human dignity
still exists even among the world's poorest peoples? For having
prepared well and with conscience before beginning our
uprising? For having brought guns to battle instead of bows
and arrows? For having learned to fight before doing it? For
being Mexicans? For being mainly indigenous? For calling
on the Mexican people to fight by whatever means possible
for what belongs to them? For fighting for liberty, democracy,
and justice? For not following the models of previous guerrilla
armies? For refusing to surrender? For refusing to sell out?

Who should ask for pardon, and who can grant it? Those who
for years and years sat before a table of plenty and had their fill
while we sat with death, so frequent and familiar to us that we
finally stopped fearing it? Those who filled our pockets and
our souls with promises and declarations? Or the dead, our
dead, so mortally dead from "natural" death, that is from measles, whooping cough, dengue fever, cholera, typhus, mononu-
cleosis, tetanus, pneumonia, malaria and other gastrointestinal

and pulmonary niceties? [...] Those who deny our people the gift and right of governance and self-governance? Those who refused to respect our customs, our culture, and our language? Those who treat us like foreigners in our own land and who demand papers and obedience to a law whose existence and justness we don't accept? Those who tortured, imprisoned, assassinated, and disappeared us for the grave "crime" of wanting a piece of land, not a big piece, not a small piece, just a piece on which we can grow something to fill our stomachs?

Who should ask for pardon, and who can grant it?

The President of the Republic? The Secretaries of State? The Senators? Deputies? Governors? Mayors? The police? The federal army? The magnates of banking, industry, commerce, and land? The political parties? The intellectuals? Galio and Nexus? The media? Students? Teachers? Neighbors? Laborers? Farmers? Indigenous people? Those who died in vain?

Who should ask for pardon, and who can grant it?
Well, that's all for now.

Health and a hug, and with this cold both will be appreciated (I believe), even if they come from a "professional of violence."

Subcomandante Marcos.

This statement left me even more perplexed. The letter exudes an aura of Dostoevskian religiosity entirely different from the verbal habits of Latin American guerrillas. I do not detect traces of Castro or the Maoists. Nothing like the Shining Path; nothing that recalls that archaic lexicon from the manuals of Nikitin or Konstantinov, which were used so often in my student days. The statement by Aspe, the finance secretary, saying that we Mexicans had invented a great myth, that of our misery, is shattered before the torrent of extreme, excessive, and desperate poverty that the cameras capture every time they do a report from Chiapas—that is, every day—as well as the statements by Salinas about our entrance into the First World through the Free Trade Agreement. Who the hell is the masked Subcomandante! A seminarian, perhaps?

22 JANUARY

...A photo on the cover of the magazine *Macrópolis* sums Chiapas up for me: a child of seven or eight years old carrying a bundle of firewood on his back, his head toward the ground, a rope across his forehead, a *mecapal*, sustains the load. The picture moves me more than any description. All the images that appear on television nowadays, especially of children and old people, are terrible. It is the hidden world we were barely able or wanted to recognize. The press says that Marcos may be a Jesuit, a former student of the Polytechnic, a student expelled from the National University, a Guatemalan, Salvadoran, Venezuelan guerrilla, a retired professional soccer player.

23 JANUARY

I just saw an account of the events in Chiapas on television. Subcomandante Marcos, as well as the other rebel officers, insist that their army has been preparing for several years and that they have people positioned in many parts of the country, perhaps in order to look bigger in the eyes of the nation and to arrive at the negotiating table with a force otherwise difficult to verify. Because Marcos is apparently now willing to hold talks with the government, or at least that's what I thought I heard. It's at moments such as this that I despise my deafness. My impression, contrary to what some of my friends think, is that the solution to the conflict is still distant and so far the guerrillas have been able to play government just like they wanted, like a cat with a mouse. There is a lot of talk that the PRI will have a big surprise before the end of the electoral campaign. At least the greyish outlook we've lived with in recent years has completely changed. We find ourselves suddenly in something that, for better or for worse, is a different Mexico. In *La Jornada*, Octavio Paz criticizes intellectuals for their irresponsibility when speaking about the events in Chiapas. I have the impression it was a veiled rebuke of Carlos Fuentes for his recent statements about a first post-socialist rebellion. The reproachful tone at the beginning notwithstanding, it is an extremely nuanced text. Paz states that the Subcomandante's letter of pardon moved him, and he recognizes that Mexican society, especially the landowners and politicians in Chiapas, owes a heavy moral debt to the Indians.

24 JANUARY

I watched the news this morning. Everything the President said about the path to peace being the only solution seemed farcical. In practice, they've begun to obstruct Camacho because he's gained too much stature. Deep down, the politicians don't give a damn about the country.

26 JANUARY

I'm stunned. I still do not understand what is going on in Chiapas. They say the government now knows who's leading and protecting the insurgency and within a week everything will be explained. Already today Camacho Solís was not mentioned on the news. During dinner someone said there was an open break between him and the president. If I only knew for sure it was true! What in fact is true is that some of the journalists that receive money from the PRI or from government offices have pounced on him with renewed ferocity. There are times when one feels very discouraged.

27 JANUARY

The Zapatistas' victory will not be military but moral. They've managed to produce a considerable upheaval, both nationally and internationally. Perhaps this will make a transformation in Chiapas possible that would otherwise be impossible to dream of. I'm not getting my hopes up about the acceptance of humanitarian changes by the Chiapas farmers and politicians. Or in the *priístas*. They still haven't swallowed their fear and are already mobilizing to put an end to Camacho Solís.

II. WATER FROM THE SAME RIVER

Toward the end of January, I felt the need to visit the theater of events in an attempt to put certain things in order. It seemed to me that around those dates I was making too much in my journal of the circumstances as well as of the Subcomandante. I had many unanswered questions. Perhaps visiting the places where most of the action was taking place, learning the opinions of the witnesses to the occupation of San Cristóbal, for example, could help me see things more clearly. I mentioned it to Paz Cervantes, and she immediately joined the project. Paz knows Chiapas well. She began to organize the trip. We would fly from Mexico to Tuxtla Gutiérrez, and there, at the airport, we would rent a car to drive to San Cristóbal and everywhere the army would allow. She would be responsible for booking the hotel, flights, everything.

On February 3rd I traveled by car from Xalapa to Veracruz, where I would fly to Mexico City, spend the night, and start the trip to Chiapas with Paz early the next morning. A few hours before leaving Xalapa, I received from Italy Tabucchi's last novel: *Pereira Declares*, the first book I would read after abstaining for several weeks. I started reading in Xalapa, continued in the car, then on the plane in order to finish it that night in Mexico City. It was the best preparation for beginning the journey, that pilgrimage deep inside myself I hoped to undertake. Tabucchi declares through his hero Pereira that every man harbors within his breast a confederation of souls, a theory that is not new; on the contrary, the concept that multiple personalities coexist for better or worse within the same individual has become a cliché of contemporary culture. Tabucchi, however, resurrects an all-but-forgotten theory of Pierre Janet in which one of the souls that inhabits us maintains hegemonic control over the others, without conceding to that hegemony the possibility of being eternal or immutable. An ego, one of the many that make us up, may, at a given moment and as a result of some stimulus, defeat the heretofore ruling ego, thus becoming the new hegemonic ego that will unify the confederation of souls that is each one of us. Tabucchi's Pereira is a cautious man in the midst of a dirty and dangerous world; he attempts to remain outside politics, to not swim in murky water, to close his eyes to certain situations. The appearance of a young man who could be the same age as the son Pereira never had will allow the emergence of a new hegemonic ego, which will turn the old man whose only desire is to escape the ugliness of his time into an active enemy of the Salazar regime.

The book was predestined for me, and I read it at the most opportune moment, as I was beginning to feel the impulses that were a prelude to the emergence of a new ego. I would know when I confronted the signs of a new reality if this was true or merely wishful thinking. Four days in Chiapas were enough to shake off thirty years or more. Excitement, astonishment, enthusiasm, pain, and anxiety were some of the feelings I experienced simultaneously during those days. It was like witnessing the outbreak of a repulsive tumor and watching the pus furrow through its edges. The nation, the body where the abscess was located, was visibly trying to come out of its lethargy, to breathe, to dust itself off. The journey to Chiapas allowed me to approach reality; at the same time, the accumulation of diffuse and distant circumstances at times made the trip seem unreal, dreamlike, free from the ties of this world.

Traveling with Paz Cervantes, a friend par excellence, was a veritable godsend: she knew the area very well; but not only that, she also knew how to observe, she was able to separate what seemed fused and unite what was dispersed. What's more, my being there with Carlos Monsiváis and Alejandro Brito for two of those days was another stroke of luck. Thanks to them, I was able to hear Camacho Solís's statements as well as those of his entourage; we spoke at length with the historian Alejandra Moreno Toscano, who gave us guidelines to orient us in Chiapas's intricate labyrinth, with politicians of different stripes, with priests, and local as well as foreign journalists. Paz and I also spoke to the everyday people of San Cristóbal. In all of them, we encountered hope for a quick peace, if not tomorrow then the next day. They wished for it, yet at the same time they hoped it would not mean a return to the situation prior to December 31, the day the uprising began. Most claimed that the uprising had been necessary so the world would know the climate of terror Chiapas had endured throughout its entire history, but above all—and they put special emphasis on this—during the last fifteen years. It was four solar days, painful, exhilarating, and hopeful. Paz and I attended with Monsiváis and Alejandro Brito a crowded press conference with Manuel Camacho Solís, in which he announced it would be only a matter of days before they knew when and where the peace talks would be held; we attended at the cathedral a mass for peace celebrated at night and officiated by Don Samuel Ruiz, Bishop of San Cristóbal, attended by the commissioner, several journalists, foreign observers, and hundreds of Indians, who saw in the bishop their most loyal defender, their father.

The four of us: Paz, Carlos, Alejandro, and I traveled one morning to Ocosingo. After passing countless military checkpoints and seeing hundreds of Indians of all ages huddled beside stationary trucks who apparently had been detained by soldiers, we arrived at the locale. I have known few cities as ugly, as lacking in appeal, as Ocosingo. Its ugliness and its clumsiness were, perhaps, the inevitable product of those days. The streets were empty, the shops were mostly closed; in the market some stalls were covered with black cloths. This was the place where the bloodiest encounters between the army and the

Zapatistas took place. The city was still tightly guarded. The air was oppressive and detestable. That evening we returned to San Cristóbal in a very somber mood.

That night we spoke to priests whose stories of oppression inflicted on the Tzotzil, Tzeltal, Ch'ol, and Tojolabal people were so atrocious that the memory of the checkpoints on the roads, the Indian families standing in the countryside next to buses and trucks, the military who did not allow even children to sit on the ground, the tanks and patrol cars, the streets in Ocosingo, seem like the details of a delightful fairy tale. The Catholic Church in Chiapas, especially the Bishop of San Cristóbal, had begun to be attacked by journalists, politicians, and the "good" people of San Cristóbal, the *coletos*, the white elites among whom racism has been endemic. According to one of the priests, they are trying to implicate the bishop in the uprising, which is wholly false. The work of the Church in Chiapas began four hundred years ago with Fray Bartolomé de Las Casas, the first great *apóstol de los indios*, and has continued until today. The bishop's actions, another priest says, remain the same. We learned that a few years ago the Church sent out thousands of catechists (I thought I heard more than eight thousand) to live in the most inhospitable regions of Chiapas. They penetrated into the heart of darkness: the Lacandon jungle. They lived as poor as the Indians, in the same conditions; taught them to have faith in Christ, but also to be proud of being Indians. And for that the Chiapas ranchers, the cultural Hispanics of the state, and the *coletos* of San Cristóbal have never forgiven them.

The ideology of the current movement was amassed from the teaching of the catechists, from the action of some student groups who survived the repression of 1968, from the branches and stumps that broke off from the most radical leftist movement of the sixties and seventies, and from the despair and the abuse of the indigenous communities. It is not difficult to imagine the many controversies that have been produced, the suspicions, resentments, internecine ruptures, defenses of orthodoxy against the onslaught of the modern, over and over and again, until that once-unformed embryo succeeded in achieving a degree of coherent efficacy and manifesting itself in the armed movement that, as the Subcomandante said with undeniable awareness, was determined not to repeat the patterns of earlier guerrillas.

The next-to-the-last day of our stay in Chiapas, Paz and I visited San Juan Chamula, that is, his church, that indescribable place where among the assorted stench of alcohol, wax, incense, urine, and sweat one approaches ecstasy. It takes time to grow accustomed to that undulating chiaroscuro. The light comes from hundreds of candles, votives, and tapers placed in different places and at different heights. There are areas that remain forever in the shadows. It was Sunday. A mass baptism was being celebrated. Dozens of infants were screaming in unison. Entire families apostrophized loudly, furiously, before this or that altar, this or that saint, as they passed bottles of *aguardiente* from hand to hand. A decrepit old Indian woman carded the wool-like hair of small children who rolled nimbly on the floor, which made the task of picking their lice more difficult. A ceremonial procession of dignitaries, the village stewards, dressed in their Sunday best, roamed the premises. They beat the floor with their canes, made speeches in their language, bowed first to one side and then the other, then continued their rounds in ritual step. In a corner, a couple slept sprawled on the ground, the man still had a bottle of *aguardiente* in his hands; several children, surely theirs, intoned a sad, monotone song. And above and beside the crowd of the vivid, haggard, and moribund chatterboxes, the sacred was imposed. They must have prayed this way once in the Roman catacombs and temples built to the new faith in Antioch and Trebizond. The shepherds would arrive with their animals and skins of wine; they would pray and sing until reaching a delirium that united them with that which was higher than themselves. And in San Juan Chamula, beside us, all this continued to live and was amazing and terrible, luminous and crepuscular. I emerged from there as if I were far away, as if I were exiting a thick, mottled dream, and while still in this state Paz Cervantes put me in the car and took me to Zinacantán, a clean and prosperous town, which in those parts was a miracle.

In the village church, small and ascetic, unlike the whirlwind we had just left, there was only a couple, most certainly married; the husband and wife, very young, were wearing clothes embroidered in splendid colors. There were also in the church a couple of children, five or six-years-old, the children of that exceptionally attractive couple. When we arrived the husband and wife were kneeling before the main altar, praying; the children sat in the front row, behind their parents, just a step away. Suddenly, the man let out a horrible, terrifying howl. Upon hearing this, the woman began to wail in anguish. Later, it was she who howled; she became a thunderclap, a whip, a relentless storm, while he rolled on the floor, crying, babbling, and pleading. Later, both of them began to moan in unison, prostrate on the stone floor. This was only the introit. They recovered suddenly, jumped up, and began to run around the walls, each in opposite directions; they crossed and kept running, screaming and crying like two desperate souls. The pain was excruciating, indescribable, unbearable. It felt as if staying there would give me a heart attack. Paz's cheeks were awash in tears. At one point, the children, who until then had behaved normally, like spectators at a play they had already seen, walked up to us as if they knew us, and one of them, the eldest, I think, said to me: *"¡Dame chicle!"* "Give me gum!" I said I didn't have any, but he returned to the charge: *"¡Dame un lápiz!"* "Give me a pencil!" I gave him a disposable pen, and they returned calmly to their seat as if the parents' wailing and mourning didn't faze them. We, however, left the temple like cockroaches that had just been given a beating. What had just happened? What was that? Suffering caused by unavoidable misfortune? The death of a close relative? An unspeakable offense that brought terrible dishonor to them and their relatives? The knowledge that one of them was suffering from a disease from which he would soon die? Or was it merely a routine ceremony, a form of catharsis that was elicited from time to time and for which the community had left them alone in church that Sunday? Just as before in San Juan Chamula, I had the feeling of moving through a strange land, in Ultima Thule, where reason was reduced to the ineffable. The enormity of my gaps was revealed to me. One learns something always in fits and starts, in fragments, he's aware of effects, but when he can't identify the causes it is as if he didn't know anything. When was the Christian liturgy that we know today standardized? What elements could be defined as Christian, and which were Quiché or Maya in these religious practices? Which were added in the last five hundred years? When everything has passed—and hopefully everything goes well!— I promised myself that I would return to San Cristóbal de Las Casas and San Juan Chamula and to Zinacantán. But then I will be better informed, with more readings to be able to discern a bit of its reality.

We returned that night to San Cristóbal. We dined for the last time in the restaurant in our hotel. We said hello to a great deal of journalists and members of non-governmental organizations, some friends from many years ago, and others we'd met during the last few days. The restaurant and bar are like a scene from a motion picture. It could be Saigon, for example, during the Vietnam War. There were war reporters and television teams from many countries. All the major languages were being spoken. According to what we heard, some of them had managed to penetrate the jungle and visit the Zapatistas. It was not clear whether it was in jeeps or on foot. They took on a mysterious air as they spoke about their experience; they seemed to imply that any misstep could jeopardize their contacts; it would be denouncing them. They themselves are amazed at what is happening. They came to Chiapas with little or no sympathy for the guerrillas. They were only interested in finding out what had happened, why that hiccup in the Mexican economic miracle and Free Trade Agreement had occurred. The guerrilla no longer enjoys the prestige that it did in the fifties or sixties. On the contrary, all of Che's followers ended up being inept or fanatics. And suddenly they've found a person and a situation they did not expect. Of course, the monstrous presence of extreme poverty in which the Indians live and the always active racism of the white landowners are the appropriate framework for this young masked man whose language is different from all previous guerrilla leaders. Among the various registers he handles—and this truly is unbelievable!—is humor.

After talking about the still incipient charisma of the Subcomandante, the conversation in every restaurant and bar in San Cristóbal branches off, but not too far. When were the negotiations finally going to take place? What role would the Bishop of San Cristóbal play in them? Would it end in a win for Camacho Solís? Would Camacho still have complete official support? Could it be true that cracks had appeared in the Mexican political system?

Suddenly, I feel that everything that Paz and I have seen today are but pieces of the same puzzle. Foreigners in San Cristóbal with their bulky film equipment, the church of San Juan Chamula, the ceremony witnessed in Zinacantán, the Subcomandante's invisible presence in the air, the indigenous mass that has come to San Cristóbal, fleeing the bombings, the Indians who surround the cathedral in vigil for their bishop are but particles, all of them fragments of the same phenomenon, water from the same river, moments from the same time.

III. FROM THEN UNTIL NOW

I left that day infected by the negotiating climate that existed in San Cristóbal. And, indeed, the meeting between the government representatives and the Zapatista Army of National Liberation took place shortly after in the city's cathedral. There were three protagonists: Manuel Camacho Solís, Bishop Samuel Ruiz, and Subcomandante Marcos. Mexico watched in fascination as the Zapatista delegation entered and exited the cathedral. The ski masks covering their faces and the rifles and bandoliers strapped to their chests added intensity to the epic story. These were scenes that took us back seventy years or more, to the time of Zapata and Villa, whom we only knew from the movies, and not to one when treaties are signed today by attorneys in suit and tie. The Subcomandante was playing his cards for the second time. The tragic engine was granting him the force needed to fulfill his destiny, as it had done the first of January of that year. The image of the Subcomandante rose dramatically among both his admirers and his detractors. No one knew anything about him save his eyes, hands, and pipe.

The drive to engage in dialogue decreased suddenly, and did so in a dramatic fashion. Camacho Solís was replaced by gray, irrelevant characters—second- or third-rate bureaucrats. His lack of imagination complemented the superior orders perfectly. It had become necessary to bog down the dialogue.

The designs of power are always difficult to pin down. Politicians speak of peace as the only way to resolve the Chiapas conflict, but they also allow the growth of the paramilitary *guardias blancas*, encourage the most virulent racist groups, especially the *coletos* in San Cristóbal, harass the supporters of Zapatista Army, co-opt anyone they can, intensify the smear campaigns against the Subcomandante and the Bishop of San Cristóbal. Those campaigns are carried out without many successes, rather with setbacks. Because as time goes by—from the beginning of the uprising until today two and a half years have passed!—the Zapatista rebellion has acquired characteristics of both gale and spring; it has toppled gigantic fallacies, and has shown a vitality, a moral strength, and an admirable political imagination. It owes its existence still to these virtues.

The armed rebellion having just emerged, its leaders are already noticing that the struggle should be fought more in the media than on the battlefield. Marcos's capabilities, his imagination, speed, humor, have allowed his figure to be taken seriously beyond our borders. Just a few months after his appearance as the Subcomandante of the Zapatista Army, Marcos announced that his destiny and that of his troops should be placed in the hands of civil society, ceding to it all his triumphs and attributes. It was civil society that should grow and take the great strides that would lead the country toward democracy. The action of civil society would cause the insurgent army to forfeit its *raison d'être*. The Convention of Aguascalientes, in the Chiapas jungle, in Marcos's keynote speech, urged parties to the convention to move in that direction: "Fight to make us unnecessary, to eliminate us as alternatives!" And he insisted in the end: "Fight relentlessly. Fight and defeat the government. Struggle and defeat us!"

His thinking is fundamentally democratic. And prominent foreign figures saw that sooner than those in Mexico. On 2 March 1995, in *La Jornada* a letter was published signed by some prestigious Italian intellectuals, among them Norberto Bobbio and Michelangelo Bovero. Allow me to quote one paragraph:

> The Zapatista movement with its demands for democracy, freedom, and justice, its proposals for constitutional and anti-authoritarian reforms, and, above all, its surprisingly persuasive ability to communicate and disseminate them has surpassed the paradigms of the old Latin American guerrillas. Even as the dramatic option for armed insurrection, in January 1994, has raised and continues to raise distressing questions, it is clear that during the course of events the movement has been able to position itself as one of the principle actors in the process of democratic transition that appears to have produced a response in a broad plan of reforms. Thus, the neo-Zapatista movement, by contributing to the debate on the different path to democracy, has benefited recently from a spirit of solidarity

THE ART OF FLIGHT

that once again has countered an attempted military liquidation of the insurgents.

One of the official obsessions was to identify the Subcomandante and reveal his true face before the country. They achieved it. They believed that the virtual unmasking would destroy the figure, eliminate his epic halo. The fiasco was tremendous. They were sure that they had found a fossil with an appalling criminal record. On February 9, 1995, what appeared to be his real name and a photo of his prerevolutionary period were shown on television. Officials said the man was a criminal, a fugitive from justice, and therefore should be immediately arrested. The information that then appeared in the press played against the persecutors: the Subcomandante "turned out to be the son of businessmen, a Catholic school student, a brother of a former member of the PRI, philosophy student, decorated by President López Portillo for academic achievement, a student at the Sorbonne. His thesis adviser was the philosopher Cesáreo Morales, who became Luis Donaldo Colosio's chief of staff," writes Juan Villoro. "The government needed an ideological troglodyte, enrolled in some 'frequent flyer' program to North Korea, or a psychopath willing to use a power saw at the direction of Quentin Tarantino. Instead, it found the perfect son-brother-in-law-boyfriend for the *Gran Familia Mexicana*."

For several weeks *Proceso* documented the celebrity's life through testimonies from family, friends, fellow students, and teachers. A photo of him taken from an experimental film impresses me because of its Beckettian loneliness, as well as the fact that during his adolescence he acted in several plays, including, precisely, *Waiting for Godot*. Despite the reports, no one calls him by name, neither his supporters nor his enemies, neither the press nor TV, not even members of the government. He continues being Subcomandante Marcos for all purposes.

It has been two and a half years, and we have yet to enter the First World, quite the contrary. We have experienced a permanent economic crisis. As for politics, if we look at the PRI party family, we seem to be witnessing something akin to the end of the world. There have been high-profile murders, that of Luis Donaldo Colosio, candidate for president of the Republic, Francisco Ruiz Massieu, the leader of PRI, others. The pressures to prevent the truth from coming to light must be immense. Investigations seem like very complex, byzantine amusements that do not allow us to get to the bottom of anything. Crimes committed by leaders and officials, tried and proven, go unpunished. Corruption among the leadership during the previous administration and its relationship to drug trafficking and organized crime have become public knowledge. This collapse, this decline in social morality, favors the development of a civil society that has rendered a military solution in Chiapas impossible. One must remember that all the public demonstrations have been for peace and none in support of the armed path. Subcomandante Marcos and the Zapatistas understood this immediately. Now we have to achieve a just and worthy peace. Not only that: there is a desire to move toward a peaceful means and defend the causes they hold through political action. And the Subcomandante, "once granted, his glittering arms he will commend to rust / his barbed steeds to stables," as a character says in Shakespeare's *Richard II*.

Are there discernible victories in Zapatista actions? It seems to me that the strengthening of civil society is one of them. It is also important, although now less visible, to support publicly in Chiapas the problem of inequality and to demand that different sectors, including the indigenous, initiate a conversation on racism. The maturity with which this discussion is being carried out suggests that we are witnessing the beginnings of an irreversible phenomenon.

During the moments when a military solution seemed imminent, demonstrations for peace multiplied. At times the motto was, "We are all Indians." The reaction of some journalists or broadcasters was sarcastic. To conceive of oneself as an *indio*? To want to be a Tzeltal, a Ch'ol, a Tojolabal? I suppose it seemed so preposterous to them that they weren't even aware of the deep racism that their rejection implied. I do not know if this attitude has softened. It is possible that after seeing the violent reaction of the powers that be of San Cristóbal against the indigenous population of the city, the lynch-mob mentality of the ranchers and of their *guardias blancas*, they will remember the King of Denmark who, during the German occupation, went out into the street wearing an armband on which was sewn a star of David, the very day it was made mandatory for the Jews to wear it outside their homes as a visible sign of belonging to a despicable race. There will be a day, I imagine, when it will not be necessary to shout that we are also Indians. I think about Chiapas and about what it might become. I think about the Indians I saw in early February 1994 detained by the dozens at military checkpoints. I think about the hunt for girls to feed brothels, about the two Indians tied to huge anthills, as a priest from San Cristóbal told me, "to teach them how to behave." I think that all of this needs to disappear. Or is that too much to ask? Maybe so. But we must think that if it is true that we are living in cruel times, it is also true that we are in a time of wonders.

Xalapa, June 1996

TRANSLATOR'S NOTE

Translating an author of Sergio Pitol's stature is a humbling task. Translating his first major work into English is both humbling and terrifying. The feelings of humility and terror are compounded by the fact that Pitol, in his own right, is a celebrated translator of, among others, James, Conrad, Woolf, Austen, Graves, Chekhov, Gombrowicz, and Andrzejewski.

I discovered Pitol in graduate school, where his "Carnival" triptych (the novels *El desfile del amor*, *Domar la divina garza*, and *La vida conyugal*) were required reading. Between 1996 and 2005, Pitol penned three literary memoirs, of which *El arte de la fuga*, translated here as *The Art of Flight*, was the first. Known collectively as the "Trilogy of Memory," these three autobiographical volumes, comprised of diary entries, personal musings, travel writing, and literary essays, are reminiscent of Elias Canetti's *Memoirs*.

About two years ago, Michelle Johnson of *World Literature Today* sent me an article written by Mexican novelist Valeria Luiselli for *Granta* that named Pitol a "best untranslated writer." The article was somewhat of a misnomer as Pitol had in fact been translated into over a dozen major languages—but notably not into English.

How, I wondered, was it possible that a writer of Pitol's stature—one of four Mexican authors at the time to have won the Cervantes Prize, the most prestigious prize given to an author writing in the Spanish language—had not been translated into English? This translation is an attempt to right that wrong.

Already in the title I have failed. Failure is something that every translator must live with. But how does one fail before really starting? Like many words, the Spanish word *fuga* is ambiguous, meaning both *fugue* and *flight*. Ever the careful wordsmith and ironist, Pitol's use of ambiguity in the title is intentional. Not only does the title refer to a life spent in constant flight, it is also meant to invoke, as in music, the use of the interwoven repetitive elements in his writing. Also intentional is the allusion to Bach's *Die Kunst der Fuge*, known in English as *The Art of the Fugue*. Unfortunately, it was not possible maintain either the semantic ambiguity or the musical allusion. To the extent that I have failed, here or anywhere else in the translation, I offer a heartfelt apology.

In *The Art of Flight*, Pitol writes, "Translating allows one to enter fully into a work, to know its bones, its structure, its silences." Pitol alludes here to translation as an act of reading. First and foremost, the translator is a critical reader. Through this act of critical reading, he becomes a mediator of meaning for readers in another language. While reading/translating the text, the translator discovers meaning at every level—lexical, semantic, and syntactic. And, as Pitol states, in the text's silences. In other words, the translator must not only listen to what the writer says, but also to what he doesn't.

Some of the features of *The Art of Flight* include Pitol's at times labyrinthine prose (the opening sentence is sixty-two words long), interspersed with short parenthetical phrases that create a staccato-like rhythm, as in the following sentence: "In my case, plain and naked exposition, without flourishes, without detours, without echoes or shadows, fatally diminishes the efficiency of the story, converts it into a mere anecdote; a vulgarity, when all is said and done."

Throughout the translation, I have striven to be faithful to Pitol's style. To that end, and because of its potential to enrich the receptor language and culture, I have adopted a foreignizing strategy. Foreignization goes beyond leaving occasional words in the target language, especially those words that are already familiar to the reader. Doing so would render the translation a parody or, to borrow one of Pitol's favorite words, a vulgarity. The translator, then, must listen for the words that call out to remain untranslated, words that express concepts that are either foreign to, or by their use will enrich, the receptor language and culture, words like *capillas* (Mexico's literary coteries), *coletos* (white elites), (paramilitary) *guardias blancas*, and *tertulia* (the uniquely Spanish version of the salon). As noted, these loanwords appear in italics and have been explicated as naturally as possible and to the extent necessary to give them meaning.

Foreignization may also occur at the syntactic level, that is, so that the syntactic features present in the source language remain intact in the translation. To that end, I have attempted to intervene as little as possible in Pitol's syntax. At the lexical level, in most cases, I have chosen Latinate and Greek cognates rather than Anglo-Germanic synonyms. In doing so, I endeavored to honor Pitol's style and vocabulary, both of which tend toward the baroque, an effect I strove to retain or, at least, echo in the translation At times, however, it was necessary to change Pitol's punctuation, especially colons and semicolons, which he uses generously, and at times completely contrary to American usage. In some cases, but few, laboriously long and subordinated sentences either had to be broken up or the clauses reordered lest the reader become lost in a maze of subordination.

Because *The Art of Flight* is a multigeneric text, written in multiple voices, styles, and literary forms, over a period of three decades, it was important to not resort to a single, unifying voice. In the case of the numerous quotations, translated from a variety of languages into Spanish, I chose to incorporate, where available, existing English translations. For the sake of consistency, I have also used extant English translations for quotations of Spanish texts, many of which are considered canonical and will be familiar to English readers.

Translating in general is an agonizing process. It is acknowledging defeat in the face of unavoidable cultural loss. Consider the word *campechano*, which can be a gentilic that refers to inhabitants of the Mexican state of Campeche as well as an adjective meaning "good-natured" with a hint of indifference. For Mexicans, it is impossible to separate one meaning from the other. To describe someone as *campechano* is to say he possesses the same carefree bonhomie as the inhabitants of Campeche. This kind of cultural loss is inevitable, but the careful translator, especially the one who sees himself as a custodian of culture, will strive to minimize it. Such is translating every writer, but especially translating Pitol.

Translating Pitol means catching a parodic reference to *The Communist Manifesto*; it means reading *The Sound and the Fury* in order to translate Caddy's *calzoncitos* as "drawers." It is knowing that "in the beginning was the Word," and that *inmundicia*, in order to maintain the biblical reference, is best translated as "uncleanness" not "dirt" or "filth." It is tracking down un-cited quotes by Galdós and Paz and Cortázar and Bobbio and Gide and James and Woolf and Duras and Beckmann. It is studying Beckmann's tryptic *The Departure* to be able to translate Pitol's painstaking description. It is reading not only the diaries of Mann but also those of his son Klaus and those of Lezama Lima. It is reading Berenson's *The Venetian Painters of the Renaissance.*

Translating Pitol is learning that "will of reason" comes from Aquinas's *Summa Theologica* and that "people of reason" is a reference to the culturally Hispanized. It is tracing idioms back to the *Quixote* and to *The Celestina*, and deciding if or how they can be retained. It is discovering titles to novels embedded in sentences. One example is "la princesita negra de los brezos" ("the little black princess of the heaths"), an arcane reference to a nineteenth-century novel, *Das Heideprinzeßchen*, by Eugenie Marlitt, translated into English as *The Princess of the Moor*, and Spanish as *La princesita de los brezos*. Pitol, however, modifies the title by adding the adjective *negra* (black) in order to describe an effeminate young black man of high rank whom he observes in a two-bit dive in Barcelona's gothic quarter. Although Pitol employs the metaphor to great effect, it demands much of the reader and poses a herculean challenge for the translator. Ultimately, I had to determine to what end Pitol was employing such an esoteric literary reference. Was Pitol, as he is wont to be, simply in conversation with himself? In other words, was it nothing more than a recondite inside joke? Or was he providing an insight into the infinite ways literature lives inside all of us at all times?

Translating Pitol, then, requires being—or becoming—familiar not only with such arcane literary references but also the breadth of Mexican and Spanish culture, as well as American, British, Polish,

German, and Russian literatures. Translating Pitol requires reading philosophy, theology, drama theory, and the Italian Renaissance.

Translating—and reading—Pitol provides an incomparable humanistic education.

In the end, translation is about making choices and having trust. A reader must accept that a translator has made good-faith decisions about how to render a word, a pair of words, an idiom, or a metaphor. Once that is done, the translation should stand on its own weight.

No translation happens in a vacuum, nor is it a solitary endeavor. Ideally, a translator enjoys the opportunity of collaborating or, at the very least, consulting with the author during the translation process. But in recent years Pitol has suffered from a cognitive disorder that has resulted in a progressive loss of language, making it impossible to consult with him on this translation. I cannot express to you how distressing this news was. Not only because of the effect that my inability to consult with Pitol would have on the translation but also knowing that he had lost the one thing that had meant the most to him in life, as he expresses throughout *The Art of Flight,* where we also learn how much Pitol valued the collaborative process, both as translator and translated writer. Finally, I recall with fondness the email he sent almost two years ago: "Your interest in my work fills me with happiness and gratitude. I would love nothing more than to see my *Trilogy of Memory* translated into English, a language that I adore and in which none of my books exists."

Absent, then, the opportunity to consult with Pitol, I relied heavily on those secondary resources to which translators routinely recur: writers, other translators, and editors, all of whom are intimately familiar with Pitol's work, and who graciously made themselves available throughout the process. My eternal thanks go out to Elena Ponia-towska, Alberto Chimal, Raquel Castro, Beatriz Meyer, María Rosa Suárez, Luis Jorge Boone, Omar Villasana, Rodrigo Figueroa, Rodolfo Mendoza, Gregorio Doval, and Miguel Kimball-Santana.

I am also indebted to Charles Hatfield and Rainer Schulte at the Center for Translation Studies at the University of Texas at Dallas for their mentorship, to Michelle Johnson and Daniel Simon at *World Literature Today* for their unfailing support, and to Scott Esposito, whose thoughtful reading of the text and many suggestions made this translation better. A special thanks to my publisher, Will Evans, for his unwavering patience and commitment to publishing not only this translation, but also *The Journey* and *The Magician of Vienna*, which along with *The Art of Flight* make up Pitol's "Trilogy of Memory."

More than anyone, however, I am indebted to *maestro* Sergio Pitol, for serving as my guide and tutor through the literary and linguistic worlds that were formerly unknown to me, for his erudition, for his boundless imagination, and, finally, for his infinite and inextinguish-able spirit.

George Henson
Dallas, Texas, 2015

BIBLIOGRAPHY OF TRANSLATED TEXTS

ANDRZEJEWSKI, JERZY. Trans. James Kirkup. *The Gates of Paradise*. Weidenfeld & Nicolson. 1962.

BAKHTIN, MIKHAIL. Trans. Hélène Iswolsky. *Rabelais and His World*. Indiana University Press, 2009.

BAKHTIN, MIKHAIL. Trans. Caryl Emerson. *Problems of Dostoevsky's Poetics*. University of Minnesota Press, 1984.

BOBBIO, NORBERTO. Trans. Teresa Chataway. *In Praise of Meekness: Essays on Ethnics and Politics*. Polity, 2000.

BORGES, JORGE LUIS. Trans. Harold Morland. "In Memoriam: Alfonso Reyes." *Dreamtigers*. University of Texas Press, 1967.

BORGES, JORGE LUIS. Trans. James E Irby. "Story of the Warrior and the Captive." *Labyrinths*. New Directions, 1962.

BORGES, JORGE LUIS. Trans. Norman Thomas Di Giovanni. "The Aleph." *The Aleph and Other Stories*. E.P. Dutton, 1970.

CHEKHOV, ANTON. Trans. Ronald Hingley. "The Steppe." *The Steppe and other Stories*. Oxford World's Classics, 2009.

CHEKHOV, ANTON. Trans. Constance Garnett. *The Letters of Anton Chekhov*. The McMillan Co., 1920.

DURAS, MARGUERITE. Trans. Mark Polizzotti. *Writing*. University of Minnesota Press, 2011.

HAŠEK, JAROSLAV. Trans. Paul Selver. *The Good Soldier Švejk*. Penguin Classics, 1995.

HERZEN, ALEXANDER. Trans. Katherine Parthé. "A Letter Criticizing the Bell." *A Herzen Reader*. Northwestern University Press, 2012.

IBSEN, HENRIK. Trans. William and Charles Archer. *Peer Gynt*. New York Heritage Press, 1957.

KUNDERA, MILAN. Trans. Linda Asher. *Testaments Betrayed: Essay in Nine Parts*. Harper Perennial. 1996.

KUNDERA, MILAN. Trans. Linda Asher. *The Art of the Novel*. Harper Perennial. 2003.

MANN, THOMAS. "The Stature of Anton Chekhov." *The New Republic*. May 16, 1955.

MANN, THOMAS. Trans. Richard and Clara Winston. *Diaries: 1918–1939*. Robin Clark Ltd., 1984.

MANN, THOMAS. Trans. David Luke. *Tonio Kröger and Other Stories*. Bantam, 1970.

MARTÍN GAITE, CARMEN. Trans. María G. Tomsich. *Love Practices in Eighteen-century Spain*.University of California Press, 1972.

PÉREZ GALDÓS, BENITO. Trans. Robert Russell. *Our Friend Manso*. Columbia University Press, 1987.

PÉREZ GALDÓS, BENITO. Trans. Clara Bell. *The Court of Charles IV.* New York, W. S. Gottsberger, 1888.

TABUCCHI, ANTONIO. Trans. Tim Parks. *Flying Creatures of Fra Angelico*. Archipelago, 2012.

TABUCCHI, ANTONIO. Trans. Patrick Creagh. *Pererira Declares*. New Directions. 1997.

TABUCCHI, ANTONIO. Trans. Margaret Jull Costa. *Requiem: A Hallucination*. New Directions, 1984.

SERGIO PITOL, one of the leading Mexican writers of his generation, was born in the city of Puebla in 1933. He studied law and philosophy in Mexico City before beginning an intellectual career that included writing and translation while working in the promotion of Mexican culture abroad, which he achieved during his long service as a cultural attaché in Mexican embassies and consulates across the globe. He has lived perpetually on the run: he was a student in Rome, a translator in Beijing and Barcelona, a university professor in Xalapa and Bristol, and a diplomat in Warsaw, Budapest, Paris, Moscow, and Prague. One of the most versatile, well-respected, and influential authors of the twentieth century, Pitol began publishing novels, stories, criticism, and translations in the 1960s. Elected to the Mexican Academy of Language in 1997, he has received his nation's most important literary awards, as well as the internationally recognized Herralde Prize, which has also been awarded to Javier Marías, Roberto Bolaño, and Álvaro Enrigue. He is also one of the Spanish language's most accomplished translators, having brought into Spanish works by Jane Austen, Joseph Conrad, Lewis Carroll, Henry James, and Witold Gombrowicz. In recognition of the importance of his entire canon of work, Pitol has been awarded the two most important literary prizes in the Spanish language world given to an author for a lifetime's body of literature: the Juan Rulfo Prize in 1999 (now known as the FIL Literary Award in Romance Languages), and the 2005 Cervantes Prize, known as the most prestigious literary prize in the Spanish language world, often called the "Spanish language Nobel." Though Pitol's works have been translated into a dozen languages, Deep Vellum will publish Pitol's "Trilogy of Memory" in full in 2015-2016 (*The Art of Flight; The Journey; The Magician of Vienna*), marking the first publication of any of Pitol's books in the English language.

GEORGE HENSON is a senior lecturer of Spanish at the University of Texas at Dallas, where he is completing a Ph.D. in literary and translation studies. His translations, including works by Andrés Neuman, Miguel Barnet, and Leonardo Padura, have appeared previously in *World Literature Today*. His translations of Elena Poniatowska's *The Heart of the Artichoke* and Luis Jorge Boone's *The Cannibal Night* were published in 2012 by Alligator Press.

ENRIQUE VILA-MATAS is one of the most accomplished writers in the Spanish language. His novels have been translated into 30 languages, and he has received numerous international honors and literary prizes.

PUBLISHER'S NOTE

Dear readers,

Deep Vellum is a not-for-profit publishing house founded in 2013 with the threefold mission to publish international literature in English translation; to foster the art and craft of translation; and to build a more vibrant book culture in Dallas and beyond. We seek out works of literature that might otherwise never be published by larger publishing houses, works of lasting cultural value, and works that expand our understanding of what literature is and what it can do.

Operating as a nonprofit means that we rely on the generosity of donors, cultural organizations, and foundations to provide the basis of our operational budget. Deep Vellum has two donor levels, the LIGA DE ORO and the LIGA DEL SIGLO. Members at both levels provide generous donations that allow us to pursue an ambitious growth strategy to connect readers with the best works of literature and increase our understanding of the world. Members of the LIGA DE ORO and the LIGA DEL SIGLO receive customized benefits for their donations, including free books, invitations to special events, and named recognition in each book.

We also rely on subscriptions from readers like you to provide an invaluable ongoing investment in Deep Vellum that demonstrates a commitment to our editorial vision and mission. Subscribers are the bedrock of our support as we grow the readership for these amazing works of literature. The more subscribers we have, the more we can demonstrate to potential donors and bookstores alike the diverse support we receive and how we use it to grow our mission in ever-new, ever-innovative ways.

If you would like to get involved with Deep Vellum as a donor, subscriber, or volunteer, please contact us at deepvellum.org. We would love to hear from you.

Thank you all,

Will Evans, Publisher

Thank you all
for your support.
We do this for you,
and could not do
it without you.

DEEP
VELLUM

LIGA DE ORO

($5,000+)

Anonymous (2)

LIGA DEL SIGLO

($1,000+)

Allred Capital Management
Ben Fountain
Judy Pollock
Loretta Siciliano
Lori Feathers
Mary Ann Thompson-Frenk & Joshua Frenk
Matthew Rittmayer
Meriwether Evans
Nick Storch
Stephen Bullock

DONORS

Alan Shockley · Amrit Dhir · Anonymous · Andrew Yorke
Bob & Katherine Penn · Bob Penn · Brandon Childress
Brandon Kennedy · Charles Dee Mitchell · Charley Mitcherson
Cheryl Thompson · Christie Tull · Ed Nawotka
Greg McConeghy · JJ Italiano · Kay Cattarulla · Linda Nell Evans
Lissa Dunlay · Maynard Thomson · Michael Reklis · Mike Kaminsky
Mokhtar Ramadan · Nikki Gibson · Richard Meyer
Suejean Kim · Susan Carp · Tim Perttula

SUBSCRIBERS

Adam Hetherington
Alan Shockley
Amanda Freitag
Angela Kennedy
Anna Zylicz
Anonymous
Balthazar Simões
Barbara Graettinger
Ben Fountain
Ben Nichols
Benjamin Vincent
Betsy Morrison
Bill Fisher
Bjorn Beer
Bradford Pearson
Brandon Kennedy
Brina Palencia
Charles Dee Mitchell
Cheryl Thompson
Chris Sweet
Christie Tull
Clint Harbour
Daniel Hahn
Darius Frasure
David Bristow
David Hopkins
David Lowery
David Shook
Dennis Humphries
Don & Donna Goertz
Ed Nawotka

Elizabeth Caplice
Erin Baker
Fiona Schlachter
Frank Merlino
George Henson
Gino Palencia
Grace Kenney
Greg McConeghy
Horatiu Matei
Jacob Siefring
Jacob Silverman
Jacobo Luna
James Crates
Jamie Richards
Jane Owen
Jane Watson
Jeanne Milazzo
Jeff Whittington
Jeremy Hughes
Joe Milazzo
Joel Garza
John Harvell
Joshua Edwin
Julia Pashin
Justin Childress
Kaleigh Emerson
Katherine McGuire
Kimberly Alexander
Krista Nightengale
Laura Tamayo
Lauren Shekari

Linda Nell Evans
Lissa Dunlay
Lytton Smith
Mac Tull
Marcia Lynx Qualey
Margaret Terwey
Mark Larson
Martha Gifford
Mary Ann Thompson-Frenk
& Joshua Frenk
Matthew Rowe
Meaghan Corwin
Michael Holtmann
Mike Kaminsky
Naomi Firestone-Teeter
Neal Chuang
Nick Oxford
Nikki Gibson
Patrick Brown
Peter McCambridge
Scot Roberts
Steven Norton
Susan B. Reese
Tess Lewis
Tim Kindseth
Todd Mostrog
Tom Bowden
Tony Fleo
Wendy Walker
Weston Monroe
Will Morrison